"The be..... ...les

"A thriller of a ride. . . . So riveting, I couldn't put it down. Jan Burke only gets better. The pace is fast and never slows down, each layer of the mystery is revealed artfully and . . . the believ-ability factor is high. Irene and the gang held me in their grasp."
—*The Snooper*

"A winner. . . . The best book in this wonderful . . . series."
—*Midwest Book Review*

"Ms. Burke is a wondrous storyteller, who deserves recogni-tion on par with Cornwell or Rosenberg. . . . Although Jan Burke writes mysteries, her novels seem much wider, encom-passing fans of mainstream fiction, romance, and suspense as well. Her who-done-its . . . are brilliantly plotted and executed, but the heart of each book rests inside the lead protagonist and her relationships."
—*Mystery Web*

"Kelly is a terrific heroine—feisty, tough, sensible, and smart—and Burke's suspenseful, action-filled plot, acerbic humor, and writing make this an entertaining entry in a popu-lar series."
—*Booklist*

"Jan Burke scores a hit once again."
—*Harvey Star* (Chicago Heights, IL)

"The biggest and most complex of her six novels. . . . Reminiscent of Ross Macdonald. . . . Conveys a constant sense of menace."
—*Kirkus Reviews*

"A simmering family feud leads to multiple murders and plenty of suspense."
—*Oklahoma City Oklahoman*

LIAR

———◆———

ALSO BY JAN BURKE

Goodnight, Irene

Sweet Dreams, Irene

Dear Irene,

*Remember Me, Irene**

*Hocus**

*Published by HarperPaperbacks

LIAR

An Irene Kelly Mystery

JAN BURKE

HarperPaperbacks
A Division of HarperCollinsPublishers

HarperPaperbacks
A Division of HarperCollins*Publishers*
10 East 53rd Street, New York, NY 10022-5299

This is a work of fiction. The characters, incidents, and
dialogue are products of the author's imagination and are not to
be construed as real. Any resemblance to actual events or
persons, living or dead, is entirely coincidental.

ISBN 0-06-104440-7

HarperCollins®, ![icon]®, and HarperPaperbacks®
are trademarks of HarperCollins Publishers Inc.

A hardcover edition of this book was published
in 1998 by Simon & Schuster Inc.

Cover illustration © 1999 Shasti O'Leary

First HarperPaperbacks printing: May 1999

Printed in the United States of America

Visit HarperPaperbacks on the World Wide Web at
http://www.harpercollins.com

❖ 10 9 8 7 6 5 4 3 2 1

TO
SHARON WEISSMAN,
JACQUELINE PREBICH,
KC PILON, JENNY OROPEZA,
TOM MULLINS, RICHARD MALZAHN,
DONALD GRANT, ENDA BRENNAN,
AND DEBBIE ARRINGTON

*For friendship over the long run, and with
the hope that I may have your company
to the farthest gate.*

PROLOGUE

The man who stood beneath the tree on the front lawn had come to hurt his mother. Of that, Travis felt certain.

The boy stood just a few feet behind the blinds, not touching them, his hands curled tightly on the edge of the desk behind him. The lights were out in the house and with the blinds angled in this way—yes, he was fairly sure he could not be seen by the man. The window wasn't open very far, just a few inches, and the screen was in place. Travis's pajamas were dark in color, wouldn't give him away. More likely his pale face would reflect the moonlight.

He's not looking at me anyway, Travis reassured himself.

The man was staring toward his mother's window. He had not moved for the last few minutes.

The small anniversary clock on the desk chimed once. Most other children who were Travis's age were in bed by now, but he was allowed to stay up as late as he liked. Travis was, his mother was fond of saying, the oldest eleven-year-old in the world.

He wasn't sure that his mother was right about that. His mother seemed not to be right about much of anything lately. At the thought, Travis glanced nervously toward the room upstairs. He hoped his mother would not awaken. She was so afraid of so many things; seeing the man out on the lawn would greatly upset her.

All together, Travis had been watching the man for about twenty minutes now. He had come downstairs to the study when he heard the car. This was a quiet street, and on these breeze-barren summer evenings, windows were open, sounds carried. Even if the engine had been turned off, the kiss of tires on the pavement would have betrayed the man's arrival. Apparently—and to Travis's amazement—none of their neighbors had heard the driver's door open and close.

The man had not parked in front of their house, though it was obviously his destination. Yet once reaching it, he had not tried to come inside, as Travis had expected. Instead, he had stood beneath that tree and stared at the room where Travis's mother slept.

The man stirred, took a step closer. Did he see Travis then? No, no, he was still staring at the upper story. He took another step, and another. Travis's palms dampened on the desk.

The man was crossing the lawn now, coming straight toward him.

Move away from the window! Run upstairs! Don't let him see you! Hide!

But Travis stayed. And watched.

He could see him clearly now, as he stood just outside the window. He was no farther from Travis than priest from confessor. Travis tried to study him objectively, to memorize his features. The man was younger than his mother, taller and stronger. That his mother would probably call the man's face handsome did not count for much with Travis, especially not if the man intended to harm them. He watched the strange, intense longing on the man's face; watched him frown in indecision.

Suddenly the man's gaze fell, and again Travis tensed, thinking he might be seen—but the man's eyes were lowered now. The man began to move again; he walked slowly out of view.

Travis let out his breath, then suddenly drew it back in

again as he realized that the man was not walking toward the street, but to their backyard gate. He heard the sound of the latch being fumbled open, the quiet click as it closed behind the intruder. Travis ran on bare feet to the kitchen, heard the man's steps clacking cautiously over the bed of black pebbles that lay between the house and fence.

Here, too, the windows were open, but curtains hung over them, blocking any view. The pebbles gave away the man's movements.

The back door! Had his mother remembered to lock the back door?

Panicked now, staying low, Travis hurried through the kitchen to the laundry room.

No! He could see the deadbolt had not been thrown.

He reached up, turned the latch, pulled his hand back just as he heard the soft sound of the man's soles on the back porch. Crouching, Travis leaned against the door, praying the man would not see him, had not heard him throw the lock.

There was a long moment of heart-too-loud silence before he watched the knob turn, heard the man lean his weight gently against the door. The man paused, and Travis looked up to see a hand pressed against the glass of the window in the door.

It was red.

Blood.

Had the man cut himself?

No. Travis could see the palm of his hand pressed there, perfect and large and unwounded.

The knob released.

The man stepped back, and Travis heard him leave the porch; he waited for his steps on the pebbles. The sound did not come.

Travis dared to rise up a little, to peer out the window in the door. He saw the man staring up again, this time toward

Travis's own bedroom window. And Travis saw the man's face, and again his expression of longing, a longing that Travis found mysterious and unsettling.

Travis stood now, and the movement must have caught the man's eye, for he was looking right at him, right straight at him; the man, with his solemn face, Travis's own pale, wide-eyed expression reflected on the same surface, boy's and man's face in one. For reasons that would elude him for many years, Travis suddenly balled his hand into a hard fist and plunged it through the glass, through the very place where the hand print had not yet dried, watched the red glass splinter and fall, did not cry out as it cut once and then cut again as he pulled his hand back, not shedding tears when his father reached in through the broken window and let himself into the house, not feeling anything like pain until his father took him into his arms.

1

I don't want to give the impression that my sister, Barbara, is a liar. I will admit that I have long thought that her flair for melodrama has been wasted on her usual audience, a family that has more often called for the hook than begged for an encore. I am the last remaining member of her immediate audience, and time has not deepened my appreciation of her skills.

The most recent performance began late one Friday afternoon at my front door; I was summoned to this makeshift theater by the repeated ringing of the doorbell. Even the overture provided by my barking dogs and yowling cat was unequal to the script she had prepared.

"Irene!" she cried, throwing herself into my arms. "There's a stranger in my grave!"

I disentangled myself and asked a question I've often asked her. "What the hell are you talking about?"

"Someone else has been buried in my grave!"

I looked her over. "From the eyebrows down, you appear to be alive. Customarily—"

"Well, of course I'm not dead yet. I mean, someone is already in the grave I'll be buried in when I die," she said.

"Who?"

"I don't know. That's why I came to you for help." She peered over my shoulder. "Why aren't you letting me in? Is the house dirty?"

"No, it's not," I said, then thought of the time I had found her carefully washing out all of the covers on the light fixtures in her home—Barbara would not wait for a burned-out bulb to necessitate the chore. "The house isn't dirty by the standards of human beings with real lives," I amended.

"Frank is too lenient with you about keeping the place neat," she said, pushing past me.

I issued an invitation to come in as she made her way to the living room. I put the cat in the bedroom and the dogs outside, as much for their benefit as hers. I offered her something to drink, but she politely declined as she took a seat in our grandfather's armchair. She often sits in that chair when she visits me. Barbara has always been annoyed that our father passed that family heirloom on to me instead of her. She ran her fingers over the upholstery and frowned. I know that kind of frown. On Barbara, it's the equivalent of a labor pain before the birth of a critical remark.

"You came here to ask for my help?" I said.

The frown became a smile. "You're a reporter—here's something you can investigate. I think this would make a great story—"

"Uh, Barbara, I don't think the *Express* is going to be all that interested in—"

"Of course it will! You don't want the LA *Times* to get this story first do you? It's exactly like that case that was in the headlines awhile back. Cemetery fraud. Illegal burial. Selling the same burial plot to two different people."

I sighed. "I'm sure it's nothing more than a simple mistake. If you're certain the plot is yours, just go into the cemetery office and show them your receipt."

"Receipt? I don't have a receipt."

"You lost it?"

"No. No one sold it to me, but it's where I'm supposed to be buried. You know that."

I felt the beginnings of a headache. "What cemetery are we talking about, Barbara?"

"Holy Family."

"Where Mom and Dad are buried."

"Yes. I'm supposed to be buried next to Mama."

"Supposed to be buried next to Mom? Let me guess who's doing the supposing."

"Of course I am! I knew her longer than you did, Irene."

"Don't start!"

"Okay, okay. I've always wanted to be buried there, but even having *you* buried there would be better than some stranger lying next to Mama for all eternity."

"Barbara, I don't own that plot and neither do you. The cemetery can bury whomever they want to in that space. It's not up to us."

"You never have cared about their graves!"

"Oh, for pitysakes—"

"You haven't. I'm the only one who visits them."

I stood up and walked over to the sliding glass door that leads to our backyard, looked out at my husband's carefully tended garden, felt myself relax a little. Trying to stay calm, I said, "For you, it's important to go to the cemetery. I respect that. But for me, it's . . . not where Mom and Dad are."

"You think someone else is buried in their graves?" she asked in alarm.

I turned to look at her. "No. I mean, the cemetery is only where their remains are—that's all that's there, what's left of their bodies. Not who they were or who they still are in my memories of them."

She shook her head. "Honestly, Irene. As if you can only have it one way or the other. Besides, if you did care about their memories, you'd honor them on important dates."

I felt my spine stiffen. "I know that Tuesday was the anniversary of her death, Barbara. If you think I've forgotten the day she died, you are seriously full of shit."

"But you didn't bring any flowers to the cemetery, or you

would have noticed that no one was in my—in the grave next to hers on Tuesday. And if you had returned on the anniversary of her funeral—"

"You think it's healthy to be that obsessed with death and funeral dates?"

"If you had returned today," she went on forcefully, "you would have noticed that between Tuesday and today, someone was buried next to our mother without our permission!"

"Maybe that person's family—whose grief must certainly be fresher than yours—has every right to bury someone there without our permission."

She folded her hands in her lap and looked down at them.

"Not the praying bit, please, Barbara."

At least she didn't say them aloud. After a moment, she looked up and said, "In the whole world, I have only one living relative."

"Am I adopted, or did Aunt Mary die? Not to mention the ones that live a little farther away—"

"One living sister," she amended. "One sister to go to when I'm upset, or need help, or any of the other things that sisters do for one another. And even though you don't like me much—"

"Barbara—"

"I hope you know that if you ever needed me, even for something much more significant than this small request I've made of you—"

"All right, all right! I'll go to the cemetery first thing tomorrow—"

She smiled. "They're open until sunset."

"Frank will be home any minute now. I'm not going to the cemetery tonight. I'll go in the morning."

"That's fine, that's fine. I'll probably find some way to go to sleep tonight."

"I'm sure you will."

She seemed to figure out that she had obtained her most important objective, and that she wasn't likely to push me into any further concessions just then. Before she left, she told me again how much she appreciated my help and gave me a kiss on the cheek—which surprised me. A sisterly hug between us isn't unheard of, but a kiss on the cheek is rare. I had some idea of how important this request was to her then, and found myself standing on my front steps, holding my hand to my cheek as I watched her drive off.

But in the next moment, I realized that once again I had let her con me into doing something I really didn't want to do. She's my older sister, but somehow I've ended up solving a lot of her problems. There was no reason she couldn't have gone into the cemetery office on her own and asked who was buried next to our mother, but I saw now that Barbara wanted to get me involved at this early stage for a reason. Later, if a confrontation was necessary, I'd be asked to do her fighting for her.

I went back inside the house, disgusted with the knowledge that the one thing that definitely wasn't buried in that new grave was my old habit of rescuing my sister.

─── ◄ ►

"Let's go over there now," Frank said when I told him about Barbara's visit. "Shouldn't take more than a few minutes."

"You just got home from work. Don't you want to relax, have some dinner?"

"No, I'm not really hungry yet. Let's go now—Jack wants to take us sailing tomorrow morning. He's invited Pete and Rachel. Cassidy might come along, too."

Although Pete and his wife are at our home quite often—Pete is Frank's partner—I hadn't seen Thomas Cassidy in a couple of weeks. He's a detective with the Las

Piernas Police Department—as are Frank and Pete. But Cassidy rarely works with them—Frank and Pete are homicide detectives, and Cassidy spends most of his time as a negotiator on the Critical Incident Team.

Jack Fremont, our friend and next-door neighbor, must have noticed the same things all of Frank's friends had noticed lately. He had lost weight he didn't need to lose, wasn't sleeping well. All to be expected, Cassidy told me, of someone who had survived being held hostage.

A day out on the water might be good for him; the companionship undoubtedly would be.

"Sure," I said. "We can go out to the cemetery now, and save tomorrow for sailing."

2

As we drove through the gates of the large old cemetery, Frank asked, "Which way do I turn?"

Throughout the drive I had worried that in the seven or eight years since I had been there, some essential landmark within the sprawling grounds would have changed, that I wouldn't be able to find my own parents' graves. In order to spare myself that embarrassment, I had a strategy prepared.

"We don't need to go out to the graves," I said. "Let's just pull into the office over here on the right."

He raised an eyebrow but said nothing as he parked the car. I got out and hurried to the office door, wanting to get this business over and done with. I planned to walk into the office and ask whoever was on duty for the name of the person who was newly buried next to my parents, Patrick and Maureen Kelly. Simple. I yanked on the glass door, but it didn't budge. I read the lettering on the glass and swore softly.

"Closed?" Frank asked from behind me.

I turned and nodded. "At five. We've missed them by an hour. I guess the office closes before they lock up the cemetery itself."

"Let's just drive over to the graves, then."

"What good will that do? Barbara said there isn't a stone in place yet. We won't be able to learn anything."

"We might be able to learn something from the surrounding graves. Besides, I've never seen where your parents are buried." He frowned, then added, "But if it's something that will be too upsetting to you, or is too personal—"

"No, no, of course not," I said.

We got back into the car and I directed him down a road that I was fairly certain would at least take us to the right section of the cemetery. I remembered that we needed to pass the oldest part of the grounds first; the one with crypts and tall, ornate headstones inscribed with poetry and scripture. Frank drove slowly, but soon there were fewer and fewer worn and weathered tombstones and more and more modern-style flat stones that lay flush with the ground. As we entered the newer part of the cemetery, I was relieved to see statuary that seemed familiar to me: various angels, one of Mary alone, and then a copy of Michelangelo's *Pietà*. I suddenly recalled that my parents' graves were across the road from a section with many children's graves in it. My parents' graves on the right side of the road, the children's graves on the left. I looked across the road and saw a statue of the Good Shepherd—Jesus depicted as a shepherd holding a small lamb.

"Stop here," I said. "Pull over to the right."

Now what? Trees, I remembered. Between four trees. I looked out over the cemetery and saw trees everywhere. At least eight of them nearby. I took a deep breath and got out of the car.

I began walking with a show of purpose, looking down at the rows of headstones, trying, as I always did on my few visits here, not to step on anybody. It wasn't really possible, but I tried I kept hoping that some unusual name or a special military headstone would jog my memory, tell me I was in the right place. I looked up and tried to recall what the trees near my parents' graves looked like. I tried to find a new grave—there were four of them, all fairly far apart. One was near a tree and a bench, so I could rule that one out. But it could be any of the others. I chose the nearest one and, feeling Frank's eyes on me, walked with determined steps toward it.

Wrong grave.

I stood still, feeling a sudden overwhelming sense of shame.

Frank, misunderstanding the cause of my upset, put an arm around my shoulders. I saw him read the nearest head-stones, saw his look of puzzlement when he realized that they were Cambodian names.

"I don't know these people," I said, then added, "I also don't know where my parents are buried. I never come out here."

He didn't say anything, but he pulled me closer.

"I thought I could find them," I said. "I've never felt what some people feel when they visit graves—what Barbara feels. She feels closer to my mother when she's here. But even when we were younger, when my father used to bring us here to put flowers on my mother's grave, I would wander off over there, across the road." I pointed to the statue. "I'd read the children's tombstones."

"We can't be too far away, then," he said. "It has to be near one of the new graves, right?"

I nodded.

He kept his arm around me as we walked. We stopped at the next nearest new grave, but my parents' graves weren't there, either. As we headed for the third one, a caretaker's truck pulled up. The driver, a gnarled old man, wore a straw hat, jeans and a light-green cotton shirt, work gloves and boots. He took a rake from the back of the truck and headed toward one of the trees. Seeing us, he asked, "You need help?"

"Yes," Frank answered before I could politely refuse. "Kelly?"

"Oh, sure. You one of Mary Kelly's nephews?"

Frank smiled. "No, only by marriage."

"I'm her grandniece," I answered. "You know her?"

"Sure." He studied me for a minute. "You ain't the one she calls Prissy Pants."

Frank laughed. There were reasons he got along well with my great-aunt.

"You must be Irene," the caretaker went on. "She's told me a lot about you. You're the reporter, right?"

"Yes. And this is my husband, Frank."

"A cop, right?"

"Yes," I said, "but how do you know—"

"Oh, I've known Mary for years. We both go to St. Matthew's and a lot of her family is buried here. Most Sundays I see her and we talk for a while after Mass. Your aunt is quite a lady. You're headed the wrong way," he added, and steered us toward the grave I had first ruled out, near the bench and tree.

"What's your name?" I asked.

"Oh, forgive me. No manners on me today. I'm Sean Grady," he said, tipping his hat. "I knew your grandfather, too. Daniel Kelly was a fine man. A fine man. The Kellys own most of the plots in this section, you know. Or Mary does, anyway."

"No, I didn't know that."

"Well, she does. She has a way about her, that one." He laughed. "I put this bench in here for her, so she'd have a place to sit when she comes to visit. She thanked me, then asked me to plant a tree so she could sit in the shade!"

"She's been trying to reach you, hasn't she?" Frank asked.

"Yes, we've been playing phone tag for the last few days," I said. "This must be why she called." Worried, I tried to think of any relatives on the Kelly side of my family who might have died—but the other Kellys lived out of state, or in Ireland. Why would any of them want to be buried in Las Piernas?

There were newly cut flowers on my parents' grave; a dozen red roses, carefully arranged in the brass vase that fit into my mother's side of the grave, probably left there by my sister. My mother would have loved them. Frank and Mr. Grady stood quietly beside me. My parents' headstone looked odd, and I quickly realized why: the side bearing my mother's name was polished, but my father's side was covered with a layer of dust. More than dust, really—it was dirty. There was even a bird dropping on it.

"That bitch," I said, to Mr. Grady's apparent shock.

"Barbara only cleaned off your mother's side?" Frank asked.

"Yes," I said, so angry I could hardly manage that one word. I started looking through my purse for a tissue, but everything was blurry, including the one, big fat tear that I felt rolling unattractively off the end of my nose.

Frank knelt down, not seeming to notice that he was probably going to have grass stains on his suit pants, and took a handkerchief from his pocket. He started cleaning off my father's side of the stone. I knelt next to him, and soon old Mr. Grady was there, too, using a big red cloth, all three of us polishing the smooth marble.

"We need some water," Mr. Grady said, getting to his feet.

Frank worked the metal vase free from my father's grave. "Is there a faucet nearby?" he asked Mr. Grady.

Mr. Grady pointed one out, and Frank left to fill the vase.

I moved to the bench, tried to pull myself back together. I made myself focus on the new grave, on the seams of earth between rectangles of newly placed sod. I silently debated whether or not I should do anything on Barbara's behalf. Ever.

"Do you know whose grave this is, Mr. Grady? The one next to my mother's?"

He shook his head. "No, no, I don't. I wasn't here the day of the funeral—I'm off on Sundays, Wednesdays and Thursdays, and I think this one was Wednesday. Must be somebody your great-aunt Mary knows, though."

"Why do you say that?"

"She owns several plots here. Nobody could have been buried next to your folks without her say-so."

Frank came back and splashed the headstone with a little water. The rest of the dirt came off, and with a little more water, the stone cleaned up nicely. Frank put the vase back in its holder, water still in it. He reached toward the roses, then hesitated, looking at me.

"Do you think she'd mind?" he asked.

"My mother?"

"Yes."

I smiled. "No, she wouldn't mind. She was always generous."

He carefully pulled three of the roses from the vase on my mother's grave.

—◆—

I tried to tell myself, on the way home, that my father was past feeling any slights from Barbara, that even when he was alive, he had an understanding of her habit of distancing herself from him, an understanding I could never share.

"You going to see your aunt Mary?" Frank asked.

"You want to come along if I do?"

"Of course. Wouldn't miss it."

I looked at the muddy spots on his knees. "Frank?"

"Hmm."

"Thanks."

He smiled, looking more content than he had in many days.

3

"No, not one of the Kellys," Aunt Mary said when I called her. "But some things should be discussed face-to-face, not over the phone. Besides, I've baked an apple pie and I don't want to sit here and eat it all by myself. Frank likes apple pie, doesn't he? Of course he does. Come over to my house after you've had your supper. See you then."

She hung up before I could accept or refuse the invitation or confirm that yes, Frank liked apple pie.

We pulled into the driveway of her small Craftsman-style home, parking behind her red '68 Mustang convertible. Aunt Mary is the original owner of both the car and the house.

Her house is small but it sits on a large lot. Her garden was in bloom, and although it was too dark to see the honeysuckle and roses and jasmine, we savored the combination of their sweet and spicy fragrances as we walked to the front door. I glanced at my watch before knocking. It was nine o'clock. For some people just over eighty years old, it might have been a little late to begin an evening's visit, but Mary has always been a night owl. As far as Mary's circadian rhythms were concerned, we had arrived at the equivalent of four o'clock in the afternoon.

When she answered our knock, a different fragrance

greeted us, that of hot apple pie. "Come on in, come on in," she said, taking an apron off.

Despite the fact that she loves to bake, she has always been slender. That night she was wearing jeans and a white T-shirt and running shoes. Her hair was in a single neat, thick gray braid, and she was wearing her favorite jewelry—a squash-blossom necklace and turquoise-and-silver earrings.

She carelessly set the apron aside and gave me a big hug as I walked in. Frank got a hug, too, but she held on to him as she stepped back and looked him over. She made a clucking noise and said, "Irene, you are starving my favorite nephew."

"No, she's not—" he began, but she interrupted.

"Pie will be ready in about fifteen minutes," she said. "Have a seat in here. Too hot in the kitchen."

"I thought you said the pie was already made," I said.

"Well, maybe I did, but what I meant to say was that if you'd come over, I'd make one."

"But you must have had the ingredients on hand," I persisted.

"Yes, Miss Smarty, I did. And since I know how that mind of yours works, yes, I knew that sooner or later you would be coming by, and if you were—well, now, I couldn't have you bring this big fellow and not offer him anything to eat, now could I? Have a seat, I said."

We sat.

"Going to extremes, aren't you?" I said.

"What? Making an apple pie?"

"That's not what I meant and you know it."

"No wonder you're off your feed, Frank. Pushy and uppity, isn't she? Here I am, offering my hospitality, and she wants to proceed at her pace, do things her way."

"Can't imagine where she gets that from," Frank said.

She looked taken aback for a moment, then laughed. "Ah,

you should come to see me more often, you two. Can I get either one of you something to drink?"

With that she took charge again, and warned off, I bided my time. She focused her attentions on Frank, asking him about his plans for his summer garden, which took the two of them into a rather detailed discussion of planting methods for vegetable gardens. Apparently, there would be no talk of cemeteries until she was good and ready to bring the subject up. I knew her well enough not to try to coax it out of her. If Mary had decided that we owed her three or four visits before she would tell me who was buried next to my mother, that's how long I'd have to wait.

As it turned out, she only held off telling me until after Frank had polished off two pieces of apple pie with double scoops of vanilla ice cream on them. She wasn't stingy with my serving, but my patience was wearing thin, and after the day I'd had, my appetite wasn't up to par. She noticed.

"No need to pout," she said. "He's my favorite nephew because you're my favorite niece."

I didn't try to hide my skepticism.

"My favorite in California," she amended. Since most of her other nephews and nieces live in Ireland, and only another handful live in other states, this was not the signal honor it may seem.

"Mr. Grady tells me you refer to your only other California niece as 'Prissy Pants,'" I said, "so forgive me if I fail to feel puffed up with flattery."

"Well, she is a Prissy Pants. And I'm damned tired of her disrespect to her father's memory."

"Is anyone buried in that new grave? Or did you just have Mr. Grady and his friends hack up the ground to upset Barbara?"

"Of course someone is buried there. And when I tell you who it is, you'll be ashamed of yourself for even suggesting such a thing."

I waited.

"You don't even have a guess, do you?" she said.

"Tell me something, Aunt Mary. If you go to that cemetery often enough to be on a buddy-buddy basis with the groundskeeper—"

"Mr. Grady is a member of my parish—"

"I'll bet none of the other members of the parish get benches and trees near their dearly beloveds' final resting places."

"Hmph."

"If you're there so often," I went on, "why haven't you cleaned my father's side of the stone?"

"Ha! You think I haven't? You think there was seven years' worth of bird crap on that stone when you got there today?"

That hurt, but I said, "It does rain once in a while."

"Rain!" She rose to her feet. "Rain! Oh, my poor nephew Patrick, with nobody to remember him but these two—"

"Mary," Frank said, quietly but firmly.

She sat down and crossed her arms over her chest. She sighed. "You're right, Frank. I'm going about this all wrong. All wrong. Irene, I apologize."

"Me, too," I said. "On more than one count. You're right, Mary, I should go out there more often—"

Mary waved a hand in dismissal. "I know why you don't, and it's all okay by me, Irene. I need your help, and I should have just asked. I guess I just wondered how long it would take your sister to get curious about that grave."

"Not long. You said you need my help—does it have something to do with the grave?"

"Yes. Do you remember your cousin Travis?"

I frowned, then shook my head. "If I've met a Travis Kelly—"

"Not Kelly. Maguire."

My eyes widened. "You mean—"

"Yes," she said. "Your mother's nephew."

"He died?" I asked, shocked. The last time I had seen Travis, he was an infant.

"No, his mother died."

"His mother? Not . . ."

She nodded. "Your mother's sister, Briana."

It was a name I had not heard in over a dozen years. Still, I could feel my face turning red when she mentioned it.

Frank straightened in his chair, his interest piqued.

"I buried her next to your mother," Aunt Mary said. "I was trying to right a wrong. Your father was a good man—please understand, I'm not denying that on most counts he was a very good man, Irene. But he was wrong to treat Briana the way he did. The least the Kelly family could provide her was a place to rest her bones."

"I haven't heard anything about Briana or Travis in so long . . ."

Mary snorted. "Of course not. Your father made sure of that, didn't he?"

I shook my head. "I could have tried to look her up after Dad died. I'm ashamed to say I'd forgotten all about her."

"I'm confused," Frank said.

"The Maguires are my mother's family," I said. "Most of them are in Kansas. My mother is one of three sisters. I never knew the oldest one, Maggie. Maggie died before I was born. But the other two—my mother, Maureen Maguire, and her sister, Briana—came out to California."

"Go on," Mary said, "tell him the rest."

"My mother married my father, Patrick Kelly, and Barbara and I were born. When we were little, we saw Briana fairly often. Barbara and I were very fond of her."

"You were much closer to her than Barbara was," Mary said.

I shrugged. "I suppose that's true."

"It's undoubtedly true."

"So what happened?" Frank asked.

"She got married, and my father never liked her husband."

"To put it mildly," Aunt Mary grumbled.

"I didn't like him either," I said.

"Do you even remember him?"

"Yes. Arthur Sperry was almost fifteen years—"

"Twelve at most," she corrected.

"Somewhere between twelve and fifteen years younger than Aunt Briana," I continued. "He was handsome and charming and still managed to give me the creeps."

"You liked him at first," she said.

"Everyone liked him at first. But not after he made a pass at my mother."

"Hmm. You always did have big ears," Mary said. "A child shouldn't have heard such talk."

"It wasn't just talk—"

"Never mind that," Mary said. She turned to Frank. "The upshot of this alleged pass—"

"Alleged!" I protested.

"Of this *alleged* pass," Mary went on determinedly, "is that the two sisters saw less and less of each other."

"It wasn't just that," I said, turning to Frank. "My mother died not long after they were married."

"So you were twelve when Travis was born?" he asked.

"Yes. He was born the year my mother died. I never got to know him, really."

My thoughts drifted to memories of those last weeks of my mother's life. At that time, hospital rules were different than they are today, and children—defined by the hospital as anyone under sixteen—were not allowed in the patients' rooms. Barbara was seventeen, but I was only twelve, so I waited alone in the hospital lobby downstairs, while Barbara and my father went up to my mother's room. I would write notes for my father to bring upstairs, to read to my mother as she lay dying of cancer, to let her know that I was there, too.

As it became clearer to everyone that she would not be coming home from the hospital, family differences were set aside. Still, Aunt Briana did not bring Arthur with her. The first time she came to visit my mother, the nuns wouldn't let her take the baby up to the room, so she asked me if I would hold Travis until she came back downstairs. I was a little afraid, because I hadn't spent much time around babies, but Travis made it easy for me. He watched me with that intense, studying stare we allow only babies to make of us. Apparently deciding I was trustworthy, he yawned and fell asleep in my arms.

Briana came back downstairs and thanked me for watching him, and said she would find a sitter next time. But I begged her to bring him back, and whether out of pity or gratitude, she told me she would. And so for three weeks, Travis and I consoled one another, his childhood beginning as mine ended. The last time I held him was the day of the funeral. Aunt Briana took my little talisman against grief away from me that day, and I had not seen him since.

I looked up to find Mary studying me, and saw that she was challenging me to tell the rest of Aunt Briana's story.

"What is it?" Frank asked, looking between us.

"As it turned out, my father wasn't such a bad judge of character," I said.

"But far too much of a judge!" Mary snapped.

"Arthur and Briana weren't legally married," I said.

"Now don't make it sound as if—" Mary began to interrupt.

"Arthur already had a wife," I said. "He was a bigamist."

One good thing about marrying a cop is that announcements like these are received with a great deal more equanimity than they might be otherwise. He merely raised a questioning eyebrow.

"Briana had separated from him before anyone else learned that he was already married," Mary said.

"Not long before. But that's not the worst of it. No one else learned that he was a bigamist until he was wanted for questioning in connection with a murder in Los Alamitos. His first wife—his legal spouse—was found dead. He was suspected of killing her, but it took awhile to link 'Arthur Spanning'—which was his real name—with 'Arthur Sperry.' Once the connection was made, guess who supplied his alibi?"

"Briana," Frank said.

"Yes, and Travis backed her up. They said Arthur had been at their home. It wasn't hard to back up his story, because on the night in question, Travis had cut his hand and was treated at a local hospital. Arthur had carried him into the emergency room. Briana was with them."

"Anyone else ever accused of the murder?" Frank asked.

"No," I said. "Everyone always thought Arthur did it, and that Briana just lied for him."

"Your father thought so, anyway," Mary said.

"He wasn't alone. He thought Briana was afraid of Arthur."

"Well, it hardly matters. They separated. As far as I know, Briana never saw him after that."

"I wish I had known about Briana's funeral," I said.

"There was no funeral to speak of," Mary said.

"What?"

"She was a Jane Doe."

"A Jane Doe? Briana?"

"In Las Piernas?" Frank asked.

"No," Mary said, answering his question first. "She was the victim of a hit-and-run accident in San Pedro. Well, perhaps 'accident' isn't the right word for it. She was walking home from the neighborhood market one morning, didn't have any identification on her. It took almost two weeks for them to figure out who she was."

"San Pedro?" I asked. "What was she doing there?"

"She moved there after all the notoriety of the murder case drove her to leave Las Piernas. She stayed here for a time, found a fairly good job as a secretary, but sooner or later she would encounter someone who knew her story. It was very painful for her—for Travis, too, I'm sure.

"So she moved. It took her awhile to find work, but she eventually got a job as a file clerk in a health clinic. Never did have a lot of money. She kept to herself. Life just kept getting harder and harder for her. She had been having health problems lately—something wrong with one of her knees, I think. A couple of months ago, it got so bad it forced her to leave her job. She was living on a small disability check. She hadn't lived in this last apartment for very long."

"Travis told you all of this?"

She shook her head sadly. "No, but I suspect Travis hasn't been in touch with her for some time. And no one over there at this new place really got to know her before she died. Oh, she'd met a couple of her more curious neighbors, but I don't think they ever learned much about her. I learned a few things from them, but they didn't even know she had a son. When the police finally figured out which apartment she lived in, they found an Easter card I sent to her a few weeks ago, and that's how they got in touch with me. I told them I would bury her."

I tried, but could not reconcile this image of a lonely recluse with that of my aunt Briana. I thought of the last time I had seen her, at my mother's funeral.

"Travis—" I said.

"That's what I need you to do, Irene. I want you to find

him. A child should be told when his mother is dead. And even if he's like you, and doesn't want to visit the grave, at least he should know where she's buried. But I also need your help—yours and Frank's—to find out who killed her."

"The LAPD is calling this a homicide?" Frank asked.

"Yes," she said, as her phone rang. Even though it was now after ten-thirty, most of Mary's friends would know that she's up late. But this wasn't a social call.

"Yes, Detective McCain," she said to her caller. ". . . No, no, this isn't too late! Not at all! As I told you, I don't usually go to sleep until just before dawn. But I promise you, you don't need to bring a wooden stake or garlic when you visit. I'm not a vampire."

She listened, then suddenly looked over at us, frowning. "Yes, I know Irene Kelly," she said into the phone. "She's my grandniece. She's sitting here right now, with her husband—did I tell you he's a homicide detective, too? Oh, I did. Yes, he's the one. Well, let me ask them."

She covered the mouthpiece. "Detective McCain is a homicide detective with the LAPD. He wants to know if he can come over to talk with you."

4

People who got their ideas about detectives from television probably would have been disappointed in Detective Jim McCain. He was gray-haired, plain-faced, a little thick in the waist, but—we quickly realized—not between the ears. He was of medium height and stood up straight, his posture neither ramrod nor slouched. He didn't smoke, didn't wear a fedora or a crumpled raincoat. His shoes had seen better days, but had leather soles, and while his suit wasn't an Armani, it was still neat and clean. He didn't look as if he had punched or shot anyone lately. He smiled warmly when Mary opened her door, thanked her politely when she let him in. I decided his voice, soft and low, was one of his assets. It was a voice that invited confidences.

He was still smiling when his dark blue eyes rested on Frank and me, but they widened slightly when Mary introduced Frank.

"Harriman?" he said, with a note of recognition.

"Yes," Frank answered. I could see him tensing, waiting for the inevitable questions: *Were you the hostage? Just how did that go down? How did they manage to get the drop on you?* Questions he had been asked just about a billion times.

But instead, McCain extended a hand and said, "An honor to meet you. Glad you came out of that okay."

"Thanks," Frank said, obviously relieved.

McCain turned to me and shook hands as we were introduced—smiling, polite and sizing me up. What the verdict was, I'm not sure.

Once he was seated and had resisted all of Mary's offers of food and beverage, he took out a little notebook, turned to me and said, "Ms. Kelly, I assume your aunt Mary has told you that I'm investigating the death of Briana Maguire?"

"Yes."

"She was your mother's sister?"

I nodded.

"And when was the last time you saw her?"

"Over twenty years ago. At my mother's funeral, when I was twelve."

"Not since then?"

"No."

"Any other type of contact with your aunt since then?"

"No." From the corner of my eye, I saw Frank sit forward.

"No phone calls?" McCain asked.

"No. No phone calls, no letters, no contact at all."

He said nothing, just watched me. I didn't try to fill the silence, but Mary did. "I explained all that to you," she said.

He smiled. "Is there a room where I could talk to Ms. Kelly alone?"

"Perhaps she should talk to you another time," Frank said. "In the presence of an attorney."

McCain's smile didn't waver. "She is, of course, absolutely free to do so, but right now, I'm just asking questions. You know how this goes, Harriman. Lawyers cause unnecessary complications, just to make their clients think they've earned their fee. I don't need that kind of grief, and neither do you. Better this way. None of us would ever get a thing done in this line of work without a little cooperation."

I knew this last line didn't necessarily refer only to my cooperation with him; I could see from Frank's face that he got the hint as well—McCain was saying, *You want coop-*

*eration from LAPD on any of your cases, don't screw with
our cases.*

"I'll talk to him, Frank," I said.

"What brings my wife into this?" Frank asked, ignoring me.

"I'll be happy to tell you in a moment," he said. "Just a
few more questions, Ms. Kelly? In fact, if your husband
wants to be present—"

"I get the picture," Mary said. "I'll go into the kitchen."

He thanked her and stood as she rose to leave the room.
She laughed and made some remark about courtly manners, then shut the door between the two rooms.

Frank, I could see, was still wary.

"Now, where were we?" McCain said, flipping though his
notes. "Oh, yes. Well, let's skip the family history for the
moment."

He flipped back a few pages in his notebook and said,
"You drive a Karmann Ghia convertible?"

So he had run a DMV check on me. And Briana was
killed in a hit-and-run accident. Didn't take a genius to figure out where this was headed. "Yes, I drive a Karmann
Ghia. It's at home in our driveway, without any damage to
the front end."

He smiled again. Now Frank was smiling, too.

"He's probably got someone over at the house, taking a
look at it right now," Frank said.

He nodded. "And I had a look at the Volvo on the way in.
But neither of your cars matches the description witnesses
gave of the vehicle that struck your aunt, Ms. Kelly."

"Which was?"

"Sorry, I'd prefer not to say. It's an open case, Ms. Kelly, and
for the moment we have all the detectives we need on it."

Polite or no, the guy was starting to irritate me.

"Do you remember what you were doing the morning of
Wednesday the eighteenth?" he asked. "That's two weeks
ago."

"Working. I work for the *Las Piernas News-Express.*"

"You were in the office?"

"Yes. Most weeks, on Tuesday nights, I cover the city council meetings. I turn in what I can on Tuesday night, but if the meeting goes later than my final deadline or some item needs a follow-up, I write about it on Wednesday."

"And you're certain you were writing about the city council meeting on that Wednesday morning?"

"Yes. Two weeks ago they took the final vote on the sale of some park land. It was hotly debated. The meeting ran late."

"You don't get to sleep in on Wednesdays after covering evening meetings?"

"Sometimes. I've worked at the paper for a number of years, so I'm not punching a clock. In general, I get to decide how I use my time—provided I meet my deadlines. As long as I continue to produce my stories on time, no one will hassle me much. But that day I needed to contact some sources I can only reach during business hours, so I showed up at about eight that morning. Lots of people can verify that."

"What brings Irene into this?" Frank asked again. "For more than twenty years, she's had no contact with this aunt. She didn't even learn that Briana Maguire had died until a little more than an hour ago."

McCain seemed surprised. "Your aunt Mary didn't tell you before today?"

"No."

"Ms. Kelly, what are your expectations of Ms. Maguire's estate?"

"Expectations?" I asked, taken aback. "From Briana? Why, absolutely none."

"But you were a favorite niece, weren't you?"

"Look, about two dozen years have gone by since I last saw her. There was a family quarrel, even before her other troubles started."

"Other troubles?"

"You undoubtedly know which ones I mean."

He paused, then said, "Yes, your aunt Mary has been very helpful. Ms. Kelly, several times your husband has asked me what brings you into this matter. Are you aware that your aunt left a will?"

"No. As I said—"

"Yes, yes. But she did leave a will, Ms. Kelly. A holographic will. You know what that means?"

"A will written entirely in her handwriting," I said.

"Yes. We found it today, among the papers in her apartment."

"She died two weeks ago and you just searched her apartment today?"

"Keep in mind that we didn't know who she was until a few days ago, Ms. Kelly. Our first concern was to find someone who could provide positive identification of the victim and claim her body, someone who could arrange for her burial. Given our caseloads in this division, I don't think we've done too badly."

"No, no, I'm sorry. So you found a handwritten will leaving everything to her son—"

"Oh, no, Ms. Kelly. Nothing was left to her son."

"What?"

"Briana Maguire's will leaves everything to you."

5

"It doesn't appear to be much of an estate, I'll grant you," he went on. "But we haven't really had time to check for assets. You know, sometimes you read about these hermits who live very simply, but end up having a million bucks stashed away in a savings account somewhere."

"Brilliant," Frank said angrily. "You think this single mother who worked as a file clerk was a millionaire? A woman who was living on disability checks?"

McCain shrugged.

"No matter how much she did or didn't have," I said, "I don't want any of it. And I have no idea why she named me in her will."

McCain studied me for a moment, then seemed to come to some decision; he appeared to relax a little. He asked me a few more questions about my childhood relationship with Briana, then said, "Any idea why someone might want to kill her?"

"No. I don't know anything about her recent life that Mary didn't tell me tonight. As I said, I haven't been in touch with Briana in a long time."

"You're certain this was premeditated?" Frank asked.

"Not absolutely. But a couple of things bothered us about it, or I wouldn't be here," McCain said, seeming to loosen up a little more. "First, a high rate of speed, coming down a street that isn't exactly known for drag racing. Second, no skid marks—and yes, maybe the car had antilock brakes, but we've got two wits that say the car didn't stop at all. You and I both know that very few people would accidentally hit someone and never apply the brakes." He turned to me. "Most hit-and-run drivers are surprised, you might say—they stop or try to stop at some point. Maybe panic sets in or they have some reason for avoiding the police—drugs in the car, car's stolen, they've got warrants out on 'em, whatever—so they take off after they realize what they've done. But they seldom just hit somebody and keep rolling as if nothing's happened. In this case, no one heard brakes or saw the driver swerve to avoid her."

"Any chance the driver just didn't see her?" I asked.

"Your aunt was in the middle of an intersection on a bright and sunny morning, wearing light-colored clothing. The direction of the vehicle's travel was away from the sun, so nothing impaired the driver's vision. In fact, the witnesses say that after the initial impact, the driver deliberately drove the car over her after she was down."

I shuddered.

"The witnesses give you a make on the vehicle?" Frank asked.

"They can't agree on the make, but between what they've given us and some of the physical evidence, we think we're looking for a Camry." He paused, then looked over at me. "As I said, the witnesses agreed that it looked deliberate. The vehicle wasn't out of control—it maneuvered to hit her. The car hits her, knocks her down, rolls over her, and drags her body a few yards. The collision breaks a headlamp and does some other damage to the car, and makes a noise loud enough to bring people running out of a little store on the corner. No brake lights, no slowing, no horn."

Even though I hadn't seen her in a long time, it was hard for me to hear this description, to imagine someone doing that to Briana. Frank took my hand. I held on.

After a moment, McCain said, "Any idea where your cousin is these days?"

"Travis? No."

"Your aunt's ex-husband?"

"He wasn't really her husband. But no, I don't know anything about him."

He asked a few more questions, then walked over to the kitchen door. As he opened it, it was clear from both her startled expression and her nearness to the door that Mary had been eavesdropping. She recovered herself quickly though, and I had to admire her regal bearing as she continued on into the living room. "Thank you, Detective McCain," she said. "It was insufferably hot in that kitchen."

McCain gave a little laugh. As he came back to where we were seated, he smothered a yawn, then said, "Excuse me. I think I'll call it a night. You'll be in the area for the next few weeks, Ms. Kelly?"

"As far as I know."

He took out a card. "Give me a call if you have any questions, or if anything comes to mind."

"One moment," Aunt Mary said.

He waited.

"I assume you aren't charging Irene with any crime?"

"No, as of now, I have no reason to do so," he said.

"Is there any reason why she can't visit Briana's apartment, take things out of there?"

He hesitated, then said, "It's no longer sealed, if that's what you're asking."

"I don't want—" I began.

"Hush!" she snapped at me. "I want you to go over there tomorrow morning and clear her things out. You can keep them in boxes and give them to Travis when we find him. That's fine."

"But her furniture—we don't have room—" I began

again, grasping at the first argument that came to mind.

"Don't worry about that. I'll even arrange to have movers bring the furniture here. I'll store it for you until we find him."

"What's your hurry?" McCain asked.

She folded her arms across her chest. "I drove over to Briana's apartment the other day. I'm sure one of your men mentioned that to you."

McCain just smiled.

"Well, he wouldn't let me in the apartment, but I spoke briefly to Briana's neighbors. They said up until you and your patrolmen started hanging around, there had been problems with break-ins in that building. I don't want thieves looting what belongs to Travis."

"Neither do I," McCain said, looking right at me.

Frank rose halfway out of his chair. I placed a hand on his arm and said, "That won't help anyone." He sat back down.

"What's your real reason for wanting her to go over there?" McCain asked Mary.

"That's real enough," she said, narrowing her gaze on him. "I don't lie as readily as some people do."

He didn't say anything, just kept smiling.

"I do have another reason. I want her to find her cousin. I'm very worried about him."

"We'll find him."

"Hah! Listen here, Mr. McCain. There are only about six or seven *states* that have a bigger population than Los Angeles County—you're going to tell me that you'll find the needle I want out of a haystack as big as that? And that's if he stayed local. Besides, you just mentioned to us that things are kind of busy in your division."

"We have other professionals who—"

"So does she!" Mary crowed. "One sitting right next to her."

"I'm sure Detective Harriman won't want to cause juris-dictional problems."

"No," Mary answered for him. "Even though you're in his right now. But he's going sailing tomorrow morning. Irene's going to hire that private investigator friend of hers to help us look for Travis."

It took all the acting skill I have not to betray my surprise at this announcement. I'm not sure I succeeded. McCain seemed skeptical. Frank was cooler under fire.

"Rachel Giocopazzi," he supplied, not missing a beat. "She worked homicide in Phoenix. She's my partner's wife."

McCain's working smile suddenly brightened into the genuine article—this one lit up his face with pleasure. "Giocopazzi? Rachel Giocopazzi got married?" He laughed. " 'Pazzi! Well, I'll be damned!" He quickly looked over at Mary and said, "Pardon me, ma'am."

She waved that away. "You know her?" A bold question, since Mary had never actually met Rachel, only heard us talk about her.

"Know her?" McCain said. "Yes. I know her. Lord, yes. We worked together on a long, tough case—two victims killed here, bodies taken to Phoenix."

This led to some grisly shop talk between Frank and McCain, during which it was obvious that Jim McCain's unspoken reminiscences were not strictly about the case.

"Married," he said again. "Your partner must be quite a guy. I don't think there was a man in the Phoenix department that didn't dream about 'Pazzi. They'd call her that, or 'the Amazon.' "

I wondered what he'd think of Pete Baird when he met him. I had a feeling he was in for a shock. I'm fond of Pete, but a page off the Hunk-A-Day Calendar he ain't.

"So you'll give Irene the keys to the apartment?" Mary asked.

He rubbed his chin, then said, "Sure, but I don't have the keys with me. I tell you what, I'll meet you and Rachel over there."

"But we go through the apartment on our own," I said.

Again he hesitated, looking at me curiously before he said, "All right, meet you there at ten o'clock. But you'll tell me if you come across anything that has a bearing on this case?"

"If someone murdered my aunt, Detective McCain, I'll do everything in my power to help you find her killer."

"Good. And no trying to get in there before ten, all right?"

"Fine. I'll see you then."

"You sure Rachel can make it?" he asked.

"I'm almost certain," I said, praying Rachel wouldn't mind giving up sailing, too.

— ▬

"Families," Rachel said on a sigh, her eyes not leaving the heavy traffic in front of us. "My brothers, we might not speak to each other for years, but one of 'em calls up and says, 'Hey, Rach, I need a little something from the dark side of the moon,' and even though my mouth might say, 'Are you nuts? I'm not going to any damned moon,' I'm already thinking, Gee, wonder how I'll look in a spacesuit?"

"You're just as good to your friends as you are to your family," I said. "Thanks for giving up the sailing trip."

Uneasy about McCain's suspicion of me, Frank had talked about canceling, too—but Rachel had shooed him out the door with the other men. When we first mentioned McCain to her, she frowned a little, glancing over at Pete, then said, "Yeah, I think I remember him."

She helped me gather up some empty boxes, and offered to drive us over in her Plymouth sedan, which was better suited to hauling boxes than my Karmann Ghia.

Now we were on the Vincent Thomas Bridge, high above LA Harbor. Rachel hit the brakes as a pickup truck made a sudden lane change into the space in front of us, and I heard her muttering something in Italian.

"Starting to regret this?" I asked.

"Aw, I don't mind this at all. Glad to come along. You think I'd be happier stuck on a sailboat all day with those clowns? No way."

"If you needed an alternative, you could probably think of something more fun than going through a dead stranger's possessions."

"Hell, I'm used to it."

"I guess you are," I said. Rachel had retired in her early forties from her job in Phoenix homicide, after putting in twenty years in the department—where she'd started as a meter maid, back when they called them that.

"Am I horning in on something you'd rather do alone?" she asked.

"No—not at all. Even if you hadn't been so willing to offer your car or to help pack boxes, I'd be grateful just to have you with me. I'm glad I'm not facing this alone."

"That's understandable. You said you don't know how much stuff is in this apartment, right?"

"Aunt Mary said the place is small and that it wouldn't take long to pack up, but she's never moved from the first house she bought in Las Piernas, so I'm not sure she's much of a judge."

After McCain left her house, Aunt Mary said she hoped we didn't mind the way she'd rescheduled our Saturday. Apparently it was her guilt over this that led her to make a generous offer—to call my sister and explain a few matters to her about the cemetery. But I had a score to settle with Barbara, so I told Mary that I would make the call myself.

Barbara's an early riser, so I called before leaving for San Pedro, and started by telling her that the "stranger" in what she thought of as her grave was our mother's sister.

That led to a brief bout of hysterical exclamations regarding Briana's unworthiness to be buried in the same cemetery as our mother, let alone in an adjoining plot. Listening to Barbara's version of family history, it would have been more appropriate to bury Benedict Arnold in Arlington National Cemetery.

I nocked my first arrow. "Then you should call the person who owns the gravesite and tell her off."

"I will!" Barbara fumed. "Who is it?"

I let the arrow fly. "Aunt Mary."

Utter silence. Bull's-eye.

I loosed the next one by saying, "Of course, if you make too much of a fuss about it, you might be the one who ends up buried in some other cemetery. Aunt Mary owns most of the nearest plots."

"She does?"

"Yes, she does. And Barbara? If I *ever* hear from Mary that only one half of our parents' gravestone is being cared for? I'm going to beg her to sell those remaining plots to me. And I think she'll do it, don't you?"

She hung up on me. William Tell never had a better day.

Briana's apartment was on the east side of San Pedro, an area named by Juan Cabrillo when he sailed into its bay in 1542. San Pedro was once a city itself, but became part of Los Angeles near the turn of the century; Briana's apartment was near the old downtown, an area once known as Vinegar Hill, on one of the streets between Gaffey and the harbor.

We turned onto Sixth Street, driving past an old theater and Vinegar Hill Books. At the corner of Centre and Sixth was Papadakis Taverna, Frank's favorite Greek restaurant. We had dined there not long ago, and now I thought of how close we had been to Briana's home that night.

We turned off Sixth and drove through the surrounding neighborhood, a mix of homes and apartments that ranged in style from Victorian mansion to postwar crackerbox.

Briana's apartment wasn't hard to find: there was a black-and-white LAPD patrol car sitting in front of it.

"Old Mac didn't trust us to wait for him," Rachel laughed.

"Mac?"

"McCain. He called me 'Pazzi, I suppose? He picked that up from those boneheads I worked with in Phoenix."

"How well do you know this guy?" I asked.

"Well enough," she answered, in a tone that made me change the subject. She was doing me a big favor and her past was none of my business—my own is by no means sterling. I was curious about her connection with McCain, but it was clear I'd have to wait to learn more.

The apartment was in a run-down fourplex. The crown of the building was a flat roof skirted by three irregular rows of red Spanish tile. The exterior walls were sun-faded brown with white pockmarks; as we came closer, we could see that the stucco was coming off—large, broken, dry bubbles of it clung to the walls—wounds in the building's hide.

The windows at the side of the building were barred. Four large picture windows faced the street; at the center of the building, a wide doorway opened onto a concrete porch. Inside this door were a short entryway and a steep set of stairs; at the top and bottom of the stairs, apartment doors faced one another. On the right-hand side of the entry, a short row of black mailboxes was attached to the wall. Self-adhesive gold numbers—the type one might find in a hardware store—adorned the locking mailbox doors, numbering them one through four. Three of the four boxes also had red-and-white tape labels bearing the occupant's first initial and last name.

The officer in the patrol car waved at us. Rachel smiled and waved back, saying under her breath, "Yeah, putz, we know you're watching us." I glanced at my watch. We were only about fifteen minutes early.

The building was quiet; I decided to see if any of Briana's

neighbors were home. I knocked on the door across from Briana's and heard a parrot squawk, but no one came to the door. I heard a phone ring in one of the upstairs apartments; it rang about ten times. I climbed the stairs anyway, but got nothing but a little exercise.

When—right at ten o'clock—Rachel saw McCain's car pull into an empty parking spot down the street, she glanced at me nervously and took a deep breath. I had never seen her less than ready to take on the world, so I was surprised by her reaction. But when McCain stepped out of his car, dramatically clutched his chest and shouted, "Married? *Married?*," she was already grinning and hurrying toward him. There was nothing sexual about their dancing embrace in the middle of the street, nothing desperate. If anything, it was the sort of happy, enthusiastic hug two football fans might give one another after their team scored a crucial goal on a Hail Mary pass. Friends, I told myself, they were just friends.

Told myself that until they came walking back toward me, Rachel a little ahead of him, and I saw how McCain watched her, saw the hunger with which he took in her way of moving, and saw her glance back at him and smile.

Show him a picture of Pete, I wanted to say, but didn't. She must have read something on my face though, because she stopped smiling and said, "I guess you two have already met."

"I guess you two have, too," I said, hating the snide little note I heard in it.

"Well," McCain said uncomfortably, bringing out a keychain with a St. Christopher medal on it. "Here are your aunt's keys."

"Thanks," I said, taking them from him. Determined to redeem myself with Rachel, I added, "Listen, you two haven't seen each other in a long time, and it's bound to take me awhile to even figure out how I want to tackle this job, so maybe you'd like to grab a cup of coffee somewhere."

"I'd love to do some catching up," McCain said, "but why don't you come with us?"

"Yeah, come along," Rachel said meaningfully. "I'll drive."

"Okay," McCain said. He went over to the patrol car, said something to the officer in it.

While McCain was out of earshot, I started to apologize to her, but she said, "Thanks for coming along. I know you're anxious to get started on your aunt's place."

Nothing was further from the truth than this last statement, but I didn't argue with her. I looked up to see the black-and-white driving off. McCain was walking back.

"You're still a suspicious bastard, Mac," Rachel said when he was nearer. "What the hell was that guy guarding? We're here to take everything we can out of the place anyway."

"As I recall, you're good with a set of lock picks. Why risk damage to the door?"

"No damage. Like you said, I'm good with them."

He didn't answer, just started to ask her about people in Phoenix. She started asking about people in the LAPD. This continued even after we were at the coffee shop, Rachel and I on one side of a booth, McCain on the other. He tried to bring me into the conversation by talking about Frank's time as a hostage, focusing on the efforts to free him. It was still difficult to talk about.

"That whole experience was awful," Rachel said. "It's still with all of us, Mac. It's affected everybody who cares about Frank. Out on the job, I don't think Pete can stand to go more than a couple of hours without knowing where Frank is. Drives Frank nuts."

"That's right," McCain said. "I forgot he was Harriman's partner." He smiled a little and said to me, "I think your husband was kind of angry with me last night."

Kind of angry? I decided I wouldn't tell him all the choice things Frank had said about him on the drive home.

"In fact," he went on, "I think he was seriously consider-ing kicking my ass."

"Then you're lucky he didn't try," Rachel said.

"Your husband as big as Harriman?" he asked.

"You don't need to worry about whether my husband can kick your ass," she said, leaning across the table.

"Why not?"

"Because we both know *I* can."

He laughed until he was wiping tears from his face, but didn't contradict her.

She dropped him off at his car, telling him she wanted his parking spot—which, of course, ensured that he had to drive off. He was no sooner out of sight than Rachel said, "Be careful around him. He suspects you—if not of murder, of—well, I don't know what."

"How can you tell that? He never talked about the case this morning."

"I know him. He doesn't trust anybody."

This time, when we came up the porch steps, I could hear the noise of neighbors at home. The parrot in apartment one was calling out "Stick'em up!" The phone was ringing in apartment four, but this time it was answered after two rings. Briana's apartment was silent.

I reached into my jeans pocket and took out the key ring; it had three keys and the medallion on it. I used the smallest key to open mailbox number four, the one with nothing but a sticky rectangle where "B. Maguire" ought to have been. The mailbox was empty. Now that we weren't being watched by the LAPD, I took out my notebook and wrote down the other occupants' names and their apart-ment numbers. Rachel watched me, but didn't say anything.

"Is that a Christopher medal?" she asked, as I moved to the door of apartment number four.

"Yes. I was sad when Christopher got taken off the A-list. All the surfers used to wear the medals anyway."

"I never did any surfing, but maybe he deserved to get ousted. He was supposed to protect travelers, right?"

"Right."

"Your aunt couldn't make it from here to the store."

I shrugged and put the key in the lock.

Above us, a door opened and an elderly woman stepped out on the landing. She was wearing a thin housecoat and a pair of slippers; her white hair was in wild disarray. "Just hold it right there!" she called, coming down the stairs at such a fast clip, I feared for her safety.

She pointed a finger at me. "Just what do you think you're doing?"

"I'm Briana's niece—"

"Hah!"

"She is!" Rachel protested.

"Let's see some identification," the woman said.

"All right, Mrs. Woolrich," I said, using the name from the tag on the mailbox. I pulled out my wallet as she continued to eye me suspiciously.

I showed her my driver's license. She pulled a pair of reading glasses out of the pocket of the housecoat and put them on. She looked between me and the license. "Irene Kelly . . . you're Mary Kelly's grandniece?"

"Yes. And this is my friend, Rachel Giocopazzi."

"I'm Esther Woolrich. Miss Woolrich, by the way, which is something no mailbox can tell you," she said with a wink. More solemnly, she said, "Mary told me she'd be sending you by for Briana's things. I'm sorry for your loss, although from what Mary tells me . . ."

"Yes," I said quickly. "Well, if you'll excuse us, we've got a lot of work to do."

She didn't move. "Sorry if I was a little brusque, but twice in the last few weeks, someone has tried to rob this apart-

ment. Now that the cops are going away, we don't want anyone to start trying to break in again."

"Mary mentioned something about break-ins, but—only
this apartment?"

"Yes. I've told the police about it, but they don't do a
thing."

"You told the homicide detective?" Rachel asked.

"No, no. As I said, this was before we knew what had
happened to poor Briana. Started not long before she died.
I called the regular number, not homicide. They think I'm
some old crackpot. You'd think I'd have to wait until the
thieves actually broke in."

"You came down those stairs thinking we were burglars?" Rachel asked. "Miss Woolrich, next time, it might be
better to call the police. If we *had* been here to commit a
burglary—"

"You probably would have run off. That's what the others did."

"What others?" I asked.

"First time, it was a man. Come right up to the front door,
bold as brass. I'd seen him here before—parked out front.
Casing the joint, that's what he was up to then. That was
before Briana died."

"I'm confused—did he try to rob Briana's apartment
while she was still alive?"

"Yes. He parked out front and watched her leave, then
came up and read the mailboxes, just like you did."

"You couldn't see that from your apartment," I said.

She sighed, then startled us by calling out, "Open the
door, Ruby."

Behind us, the door to apartment number one opened a
crack, and a short, stout woman who appeared to be near
Esther Woolrich's age peered out.

"Put the gun away and come out and meet Mary's grandniece," Esther said.

Rachel and I quickly exchanged horrified looks.

"Oh, don't worry! She's trained to use it," Esther said.

We were not entirely reassured. Anyone with a parrot that had learned to say "Stick'em up" might be a little trigger-happy. But when Ruby stepped out into the hall, she greeted us warmly, with no sign of any intention of shooting us.

"You ever ridden with Mary in that car of hers?" she asked me as she shook my hand.

"Several times," I said.

Rachel looked at me questioningly.

"A cherry '68 Mustang convertible," I said, getting nods of agreement from Esther and Ruby.

"I've got to meet this woman," Rachel said.

"Who lives in the other apartment?" I asked, pointing to the one across the hall from Esther's.

"Oh, that guy. He's spending a month back east with his grandkids," Esther said, then added with a note of disapproval, "He's like your aunt was—he keeps to himself."

"But I take it you all keep an eye on one another?" I said to Ruby.

"Yes. That's how we caught the burglars. Esther scared them off—didn't have to use my little semiautomatic. Only a twenty-two, not much stopping power. But it will do in a pinch. I must say I'm relieved to have you take Briana's belongings away from this place."

"Tell us more about these attempted burglaries," Rachel said. "The first time you saw him, he parked out front, came up to look at the mailboxes, then left?"

"Yes," Ruby said. "Esther spotted him first, and called me. We watched him while he was watching the place. But he didn't try to get in that time. Later, we sat down and figured out that it had been just before the accident." She shook her head. "I feel so terrible about that! Briana kept to herself more than most, so we didn't always know what she was up to, if you know what I mean. We knew she wasn't home, but recently she'd taken to leaving for a few days at a time, and we just thought she might have gone visiting some friends or relatives. But then to find out . . ." Her voice trailed off as she caught Esther's censorious glare.

"To answer your question," Esther said, "the man showed up just before Briana died, and watched the place. Then he came by again, after the accident, but before we knew what had become of her. He had a set of lock picks with him."

"Lock picks?" Rachel said. "Are you sure?"

"Yes," Ruby said. "Saw them plain as day through the peephole." She pointed out a small opening in her apartment door.

"I scared him off," Esther said. "And I got a good look at him, too."

"Mind describing him for me?" I asked.

"He's tall," Esther said, "about six foot, I'd say, and handsome enough, I guess."

"Hoo!" Ruby exclaimed. "A regular silver fox!"

"Control yourself," Esther said, but added, "To be fair, he was a somewhat attractive man. I'd put him in his mid-to-late fifties. Broad shoulders. He must have been dark-haired at one time, but mostly gray now. Cut short. And he was clean-shaven."

"I smelled booze on him," Ruby added.

"Oh, now, Ruby!"

"I was right down here near him, Esther, and I tell you I smelled booze." She turned to us. "Do you know him?"

"Now Ruby Hambly, why on earth would they know a drunken burglar?" Esther exclaimed. "Of course they don't."

"You said there were two attempts?" I asked.

"Yes," Esther said. "The second time was just a day or two ago. Didn't get as good a look that time—slender fellow, trying to break in through a back window."

"How tall?" Rachel asked.

"That's hard to say, too. I only saw him at night, and from

my upstairs window. Saw someone in dark clothes and a knit cap, which was an odd thing to be wearing on a spring evening. Heard him trying to pry the bars off. Stupid thing to try. I shouted down at him and he ran off. I'd guess him to be younger than the fellow who was at the door, and definitely not as tall."

"Sure it wasn't the same man?" I asked.

"That much I'm sure of. Different build."

Rachel asked a few more questions, but the ladies seemed not to be able to recall much more. There was an argument over the make and color of the drunken burglar's car. It was American, a sedan, dark green or brown.

"I appreciate your watching over things," I said. "I'm going to try to get everything moved out this weekend, so with any luck this place won't seem so attractive to thieves."

They again expressed condolences, then went back to their apartments.

I unlocked Briana's apartment door, and Rachel followed me in and shut it behind us.

"I'll open a couple of windows," she said.

The room we stepped into was warm and close. I felt a mild sensation of claustrophobia, and if Rachel had not hurried to let some air in, I might have stepped back outside. I glanced back at the door and saw a crucifix above it, dried palm leaves from a Palm Sunday Mass placed behind the cross. I turned my attention back to the job at hand.

I reached over a small, tattered sofa and raised the blind on the picture window, filling the room with sunlight. Looking more closely at the sofa, I saw tufts of shredding on the corners and arms; the type that can only be made by a cat who has decided to use the upholstery as a scratching post. For a moment I worried that some feline had been horribly neglected after Briana's death, but saw no other signs that a cat had been living in the apartment—no scent of a cat or a litter box, no fur, no food dishes, no cat toys.

This front room was a parlor of sorts, a room that could be closed off from the rest of the apartment by pulling two sliding wooden doors shut. The carpet was a faded floral pattern of large, pale roses on a beige background. On one wall, there was a framed print of the Sacred Heart. On top of a set of built-in bookcases, Briana had made up a small shrine to the Blessed Virgin: a little plaster statuette surrounded by five blue-glass candle holders. A pink-glass rosary lay to one side, on top of a holy card with the prayer "Hail Holy Queen" printed on it. One shelf of the bookcase held a dog-eared, leather-bound Bible and a worn *St. Joseph's Sunday Missal*, as well as *Butler's Lives of the Saints*. There were no other books, only two solemn ceramic angels, one with its guiding hand on a small boy's shoulder, the other like it, but guiding a little girl. The lower shelves held a few seashells.

If Briana was this religious a couple of decades ago, when we were closer, I didn't remember it. Devout Catholics though Briana and my mother had been, that devotion hadn't overwhelmed the decor of their homes.

Rachel had already moved to the rear of the apartment. I continued to walk through rooms, but more slowly. I moved from the front room into a larger room that contained a small dining table and a set of built-in cupboards. The cupboards contained a few pieces of mismatched crockery. On the table, facing the single chair, was a small, black-and-white TV with a crack in its case; a bent hanger did duty as an antennae. In front of the TV was a plastic placemat—a photograph of a meadow blooming with small yellow flowers. Although it was clean, there was an indentation where hot cups of tea had been placed. I caught myself making this supposition of tea and stood remembering that unlike her sister, Briana had never acquired a taste for coffee; that on Sundays after Mass, Briana would come to the house and my mother—who had shopped at special stores to find the type of tea her sister liked to drink—would bake scones. Tea and scones to make Briana feel welcomed in our home. I ran my fingers across the indentation in the plastic mat and wondered if Briana ever thought of those long-ago Sunday mornings.

I went into the small, bright kitchen at the back of the apartment. I opened cupboards, found a can of peaches, two cans of chicken noodle soup, a tin of Hershey's cocoa, a box of powdered milk, a box of baking soda, a small box of sugar and half a bag of flour. Nothing more. The refrigerator was empty, but Mary had warned me that the landlord was going to clean it out—it belonged to him, along with the stove. In a drawer next to the stove, I found a box of generic-brand tea bags. I felt my throat tighten.

I shut the drawer and moved through another door, which led to a bathroom. Here there was a sink, toilet and claw-foot tub; a small mirror that was losing its silvering; a pink toothbrush in a water-stained glass; three hairpins near the faucet; cracked linoleum; a set of thin towels neatly folded over a single towel rack. I moved on.

I found Rachel sitting at a small rolltop desk in the bedroom, lost in thought. It didn't look as if she had been searching the contents of the desk, which surprised me—we're both curious by nature.

"You doing okay?" she asked as I walked in.

"Yes. Sorry to take so long—I guess I've been looking for—well, it's hard to explain."

"Something to tell you who she was?"

"Yes."

"This is the room you've been looking for."

As I glanced around the bedroom, I saw that she was right. There were a number of photographs on display on top of a plain wooden dresser. The small bookcase in the room was not filled with religious books but with two types of paperbacks: westerns and Georgette Heyer romances. Near the end of the neatly made twin bed was a rocking chair; a basket of knitting—blue and gray yarn to make an afghan, it seemed—lay on the seat.

There were a crucifix and a rosary on a nightstand next to the bed, and above it, a print known to any Catholic school child. An angel with flowing blond tresses and a white star above her head hovers serenely behind two barefoot children, a little boy in a straw hat and his sister, who carries a basket over one arm and comforts her brother with the other. Dark woods rise in the background as the children cross a dilapidated bridge over a treacherous river, but we fear not—their guardian angel will see them to safety.

The nightstand also held a plastic statue of the Blessed Virgin Mary that was about ten inches high, the type that has a little night-light bulb in the base and glows from within when plugged in, although this one wasn't. But even with these items, the bedroom had less the feel of a religious articles store display than the front room.

"Is this you?" Rachel asked, holding out a small, framed snapshot.

I took a look. "Yes, with Barbara. Judging from the missing front teeth, I was probably about seven, so Barbara was about twelve."

Barbara and I were a study in contrasts—she, a redhead with green eyes, was looking at the camera with a bored, half-pouting regard: how awful to be asked to pose with her little sister. I, with dark hair and blue eyes, looking more like the Kellys—my father's side of the family. In the photo I was grinning up at the lens with my goofy gap-toothed smile, oblivious to Barbara's sullenness.

I began studying the other photographs. One was of a thin, gray-haired woman with a cane, standing next to a priest, in front of a church. I saw the family resemblance and thought perhaps this was a photograph of my grandmother, in Kansas, until I noticed a palm tree in the background. A closer look made me realize—with a shock—that this must be Briana herself. In that instant it was brought home to me that she had not stopped aging when my mother died; that while my mother would forever be fixed in my mind as a woman in her early forties, Briana had gone on, had become a woman in her sixties. She was my mother's younger sister by a number of years, but I could not remember exactly how many, and now, looking at the photo, I wondered what my mother might have looked like at a similar age, had she lived.

Even taking a high estimate of Briana's age, she could not have been past her early sixties. The years, I was sad to see, had not been kind.

Another photo showed her when she was younger, looking much as I remembered her—probably in her late thirties or early forties—holding a toddler. Travis, most likely. There were several photos of Travis at various ages, sometimes with other adults and children, other times alone. None showed Travis with his father, Arthur. There were no photos of Arthur.

I looked for the most recent of Travis, which seemed to be a senior yearbook portrait. I picked this one up and studied it, trying to be objective. With dark hair and light-green eyes, Travis resembled Arthur to a great degree—but some of the Maguire looks were also in his features. Perhaps he had not grown up to be quite as handsome as his father, but he wasn't hard to look at.

"Your cousin?" Rachel asked.

"Yes. This must be from high school. He's in his mid-twenties now."

"He looks like his dad?"

"For the most part. You're wondering if Arthur was the man who was trying to pick the locks on the front door?"

"Yes. Do you think it could have been him?"

"It's possible. Allowing for a few changes since I last saw

him, he'd probably fit the description—but so could any number of other men. The age would be about right. If it was Arthur, why wouldn't he just knock on the door?"

"He could have been looking for something she didn't want to give him."

"What? A copy of *Butler's Lives of the Saints?* A pink rosary? An old tin of cocoa?"

"We haven't looked through this desk yet. Maybe he wanted something that had to do with the murder of his first wife—"

"Only wife, as far as I know. And that was more than a dozen years ago," I said.

"Was he ever tried?"

"No. Never even charged."

"Look at it another way," she said. "If he had been tried and acquitted, he'd be protected."

"Because of double jeopardy—he couldn't be tried twice for the same crime."

"Right. So he'd feel safe. But as it is, he's still vulnerable. No statute of limitation on murder."

"So if she blew his alibi apart . . . but this is nonsense," I said. "She wasn't the only one who alibied him. They were at the emergency room that night with Travis."

She crossed her arms and tapped a toe. "You know the details of the murder case?"

"Not really. I wasn't living around here then. I was working up in Bakersfield."

"But . . . well, that's your business," she said, throwing her hands up in exasperation. "And what's done is done."

"What's that supposed to mean?"

"I mean, you ignored your aunt for more than twenty years, and there's not exactly any way to make up for that now, is there?"

I didn't answer.

"Sorry," she said.

I studied the photo of Briana and Travis, the one taken when he was a toddler. Like my mother, Briana was a redhead. Her eyes were blue, her smile shy. "She was timid," I said. "Quiet and unassuming, for the most part. I'll admit she could have changed over the years, but it's hard for me to imagine her blackmailing Arthur."

She shrugged. "Who knows?"

"So you think he came around here and tried to shut her up?"

"Right," she said. "A possibility, anyway."

"Maybe you're right. Maybe she had some kind of proof that he did it, alibi or no alibi. Otherwise, what the hell would anybody try to steal from her? I mean, even the most rabid Georgette Heyer fan wouldn't go to the trouble of prying off the bars on the back windows to steal these paperbacks."

"Georgette Heyer?"

"The author of these genteel Regency romances," I said, pointing to the books. "Not the sort of reading that leads to a life of crime."

"No, I guess not."

"It wasn't a random break-in, though. He was looking for her place specifically—Esther said he had been watching the apartment, checking mailboxes."

"*Bene.* We agree."

"Tell you what. Let's take a quick look through whatever papers McCain left in the desk and then pack up here. If we have time, maybe we can find the little market she was walking to, try to locate the place where the accident happened. It's supposed to be close to here."

"Sounds good. Monday morning, I'll see if I can learn anything more from McCain."

"You don't need to get involved—"

"You think you can keep me out of this? Besides, your aunt Mary was right. You're going to need to find your cousin—and fast. If the alibi can be broken, he's probably next on his dear old dad's hit list."

Just as she said this, we heard an urgent knocking on the front door.

I opened it to see Ruby looking flushed and excited. "He's here!" she shouted.

6

"Who's here?" I asked, still thinking of Travis.

I heard a car driving off just as Esther, hurrying down the stairs, hollered, "Damnation, Ruby! You scared him off. Didn't even get a chance to look at the plates!"

"Who are you talking about?" I asked, stepping out of the apartment to look up and down the street. Rachel joined me, but neither one of us saw any moving vehicles.

"The one who tried to break into the apartment!" Ruby said. "I noticed him first," she added, glancing back at Esther with a look of reproach. "Maybe if I hadn't taken the time to call Esther, we would have been able to surprise him."

"Did you get a better look at the car?" Rachel asked.

She blushed, then shook her head.

"The color?" I asked.

"Green!" she answered quickly.

"Brown!" Esther countered.

I asked them to wait, then went inside the apartment to get my purse, pulled out a couple of business cards and a pen. I wrote my home phone number on the backs of the cards, then handed them to Briana's neighbors. "If you see him again, call me—doesn't matter what time of day."

"You're a reporter?" Ruby asked. When I said yes, Esther began to give me some ideas for improving the *Express*— although she admitted that she had stopped taking it about ten years ago—continuing until Ruby said, "For crying out loud, Esther! She works there, she doesn't own it. They ever ask you how the wing on a plane ought to be built when you were answering phones at Douglas? If the answer is yes, I'm never going to fly anywhere again!"

Rachel started laughing, which made Esther put her chin up in the air. I did my best to smooth her ruffled feathers, thanked them both, and Rachel and I went back into the apartment.

"Think he'll be back?" Rachel asked as she shut the door.

"No," I said. "Not unless he thinks we failed to find whatever he's looking for."

She looked around the room thoughtfully, eyeing the ceiling, walls and floor as if looking for a secret compartment.

"You said your aunt Mary arranged for movers to pick up the furniture?" she asked.

"Yes, they're coming Monday. And she's hired a cleaning crew to come by on Tuesday. So we're just taking the personal items—clothing, papers, dishes, pictures—things like that."

"Yeah, all right," she said absently.

I wasn't surprised when she started pulling the built-in drawers all the way out, inspecting the bottoms, looking for hiding places. I started doing the same to the furniture in the bedroom as I packed Briana's things away.

Even with this check for secret compartments, packing up the meager contents of the apartment took little time. I didn't search through the items we were taking—the actual contents of the drawers and cabinets—figuring I could do that later. Like Rachel, I wanted to have a look at anything we weren't taking with us.

Only once was I tempted to linger over the contents of a drawer—when I found one that was filled with photographs, including some black-and-white photos of my mother and grandmother. But I heard Rachel working steadily in the other rooms, and rather than reminisce while she worked, I boxed the photos gently but quickly.

The desk had an assortment of loose papers in it, no more organized than the photographs in the drawer. I took a quick look at the papers, but none seemed to have black-mail potential, nor did they immediately identify Travis's whereabouts.

None of my searching revealed any secret hiding places, but when I was ready to start loading the car, I couldn't find Rachel. I went from room to room, and didn't see her. I glanced out at the car, thinking perhaps she had already started loading it, but she wasn't there. I walked into the apartment again, this time loudly calling her name. Her voice came back muffled, as if through a wall. I found myself wondering if she was in a secret passageway, per-haps having pressed some button on a built-in bookcase. But her voice had seemed to come from the kitchen, not the bookcases.

In the kitchen, though, I still couldn't see her. I called out again and when I turned toward her voice, she startled me by briefly popping her face up in the window over the sink. "Out here!" she shouted. I looked out. She was standing beneath the window, in the backyard. As I started to unlatch the sash, she shouted, "Don't! Don't move it! Come back here—I want to show you something."

I went outside, down the porch steps and through a side gate to a small backyard shared by the four tenants. It was basically a patch of grass with a couple of rusted metal lawn chairs on it, but Rachel wasn't touring the gardens. She was staring at the window.

At first I didn't see what was holding her attention, but as I drew closer, I saw that she was studying some sort of strange symbol, drawn in pencil on the windowsill, near the bars. It was small, not more than a few inches wide, and looked like a rectangle with the bottom side missing; a small, single straight line rose perpendicular from the top side:

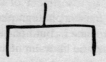

"A gang symbol?" I asked.

"I don't think so," she said. "It's not really in that style, and it's way too small. But maybe it had some meaning to the burglar."

"Why do you say that?"

She pointed to tool marks left on the bars of the window. "I think it marked this window as the one to break into. Or maybe it marked your aunt's apartment. Or maybe it was left here as a kind of warning to your aunt."

"Awfully small warning in an obscure place. She might not have ever come out here, or seen it if she did. And it could have been drawn a long time ago. Some kid could have drawn it."

"Not too long ago," she said, pointing at, but not touching, other areas of the sill. "See? Someone wiped at the dust on the sill before they drew it. It's less dirty than these other places. And rain or more time would have left it looking like the rest of the sill."

"Hmm. And now that I think about it, I guess no little kid drew it. Not up this high."

"No. Older kid, maybe, but you'd expect more than one little mark if some teenager wanted to doodle." She studied it for another minute and said, "I've got a camera in the car. Mind if I take a photo of this?"

I shrugged. "Be my guest."

After she had photographed the drawing (at one point making me hold a ruler near it), we began loading boxes into the car.

When we had finished, Rachel peered into her trunk. "Been a long time since I could fit all my worldly possessions into the trunk and backseat of a Plymouth."

"Look, if you're hinting that I ought to feel ashamed of myself—"

"Hey, relax! I'm sorry about what I said earlier. Nobody's trying to blame you for anything. All right?"

"Sorry. Guess I'm on edge. Maybe it's because your friend McCain *is* trying to blame me."

She closed the lid of the trunk a little more forcefully than necessary. "Let's see if we can find this little grocery store," she said, opening the driver's side door.

"It's probably within walking distance."

"I don't want to leave the car sitting here—not with all her belongings in it."

No sooner had she said this than a now-familiar car pulled up. McCain. He double-parked, blocking us. Even though Rachel was the one standing between the two cars, I took a couple of steps back on the sidewalk, a brief, wild urge to run passing through me. Run? From what? Maybe it was just that McCain was starting to make me feel hemmed in.

There was a humming sound as he lowered the passenger window.

"You live in this neighborhood, Mac?" Rachel asked.

"Just wondered how you were doing," he said. "And I brought you a little present."

"We're fine," she said coolly. "We just finished up, in fact. You caught us just as we were leaving."

"Find anything?"

"Nothing we could walk off with," she answered. "But you ought to turn on the famous Mac charm with the old ladies in the neighboring apartments. Ask them about break-ins." She laughed. "Or ask the knuckleheads who took the breaking-and-entering complaint calls before Briana Maguire was killed."

"Briana Maguire called in a burglary in progress?"

"No, but her neighbors did. You didn't run a history on this address? Mac, Mac, Mac. You're slipping."

"Planning to do it Monday," he said, turning red.

"Well, we have to get going."

He extended a manila envelope. "Your present."

"What is it?" she asked, taking it.

"Copies of her bills. Maybe they'll help you find the kid."

"All this time, you been down at the PD, running copies of all this for me?"

He nodded.

She gave him a brilliant smile. "Thanks, Mac. I owe you."

"No, no, you don't."

"Tell you what—wait just a second." She turned to me. "Come on, get in." I obeyed. She got in on her side and rolled the window down. "You can have your parking spot back. Talk to those other tenants—it will make you look good."

If he was disappointed that she was leaving, he hid it well. "Thanks, Rach."

She pulled out, let him park, then backed up to block him as he had blocked us, only McCain couldn't even open his door. When he lowered the driver's side window, she said, "You know what, Jimmy Mac? Those old gals just might make you let up on Irene."

She put the car in gear, laughing as she pulled away. I picked up the envelope and started looking through it, hearing her hum a catchy oldies tune. She had stopped the car again by the time I realized the song was "Jimmy Mac."

It hadn't taken long to find the small tienda, which was about two blocks from Briana's apartment. We parked on the street, at the corner beneath a shady tree. As I stepped out of the car, I noticed a little white cross was planted in the crook of the tree roots, a small, dusty cluster of artificial roses entwined at its base. I looked away from it and strode resolutely toward the store.

The store owner, Mr. Reyes, smiled and welcomed us in English, but when he learned that we spoke Spanish, he was happier to converse in it. My Spanish is passable, but Rachel speaks it fluently, so I let her do the talking. She explained my relationship to Briana, and at his questioning look, added that Briana was the lady who was killed in a hit-and-run accident. Wasn't the accident at this corner?

His face changed entirely, and once again I received condolences I had not earned. Yes, he told us, this was the corner where the lady was killed. He was obviously upset about it.

His wife, who also worked at the market, was visiting their daughter today—she would feel sorry to have missed us. They were both in the store on the day of the accident. They had not seen the accident itself; they had heard the sounds of the impact and of the car speeding away. When his wife looked outside and saw what had happened—he shook his head sadly. After a moment, he went on, saying that he was the one who had called 911. The ambulance came, but everyone knew it was too late. He glanced at me and quickly said that they were told the lady had not suffered.

Although the police had questioned them, they had not been told of any outcome of the police investigation. They had been worried that the woman was still unidentified.

"¿Su tía?" he asked me again.

"Sí, mi tía," I answered. *"La hermana de mi madre."* Yes, she was my aunt, my mother's sister.

Again he expressed condolences, and then asked me if I would please say my aunt's name again. He repeated it softly to himself several times, as if memorizing it, changing it slightly but making it sound no less beautiful with Spanish pronunciation. He patted his pockets and found a pen, wrote *Briana Maguire* on the back of a receipt, then paused and looked up at me as if to verify the spelling.

"Bueno," I said.

He talked to us again of his concern over the accident, and was obviously relieved that someone had claimed the body; he was Catholic, and knew my aunt was Catholic— they were concerned that my aunt had not received a Catholic burial.

How did he know she was Catholic? Rachel asked. Did she belong to his parish?

He wasn't sure if she was of his parish; he attended the Spanish-language Mass at nine o'clock and he didn't think the lady spoke Spanish. But he knew she was Catholic because she carried the key chain with the St. Christopher medallion on it, and because she had ashes on her forehead when she had shopped on Ash Wednesday.

The lady had been coming to his store only for a few months, but he liked her. She was shy, he said, and he never asked her name. Now he regretted this, too, but at the time he had not wanted to be presumptuous. Once, he said, she told me that she was sorry she had never learned Spanish, and told him that her son spoke it very well. "I think she missed her son," he said. "She only mentioned him once, but when she did . . ." He gestured to his face. "She looked sad."

A man came to the register, and Mr. Reyes introduced us to his customer, and again a round of condolences was offered. Did we need any help? Was there something they could do? Did I know, the customer asked me, that the store owner's wife had made an *altarcito*—a marker, a little shrine with a small cross—and put some flowers out on the corner where the accident happened? That she had even arranged for a Mass to be said for my aunt? That she had asked everyone if they knew anything about the lady?

After expressing my gratitude, I listened as Mr. Reyes and the customer told us more about Mrs. Reyes's activities following my aunt's death. Soon I saw that I was indebted to this woman I had not yet met—and saw how it was that the LAPD eventually discovered where Briana lived.

Mrs. Reyes had described the lady who had been killed to anyone who would listen, and some of her customers, who lived in this neighborhood, remembered seeing the lady with the cane. One customer had often seen her walk from this street to that, another had once seen her walking back from the store in a certain direction. Mrs. Reyes passed her information along to the police, who thanked her, but had not told her the results of her efforts.

Rachel asked a few more questions, confirming that none of them had ever seen Briana come to the store with anyone else; no one they knew had seen the car that struck her, although they were told there were witnesses who had talked to the police. No, Mr. Reyes told us, she was not carrying a handbag—she always arrived with nothing more than a small coin purse, which she kept in the pocket of her sweater or coat. It was perhaps, he ventured, a little cool for her, living near the water, because she always wore a sweater or coat. On that day, a warm spring day, he recalled, she had worn her blue sweater.

We thanked him and the customer for their time, and I asked him to please convey to his wife that my family deeply appreciated her help, that it was very kind of her to remember my aunt with the shrine and the Mass. If ever I could do anything for them—

"De nada," Mr. Reyes protested. "It's nothing."

We stopped off at Aunt Mary's house on our way back home. As might be expected, Rachel and Aunt Mary hit it off instantly. While I worked at hanging Briana's clothes in the closet of one of Mary's guest rooms, Rachel told Mary about our day's discoveries.

"I didn't know you spoke Spanish," Mary said to me.

"Not as well as Rachel, but I studied it even before the *Express* started requiring all of its reporters to learn Spanish."

"Hmm. Paper should have done that years ago. You said you went back to the apartment after you talked to Mr. Reyes. Did the neighbors recognize Travis from any of Briana's photos?"

I still wondered if James McCain had more to do with Rachel's decision to make the return trip than Travis did, but McCain had left by the time we got there. To Mary, I said, "Not really. They said Travis might have been the younger of the two men who helped her move in, but they weren't certain—Briana and that young man hadn't behaved toward one another as a mother and son would, they said—hardly spoke to one another, and the young man had not been back since."

"Who was the other man?"

"A priest. When he came to visit other times, he was wearing a collar, they said."

"What priest?"

"We asked that, too. They didn't know."

Mary looked troubled, then straightened her shoulders and began to ask Rachel a lot of questions about her work as a cop in Phoenix and as a private eye here in Las Piernas. When I hinted that grilling the volunteer help might show a lack of manners, she told me to mind my own damned business.

I was hanging up Briana's moth-eaten wool coat, half-listening to them, when I impulsively reached into one of the pockets, thinking the trait of forgetting to empty one's coat pockets might run in the family. My fingertips met a stiff piece of paper, and my imagination ran ahead of me—this would be a three-by-five card with Travis's address on it. Instead, to my dismay, I withdrew a holy card.

I might have sworn, but Saint Somebody-or-another was looking right at me, and there are limits to my sacrilegiousness. It was a familiar image, a monk in long brown Franciscan robes, holding a stalk of lilies and the child Jesus. I turned the card over to see who it was and received a shock that made me reach clumsily for the edge of the bed, where I sat down hard next to Rachel.

"What's gotten into you?" Mary said sharply.

"Arthur—"

"What?"

"Arthur Spanning. He's dead. This is a holy card from his funeral Mass."

7

On the back of the holy card—a likeness of St. Anthony of Padua, as it turned out—was a prayer for the dead. A few added lines of print indicated that Arthur Anthony Spanning had died three weeks ago at the age of forty-eight.

We each took turns looking at the back of the card, not speaking for several moments.

"Poor Travis!" Aunt Mary said softly. "Both parents in such a short period of time!"

"They followed one another to the grave a little closely, didn't they?" I said. "A week apart."

Rachel nodded. "Exactly what I was thinking."

"This funeral home," I said, studying the card, "is in Las Piernas. Do you think he died here?"

"Kind of strange to think of him living here in town all this time, isn't it?" Rachel said.

"Yes. And Briana must have been in contact with him, or kept track of him, anyway. Otherwise, how would she know about his funeral? I wonder why she went to it?"

"Maybe to make sure he was really dead," Rachel said. "You know, if he faked the wedding . . ."

Aunt Mary was pacing, ignoring these remarks. "This is going to be very hard on Travis," she said.

"Was he close to Arthur?" I asked.

"I have no idea. I used to see them once in a great while when Travis was little. After Briana moved from Las Piernas, she and I never exchanged more news than would fit on a few lines at the bottom of a greeting card. She never mentioned Arthur, and only wrote 'Travis is doing well in school,' or 'Travis is growing so tall,' things like that. She did tell me that he wasn't going to be living with her at the new apartment, but I suppose I just thought it was high time he was on his own. I asked for his new address, but she never sent it."

"Maybe he already knows about his father's death," I said. "He may be the one who told Briana about it."

"But to lose his remaining parent so quickly!" Mary said, pacing again.

"You have her old address? The place where she lived before she moved to this apartment?" I asked.

"Yes, I think I have it somewhere around here."

"That might help us find Travis," I said. "Maybe one of her former neighbors will know where he's living these days."

She searched for it and found it. I made a note of it and asked, "So she was at this place from the time of the murder until recently?"

"No, she didn't leave Las Piernas immediately after the murder. But she was at this place for a number of years."

"Do you remember anything about the murder of Arthur's first wife?" Rachel asked.

"Certainly. Arthur's wife was Gwendolyn DeMont, the sugar beet heiress."

Rachel raised a brow. "Sugar beet heiress?"

"Yes, this area used to have lots of sugar beet fields. That's how her grandfather started out, but that was just the seed money for their wealth. He made money in real estate and by investing in aerospace and oil companies—with a sense of timing that made the rest of us wish we had his crystal ball."

"You said this was her grandfather?" I asked.

"Right. He raised her. Her parents died when she was just a baby, not long after World War I, I believe."

I looked at the holy card again. "World War I? She must have been at least thirty years older than Arthur!"

"Yes, she was much older than he. I know you think of him as being much younger than Briana, but after Gwendolyn, Briana must have looked like a regular spring chicken to Arthur."

"Did you know Gwendolyn?" Rachel asked.

"Oh, no. But the family was wealthy and Los Alamitos isn't so far away, after all. Irene's grandfather used to like to go to the Los Alamitos Race Course, which is in Cypress, not Los Alamitos—but that's another story."

"What else do you know about Gwendolyn?" I asked, knowing where racetrack discussions could lead, and not especially inclined to have Rachel learn all about my grandfather's various pastimes and diversions.

"Not too much. She was a very shy woman. A recluse, really."

"Arthur was apparently attracted to shy women," I said.

"Perhaps he was—what of it?" she snapped. I didn't answer, and she scowled at me. "Maybe there are two pairs of Prissy Pants in the family."

Rachel didn't even try to hide her amusement.

I was saved further humiliation only because the doorbell rang. Mary answered it, and soon we heard our husbands' voices and the sound of their laughter. Rachel's face reflected nothing but pleasure when she heard it, and I hurried after her into the living room, where Frank and Pete were chatting with Mary.

"*Caro*," Rachel said, running a hand over Pete's sunburned bald head. "You didn't put the sunscreen on like I told you to!"

"See what happens when you don't go with us?" Pete said.

I found myself wondering what on earth had ever made me think she was flirting with McCain.

Frank put an arm around my shoulders. "Thought you'd like a ride home."

"That would be great," I said, perhaps a little too enthusiastically. "I need to get a few things out of Rachel's car."

We divided up the rest of Briana's belongings as planned, and Frank helped me to move the photos and desk papers from Rachel's car to his.

Once, while Frank was out of earshot, Pete asked, "You want us to try to look up this cousin of yours in DMV records?"

I shook my head. "McCain has undoubtedly already tried that. And things have been bad enough for you two at work lately. You might get in trouble."

He laughed at that and told me not to worry.

I thanked Rachel again, and we said good night to Mary and the Bairds. As we drove home, I made Frank tell me about his day first. He told me where they had sailed, about the dolphins they had seen, of a predictably futile but hilarious attempt by Pete to win an argument with Cassidy, of Jack's surprising ability to actually get the better of Cassidy once or twice—which had made Pete look at Jack with new admiration. "I kept trying to figure out if Cassidy was orchestrating the whole thing—you know how Pete is sometimes a little jealous of Jack? Maybe not jealous—"

"Yeah, jealous."

"Right, well, you know how Pete is—anyway, by the end of the day, Pete is treating Jack like he's his best pal. Inviting him over for dinner, asking Jack to tell Cassidy about his days in the motorcycle gang—and through all this, Cassidy—" He glanced over at me, stopped his spirited narrative and said, "Missed you, though."

"That was an afterthought if I've ever heard one."

He laughed. "No, really. Jack's talking about taking everyone to Catalina in a couple of weeks. You should come with us. I have the feeling your day wasn't so relaxing."

I shrugged.

"Tell me what happened."

I did, but didn't want to trouble him or bring down his mood, so I put the best face on it I could. He caught me at it. As we pulled into the driveway he said angrily, "You don't have to treat me like I'm going to break into pieces, you know. It's goddamned insulting. I'm tired of it. Bad enough to get it from the guys at work. Tiptoeing around me like I'm— like I'm a basket case or something."

"Sorry," I said. I tried to think of something else to say and only managed another lousy, "Sorry."

He kept going on about it for another ten minutes or so, long enough for me to stop feeling apologetic. Maybe I would have kept my cool if I hadn't spent the last two or three days looking at the ends of fingers pointed in my direction. I did manage to stay silent. At some point it must have dawned on him that I wasn't participating in the conversation, though, because he broke off and asked, "Do you understand what I'm saying?"

"You're treated like a leper at work and coddled at home. You want it to stop. I can't do anything about what happens to you at work, but it will be a damned pleasure to stop coddling you. Will a bell ring at the end of this lecture period, or will you dismiss class in some other way?"

He didn't answer, just swore under his breath and got out of the car. I sat there staring at the glove compartment as he opened the trunk, got the boxes out, and took them into the house, greeting the dogs as they ran outside. He came back out, walked over to my side of the car and lifted his hand, as if he were going to tap on the window. He hesitated, put his hand in his pocket and stood there. I went back to staring straight ahead, even when the dogs jumped up against the passenger door. I heard Frank tell them to get down, and they ran off to wrestle with one another in the front yard.

After a minute, Frank tapped his knuckles against the glass. I rolled the window down. He leaned over, so that his face was level with mine.

"Come inside," he said.

I didn't answer.

"Please."

"For most of the weekend," I said, "I've been doing whatever someone else wanted me to do. The results have not been great. Childish though it undoubtedly is, right now I just want to have a really terrific pout."

He moved a short distance away, but didn't go inside the house. He played with the dogs until they lay panting in the grass. Then he came over to the car again, but stood a few feet away. He squatted down, resting his elbows on his thighs. He plucked a piece of grass from the lawn, fiddled with it.

"Cassidy said something strange to me today," he said.

"No kidding."

He ignored that and said, "Yeah. He asked me if you and I had been fighting lately."

I looked over at him.

"I told him, no, we hadn't. He said he was sorry to hear that."

"What did he mean by . . . oh," I said.

"Right. All this peace and harmony—not exactly natural for us, is it?"

"No."

"Not one fight. Not once since . . . not since the morning I was taken hostage."

I opened the car door, rolled up the window and stepped out. He stood up and I moved closer to him.

"Put up your dukes," I said, and he pulled me into an embrace.

We stood there together for a while, then he glanced at

his watch. "There are about four hours of Saturday left," he said. "What would *you* like to do?"

I told him. In detail.

I got everything I wanted, my way, and still had no reason to feel selfish.

8

I didn't have much time to sort through Briana's belongings on Sunday; there were household chores that couldn't be put off, and just after one o'clock I was called into work to help write a memorial piece on a civic leader. The man had had the discourtesy to die of a heart attack after deadline on Saturday night. Having no suspicion of his health problems, the paper didn't have one of its instant obits ready to go.

If I had only needed to write a history of his generosity to the community, it wouldn't have been so bad, but I had to get comments. As a result, several times I was placed in the unpleasant position of being the first person to tell one of his friends that he had died. I would wait for the stunned silence or shout of disbelief to pass, express condolences, tell the friend that I knew he or she had worked closely with him, and coax comments. I did get one break—another reporter was sent to talk to the widow.

By the time I got home, I was emotionally drained. Frank was making dinner. I was changing into more casual clothes when Aunt Mary called.

"Did you go to Mass today?" she asked.

"You've been hounding me about my sense of duty to my family," I said, ready to tell her straight out that I was in no mood to talk about the dead. "Are you going to start pestering me on the subject of religion, too?"

"Hmm. I probably should. But here I've started out all

wrong again. I called to apologize. Realized I needed to when I went to Mass this morning."

"You don't owe me any apologies," I said.

"Yes, I do. Don't interrupt. I went to Mass this morning, and afterwards, I spoke with Mr. Grady—the gentleman you met at the cemetery?"

"Yes, the one who is redesigning the grounds there for your personal comfort."

"Now, don't get smart with me or I'll lose sight of my purpose. Sean—er, Mr. Grady—told me that I was cruel, and he's right. He told me—well, I didn't realize you had been so upset. You should have said something. Better yet, I never should have let things come to such a pass. I should have just called and asked for your help. That's all."

"Don't worry about it. I'm all right," I said. "You weren't trying to hurt me."

"No, but I did, and I wouldn't for the world. You know that, don't you?"

"Yes, Aunt Mary."

Frank, who was only hearing my half of the conversation, said, "Invite her over for dinner. There's plenty."

I made a face, but issued the invitation.

"Well, thank you," she said, "but I'm already engaged for the evening."

"Mr. Grady?" I asked.

"None of your beeswax. But you listen to me. Just enjoy your time with Frank this evening. Forget about all your horrible relatives and take care of him."

I was happy to obey this directive.

I hadn't been in the office long on Monday when the intercom line buzzed. John Walters, now the managing editor of the *News-Express*, commanded me to come into his office.

The workload ahead of me was routine stuff—I knew I would be spending most of the day on the phone, trying to track down some out-of-town contributors to a local campaign fund—so I answered his summons with a sense of anticipation. Maybe he had a more exciting story in mind.

He answered my knock with a scowl and waved me in. He now had a slightly bigger office and a bigger desk and chair, but he's a large man who seems to crowd any room he's in.

"Shut the door," he growled, and used his meaty fist to jab his ballpoint pen into his desk blotter.

He was pissed off. Didn't look like I was in for anything good after all. But his usual level of sweetness is nearly that of a lemon, so the mood itself didn't faze me. His next words did.

"I thought we agreed that since you insist on bedding a cop, Mark Baker covers crime stories around here."

"Right," I snapped, "whom you bed makes a difference around here—although if it's Wrigley, you still get to write about jackasses. And did anyone question the guy who wrote about the wool—"

"Enough!" He looked away, and if I hadn't known him for so long, I might not have understood that he was calming himself down. "One of these days, Wrigley's going to hear what kind of remarks you make about him, and he'll can your ass."

I shrugged. "You haven't always complimented your boss's judgment. But you didn't call me in here because I'm making nasty remarks about Wrigley. What have I done to make you accuse me of trying to butt in on Mark Baker's territory?"

"I got a call this morning," he said. "A Los Angeles homicide cop. Guy named McCain. Said he just needed to verify your whereabouts on Wednesday the eighteenth. Wouldn't tell me anything more."

"What did you tell him?"

"Nothing."

"John!"

"I told him that without more information from him, I wasn't ready to talk to the LAPD about what my reporters were up to. I don't make a habit of telling the police everything I know—unlike some people around here."

"You have no right to imply that I talk to Frank about what goes on here at the paper."

He scowled down at his desk, but eventually said, "No, no, I don't. I'll give you that."

But I had already started thinking of the more important implications of what he had said. "God, I wish you had just talked to McCain! Now you've probably made things worse."

"You want to tell me what's going on?"

"He suspects me . . ." I discovered it wasn't so easy to say. "It sounds ridiculous, I know, but he suspects me of murdering my aunt. Or arranging her murder."

"What?!"

I explained as best I could.

He was silent for a long time, then said, "You have a lawyer?"

"If you had let McCain know I was here that Wednesday morning, I wouldn't need a lawyer."

"I wouldn't be too sure about that."

"Why?"

He shrugged. "I don't know. Feeling I get about this guy. He isn't going to give up easily. Seems like he's not short on dogged determination."

"Then he'll learn that I didn't have anything to do with Briana's death. Besides, I can't afford to hire an attorney just because McCain's asking questions."

"Frank aware of this situation?"

"Yes."

"Hmm. I suppose he'll be able to tell when this guy

McCain represents a threat to you. Anyway, I'll tell Morey to be more cooperative with McCain than I was."

Until John's former position could be filled, Morey was our acting news editor. I wasn't sure that Morey, with his far from forceful personality, would be able to convince McCain of the truth after John had been so evasive.

John and I talked a little longer, then I went back to my desk. I tried to concentrate on finding people who would talk to me about the campaign funding story. I didn't have much luck, even though I was carrying the holy card of St. Anthony (who's supposed to help one find that which is lost) in my pocket. The few out-of-area contributors I did locate were either former Las Piernas residents or relatives of the candidate. A few questions to the latter group made it clear that they were completely uninterested in Las Piernas politics. Four hours of phone calls and I had nothing worth putting into print.

But my sense of frustration wasn't just a result of my problems with the story, or because of John's reticence to talk to McCain. It increased not long after I left John's office, during a phone call from Pete.

"Looks like your cousin goes by Maguire," Pete said.

"You found him!" I said.

"Got an address, anyway." He read it off—and the balloon popped.

When I didn't respond right away, he said, "That help?"

"Thanks for trying, Pete, but it's Briana's apartment address. As far as I know, Travis never really lived there."

"Oh."

"At least I know he's going by Maguire."

There was a short silence, then Pete said, "Maybe. If the address checked out, I would have felt a little more certain about that. Better not assume anything yet."

A couple of friends on the staff asked me to join them for lunch, but I had the feeling they were curious about why (according to a newsroom rumor that quickly made the rounds) an LAPD homicide cop was asking if I had been in on a certain Wednesday morning. So I begged off—told them, quite truthfully, that I was waiting for return calls.

My stomach growled, so I went from desk to desk glancing at take-out menus (more standard on newsroom desks than dictionaries) and found a good one on Stuart Angert's—a deli that delivers to the *Express*. I called it and ordered a turkey sandwich.

While I waited for the delivery, I logged on to the computer and went to a program that has replaced our old reverse phone directories. I typed in Briana's old address, the one she lived at before moving to the apartment, and within seconds the computer came up with a list of names, addresses and phone numbers for some of the residences on the same block. I printed this list, but decided I'd wait until later in the day to actually start phoning. I'd make the calls when people were more likely to be home from work.

I logged off, opened a desk drawer and pulled out McCain's manila envelope. That morning, before leaving the house, I had added to it, stuffing the envelope full of papers from Briana's desk; I opened it now and began sorting through them. In a few moments, the papers were stacked in four piles: church bulletins, grocery lists, bills and—the biggest category—flyers and advertisements.

The two grocery lists were short, and only included a few everyday items—they didn't reveal anything the tour of her kitchen hadn't already told me. I put them back in the envelope.

Next I looked through her bills. There weren't many of these either—her lifestyle didn't include flashing a lot of gold cards all over town. In fact, there were no bills from any kind of plastic. No yuppie necessities such as cellular phones, dry cleaning or cable television. Like her grocery lists, her bills were for the basics: electricity, gas, water and the telephone. Among the older bills, there was a large amount due to an orthopedic surgeon, but as I studied it, it was clear that her medical insurance company was being billed for the full amount.

But there would be other expenses, of course. Her food, rent, taxes and probably some bus or cab fares. Donations to the church. Postage, laundry—all the other little things that might cause her to feel anxious about the ways she must divide a dollar. Living on disability checks, it would have been difficult to make ends meet.

"Where was your strong young son?" I wondered aloud. *Where the hell was your niece?* an inner voice quickly answered.

I forced myself to focus my attention on the phone bills. Most were for little more than the basic service rate, but the most recent telephone bill was extravagant by comparison—it included over sixty dollars' worth of long-distance calls, all to numbers in California cities.

The calls were made within a three-day period—and when I saw which three days, I felt the hair on the back of my neck stand up. I pulled out the holy card just to make sure I had correctly remembered the date of Arthur Spanning's death. Yes—and the calls were made in the three days following his demise.

Geoff, the *Express*'s security guard, called to tell me my sandwich was waiting for me at the front desk. I went downstairs to get it, thinking about the phone bill all the while. When Briana had learned of Arthur's death, she would have called Travis. Even if he had been the one to inform her of his father's death, it was likely that they had spoken. His number must have been one of the first ones she called. But who were all the other people she had phoned?

Back at my desk, I ate the sandwich without really tasting it as I studied the bill more closely. The cities called ranged across the state—from Crescent City in the far north to El Cajon in the south, from Eureka on the coast to Blythe at the Arizona border. Most were very brief calls, but three lasted longer—the ones to El Cajon, Mission Viejo and Lake Arrowhead. I wrote these numbers down.

Did Arthur have friends all over California? And why would Briana be the one to contact them?

The more I studied the bill, the more I became aware of a pattern to the calls. They began to follow a kind of geographical order: the call after Crescent City was to Eureka, then Leggett, Santa Rosa and San Francisco. A straight line down the Northern California coast. Following San Francisco, she called Vallejo, then Sacramento, Stockton, Fresno and Visalia.

I pulled an atlas off a reference shelf in the newsroom and opened it to a map of California. As I had thought, this group of calls followed a line inland from San Francisco to Sacramento, and then down the San Joaquin Valley along Highway 99. The other calls were the same, as if the caller—Briana—had also looked at a map, using the course of major highways to decide where to call next. There were some leaps (as I began to think of them) here and there— places where the pattern jumped to another area, a separate highway. But after each leap, the pattern continued.

With this pattern in mind, I logged back on to the computer and accessed the same database. The program can also search by phone number—enter the phone number, and it produces the name and address of the listed party. I decided to try the numbers for the three longer calls and entered the Mission Viejo phone number.

When the listing appeared on the screen, I double-checked the number on the phone bill, thinking I must have made a mistake. I hadn't.

The number was that of the Mission Viejo Public Library. I tried Lake Arrowhead and El Cajon. Both were public libraries. Puzzled, I tried a few of the others. More libraries. I looked up every phone number; almost all were public libraries. The only exceptions were four elementary schools and two children's bookstores.

I tried running the name "Travis Maguire" through the program and came up with zilch, but found thirty-eight listings for T. Maguire and about a thousand other Maguires. There were forty-two T. Sperry listings and nothing for T. Spanning. There were very few Spannings; Arthur Spanning wasn't listed. I printed out the T. Sperry and T. Maguire listings.

I was about to try running the name DeMont when the phone rang. "Kelly," I answered, somewhat distracted.

It was Rachel. "You hear the news?"

"What news?"

"Our boys are going to Idaho."

"What?".

"Yeah, they're trying to find a witness for one of their cases—guess it's about to come to trial."

I didn't say anything for a moment.

"Don't worry about Frank," she said, guessing the direction of my thoughts. "He'll be fine, except that Pete will probably make him crazy. Might do him some good to get out of town for a few days."

"Yes," I said, "you're probably right."

"You don't sound convinced. I guess I should have let Frank tell you."

"No, it's all right. Glad to have some warning. It will help me to not overreact when Frank tells me. I mean, it really isn't a big deal, is it?"

"Unless maybe you were recently forcibly separated from someone, and spent time worrying about whether he was alive or dead. Then you might be forgiven for being a little worried the next time he says he's going out of town to find a witness."

"Thanks," I said, vowing to keep silent on the issue of her connection with McCain. Which was not an issue, I reminded myself.

"Look, I'm between cases here. I know you and your aunt were just yanking McCain's chain when you told him I was working with you, but I'd be happy to help you out. You want some help locating this cousin of yours?"

"Sure. But don't call in any favors at the DMV or the voter registrar's offices just yet. I think her phone bills may lead us to him."

"Found a number for him?"

"Not exactly," I said, and told her what I had learned so far.

"Libraries, bookstores and elementary schools?"

"Maybe he sells children's books," I said. "All of this is assuming it was Travis she was trying to reach."

"Were the calls made during the day?"

I looked at the bill again. "Most were. Some of the library calls were made in the early evening. But more interesting are the dates; I think she was trying to tell him that his father had died. Maybe she wanted him to go to Arthur Spanning's funeral."

"It must have been Travis. You want to fax me that list of Maguires and Sperrys? I could start checking them out for you."

"You sure you have time for this?"

"One day I'm going to convince you that I don't make offers just to hear the sound of my own voice."

"Okay, okay. Thanks. Give me your fax number."

I wrote it down, then said, "I'll call these last three numbers—the ones for the longest calls. If I get a little time, I'm going to try to look up the story of the DeMont murder. If I learn anything, I'll let you know."

"Same here."

I went back to work on my story, getting interrupted only when Frank called to break the news of the Idaho trip to me. When I reacted calmly, he said, "Rachel already told you, didn't she?" I confessed. He laughed, then told me he'd be home late.

If he was going to be home late, I wasn't going to have the luxury of staying late at the paper; two dogs and a big cat can only be kept waiting for so long. Jack, the best of neighbors, was always more than willing to help out with pet care, but I didn't like to abuse his generosity.

I called the Lake Arrowhead Library and asked if anyone there recalled speaking to a Briana Maguire within the last month. I was politely told that the library received many phone inquiries in a given month, but the librarian was kind enough to ask other staff members anyway. No one recalled speaking to her. I asked if someone named Travis had visited the library recently. That got a laugh. I mentioned that he might have been selling children's books; no, the library did not buy children's books from traveling salesmen.

She transferred me to someone in acquisitions, who went on to give me a brief explanation of the library's acquisitions procedures. They involved a complex decision-making process that made me feel a new respect for children's librarians, but left me no wiser about Travis or Briana's call.

I drew a blank with the other libraries as well.

I decided to look up the DeMont murder. I knew the year, but couldn't recall the month. I called Mary and asked her if she remembered.

"Of course I do. It was summer. July or August. Hotter than Hades. Are you making any progress?"

I told her what I had learned so far.

"Hmm. I expected more by now, I'll admit."

"Your faith in me is inspirational. Do you know what Travis does for a living?" I asked.

"No idea."

——

The DeMont story was too old to be indexed on the computer, which meant I'd have to look it up on microfilm in the library—the place formerly known as the morgue. This type of search was much slower, but it would have the benefit of letting me see the story in a context, next to other stories.

I asked for the appropriate roll of film and threaded it through a reader. Context. Gwendolyn DeMont had been murdered a month before Elvis died, in one of the years I had spent in Bakersfield as a green reporter, years away from Las Piernas by much more than a fixed distance. I hit the forward switch and stopped the reel on an early July issue. I adjusted a few knobs and the images of old news came into focus. The late seventies.

Nostalgia wasn't going to get me anywhere, so I ruthlessly hit the forward switch again. Eventually, I found the headline I was looking for. It was an Orange County story, so the *Express* didn't give it big play on the first day. It ran on the inside of the B section.

"HEIRESS FOUND SLAIN." About a twenty-four-point headline. Beneath it, in slightly smaller type, "HUSBAND MISSING."

Husband missing. Not, I supposed, for the first time.

9

The story was told in a straightforward fashion. The previous morning, a Monday, Gwendolyn DeMont Spanning had been found dead of multiple-stab wounds. The body of the sixty-two-year-old heiress to the DeMont sugar beet fortune was discovered in her bed by her housekeeper, Mrs. Ann Coughlin. No weapon was found at the scene. Time of death was uncertain, but Detective Harold Richmond of the Los Alamitos Police Department told the reporter that police estimated Mrs. Spanning died late Friday night or early Saturday morning. The home, which was surrounded by strawberry fields—the only crop now raised by the family—was somewhat isolated. Nothing appeared to have been stolen and the motive for the murder was unknown.

Police were trying to locate her husband, Arthur Spanning, who was apparently out of town on business. According to the housekeeper, Mr. Spanning had been home when she left the house on Friday. However, she told police, he traveled frequently. She was unable to say where he might have gone on his most recent trip.

The Spannings had no children; Mrs. Spanning was survived by an uncle, Horace DeMont, and three cousins, Leda DeMont Rose, Douglas DeMont and Robert DeMont, all of Huntington Beach.

I glanced at my watch. I needed to leave soon to get home in time to walk the dogs before dark. I raced through the issues that followed, seeing the stories about the murder getting more and more play. I made copy after copy of articles I told myself I could read at home, and tried not to be lured by lurid headlines:

MURDER OF RECLUSIVE HEIRESS STUNS QUIET
COMMUNITY

SPANNING ALIBI IS BIGAMY: HUSBAND OF SLAIN
HEIRESS ADMITS HE LED DOUBLE LIFE

BIGAMIST NOT CHARGED WITH WIFE'S SLAYING

DEMONT FAMILY BRINGS SUIT: SEEK TO PREVENT
BIGAMIST FROM INHERITING

I thought of shy Briana, suddenly the object of this type of scrutiny. Of Travis, at eleven, certainly old enough to read these headlines. I rewound the reel of microfilm and shut the machine off.

Later that night, I sat on the living room floor, surrounded by the boxes from Briana's house. Cody, my cat, was eyeing the piles of paper with twitching tail; I tensed as he tensed, and saw him ready to pounce. As on all his previous forays, I was able to shoo him off before he did much damage, but the scuffle woke the dogs. Worn out from a long run on the beach, Deke, a big black Lab, quickly went back to sleep, but Dunk, the shepherd, decided to gently sniff at all of the boxes again. Apparently satisfied, he lay down with a paw across my ankle and went back to sleep. This show of possessiveness was oddly comforting. Technically, he's Frank's dog, and like his master, he was soon snoring.

I stretched a little, then went back to work. The phone calls to Briana's former neighbors hadn't been of much use; only two of the neighbors remembered her, and neither knew what had become of "Mrs." Maguire or her son. They told me that she and her son had kept to themselves, had been polite but very private. After reading the headlines, it was easy to understand why Briana and Travis had sought privacy.

I made notes based on the articles I had copied, recapping what I had learned, putting the information in chronological order.

As Mary had remembered, Gwendolyn DeMont was raised by her grandfather after her mother's death. Gwendolyn's father, who died a hero's death in World War I, was one of two sons, but apparently her grandfather had quarreled bitterly with his surviving boy, Horace DeMont. When the old patriarch died, this son was left only a small monetary bequest; the bulk of the estate, including all the DeMont lands, was left to Gwendolyn.

At the time of her grandfather's death, Gwendolyn was forty-five years old. Within a month of his death, and to her uncle Horace DeMont's shock, she married one of the few men who had ever made her acquaintance: the estate's sixteen-year-old gardener, Arthur Spanning.

In the articles, her uncle made much of the fact that throughout her life, Gwendolyn seldom ventured outside the family home. She was shy of strangers, especially male strangers. It was Horace DeMont's contention that Arthur Spanning had connived his way into the household and then taken advantage of her grief. That Arthur bore no real affection for her was now proven by his illegal second marriage. Greed and impatience, DeMont said, had led Arthur to murder his rich wife.

This was vigorously denied by Arthur's older brother, a man named Gerald Spanning. Gerald Spanning had once been Arthur's legal guardian—like Gwendolyn, Arthur had lost his parents at an early age. He speculated that this might have been one reason Gwendolyn felt drawn to Arthur, who had worked on the estate from the age of twelve. Perhaps she took advantage of a young man's first crush, but Gerald Spanning had consented to the marriage of his underage brother because Arthur's heart was set on it.

However set Arthur's heart had been at sixteen, it roved by the time he was twenty-two. Briana, who was then working in a nursery and landscaping supply company, was courted by and married the charming young man she knew as Arthur Sperry. His landscaping business required frequent absences.

The articles in the *Express* supplied few details about this business, but apparently Gwendolyn had indulged her young husband's whim to have his own business, to earn his own money. If this business required him to travel, she did not seem upset by her days alone.

The cook and housekeeper, Mrs. Coughlin, was interviewed. She had worked for the Spannings for twelve years. She worked there every weekday, with weekends off, and did not live on the premises. She declared that the Spannings had always seemed to be a happy couple, that Arthur was an attentive husband. True, she admitted, they slept separately, but she had never heard them argue or complain of one another. Mrs. Spanning seldom ventured away from the house, and was rarely seen outdoors except in her own very private garden—a garden Mr. Spanning tended for her. No, Mrs. Coughlin was sure Mrs. Spanning had never had the least idea of Mr. Spanning's other life.

Police said that Mr. Spanning's claims concerning his whereabouts on the evening of the murder were borne out both by emergency room personnel at Las Piernas General Hospital and the Las Piernas Police Department. At the hospital, Travis received treatment for a severely lacerated hand. The boy said he had been sleepwalking and thrust his hand through a back-door window. To add to the upheaval in Mr. Spanning's life, his car had been stolen from the hospital parking lot. Ironically, police had taken the report of a stolen vehicle for "Mr. Sperry" and later, when Gwendolyn Spanning's body was discovered, this report was used to further back Mr. Spanning's claims regarding his whereabouts on the night of the murder.

Not much was revealed about Arthur Spanning's double life, possibly because Arthur was able to engage excellent legal help, but also because Arthur, Briana and Travis refused interviews. The "double life" article was largely conjecture, but not wild conjecture. The reporter noted that although Las Piernas and Los Alamitos border one another, they are separated by a county line. It was theorized that this division helped Arthur to keep his two identities separate—many tax, business, birth, marriage and other records were maintained separately in each county.

Arthur Spanning was a man unknown to his neighbors, not active in the community in any way, a person who lived behind high fences and strong gates, and who dealt with most others through his lawyers. Mrs. Coughlin and the lawyers were the only persons who saw much of either of the Spannings. With the exception of rare and rather strained contact with the families of Horace DeMont and Gerald Spanning, Mr. and Mrs. Arthur Spanning shunned the world around them.

If the Spannings had been more active socially, Sperry's friends might have noticed that he resembled the heiress's husband. As Arthur Sperry, head of a middle-class family, he had many friends and admirers. All admitted that they knew little of his history or work, but all described him as charming and helpful, an excellent listener who was loyal to his friends. He was active in his local parish.

To the great frustration of the DeMonts, no criminal

charges were filed against Spanning; their lawsuit to prevent him from inheriting Gwendolyn's estate was also unsuccessful.

What happened with the bigamous marriage to my aunt was typical of cases where there is no clear attempt to defraud the second spouse. Although the marriage to Briana was invalid, it was apparent that Arthur didn't marry Briana for financial gain, so no criminal charges were filed against him. She was given custody of their son, and refused Spanning's offer of child support.

I made a quick search of the remaining boxes from the apartment; there were some photos of Travis that might come in handy, but not much else.

The dogs suddenly scrambled to their feet; I heard Frank's car pulling into the driveway. I began to put the papers away. I was putting the stack of bills into one of the desk boxes when something caught my eye. It was a puce-colored flyer, announcing that Cosmo the Storyteller would be appearing in a free program for children at the Crescent City Public Library on the second of January at one o'clock.

Crescent City. The first library on the phone bill. And one so far north of San Pedro, Briana would have no reason to check a book out of it, let alone attend a children's program. Cosmo the Storyteller.

Frank called a greeting from the front door. I set the boxes and papers aside and hurried to give him a proper welcome home. I was patient, which is not the first attribute anyone will mention in my eulogy. I listened to him talk about his day, let him vent some steam about cases that would suffer while he was away, even waited until he had changed clothes and was starting to pack for Idaho before I told him that I thought I had figured out how to find Travis.

10

We rode to LAX with Pete and Rachel early the next morning; the flight to Boise from Los Angeles International had been cheaper than any out of Las Piernas, but involved ten times the headaches. The department doesn't have to justify headaches, only dollars.

While we watched brake lights on the San Diego Freeway, I repeated to Rachel what I had told Frank the night before.

"I don't get it," Pete said, listening in on our conversation. "How can you be sure Travis is this storyteller?"

"I can't," I said.

He snorted. "So this is just a hunch? Woman's intuition?"

Don't be such a pain in the ass! I wanted to shout, watching Rachel scowl at him. "Just leave Pete up there in Idaho—okay, Frank?" she said.

Oh, God.

Frank, who was driving, glanced into the rearview mirror to look at Pete, then shook his head. "Even the governor couldn't pardon me for doing something like that."

"It was more than a hunch," I said. "And I'm not saying he's the storyteller—just that this storyteller probably knows where to find him. Briana made calls after Travis's father died. Probably trying to find Travis."

"An assumption," Pete pointed out.

"Yes, I'll admit that."

"A logical one, Pete," Frank said. "This woman was such a

loner, she didn't even have an address book. She was dead for some time before anyone noticed she was missing. She didn't have much money—seemed to be barely getting by. But when the father of her son died, she spent over sixty dollars calling public libraries. I doubt she was trying to hunt down a book."

Pete shrugged. "Okay. Go on."

"The calls were to libraries up and down the state," I said, "but they started with Crescent City—which is not far from the Oregon border. Crescent City is the same place the flyer comes from. Briana didn't have a car, but even if she did, I doubt she would have driven seven or eight hundred miles to see a storyteller. So why would she have a flyer from a distant library for a children's event?"

"You call this library yet?" Pete asked.

"Pete," Rachel said with exasperation, "we left the house at six o'clock in the morning. You think the average public library was open for business by then?"

He shrugged, and took out a stick of cinnamon gum. The only time I ever see Pete chewing gum is before he gets on a plane.

"Ha qualcosa contro il mal d'aria?" Rachel asked in a low voice.

"Yeah," he said, "I've got the pills. But it isn't really air sickness that bothers me, you know?"

From that point on, there was a concerted effort to distract him from his fear of flying.

It was probably a good strategy where Frank and I were concerned as well. Distracting Pete kept our thoughts away from the last time Frank had gone to interview a witness. That time, he ended up a hostage. This trip was coming too soon after that ordeal. Neither of us had been able to sleep well—his nightmare had awakened both of us at about three in the morning. Knowing the alarm would be going off in a couple of hours, we lay there in a too-tired-and-too-wired state, worried minds continually snatching our weary bodies back from the brink of sleep.

At the airport we behaved in a perfectly respectable fashion, focusing our efforts on having a pleasant conversation until the flight was called. Frank gave me a brief hug, a kiss and a smile, then said, "I'll call you tonight," in the same way anybody else might have said it to a spouse. Said it as if he were going to Idaho to talk someone into buying a copier rather than to convince some weasel-faced, scared-ass, hiding-out known associate of a criminal to admit under oath that he had seen said associate kill a man in cold blood.

I understood, took my cues and ignored the knot in my stomach. It would be an ordinary day with an ordinary good-bye, and no one would question anyone's ability to face it, no one would say aloud that there were damned good reasons for nightmares that woke everybody up, that there was no shame in it, that it was too soon, too soon— because that would be akin to saying the aftermath of his captivity still had legs to run on. Which it did. Trauma runs the marathon, not the fifty-yard dash.

I thought he might go all the way down the jetway bantering with Pete, might get on the plane without glancing back, so I relaxed my guard and failed to have the correct devil-may-care expression on my face when he looked over his shoulder. But he wasn't wearing a smile either, not until I tried to come up with one. I hoped mine didn't look as forced as his did, and raised my hand to wave—or beckon him back, I'm not certain—but he didn't see the gesture, because Pete said something to him just then. They took another step and were past the point where Rachel and I could watch them.

Rachel didn't object when, instead of leaving the nearly empty waiting area, I moved to the wall of tall windows, squinting in the bright morning sun, watching until the plane was pushed back from the gate. There was nothing to be done now, I told myself. Once again, being on my best behavior had proved damned unsatisfying.

* * *

I turned in my story on campaign contributions and left the office. I had a council meeting to cover that night, so I took a few hours off in the early afternoon. I went home and spent some time with Cody and the dogs, then stretched the phone out onto the back patio. It was a warm day, bright and breezy. Frank's garden lay before me, the dogs plopped down at my feet, and Cody settled on my lap and purred his approval of the arrangements.

I opened my notebook and resumed my search for my cousin.

I decided to make my first calls to the El Cajon, Mission Viejo and Lake Arrowhead libraries, the ones Briana has spoken to on her longer calls. I tried Mission Viejo first, since it was the closest to Las Piernas. I thumbed through my notes while waiting for the call to go through, and found the name of the children's librarian.

"Sophia Longworth, please," I said, and was transferred to her desk.

At the risk of being immediately identified as someone as cheerfully annoying as a gnat in a nostril, I told her my name and reminded her of my previous call.

"Oh, yes," she said, but nothing more.

"I have more information now. Do you know anything about a storyteller named Cosmo?"

"Yes, yes, of course! He was here about three weeks ago."

"Ms. Longworth, did a woman call to talk to you about him at about that same time?"

There was a brief pause. "Oh! So this is what you were asking about. Well, I'm not sure I should go into this with you. It was a personal call."

If it was a personal call, I decided, Cosmo and Travis were

likely one and the same. "The woman who called said she was Cosmo's mother, right? Trying to leave a message for him at your library."

There was a little more hesitation, then, "As I said—"

"I'm his cousin. It was my aunt who called. She probably just asked him to call her"—I thought of the phrase my mother might have used—"on an urgent family matter."

"Yes," she admitted. "Yes, that was the call. His mother. But I'm sure she can tell you why she was calling. I think that would be best, so—"

"Wait," I said, sensing that she was about to hang up. "Ms. Longworth, I can't ask my aunt. She—she passed away recently."

"Oh!"

"Yes. Now you know why I want to reach my cousin."

"Oh, yes, of course! Oh, I'm so sorry. I wonder if—your aunt seemed quite distraught, but she didn't mention that she was ill . . ."

I didn't say anything to dispel that notion. "I guess she had a hard time reaching him," I said.

"Yes. Cosmo—your cousin—travels constantly."

"Did he receive the message my aunt left for him?"

"Yes, of course."

"Did he call her back?"

"Immediately? No, but he was about to give a performance. I'm sure he must have called her later."

"Exactly what is it he does?"

"Oh, he's wonderful!" she said. "I'm surprised your aunt didn't brag on him to you."

I didn't answer.

"He tells stories," she went on, a little less enthusiastically. "The kids love him. He doesn't just entertain them, he encourages them to read. And as you know, he's bilingual— he can tell stories in Spanish and English."

I didn't know any such thing, but I said, "Any idea where he is now?"

"No, I'm sorry."

"Do you have an address for him?"

"No," she said. "I'm not sure he has a permanent address—"

"Would someone in your accounting office have one for him?"

"Accounting? Why?"

"Surely someone will be mailing a check to him?"

"Didn't your aunt tell you? He donates his time. It's so good of him. In libraries that are facing severe budget cutbacks—and most California libraries are—children's programs often suffer. He helps us to keep the kids interested in reading without sacrificing book budgets. We're very grateful to him."

While trying to absorb that piece of information, I pressed on. "Ms. Longworth, as you've probably figured out, my cousin and I haven't been in touch lately." I paused. Lately. The past quarter century or so. I shook that off. "I just want to let him know what has happened to his mother. How did the library get in touch with him?"

"Well, I was going to suggest this a moment ago. Are you on-line?"

"Yes," I said.

"Then you could send him e-mail."

"He's on the Internet?"

"Yes. That's how we put in our request and verified all the arrangements. Let me look it up." I heard her tapping on a keyboard. "Here it is." She spelled it out for me. "Cosmo, with a capital c, o-s-m-o, at g-e-o-k-e-r-b-y dot com."

I wrote it as she spoke. Cosmo@geokerby.com.

I had thought of Cosmo as a magician's name, or something sort of New Age, until I saw it coupled with that Internet domain name. "George Kerby?" I asked. "As in George and Marion Kerby?"

"Yes, the ghosts in the film *Topper.* Remember it? Cary Grant played George Kerby. Lord, he was handsome. I love that film, don't you?"

"Yes . . ." But I was distracted, thinking not of Cary Grant, but of Roland Young's role as Cosmo Topper, a meek businessman beleaguered by the Kerbys' ghosts.

She went on to say that she had learned of him through the recommendations of other librarians on a children's librarians' Internet list, and would post a message to that list to ask if Cosmo was booked to appear at other libraries anytime soon.

I thanked her and gave her my phone number and e-mail address at the *Express.*

So my cousin managed to travel all over the state and donate his time to libraries while my aunt lived a spartan existence in San Pedro. He had taken on the name of a character in a movie, a rather bumbling businessman pestered by two mischievous phantoms who couldn't quite get used to the idea of being dead.

Who had Travis become?

I left the house a little earlier than planned, stopped by the paper to send an e-mail message to him. As I passed the security desk, Geoff, the guard, motioned to me to wait as he finished a call. Nobody at the *Express* has ever been able to tell me Geoff's age, and he only smiles and shakes his head if he's asked directly. He's probably well over seventy years old, and while I wouldn't expect him to wrestle anyone to the ground, he's got plenty of good sense—which means he does just fine at his job.

"Something happened while you were out," he said, "and you've got to know about it, but I hope to heaven you won't blame it on me."

I waited.

"I took my lunch break," he said, "and someone from the mailroom watched the desk while I was gone. Supposedly watched, I should say. Well, you know how careless those boys can be."

Since Geoff was liable to refer to any other male as a boy, I did not assume that some youngster had been left to guard the foyer of the *Express*. "I suppose you checked the tape?"

I wasn't sticking my neck out there. Geoff was famous for reviewing security tapes made during his breaks. He was seldom satisfied with the work done by those sent to relieve him.

"Yes, I sure did," he said. "And I saw something that made me ask that boy a few questions. Look here."

He pointed to one of his video screens, one that was dark. He pressed a button, and the screen lit up as a tape played. A grainy black-and-white image of the lobby appeared, with the security desk near the bottom of the frame. I smiled to notice that the "boy" from the mailroom staff was in his forties. Today's date appeared in small white letters in the lower left corner; the time marker showed that this segment had been taped at just after one o'clock.

"What's he reading?" I asked Geoff.

"He claimed it was something called a *manga*," Geoff said, with an expression of disdain. "But it was really some Japanese comic book. Now watch here—see that?"

On the screen, a tall, well-built man wearing jeans and a windbreaker entered. His dark baseball cap was pulled down low, but he also kept his head down and turned slightly to one side. I could see why Geoff found this worth noting.

"Doesn't want his face to be seen by the camera," I said.

"Sure doesn't. Look where he stands."

At the security desk, the man turned his back to the camera, standing slightly to the side of the desk, not approaching it at the front as most would do. He did not slouch or lean against it; the man's posture was—although not rigid—somehow reminiscent of those who were more used to giving than receiving orders.

Another person came gliding into the frame. I recognized this one. Our society columnist. "Margot Martin," I said.

Geoff nodded.

The camera saw Margot clearly assessing the man while he apparently spoke to the temporary guard—who barely glanced up from his comic book. Although there was no soundtrack on the tape, actions spoke as plainly as words—if not more so. Margot said something and the man turned his attention to her, still keeping his face from the camera. Margot moved closer and the guard seemed to enter the conversation.

"Now watch," Geoff said, narrating. "Margot gives the mailroom boy a sour look. And there—see? She takes the other fellow's arm and walks outta here practically licking her whiskers."

I smiled. "Geoff, if Margot is meeting men in the lobby, that's her business."

"Oh, no. Not this time. I asked my comic-book-reading friend who this fellow was, especially since the fellow was acting a little suspicious. He says he don't know, he didn't even get the fellow's name." Geoff sighed, then went on. "The boy says the fellow in the cap came in here asking if *you* were in."

"Me?"

"Yes, you. Were you expecting anybody?"

"No." I looked at the monitor again.

"It didn't look like Frank to me," Geoff said. "Besides, he wouldn't have gone off with Margot."

"Frank's in Idaho," I said absently. I couldn't identify the man who appeared on the tape.

"Oh, well, I knew it wasn't Frank. I asked this old boy

what had happened. He said the fellow come in asking for you, and before he can even ask the fellow for his name, Margot Martin lays *her* peepers on him and says, 'Miss Kelly is gone for the day, is there something I can help you with?'"

"What?!"

He nodded. "Flabbergasting, ain't it?"

Maybe not, I thought. "I suppose he was good-looking?"

Geoff rubbed his hand over his face and said, "Well—I didn't get much of a description out of my so-called helper, but I suppose the fellow probably was, because Margot is durned man-hungry, but she's not without refinement. She wouldn't just walk out of here with anybody."

"The man seemed perfectly willing to go with her."

"Yes, my replacement said that the fellow was smiling, seemed happy to make her acquaintance. I guess Mr. Funny Papers finally figured out that your guests ought to be directed to you and he tried to stop Margot, but old Margot just gave him that sour look and then told the gent she'd take him to you personal."

"Take him to me?" Once again, it was, as Geoff had said, flabbergasting.

"The mail clerk said he figured if she could take him to you, you and Margot were friends. I told him you weren't enemies, but you weren't great pals, either."

"I hardly give her a daily schedule. But almost everyone knows where I'll be on a Tuesday evening." I shrugged. "So Margot's probably going to be at the city council meeting."

"That's what I figured. No other way she'd know where you'd be. I don't imagine she even knows where you live."

"No, we haven't thrown any debutante balls lately, so there's been no need to invite her over."

"Count your blessings. But the fellow worries me more than Margot. There's no real harm in Margot, but I tell you, the fellow's up to something sneaky."

"Hmm. You said the mail clerk gave you a description?"

"Sort of. He said he's tall, maybe in his fifties, maybe older. Close-cropped gray hair. Thought his eyes were blue or green, some light color." He paused, pointing at a frozen frame on the tape. "See the design on the door? From where he hits it, I'd guess he stands over six-foot, maybe six-two or more. Big build."

"Could I look at the tape again, Geoff?"

He replayed the segment for me. As we watched the man first approach the desk, I noted again how straight his back and shoulders were. Except for keeping his head down, his posture was perfect. "Carries himself like an athlete or a military man."

"Hmm, yes. So he does," Geoff said. "But I can't like him hiding his face like that." He looked up and said, "Watch yourself tonight, Irene."

"Thanks for letting me know about him, Geoff, but I wonder if he'll be able to escape from Margot long enough to show up?"

"You've got a point there," he said.

I glanced at my watch, saw that I didn't have much time left before the meeting, and hurried up to the newsroom. I logged onto the computer, went to the mail program and got as far as the subject line before I stalled. Subject? I settled for "Urgent family matter."

I moved the cursor to the message section and stalled again. What to say? "Dear Travis, how are you after all these decades? And by the way . . ." No. All I could do was ask him to make a phone call.

> To: Cosmo@geokerby.com
> Subject: Urgent family matter
> Dear Travis,
> Urgent that you contact me. Please call as

soon as possible.
Your cousin,
Irene Kelly

I added my home and work numbers and, although not
perfectly satisfied with it, sent the message off into cyber-
space.

Since I was already logged on, I decided to look for
Gerald Spanning among the Spannings I had seen the last
time I had checked phone numbers. I found a "G. Spanning"
in our area code, but no address listed. I dialed the number
on the screen.

After two rings, a male voice answered.

"Gerald Spanning?" I asked.

"Who'd like to know?"

"My name is Irene Kelly. I'm trying to locate my cousin—
your brother Arthur's son?"

There was a pause before he said, "I've never met my
brother's b—" He caught himself, started again. "I've never
met my brother's son. Sorry I can't help you." He paused
again. "If you find him, tell him to give me a call someday."
He hung up.

Well, that was quick, if not painless. I suspected the
"b-word" wouldn't have been "boy." "My brother's bastard,"
he'd been about to say. It might have been easier to judge
him harshly for that if he'd said he never wanted to hear from
Travis—or if my own family hadn't also disowned Briana and
her son. Arthur and Briana's false marriage had probably embarrassed the Spannings, too. Gerald, I reminded myself, had
at least stuck by his brother when he was accused of murder.

I gathered my belongings and headed over to the city council chambers. The chambers were all but empty when I

arrived, and except for a few resident gadflies, not many other people showed up. The most interesting item on the agenda was not one most folks would recognize as such—a change in plans for use of a navy property that was coming back into the city's possession—but that item was quickly tabled. The rest of the meeting plodded along over relatively unimportant issues. Even the usual sideshow was dull—when long-standing opponents took their expected potshots at one another, the remarks lacked heat.

I had positioned myself so that I could see latecomers entering the audience, but never saw anyone who even faintly resembled Geoff's description of the man who had asked for me.

The meeting finally came to a close, and I rushed back to the paper to file my story. I had already called in to let Morey know that there was no need to hold much space for the council story.

I knocked the story out fairly quickly, then checked my e-mail. Nothing from Travis. I said good night to the few remaining staff members and hurried home.

The dogs bounced and bounded to communicate their joy at my return. Cody gave one yowl and then managed to regain a proper cat sense of aloofness. The light on the answering machine was blinking.

I pressed the play button.

"Irene? Are you there?" Frank's voice. He sounded tired. "Oh, wait, it's Tuesday—you're probably at the council meeting. The flight went fine and the hotel is okay, but we've already encountered some problems with the job, so we may be here a little longer than we expected. Sorry to have missed you. I'm pretty beat, so I'll probably turn in. I'll call you again tomorrow if I get a chance." He left the hotel number, said again that he'd try to call the next day, then hung up.

Well, hell.

I went to bed, pulled Frank's pillow close before Cody could claim it. I was tired, but I didn't sleep.

I wondered if Margot got lucky. I wondered who the guy was. I was ticked off at her for interfering, but at least she might be able to tell me his name.

I wondered if Travis would call.

I kept thinking about Frank.

The phone rang. I'll own up to a perverse wish that my husband had been having trouble sleeping, too, and was the caller. But the caller was Rachel.

"Did I wake you up?" she asked.

"No."

"You, too? First night Pete's away is always a bitch. And I missed his call tonight—I was out at the store."

I couldn't tell her that her disappointment sounded wonderful to me. "I missed Frank's call, too. Do you have dinner plans for the next few nights?"

"No. Want to get together? That's exactly what I was calling to suggest."

"Why don't you come over here tomorrow?"

"Okay."

We talked of inconsequential things for a few more minutes, then hung up. I was drowsy by then, and managed about an hour's worth of fitful sleep before the phone rang again.

"Did I wake you up?" my husband's voice asked.

"No," I said.

"Liar."

"Okay, so I am, but talk to me anyway."

He did. He couldn't sleep, had gone for a walk, finally decided to call. We had a long conversation, not about anything special, but one we were reluctant to end. "I should let you get some sleep," he'd say every so often, and we'd keep talking, remembering something else that had happened that day, or discussing some plan to do something together when he returned, or recalling something we'd meant to ask about.

"Don't bother with that leaky faucet in the kitchen," he said at one point. "I'll fix it when I get home." He knew I could fix it if I wanted to; I knew he wasn't trying to tell me not to fix it myself. There was only one phrase in all of it that mattered: "when I get home."

The reassurance of the mundane, wearing down our troubles.

━ ━

I didn't make much progress in my efforts to find Travis on Wednesday. At work, two vague leads suddenly turned into hot but demanding stories that had nothing to do with one another; trying to do justice to both stories, I was too harried to try to locate my cousin—and was forced to cancel my dinner plans with Rachel. I ended up catching about three hours of sleep between Wednesday and Thursday, worked furiously and turned in both stories Thursday afternoon. I was whipped.

In the long run it was worth it, though. Between the time I had spent on the obit on Sunday and his pleasure with the stories I turned in on Thursday, Morey agreed to give me Friday off.

Late Thursday afternoon, by driving like a demon and begging a favor from a clerk I knew in the county records office, I did manage to get a look at Arthur Spanning's death certificate for about five minutes before the office closed.

As the holy card from his funeral had said, Arthur Anthony Spanning had died a little over three weeks earlier, at the age of forty-eight.

I glanced at the bottom half of the certificate and learned that the cause of death was bone cancer; I was a little startled to see that he had died at St. Anne's, where my parents died, and that he had been seen for some time by the same oncologist who cared for my father before his death—Dr.

Brad Curtis. Later I would consider the irony of Arthur, a man my father had despised, struggling for his life with the help of the same physician, but in that moment I was thinking only of the suffering he had probably endured—the kind of suffering I had witnessed when my father was ill—and for the first time in a long time, I felt something other than anger toward Arthur Spanning.

The clerk reminded me that it was closing time and so I hurriedly turned my attention to the top of the form, "Decedent Personal Data."

Arthur's father was listed as Unknown Spanning; his state of birth, unknown; his mother's maiden name, unknown. Past experience with death certificates had taught me that this did not mean he was illegitimate—only that the doctor filling out the certificate didn't have the information.

Arthur had not served in the military, and his years of education completed were listed as six—a surprise to me, since I remembered him as a man who could converse easily on all sorts of subjects. I wondered if this was a typographical error. Then again, he had married into lots of money when he was very young, so perhaps he was self-educated.

I wrote down the Las Piernas address listed in the "Usual Residence" section and tried to picture its general location. Downtown; perhaps one of the new lofts or condos. Not really as snooty an address as I would have guessed, especially supposing he had inherited the big bucks after Gwendolyn DeMont's death. Maybe it was a case of easy come, easy go. Arthur might have blown that fortune in the first few years after her murder.

There was one other surprise on the form. In space number fourteen, "Marital Status," the word "Married" was typed in; and in space number fifteen, "Name of Surviving Spouse; If Wife, Enter Maiden Name," was "Briana Maguire."

"You liar!" I said aloud, causing the clerk to look up at me. I calmed down. Why should I be surprised that Arthur was still occasionally faking people out about his marriage to my aunt? Grudgingly, I also had to admit the possibility that if Travis spent much time around him, he might have been trying to hide his son's illegitimacy. But why not say they were divorced?

The clerk finally lost all patience and all but snatched the form back from me. When I asked if I could make a copy, she said, "You should have thought of that option four and a half minutes ago. Come back tomorrow."

A friendly, helpful clerk in county records is an asset in my line of work, and not someone you want to piss off, so I apologized profusely, and told her I owed her big time.

She laughed and said, "Honey, I hear that every day from one person or another, and I ain't seen no 'big time' yet."

＊ ＊

Rachel called on Thursday night to say she hadn't been able to find anything on Travis, but had some luck locating the DeMonts. I told her I had Friday off, and we decided to meet in the morning.

"You hear anything more from Jimmy Mac?" she asked.

I told her I hadn't been contacted again by McCain and was beginning to believe he wasn't much interested in me as a suspect, but she warned me against this kind of thinking. I tried to get her to talk about how she had come to know so much about him.

"See you tomorrow morning," she said, once again shying away from any discussion about her past connection to him.

But our Friday plans were changed about ten minutes later, when Sophia Longworth called from the Mission Viejo Library.

"I think I know where you can meet up with your cousin," she said.

"Great!" I said, not realizing that all hell was about to break loose.

11

Sophia Longworth asked if I had heard back from my cousin by e-mail.

"Nothing yet," I said.

"He travels a lot," she said, "and he may not be checking his e-mail from the road. That's why I posted a note on PUB-YAC."

"PUBYAC?"

"It's an Internet list for librarians who specialize in services for children and young adults. I received several responses, but most of them were places where he had been, not where he was scheduled to appear in the future. Only one of the librarians responded with a future date. It's not much notice, I know, but if you can get up to North Hollywood tomorrow morning, you might catch him at the Valley Plaza Branch of the Los Angeles Public Library. He's doing two performances there, one in Spanish, one in English."

"What time?" I asked.

"The Spanish performance is at nine, the English at ten."

When I called Rachel back to tell her that my plans had changed again, she offered to come with me. "That way, you can use the carpool lanes," she said.

"Don't give me that," I said. "You'll never convince me that you're just volunteering to be my diamond-lane dummy."

"You can be the dummy. We'll take my car."

"The Karmann Ghia will get us there."

"Yeah, well, my car will get us there and back. I don't mind driving. Besides, I want to talk to you about what I've learned so far."

So the next morning we were on our way to North Hollywood. North Hollywood, like Hollywood itself, isn't a city. West Hollywood is, but Hollywood and North Hollywood are part of the City of Los Angeles. Los Angeles is full of irregularly drawn boundaries; some of them can be seen on maps.

North Hollywood is near the eastern edge of the San Fernando Valley, about forty miles from Las Piernas. There was no way to get to it during business hours without going through some patch of traffic hell.

Not all of the old freeways between Las Piernas and North Hollywood had been retrofitted with carpool lanes, though, so although we were both curious about Travis's storytelling, neither of us had wanted to leave at five in the morning and then hang out in the Valley for three hours, which is what we would have to do to be at the library at nine. We had decided we'd aim for the ten o'clock English performance and try to miss some of the morning rush hour—an "hour" that begins around six and often lasts as late as ten.

As we made our way up the San Gabriel River Freeway to Interstate 5, my nervousness over the upcoming encounter with Travis increased. Rachel was humming "Jimmy Mac" to herself again, but I was too preoccupied with more immediate worries to pursue that line of conversation. I feigned an interest in the passengers of other cars, all the while trying to rehearse what I would say to Travis. It occurred to me that he might not even know he had cousins.

It suddenly seemed hot and stuffy in the car, and though I knew the sensation had nothing to do with the climate inside the car, I rolled the window down a little. I was

immediately greeted by a puff of diesel exhaust and the rat-
tling, banging metal clamor of a semi in the next lane. I
rolled the window back up. Rachel looked over at me, then
turned the air conditioner on.

"That won't help," I said.

She shrugged and turned it off.

After a minute or two had gone by, she said, "I've managed to track down most of the people who were mentioned in those articles."

"The articles about the murder of Gwendolyn DeMont?"

"Right." She cast another quick look in my direction, then
said, "You know, even if he has no interest in getting to
know you and your sister, maybe Travis will want to contact
someone in his father's family."

"Maybe," I said, trying to sound nonchalant about that possibility. I pulled the sun visor down, adjusted it up and down
as I looked in the little mirror on it—as if I were checking my
makeup. It might have been more convincing if I had been
wearing any. In the car behind us, I noticed a man in a baseball cap driving a dark green Oldsmobile sedan, a car that
been behind us once or twice before. I couldn't make out his
face, but there was something vaguely familiar about him.

"Well, if he does want to contact them, I've got an
address for Gerald Spanning," Rachel said, getting my full
attention.

"Arthur's brother? I talked to him."

"The one in Los Alamitos?"

"I didn't have an address for him, just a phone number.
So he stayed in the same town all these years?" I said.

"Looks like it. You've talked to him?"

"Very briefly. Says he never met Travis, and didn't seem to
hold doing so as one of his life's ambitions. You talked to
him, too?"

"No, just found out where he lived."

"Do I want to know how you managed to do this?"

She laughed. "Probably not."

Curiosity got the better of me. "How?"

"From a voter registration list."

"Voter registration? That information isn't available to just anybody. Don't tell me you—"

"No, I didn't have to call in any favors," she said.

"For some reason, I have a suspicion I'm not going to like the answer anyway."

This apparently did not cause her much concern. "Well, I'll tell you how someone might get them, then you can stop imagining that I'm bribing people who work in the County Registrar of Voters office." Making a wholly unconvincing attempt to look as if she were working from imagination rather than memory, she said, "Let's say a person files as a candidate for an office."

"Okay . . ."

"That person, who is not obliged to put on much of a campaign, may obtain voter registration information, such as the names and addresses and—sometimes—the phone numbers of voters. The information is printed out by a computer."

"Yes. Precinct lists. Are you a candidate?"

"Oh, no, I haven't lived here long enough to be a candidate. And I'm speaking hypothetically, remember?"

"Certainly."

She laughed again. "And those who don't want to go to the trouble of filing for candidacy just volunteer to work on a campaign, then make copies of the lists."

"I know you haven't worked on any campaigns," I said, "because there hasn't been an election since you've moved here."

"No, but I do know certain enterprising individuals—"

I groaned.

"And I know you are going to find this hard to believe," she went on, "but there are actually people who have worked on campaigns who will sell copies of those lists!"

"No!" I said in mock horror.

"So," she went on, "Arthur's uncle is registered without party affiliation. Lives in Los Alamitos. I'll give you the address."

"Does your husband know that you're going around—"

"Don't be an imbecile!" she said. "Of course not."

"Of course not."

"You and Frank, your jobs don't always put you on the same side of the fence, right?"

"No, but—"

"But nothing. Same with me and Pete."

It wasn't really the same, but I decided not to press the matter.

"No luck trying to find the housekeeper, Ann Coughlin," she said. "But like I told you last night, I did find the DeMonts."

"Gwendolyn's family?"

"Yes, the ones who tried to keep Travis's father from getting a penny of his dead wife's estate."

"There was an uncle, right? But he must be—"

"No, he's alive. He's still collecting his Social Security."

"I'm almost positive I don't want to know how you found that out," I said.

She laughed. "It wasn't that hard. I looked him up in an old phone directory—he has an unlisted number now, but he wasn't as private about it ten years ago. The old phone book didn't list the address, but the name and number were there."

"So you called and asked for him?"

"No, Horace DeMont's an unusual name. Not likely that I would have mistakenly found some other Horace DeMont living in Huntington Beach. So first I did a reverse check on this number and found out it's currently the number for a Leda Rose. That's his daughter. 'Rose' turns out to be her married name. I think she's a widow—I'm checking on that. Anyway, I called and asked for Horace, since he wasn't listed in the current directory."

"But you figured he might be living with his daughter?"

"A guess. Leda answered the phone. She said he was asleep. I told her I was with a unit investigating Social Security fraud—"

"Oh, my God—"

"—and that some checks had recently been stolen through a mail diversion scam. Told her I needed to know that Horace was receiving his checks. She said yes, and of course I had to make sure the checks were going to the correct address, which she happily gave me."

"Rachel—"

"Yeah, yeah, not your style. Your journalistic ethics and all that. That's why it's good you hired me."

"Not hired, exactly—"

"So you owe me a buck. Anyway, Horace may not be of much use to you; he's in his nineties." She paused, frowning as if trying to calculate something, then said, "Ninety-three."

"You've learned a lot about them."

"Just getting started. I also looked at county records and did a little snooping around at the family cemetery. Douglas, Horace's oldest son, died in the 1980s. But Robert is still alive. He also lives in Huntington Beach, on the same street. Judging by the addresses, I'd say they can look out their kitchen windows and wave to one another."

She stopped talking long enough to negotiate the ramp to the northbound Golden State Freeway. As if the change of freeway signaled a change of subject, she said, "So, your society columnist ever show up again?"

"No, but that doesn't mean there's anything to be alarmed over." Even as I said it, I thought of the man in the baseball cap. The green sedan. Was it the same man? Or did the cap just register with my memory of Geoff's security tapes? I glanced behind us, but all I could see were two big trucks. I couldn't see the Olds.

"Who's alarmed?" Rachel was saying. "I just wondered if you ever talked to her to find out what that guy wanted."

"Margot doesn't work full-time for the paper," I said. "She writes a weekly column, sends it in by modem. She stops by to make sure photo captions are correct and to pick up her mail. When she's in the building, she's over in features, I'm over in news. I rarely see her in person."

"Why don't you call her, find out who was asking for you?"

"I could do that, I suppose."

She laughed. "You don't like her or her column, do you?"

I didn't commit myself by more than a shrug. I went back to studying cars and passengers. Traffic was still moving, but it had slowed to about forty miles an hour. For an LA freeway, that's about half-speed. In the side mirror, I saw the green Olds again.

It was farther behind us now. I told myself that all of the cars in at least two lanes of the San Gabriel River Freeway had also made that same transition to the northbound Golden State Freeway, but I was still uneasy.

"What's wrong?" Rachel asked.

"I'm being paranoid."

"Oh yeah? That's much more fun as a group activity. Tell me what's making you nervous."

"There's a green Olds, two cars back in the lane to our right—see it?"

"Yes. You think we're being followed?"

"I don't know. He was behind us on the other freeway, too."

"An American-made sedan," she said.

"An unmarked cop car?"

"Maybe. Makes me wonder. Well, whoever he is, if he gets on the Ventura Freeway with us, we'll ditch him."

But when we hit downtown LA, traffic slowed to a crawl, and short of getting off the freeway all together or driving on the shoulders, there was no real opportunity to lose the green Olds. It was two cars behind us now, and in our lane. I still wasn't entirely convinced that we were being followed. The Olds had moved to the Ventura Freeway, but so did most of the other cars in our lanes. Tens of thousands of drivers would make this same set of lane changes on these same freeways every day.

We had two concerns by then: ditching the Olds and arriving at the library before Travis left. But traffic finally eased up and Rachel began to weave her way along, watching to see if the Olds followed. When it did, I heard her laugh. It was the kind of laugh you hear the mad scientist make in monster movies. I checked my seat belt and scrunched down.

We were approaching the Hollywood Freeway, the last one we needed to take to get to the library, but Rachel seemed determined to stay on the Ventura. She stayed on it beyond what a reasonable person would call the last minute, crossing two lanes and that wedge-shaped separation point between freeways known as the gore point. "Gore point" was an old term that had nothing to do with what you'd make of yourself if you didn't get across this dividing point in time, but seeing concrete and steel suddenly loom up in front of us made me wonder if we'd be hosed off of this one.

The Olds stayed on the Ventura. Rachel didn't take anything for granted, though, and made the trip up the Hollywood Freeway to the Victory Boulevard off-ramp at a speed that made me wonder if Travis's family was about to become even thinner of company.

She slowed on the surface streets, but my heart didn't.

"What time is it?" Rachel asked, turning at Whitsett.

"Ten-thirty," I said.

She sped up a little and made a quick right on Vanowen, and we soon saw Valley Plaza Park, which surrounds the library. We passed back under the freeway. The left she made onto Laurel Grove took out the last of my adrenaline but she slowed the car once she was through the intersection, and pulled cautiously into the parking lot behind the library.

Our fears of missing Travis were immediately relieved. Parked in a space along the back wall of the library was a purple pickup truck with an equally purple camper attached, both covered with yellow stars. On the sides of the camper, the words "Cosmo the Storyteller" and *"Cosmo el Narrador"* were painted in big yellow letters. Rachel, who didn't hide her amusement over my cousin's lack of subtlety, took a page out of McCain's book and pulled up behind the pickup, blocking it in.

"Just in case he walks out of the library while we walk in," she said.

The Valley Plaza Branch Library is not an imposing structure, and there isn't anything fancy about its architecture, but there is also nothing lacking in its warmth or friendliness. A librarian, whose name tag identified her as "I. Galvan," saw us looking around anxiously, and asked if she could be of help.

"Cosmo the Storyteller?" I asked, seeing that the children's section was all but empty.

"Oh, he's outside, in the park!" She led us back out to the parking lot and pointed to a cluster of people sitting on the grass a little distance away. We could see a brightly clad figure standing before them. Travis, I thought, although we weren't close enough to make out his features.

We thanked her and walked quietly toward the group, slowing as we neared a cluster of young mothers seated on the lawn near their preschoolers. One of the women held a sleeping baby on her lap. The attention of both parents and children was riveted on a tall man wearing black booties and tights, white gloves, a colorful tunic and a comically large red beret.

Travis? Yes. Dramatic clothing or no, I recognized his face from Briana's collection of photographs.

He was moving with an exaggerated tiptoeing step. "Shhhh," he said, gesturing with his gloved finger to his lips, although his wide-eyed audience wasn't making a sound.

We came nearer, and sat on the grass a few yards behind the mothers. A couple of them glanced back at us. Neither Travis nor the enthralled children seemed to notice us.

He crept forward, eyes wide, saying, "Wally was very scared. He didn't know if the dragon was really asleep. But then he heard the dragon snore."

He held his hand to his ear. The children began making loud snoring sounds. Travis smiled. "Ah, yes, that dragon is sound asleep!"

Stepping quietly around the invisible dragon, he moved to a big steamer trunk and gingerly removed a pair of square, papier-mâché boxes—one red, one yellow. He held the yellow one out to the audience with a questioning look.

"No!" they said, nearly in unison.

"What color is this box?" he asked, scratching his head.

"Yellow!" they chorused.

"Oh, isn't this the box I want?"

"No! The red one!"

"That's right, that's right!" he said, as if remembering, while the children laughed.

He put the yellow one back inside the trunk again. From time to time, he peered cautiously over his shoulder at the place on the lawn where the audience knew the beast still lay sleeping. Taking the red box closer to the children, he asked, "What did Wally find in the box?"

"The key!" a boy shouted. "The key!"

"Yes!" Travis said, bestowing a smile on the boy as he took a large gold key from the box. "He found the golden key. Now what did Wally do? Did he run home?"

"No!" A resounding chorus.

"But he's afraid of the dragon!"

There was a jumble of answers, which Travis seemed to understand perfectly. "Oh, he rescues the knight?"

"Yes!" The chorus again.

"You're absolutely right!" Acting out the story, he said, "Wally sneaked past the dragon and out of the dragon's fine hall. Then, carefully tucking the golden key in his pocket, Wally ran down the long staircase to . . ." He paused, scratching his head again. "Now where did that dragon put that knight?"

"The dungeon!" the children shouted.

"Oh, yes, that's where he went." More running. "And when he got to the door of the dungeon—uh-oh!" He began patting the tunic. "Where did I put that golden key?"

"Your pocket!" a girl yelled.

"Oh, yes! Thank you," he said with a bow.

"You're welcome!" the girl said in a quieter voice.

As the rest of the story unfolded, Wally freed the knight; Wally and the knight went safely back to their home; the sleeping dragon awoke and, seeing his meal missing, decided to become a vegetarian—a term which one of the children already knew. The same one who asked, "Was he a vegan?"

"I believe he was," Travis said. When the story ended the children and parents cheered him. He bowed humbly, sat on the grass with them, and began asking them about their favorite stories and books. To their delight, he gave away stickers of dragons. "Let's go back inside the library," he said at last.

He picked up one end of the trunk, which I could now see had wheels on the other end. He rolled it along as the children and their mothers followed him.

Rachel and I looked at one another, then tagged after him and his troops at a distance.

"Is that him?" Rachel asked, and I could see a look of unholy glee on her face.

"Shut up," I said.

"Love the outfit," she whispered. "Do you suppose he makes his own booties?"

I didn't answer.

"And the panty hose. You think he has to wear queen-sized?"

"Tights. I'm sure he has many costumes—" I began.

"Oh, I'm sure he does, too!" she said, laughing.

"What's your problem?" I asked, losing patience. "Didn't you see how those kids looked at him?"

"They loved him, of course," she said, but kept grinning.

I walked a little faster, pulling ahead of her, then stopped and threw back over my shoulder, "You've forgotten why we're here."

Somehow, watching her face fall wasn't as satisfying as I thought it would be.

Inside, Travis sat at a small round table that had several plastic dinosaurs on it. He was perched on the edge of one of the sturdy wooden children's chairs that surrounded the table, being smothered in hugs as his pint-sized admirers took their leave. I could see that more than one of the mothers were eyeing him with something that went beyond gratitude for entertaining their children. We stayed back, but from time to time he glanced up at us, a little uneasy, more aware now that we were there without children. Once or twice I caught him briefly studying me.

Before he was entirely free of the group of mothers and children, he excused himself and went into the library office.

"Think he's taking off?" Rachel asked, folding her arms.

"No," I said. "He'll be back out. The trunk is still here. And I don't think he knows who we are."

Ms. Galvan came over to stand by the trunk, apparently keeping an eye on it for him. Seeing that we were waiting for him, she asked, "Did you enjoy the performance?"

We agreed that we had.

"Is this the first time you've seen him tell stories?"

"Yes," Rachel answered, and continued small talk while I found myself growing more and more uneasy over the task at hand.

When he emerged from the office he was carrying his costume in a bundle. He was dressed in a pair of blue jeans and a green T-shirt, wearing a pair of running shoes. The beret off, I could see that his dark hair was cut short. He seemed serious and distracted, but as he looked toward us his face broke into a smile, making him look quite handsome.

"Think he's got a girlfriend?" Rachel whispered.

"For all I know, he's got a wife," I said.

"Or two," she said, not repenting in the least when I turned to scowl at her.

In the next moment, I was shocked to hear my cousin say, "Irene, I can't thank you enough!"

Rachel and I turned to him, mouths agape, but he was extending a scar-thatched right hand to the librarian.

"I should be thanking you," she said.

"Irene?" I said weakly.

She looked over at me. "Yes?"

"Oh. That's my name, too. I'm Irene Kelly."

She smiled. "I guess those of us whose mothers liked that song—"

But Travis interrupted her, saying in utter disbelief, "Irene Kelly?"

"Yes," I said, not hiding my relief at his recognition of my name. "Your cousin."

He stared at my outstretched hand as if he didn't know what to do with it, then suddenly turned and picked up the handle of the trunk. When he turned back to me, the charming smile was gone. His face was flushed, his eyes were blazing, and his mouth was drawn tight in a look of undisguised fury.

"Frankly," he said, as he began to move away from us with long strides, "I expected more of you."

Stunned, it took me a moment to find my voice, and then all I could manage was "Travis?"

But he was almost out of the room by then.

"Travis!" I called out.

He stopped and said, "Forget it. And don't try to follow me."

Everyone in the place was staring at us by then. The librarian said, "I don't understand—"

"They're family," Rachel said, as if that explained everything. She took hold of my elbow and began steering me out the front door.

"He's not going anywhere," she said calmly, moving toward the parking lot.

"In the mood he's in, he just might back over your sedan," I said.

"Naw," Rachel said. "That pickup truck looked new. And he won't want to mess up that purple paint job."

"You don't know—"

We heard a loud bang.

"—the Maguires," I finished, just before we heard the second bang.

12

Rachel's legs are a little longer than mine, but I do a lot of running, so I was around the corner of the building first. Travis was stepping out of the pickup, looking shaken. Rachel started shouting in Italian—what I understood of it made me pray all other Italians were out of earshot. But anyone who didn't speak the language could read the gestures.

The right front side of the car was not looking good. The wheel stood at a crazy lopsided angle, antifreeze was puddling onto the asphalt, and the headlamp was history. The pickup had surprisingly little damage. Its rear bumper was scraped and dented.

Travis stared at the car and his truck, as if he had only just awakened and found unexpected chaos. Rachel bounded over to him and grabbed him by the shirt collar, shoved him off balance and smacked his back up hard against the camper shell.

"No! Don't hurt him!" I shouted. She gave me a sharp look that said I just might be next, but let him go. She turned away from him, put her hands on top of her head, clenched her teeth and closed her eyes tightly, as if trying to contain an explosion.

He slumped a little, but otherwise didn't move. "I'm sorry," he said. "I'm terribly sorry. I'll pay for the damage."

She opened her eyes. "You're goddamned right you will!"

"I will! I will! Every cent. And I'll—I'll take you wherever you need to go—rent a car for you. Whatever is necessary. I'm so sorry. I don't know what came over me."

I could have told him that I knew what came over him and that it runs in the family, but just then Ms. Galvan opened the back door of the library. "Oh, no!" she said. "Is anyone hurt?"

"No, no one is hurt," I said. "We were in such a rush, afraid we'd miss my cousin. We stupidly left the car here and of course Travis—er, Cosmo—didn't see it." Rachel was glaring at me, but I went on. "Is there a good body shop nearby?"

Throughout the process of arranging for the car to be towed, nobody seemed to want to do much talking. Travis was still shaken, and didn't make much eye contact with me. I was fine with avoidance. I certainly didn't want to follow up this scene with the news I had to give him.

Rachel was probably thinking about that, too. Even though he had just battered her car, she seemed to make an effort to be friendly.

This began while we followed the tow truck to the body shop; on the way over, she apologized for being rough with him, and asked if she had hurt him. He shook his head.

"No? Well, you're either made of steel or you'll be feeling it later."

He smiled and said, "I'm not made of steel."

She laughed.

At the body shop, Travis looked over the loaner cars and told the shop owner that he would rent something for Ms. Giocopazzi elsewhere. It was decided that elsewhere would be in Las Piernas; if we were up in Los Angeles much longer, we'd hit the evening rush hour. Evening rush hour is also about four hours long. Travis offered to drive us home. "I'll buy you a late lunch there, too," he said, although only to her. "It's the least I can do."

We got into the pickup, all of us in the front seat. Rachel took the middle. Before starting the engine, Travis curled his fingers tightly on the steering wheel, leaned over and spoke directly to me for the first time since trying to take leave of me in the library.

"How much?" he asked.

"How much what?"

"Look, your friend Ms. Giocopazzi is being very decent about all of this, so I owe it to her to at least hear you out. You might not get what you came for, and I'm sad to see that Patrick Kelly's children aren't as proud as he was—not that I ever had any great admiration for your stiff-rumped old man, but at least he did have pride."

I swallowed a little of mine along with a retort about someone else's admirable old man and said, "Forgive me, Travis, but I don't know what the hell you're talking about."

"How much?" he demanded.

Rachel said, "Travis."

He looked at her.

"You're about to make a Clydesdale-sized horse's ass out of yourself—for the second time in less than two hours. It's kinda amusing to me, because your cousin here gets herself in trouble the same way you do—she's a hothead, too."

"I'll fight my own fights, thank you very much," I said.

"See what I mean?" she went on. "But what I'm trying to tell you is, Irene isn't here for your money."

"Is that what you thought?" I said to him, outraged. "You thought I came up here to borrow money? From someone I haven't seen in over twenty years? Of all the—"

"Irene—" Rachel said.

"If it's true that you aren't after money," Travis said, "then I'm sorry. Perhaps I jumped to a conclusion."

"No perhaps about it," I said.

"Then why are you here?"

I hesitated. "Because—"

"Not now," Rachel said firmly. To Travis, she said, "Drive us back to Las Piernas. You know where Mary Kelly lives?"

He thought for a moment. "Irene's great-aunt? The one who drives the Mustang?"

"Yes."

"Not exactly. I haven't seen her in over a dozen years. Is she the one who needs money?"

"For godsakes," I said, "nobody wants your damned money."

"You couldn't be more wrong about that," he said.

"Well, Aunt Mary doesn't. I don't. Rachel doesn't want more of it than will be needed to fix her car."

"Mary asked Irene to find you," Rachel said, holding a hand up to silence me. "It wasn't easy, and—well, I think we should go to Las Piernas, to Mary's house, and we can explain it there."

"All right," he said, starting the motor. "But now you've really piqued my curiosity."

That was enough to shut me up. At least for a few minutes. Until Travis said, "Rachel, Irene did warn you that you're accepting a ride from the bastard son of a murdering bigamist?"

"Oh, for pitysakes—" I began, but Rachel elbowed me.

"I've heard something of the family history," she admitted. "Maybe I should hear your version, though."

He smiled again. "I'll warn you ahead of time—I'm a liar. Being my father's son, what else could you expect—right, Irene? That's why I went into storytelling—a gratifying way to use my natural abilities."

I thought of taking a different tack, of telling him how much we had enjoyed watching his storytelling performance, but I saw him look over at me, trying to see if he had riled me. There was something smug about that look. I started watching cars again.

I heard him laugh. "Should I begin at the very beginning?" he asked.

"Sure," Rachel said.

There was a moment's silence.

"Once upon a time," he began, "a long, long time ago, in the time of our fathers' fathers, there was a rich old king who owned a kingdom of sugar, a magical land of green fields and blue skies.

"The king loved his queen, who had given him a fine son. The king said, 'I have everything in the world a man could want. Rich land, a beautiful wife and a fine son.' But then the king began to worry, began to fret in the way so many of us do when everything is going well. 'What if my wife should leave me? What if a dragon should take my son? What if my fortune should be lost?'

"Nothing could ease his sense of foreboding. Even when his wife announced that they would have another child, he only worried. He worked harder and harder—for he was a hard-working king, not one of the lazy sort of kings who sit about on big thrones all day. Soon he had a great deal of money in the castle, and said to the queen, 'Now I can protect you and our children from anything.'

"A little brown sparrow dared to speak up and say, 'Your highness, this life is hard. Nothing can protect us, except God in a good mood.'

"The king had no love of sparrows, and certainly did not want to hear them talk. He shooed this one from the castle. Some believe that sparrow cursed him as she flew away, but others simply believe that God had a mood swing.

"Whatever the cause, tragedy struck. Shortly after giving birth to their second son, the queen died. The king was nearly inconsolable, saying 'Just as I feared! My queen has left me!'

"In his grief, the king only worked harder. As his children grew up, the first son became a strong, brave young man, who pleased his father in every way. The second son was weak and bitter, and had a stone where his heart should have been."

"Do these young princes have names?" Rachel asked.

"Name them, if you'd like," he said.

"The younger one should be Horace DeMont," she said.

"And the older?"

"You'll have to tell me."

"Richard," he said. "Prince Richard. And like another Richard before him, he was lionhearted. He chafed at his father's protectiveness, and was something of a daredevil, and even learned to fly airplanes. He married a beautiful princess from the east, a lively woman who understood him, and he brought her to live at the castle. She was a good woman, and for a time, seeing his son's happiness, the king forgot his grief.

"Prince Horace became jealous, for he was already in the habit of looking about the castle and thinking of how much he would like to sit in this chair or own that painting when the old king died. He did not like the idea of sharing these things with the new princess, and complained about her frequently. The king tired of this, and banished him from the castle, giving him a home in another city, and telling him to stay away."

"Huntington Beach?" I asked.

"Yes. In those days, that part of the world was far away from the castle. But over the years, the land began to shrink and shrink and shrink, and it's much closer now."

He was quiet for a time, and I wondered if he would go on, or if my speaking was enough to bring an end to the tale. But then he said, "The king's worries were soon to begin again. A Great War was being fought in Europe, and Richard volunteered—enlisted in the fight even before his country did.

"While Richard was in France, his wife came to the king and told him that she was expecting a child. The king at once sent a message to Richard, to tell him of this wonderful news, but poor Richard was slain before the message could reach him. He had died a courageous death, but the king found little comfort in that, saddened that a dragon had indeed taken his son.

"Horace now asked his father to welcome him home as his only remaining son, and to remove the princess. This angered the king, who cut Horace out of his will. He saw to it that the princess had the best of care. He was overjoyed when the princess gave birth to a little girl, and was especially pleased when she named her new daughter Gwendolyn, after his late and much beloved queen.

"Again tragedy struck, and there are those who will tell you that this one disordered the old king's mind. The king and the princess traveled to the east, so that the princess might see her family, and to show them the fair Gwendolyn. And while they were there, a plague struck, the worst in five hundred years."

"The influenza epidemic?" I asked.

"Yes. Do you know about it?"

"Not much," I admitted.

"Twenty-one million people died because of it—more than twice the number killed in World War I. So many died in Washington and Baltimore, they ran out of coffins."

"Sounds as if you've studied about it," I said.

He smiled. "My father told me about it. He lies about a great many things, of course, but I checked up on this."

His use of the present tense was not lost on me, or on Rachel. We exchanged a look of dismay.

"Oh, I know a son shouldn't speak ill of his father," Travis said, misreading it, "but I know you'll hardly blame me, Irene."

"Forget about that," Rachel said quickly. "I want to hear the rest of the story you were telling. They went back east and caught the flu."

"Yes. All three of them. But despite his age, the king survived, and despite her youth, Gwendolyn did as well. But the poor princess did not. Heartbroken, the king left the east as quickly as he could, and came back to his castle. He loved Gwendolyn, but his protectiveness of this new little princess became extreme. He rarely allowed anyone else near her. A few governesses, a housekeeper or two.

"She grew into a woman, but since her grandfather believed all men to be fortune hunters, he did not allow her into their company. He forever saw her as much younger than she was. She did not mind this protection; she had known it all her life. She was extremely shy of other people, most especially men.

"But one day, when she was outside, sitting in her garden, she saw a big snake sleeping in the sun. Frightened, she cried out, awakening the snake. But a boy who was working nearby heard her, and hurried to help her. He removed the snake from the garden, then went back to see if she had been bitten or harmed in anyway. She told him she was not, but even though he was only twelve, he could see the princess—whom he thought quite silly—was shaken.

"The boy began to tell her a story, one that made the shy princess laugh, and when he had finished, the princess asked him to tell her another. He told her one, and then another, and so it went, until the boy's brother—who was much older than the boy—called to him that it was time to go.

"She begged the boy to return to her, and he did. When the king died four years later, the princess was very lonely, and soon married the only male who had ever formed an attachment to her."

He paused, then said, "There are those that would tell you that she was safer with the snake, and maybe they are right. But they do not think, perhaps, of the boy being only a young man of sixteen, and of her, however shy, being over forty. Perhaps it was the boy who would have been better off with the snake.

"What is certain, however, is that one should not ignore the advice of sparrows, for everything the king most feared came true."

— ～

We had reached Las Piernas by then and he asked for directions. I made a decision. He didn't like me much, and the easiest thing would have been to take him to Mary's house, to leave everything on her shoulders.

"Take the next exit," I said, ignoring Rachel's look of surprise.

I was as much a Maguire as I was a Kelly. It was time to stop letting my father's prejudices ruin any chance of getting closer to my cousin. I just hoped God found that funny enough to laugh himself into a good mood.

13

I was surprised when we were able to find a parking space in front of the house; it was the only one available on our block. We live near the beach, and at that time of year, as the weather was warming, the crowds were showing up.

I took Rachel aside and gave her the keys to the Volvo, asking her to give me some time alone with Travis. She hesitated, then relented. She told me to give her a call if I needed help. When he saw that she was leaving, Travis protested that he had promised to pay for a rental car, but she told him not to worry about it. "Just spend some time getting to know your cousin," she said. "You might find out she's not so bad."

He made a face that looked like the warm-up for a sarcastic reply, then caught her disapproving glance. "Will we see you later?" he asked.

She promised she'd be back.

I stalled for a while, introducing him to our pets, showing him the house, feeding him lunch outside on the patio. The dogs took a liking to him and lay on the lawn, watching him. Cody reserved judgment, and busied himself rolling around in a patch of mint that Frank had planted for him.

I answered Travis's questions about Frank, Pete and Rachel, none of which seemed to be designed to elicit more than small talk. He steered the topic of conversation away from himself, so I stopped asking questions, too anxious about coming up with a way to break the news about his parents to worry much over his reticence. I decided I would make a determined effort to discover more about him later. For the time being, I tried to learn what I could from what he chose to ask me. I suppose I learned more from what he didn't ask.

He didn't ask about me or Barbara. I told myself there was no reason to feel hurt over that, that he was a stranger. But he wasn't.

And yet, what was there to bind him to us? I began to feel sure that as soon as I told him of his parents' deaths, he would flee. It seemed to me that would be yet another loss, another unnecessary separation in our family saga of indifference. I wanted it to stop.

"I was wondering," I said, "if you could stay a few days?"

He didn't try to hide his surprise. "Here? With you?"

"Yes. In the guest bedroom."

He stared at me a moment, and I half-expected one of his sarcastic replies. But he shook his head and said, "No, I've got my camper. It's all I need—I prefer it, really."

As if on cue, we were interrupted by a loud noise—a series of whoops and honking sounds—a car alarm. He was up on his feet and hurrying through the house. I followed him, but by the time we reached the front yard, there was no one near the pickup. He pressed a button on his key-chain and the noise subsided.

"Think someone tried to break into it?" I asked.

He glanced around and shrugged. "Hard to know. It isn't one of those that goes off every time the wind blows, but I've had more than one false alarm from it."

"There's a stairway to the beach at the end of the street," I said, "so a lot of beachgoers walk past the house. Maybe someone walking by was curious about 'Cosmo the Storyteller.' "

He smiled, "Remarking on the paint job?"

"It is designed to grab attention, right?"

"Right." He glanced between the camper and the house and said, "Mind if I move a couple of things into the house for safekeeping?"

"Not at all. But as I was saying, why don't you stay?"

"No need to," he said, walking to the back of the camper. "I have a place to sleep."

"Well, then, stay here in your camper."

"Why?" he asked suspiciously.

"Maybe we could get to know each other."

He laughed as he opened the camper door. "Same question: why?"

I waited while he stepped into the camper and retrieved the rolling trunk. When I suggested he put it in the guest room, he seemed amused, but did as I asked.

We went back out on the patio.

"You asked why I wanted you to stay," I said. "What happened—between our parents—it wasn't right."

"Oh? So we should suddenly become cousins? Real cousins? Just ignore the past few decades of neglect?" He shook his head. "You Kellys are unbelievable."

"I'm as much a Maguire as you are!"

"Forgive me for saying so, but so what?"

"Do we have to perpetuate something our parents started? Make it worse?"

"Why start with me? Go ask my mother's forgiveness, not mine. God knows Mom has always been more interested in you than I am. In fact, the last time I saw her, she told me she was going to cut me out of her will in your favor. Even showed it to me." He laughed. "Some day you'll be the proud owner of a couple of religious statues and a dozen or so Georgette Heyer novels."

Well, that shut me right up.

"What?" he asked, seeing my dismay.

"I've tried to think of a way to tell you this," I said miserably.

He stared hard at me.

I drew a breath. "When your mother called you at the Mission Viejo Library, did you call her back?"

"No," he said warily. "But what business is that of yours?"

"I think she called to tell you about your father," I began. "Was—was he ill?"

"Yes," he answered, then his eyes widened. "*Was* . . . ?" he repeated, then said, "Not already! It's too soon! He's . . . he's not . . . he died?"

"Yes."

All the color left his face. He lowered his head, exhaled loudly. He made no other sound for several long minutes. But then, as the shock seemed to wear off, he stood up, fists clenched. His face, so pale just moments ago, was now flushed with rage. "I can't believe it!" he said angrily. "I can't believe she—she asked you to tell me—"

"She didn't!" I said quickly.

"You just took it upon yourself? Why on earth—"

"Because . . . maybe you should sit down again."

"No," he said, narrowing his eyes at me, as if trying to read my mind. "Something's happened—what's wrong?"

"Travis, I'm sorry, I'm—so sorry to have to tell you this, but your mother was in a car accident and—"

"She's hurt? Where is she?"

I shook my head. "She was killed, Travis."

"Killed?" he said blankly, as if it had become a foreign word. "Killed?"

I nodded.

"By a car?" Still unable to grasp it.

"She was crossing a street . . ." I said, but trailed off as I saw his face twist up with grief. "Oh, Travis—" I reached out toward him.

"No!" he said.

He turned his back to me, took a faltering step, then sat down hard in the chair. He brought his knees up, sitting sideways, curling himself up in the chair, hiding his head in his arms. "No, not her. Not her," he said, again and again, until he began sobbing too hard to say it.

The dogs had gingerly stepped onto the deck by then, and stood with hips leaning against my knees in what I took to be some sort of pack formation against danger, their ears forward and watching him with concern. Deke looked back at me, then ventured forward first, sniffing at his shoes and singing a single, high-pitched note of anxious sympathy to him. I was going to call her back, but he reached for her and held on to her soft black coat, and soon Dunk was also sidling in to offer whatever comfort he could.

I started to go inside the house, to give him some privacy, but turned back at the last moment, unwilling to let the dogs be smarter than I was, deciding that the family stubbornness that had pitted the two of us against one another might be put to better use.

The dogs moved away as I knelt next to him. I put an arm around his shoulders. He stiffened. I half expected him to tell me to go to hell, but instead he tentatively took hold of my hand, then squeezed it tightly, not letting go. After a time, he shifted in the chair, uncurling enough to put his head on my shoulder, and we held on to one another until this first wave of grief was exhausted.

He quieted, then pulled away awkwardly and went into the house without saying anything to me. I stretched and got up off my sore knees, waited a minute or two, then followed him in, dogs trailing. I heard the sound of the bathroom tap running, and figured he was washing his face. I went into the kitchen, busying myself with wiping off the counter and rinsing the dishes from lunch.

He hadn't come out yet by the time I finished, so I sat on the couch and waited for him. Cody took advantage of this time to lie on my lap, splaying paws and purring loudly as I scratched the particular place under his chin that cannot receive enough attention.

Eventually Travis came into the living room. He seated himself on the couch, but as far away from me as possible. Staring at the empty fireplace, he said, "Tell me what you know."

"About the accident?"

"Whatever you know about—what happened to my parents."

I began by talking about his father's death, because he seemed to have known of Arthur's illness. "I don't know much," I said, "only what was on the death certificate."

"He had cancer," Travis said quietly.

"Yes, that was listed as the cause of death."

After a moment, he said, "I guess you know something about that. Mom told me about your mother."

"My father, too," I said.

"Really? Patrick died of cancer?" he said, with a kind of mild curiosity, as if I had just told him that we had graduated from the same high school.

"Yes. In fact, the doctor who treated your dad was my dad's doctor."

He didn't react to that. He seemed to be caught up in some distant memory. After a long silence, he said, "Mom used to tell me this story about you. That you held me when I was a baby."

"Yes," I said, hoping to God he wouldn't ask me to talk about it just then.

He seemed to sense that, though, and said, "What happened to my mother?"

I tried to be gentle in the telling, but the facts of the matter were like axes, and couldn't be used for fine work. After a time he again grew very pale, held up a hand, then murmured, "Excuse me."

He hurried into the bathroom; I could hear him getting sick.

———

When Rachel came over a few hours later, exhaustion had led to a truce on both grief and bickering.

"Where is he?" Rachel asked, as she walked into my kitchen bearing a large, foil-covered baking dish.

"Taking a nap out in the Cosmobile," I said.

"His camper?"

"Yep. He turned down the guest room."

"You told him about his parents?" she asked.

"Yes. He took it pretty hard. Anyone would."

"You didn't have such an easy job, did you? You okay?"

I nodded. She didn't say anything for a moment, then asked, "Aren't you afraid he'll just drive off?"

"He might, but I don't think he will. He wants to see Aunt Mary and to visit Briana's grave. But he said he'd like to wait until tomorrow—wasn't ready for either one today. I don't blame him. And as for driving off, I suppose he'll probably bring my cat in first."

"Cody?"

"Yes. Cody was fascinated by the camper. Full of interesting scents and all kinds of nooks and crannies. Travis seemed to like having his company, and even left a window screen open so that Cody could get in and out if he wanted to. But I think Cody's there for the duration."

"So that's why Cody isn't in here begging. I brought lasagna," she said, putting the dish in the refrigerator.

"Sounds great, but Travis might not have much of an appetite."

"You two getting along any better?"

I shrugged. "Hard to say, under the circumstances."

There was a soft knock on the front door. I opened it to find Travis standing on the front steps, sleep-tousled and pale. His fists were shoved into his pockets and he was staring at a point somewhere near my shoes. "I don't think I can sleep any longer," he said. "Mind if I come in for a while?"

"Of course not. Did you lose the key I gave you?"

He shook his head. "No. But your privacy . . ."

"Next time just use the key. You won't disturb me. You're here as my guest."

He saw Rachel as she walked up behind me. She took one look at him and said, *"Mi dispiace molto . . . ,"* stepping forward to embrace him. He didn't refuse the embrace, but it seemed nearly to undo his struggle to maintain his composure. He looked over her shoulder at me, and I decided to see it as a request.

"Where's my cat?" I asked brusquely.

"He didn't want to leave the camper," he said, stepping away from her, visibly relaxing. "He found a spot he likes at the foot of the bed."

As he continued to babble on about the cat, Rachel picked up her cue, and made no more sympathetic comments. She told him that she had made something for our dinner, a lasagna from an old family recipe, and proceeded to try to distract him with stories about her grandmother's skills in the kitchen.

Dinner passed without much comment, and we probably could have served just about anything to Travis with much the same result—he didn't even bother toying with Rachel's culinary masterpiece. He was silent during the meal, not responding when we asked questions. We weren't ignored, really—to say he ignored us would be to suggest a choice I'm not sure he made. He was obviously too lost in his own thoughts to hear us.

When we stood up to clear our plates, he suddenly said, "Rachel, you're a private detective?"

"Yes."

"I want to hire you."

"To find out who killed your mother?"

"Yes."

"Can't do it."

We both looked at her in surprise.

"Why not?" he asked.

"I'd need the permission of my current client. I'm already working for Irene."

He was openly dismayed.

"I don't mind working together," I said. "I'd prefer it."

He didn't respond.

"We better tell McCain we've found him," Rachel said, then explained to Travis, "He's with LAPD Homicide. Lots of people have been looking for you lately."

"I'm sure they have," he said, his voice full of sarcasm. "Slay the fatted calf, the bastard has returned! And he's a rich bastard!"

"Why do you insist on using that term?" I snapped. "I've never referred to you in that way."

"I insist on it because for several miserable years, I lived with being called a bastard—and worse. And the truth, Irene, is that the term is accurate. My parents were not legally married when I was born."

"Well, maybe that changed," I shot back without thinking. "According to your father's death certificate, they were married."

For a moment, he was completely silent, then he shook his head and said, "Impossible. He lied or the doctor lied." He smiled. "Or you're lying now."

14

Rachel held up a hand and said, *"Basta!"*

"That's Italian for 'Enough!'" I said quickly, and Travis, realizing exactly what had caused me to be anxious over her choice of that particular word, started laughing at me.

I marched over to the phone, pulled out the directory and started thumbing through it.

"What are you doing?" he asked.

"Looking up Brad Curtis's number. I'm going to leave a message on his service. He can call me back and tell me why he's falsifying information on death certificates."

"The man is probably busy helping cancer patients. You want to disturb him with this nonsense?"

"Hold on," Rachel said, "hold on. Travis, humor me, and assume for a moment that your parents did marry."

"I'm telling you, she wasn't even speaking to him. She wasn't speaking to me because I dared to make contact with him."

"But—"

"Why would they marry?" he asked. "It wasn't to give me his name before he died, if that's what you think. He openly acknowledged me as his son, even during the years I didn't want him to."

"Why didn't you want him to?" Rachel asked.

He didn't answer.

"What would have happened to the estate if your father died unmarried?" I asked.

"Unless he changed his will, what's left of his estate passes on entirely to me," Travis said. "He had no other children; I'm his sole heir. Oh, God—I should try to reach W, and Mr. Brennan."

"W?" I asked. "Who is W?"

"Ulysses Ulkins. Double U. My father's assistant. Mr. Brennan is my father's lawyer. I'll call—maybe on Monday. W will probably be in the office tomorrow, but—I can't. Not yet," he said, struggling to keep his composure.

We were all quiet for a moment.

"You said something about 'what's left of the estate,'" I said. "What did you mean?"

"Most of my father's money has already been given to me. He set up trusts."

I glanced over at Rachel; she gave me a look that said she was going to leave everything up to me.

"Travis," I said, "I think you're in danger."

"Of course I am."

That took both of us by surprise. He seemed amused by our reaction.

"Remember when you caught up with me today? I thought you wanted money. Some of the DeMonts, the family of my father's wife—I mean *Gwendolyn*," he said, looking at me. "Some of them believe my father robbed them of their inheritance."

"They think your father murdered Gwendolyn DeMont," Rachel said.

"Yes," he answered. "They believe my father murdered her for her money and so that he could be free to live with his other family—my mother and me."

"Did he?" I asked.

With a small smile, he said, "You should have asked years ago."

"Did he?" I repeated.

"Kill her? I honestly don't know."

As I sat trying to absorb the implications of that statement, he added, "If he was the one who killed her, he didn't kill her to be with us. My mother and I had discovered his marriage to Gwendolyn, you see, and that caused—a certain number of changes in our happy little family."

"Start from the beginning," I said. "Tell me what you know about Arthur and Gwendolyn."

"You've already forgotten the story of the princess in the garden?"

"No, but maybe you could tell the sequel to that story in a little more straightforward style."

"I liked the way he told it," Rachel said.

"Thank you," Travis said. "It's nice to be appreciated."

I held my tongue.

We waited. He sat quietly, looking as if he were mentally composing another tale. He stared down at his scarred hand; his expression changed to one of profound sorrow. Suddenly he stood up. "I'm sorry, I can't," he said. "Not tonight. It's too soon. Excuse me."

He murmured thanks to Rachel for the meal, said good night, and walked to the front door. I followed him.

"Travis, wait," I said, as he opened it.

"What do you want?" he asked.

I stepped outside with him on the front porch, closing the door behind us. It was dark there, and somehow that made it easier to talk to him. The porch lamp wasn't on, and there was no moon. A street lamp down the block provided the only light.

"You're a member of my family. No ifs, ands or buts. And if you need my help, I don't want you to feel—what happened between our parents—that was—that had nothing to do with you."

I saw him smile a little in the darkness. I heard him pull his keys out of his pocket. "If you're talking about the infamous pass my father supposedly made at your mother, I probably know more about it than you do."

There was that word "supposedly." Mary had used it, too. "I was there," I said. "You weren't even born yet."

He didn't say anything for a moment. It was a warm night, and the scent of salt air on a light ocean breeze was mixed with wood smoke from fires on the beach. A couple of cars drove past the house. Finally he said, "Close your eyes and picture that day. You were what, about ten years old?"

"Eleven."

"Ah, yes. Eleven. An age when girls are thinking much more often about what goes on between men and women. Are your eyes closed?"

Reluctantly, I went along with the program. "Yes, now they are."

"My mother was out of town, visiting our grandmother in Kansas, right?"

"Right."

"My father was injured while working on a tree."

"Yes. He fell from a ladder. He hurt his shoulder, I think."

"Yes, his right shoulder and elbow. He fell on his right side. He had been treated at the hospital, but he needed a ride home. You and your sister were with your parents when they met him at the hospital."

I nodded. "He had a cast on his arm, but they were going to let him go home. We were going to drive him home."

"Right. But on the way home, you stopped at a pharmacy, so that he could fill a prescription."

I opened my eyes. "How do you know so much about this?"

"Close your eyes. My father told me, of course. No, don't look. Just try to go back to that day. I think you'll be able to see it a little differently."

"Okay, so we're in the drugstore," I said.

"Yes. You stay with my father and your mother, your sister Barbara goes off with your father, trying to talk him into buying something for her."

"Yes. I don't remember what it was, though."

"My dad said she wanted some sort of curlers that could be preheated?"

I laughed. "Yes!"

"Now think of my father and your mother standing at the counter, and you, nearby."

"Just on the other side of my mother, a little behind them."

"And what happens?"

I frowned. "Your father reaches over with his good arm— beneath the counter, out of sight of the clerk—and takes my mother's hand and squeezes it in his own. My father is just walking up the aisle behind them. He's seen your father take her hand, and he has a fit." I opened my eyes. "Or did your father tell it differently?"

"No. He told me all of that. But you're forgetting part of the story."

I frowned.

"Close your eyes again, think of what happened."

"Wouldn't it just be easier to tell me?" I said.

He shook his head. "Better if you remember it on your own. It's funny—whenever I dared to ask my father questions about the night of the murder, he said the same thing—if he just gave me the answers to my questions, I'd never know whether or not he was telling the truth. I'd either come to trust him for other reasons, or learn the truth for myself. So think about that moment in the pharmacy just before you go to sleep tonight. Maybe you'll dream the answer."

"Dream it? You're kidding."

He shook his head in resignation, pointed the plastic alarm remote on his keychain toward the camper and pressed a button.

The explosion blasted out the windows of the cab and sent the hood of the truck rocketing up into the air, mak-

ing it into a strange, careening metal kite. We were both
knocked back through the doorway into the entry. I sat
up, dazed, and saw that both truck and camper were on
fire.

"Cody!" I cried.

15

We ran toward the camper, but by now smoke was pouring out of it, and the heat was too fierce to get close to it. Travis tried, but I pulled him back, afraid that he would be burned.

"Get the hose!" I said. "Near the front steps!" As he ran for the garden hose, I bolted over to the Karmann Ghia, opening the trunk to get the small fire extinguisher I carried there. Rachel charged out of the house just as Jack came out of his. Seeing the fire, he hurried to his van to get another extinguisher. Rachel ran back inside to call 911.

I aimed at the door of the camper shell, as did Travis; I felt a hard lump in my throat and tears stinging my eyes, but tried to hold on to a slim hope that Cody was alive. Despite the heat, Travis reached for the door handle, but the instant he opened it flames and smoke roared out, pushing him back.

"Get away from it!" Rachel shouted at us. "Let the fire department take care of it!"

"Cody!" I said. "Cody was sleeping inside!"

Jack's extinguisher was empty; he was pulling Travis back. Soon mine was empty as well. I tried to reach for the hose, but Rachel grabbed my arms from behind. Horrifying images of Cody burning alive in that camper drove me into a frenzied struggle against her. She quickly maneuvered me down to the lawn and pinned me there. My face in the grass, my breath coming hard, I heard sirens howling their way closer. The sound somehow got through to me in a way all my discomfort did not; I realized that if Cody was in that camper, there wasn't a chance in hell that he was alive. I heard myself groan as the fight drained out of me and an agonizing ache replaced it. Rachel let up a little. I wasn't going anywhere.

"I'm sorry about Cody," I heard her say as she moved off of me, "but keep in mind that it could have been Travis."

"Small consolation," I heard Travis say as he sat down next to me.

I found myself wishing that they would both go away. Or shut up. Just shut up.

Or better, maybe I could just disappear, be somewhere where I didn't have to smell smoke and didn't have to think about what was burning in that camper. Where I could get sick or scream or sob or smash something to pieces, or follow any of the other impulses warring within me. Perhaps, I thought, it would be nice to faint. Unfortunately, I have some idea of what it takes to make me do that, and—damn it all to hell—I knew I wasn't even close.

Cody. Poor Cody. I should have never—but I stopped myself from taking that road.

I started wishing that Frank were home, because I knew he would know what not to say, but then I was glad that he didn't have this addition to the list of things he was trying to cope with.

"I left a window open," Travis reminded me. "Maybe Cody got out before the camper caught fire."

I pushed myself up.

Travis had already started looking in the bushes near the house, calling, "Co-dy . . . kit-kit-kit . . ." I checked under the Karmann Ghia and the Volvo. Jack started investigating hiding places in his yard.

The fire truck pulled up, its occupants perhaps a little

baffled to find three adults ignoring a vehicle fire, stooped down and talking in coaxing voices to plants and bushes. Rachel was cautiously using the hose to keep the lawn wet, trying to prevent the fire from spreading. She was the reason some of my other neighbors were at a distance; she had warned one of them off in an authoritative voice when he ventured too near—when he approached again, she squirted him in the crotch with the hose. He swore at her, but retreated. The others were now murmuring to one another in a rubbernecking huddle.

The firefighters made quick work of putting out the blaze, and began talking to Rachel.

I looked over at Travis, and saw that he was cradling his right hand, wincing. I moved closer to him and saw that his palm and fingers were red and swollen, covered with blisters—in a peculiar pattern. "You burned it on the door handle . . ."

"Yeah, pretty stupid, huh?"

I shook my head. "It must hurt like hell. Let's ask one of the paramedics to take a look at it."

We both turned then to take our first real look at the camper. It was a charred hulk. I heard Travis moan softly. That small sound made me realize how wrapped up in my own concerns I had been.

"Pretty lousy day for you, isn't it?" I said.

He choked out a laugh.

"Sorry," I said. "Irene Kelly, master of understatement."

The police arrived while a paramedic was placing Travis's hand in a saline soak. More law enforcement soon showed up; investigators interested in everything from bombs to arson to attempted murder.

They left a long time later, towing the remains of the camper off with them, saying they needed it for further study. The fire had left little for Travis to salvage from it. The detectives were frustrated. The only names Travis could supply for potential enemies were those of the DeMonts.

"But they had no way of knowing I'd be here in Las Piernas," he said. "I didn't know I'd be here myself."

They asked for information on them all the same. He told them the DeMonts lived in Huntington Beach, then said, with a glance at the place where the camper had been parked, "I'd give you their addresses, but—"

Rachel gave me a warning look, then said, "Don't worry about it, Travis, these guys will be able to find them."

The detectives reassured him on that point, and left soon after. Two uniformed officers in a cruiser were left behind, to keep an eye on the house. Things began to settle down.

The paramedics had wrapped the hand lightly in a gauze bandage, but said that as soon as Travis was done talking to the police, we should take him to an emergency room, to have the hand treated.

I went into the house to get my keys and to quickly change my blouse, which, after my time facedown on a wet lawn, made me look like the loser in an outdoor mud-wrestling competition. On my way back out, I passed by the kitchen, glanced in and saw a sight that stopped me in my tracks.

"Cody!"

Peering up from the kitchen counter, where he had evidently been having a grand old time demolishing the leftover lasagna, Cody mistook my shout of relief and figured he was in trouble. He streaked out past me into the front yard.

Apparently the others saw him, for by the time I got out to the front yard, Jack, Rachel and Travis were all surrounding the Karmann Ghia, bent low and talking sweetly to him. I joined them, and saw that he was twitching his tail, watching me warily.

"Come here, you big oaf," I said, but I was crying.

Cody, all orneriness aside, is usually attuned to my

moods. Demonstrating this, he came closer and peered up at me—his gray face covered with lasagna sauce—and then ventured out from under the car.

I picked him up carefully, still worried that he might be hurt. He was impatient with my attempts to fuss over him, twisting and clawing, but when Travis began petting him, he sniffed delicately at Travis's lightly bandaged hand, and settled down. Soon I realized that other than a messy face, the cat was fine.

"Sorry for the delay," I said to Travis. "I'll take you to the hospital now."

"Which one?" he asked.

"Las Piernas General. It's closest."

He seemed relieved. Seeing that I had noticed, he said, "St. Anne's is a good hospital, but since my dad—well, I don't think I can go over there yet." He quickly changed the subject. "Will eating lasagna make Cody sick?"

"It's not good for him, but God knows he's eaten worse things."

The cat, who was sauntering back into the house, flipped his tail at me in a manner reminiscent of an obscene gesture.

"I see Cody speaks Italian, too," Travis said.

By the time the emergency department doctor finished working on his hand, Travis's ability to hide the pain of his injury was failing. The doctor offered to give him an injection of morphine, but Travis said the prescriptions he'd been given would be enough and he'd wait until he got home.

It was about two in the morning when we got to the pharmacy, but it was a busy night. Throughout the time we waited for the prescriptions, Travis was silent. He sat with his head resting against the wall, his eyes closed, his brows drawn together in pain or concentration, I wasn't sure which. His face was pale.

I tried to imagine what it would be like to be told both of your parents were dead, then on the same day, see all your possessions—everything but a trunkful of costumes—destroyed by someone trying to kill you with a bomb. This on the same day you had been involved in a car accident, infuriated because a cousin—from a branch of the family that had disowned yours—showed up unexpectedly and hounded you. The same day you had suffered a second-degree burn on your hand because you thought a cat was being burned alive in your camper.

All things considered, I had to admire how well he was holding up—but he wasn't looking so great at the moment.

"Do you want to go back for that injection?" I asked.

He opened his eyes. "No, I can wait. Listen, I'm sorry you've had to pay for all of this. I have some cash in the trunk. When we get back to your house, I'll pay you back."

"Forget it. I would have paid for it anyway," I said to him. "You were wounded trying to rescue my cat."

He looked as if he might argue, but seemed to change his mind and lapsed back into silence.

I returned to thinking about what an awful day he'd had, kept trying to think of comforting things to say, but none seemed adequate.

When the harassed pharmacy clerk finally called Travis's name, we walked up to the counter together. It was then, as we were standing at the counter, that—with his help—the memory came back to me.

I was standing to his left. The weary clerk shoved two plastic bottles of pills and a tube of ointment toward us.

"Which of the pills are for the infection?" Travis asked.

She tapped the top of one of the bottles, then started to ring up the charges.

"Can I take that on an empty stomach?" he asked.

"Directions are right on the label," she said.

"Do I need to eat something before I take it?" he asked again.

She sighed with long-suffering, picked up the bottle and glanced at it. "Yes. Take it with meals." She rapped it down on the counter as if it were a gavel.

She had just finished entering a second set of numbers on the cash register when he said, "If I take the pain medication, will it make me drowsy?"

"Read the label!" she snapped.

"Can I operate machinery?" he persisted.

Wondering what was wrong with him, I picked up the bottle and said, "No, Travis. You shouldn't take these and drive."

"How many times a day do I take them?"

"As needed for pain, but not more than two every twelve hours."

I set the bottle down. He reached over with his left hand, and squeezed mine—quickly, quietly and as if in gratitude. Nothing flirtatious about it.

I looked into his face. Suddenly remembered his father asking similar questions twenty-some years before. Remembered the clerk growing more and more angry with Arthur's persistent refusal to read the label. But why? Why hadn't he just picked up the bottle and read it himself?

Something had happened just before Arthur squeezed my mother's hand. She had picked up the bottles and read the labels aloud.

Comprehension finally dawned.

"He couldn't read," I said softly. Travis nodded and smiled a little.

Mistaking my meaning, the woman behind the counter first looked shocked, then turned red. "I'm so sorry, sir," she said quietly. "I didn't mean to embarrass you."

"Nor I you," Travis said.

He took the first pain pill at a water fountain before we left the building. I held my questions until we were in the car.

"Your father—" I began.

"As you guessed."

"Arthur was illiterate?" I said, still not believing it.

"Yes," he said.

"But he had his own business!"

"Yes. Landscaping—that was how he began, anyway. He had a wonderful sense of color and placement, loved making things grow, loved the outdoors. Even when he no longer earned most of his money that way, few things made him happier."

"But not being able to read! I just can't imagine how he managed to get by!"

"It wasn't easy," he said, closing his eyes, leaning his head back.

"I'm sorry, you probably aren't up to talking about this right now."

"To be honest, no, I'm not." He yawned. "But I'll talk more about it with you tomorrow—if you want to." He yawned again. "You've got a lot to think about now, anyway," he said drowsily.

I started the car, pulled out of the parking lot.

"Did my mother know?" I asked, unable to let this one question keep overnight.

He opened his eyes, looked over at me, then watched the road for a little while before he closed them again. I thought he wasn't going to answer. But then he said, "According to my father, yes, she did—but only after that day in the pharmacy." He smiled sleepily. "He always spoke highly of your mother. She kept his secret."

"But he could have explained to my father—"

He looked over at me again. "He was ashamed that he couldn't read. Can't you imagine what that was like for him? My dad knew that Patrick would blame him, not your mother, for that little squeeze of her hand. That's exactly what happened—your father assumed he made a pass at your mother. He worried at first that she would tell Patrick the truth, and his secret would be exposed to a man who already disliked him. But your mother must have seen how painful that would have been to him, because she let my father decide whether Patrick would know or not know." He smothered another yawn, closed his eyes again. "She never told Patrick. Never told anyone. My father admired her for that." I thought he had fallen asleep, but then he murmured, "I wish I had known her."

As I drove home I thought about Arthur Spanning—my uncle, not my uncle, perhaps my uncle again. A man who preferred having my father think of him as an unprincipled sleazeball rather than as someone who was unable to read. Did he have a learning disability—something like dyslexia? Or had he simply never learned to read? I remembered the "six years" of education on the death certificate.

I thought of my mother, keeping secrets from the rest of us, letting us think Arthur was a womanizer, letting the rift grow between our family and her sister's husband.

But he *was* a womanizer, I reminded myself. A bigamist. His illiteracy had nothing to do with that. Travis was probably right; it was impossible to imagine his parents were remarried—or whatever it would be called in this case. Why would Briana ever take him back? Because she pitied a dying man? Because of Travis?

I looked over at my sleeping cousin, his bandaged hand lying palm up in his lap.

That unexpectedly strong sense of protectiveness I had been feeling toward him all day resurfaced. The idea that someone had tried to harm him while he was staying at my home made me furious. I decided that if Rachel were awake when I got back to the house, I wanted to have a talk with her about the DeMonts.

Then again, maybe it wasn't a smart idea to bring him home. Whoever had tried to kill him knew exactly where he was staying.

How? I wondered. How did anyone find out?

No one other than a librarian in Mission Viejo knew that Travis was the storyteller, and she knew very little of his background. And even if she had revealed to the world that Travis was Cosmo the Storyteller, she didn't know where I lived. For that matter, she couldn't have been certain we were going up to the Valley Plaza Branch Library; for all she knew, I would just make a phone call to that library. Certainly no one knew he'd be coming back with us. Rachel and I hadn't known it ourselves.

I thought briefly of the car that had tailed us on the freeway. But not only had Rachel lost the tail, we weren't in the same vehicle when we headed home. Where had the tail started?

There was a Las Piernas PD patrol car sitting outside our house when I pulled into the driveway. Jack and Rachel were sitting on the front porch, talking.

"They're here to keep an eye on things," Rachel said, indicating the patrol car.

"I thought you two would be gone by now," I said.

"I think I'll stick around," Rachel said. "If you don't mind. At least for tonight."

"Not at all," I said. "I'll put Travis on the foldout couch."

"Forget it!" she said. "He's been hurt. Give him the guest-room bed. I'll be fine on the couch."

"He could stay at my place," Jack offered.

But we both turned that idea down—we wanted to be able to keep an eye on him.

"I wonder if he realizes he's got a couple of mother hens looking out after him," Jack said.

"And what are you still doing here?" I asked.

He laughed. "Making sure the guy Rachel hosed down doesn't come back. Not sure those two cops in the patrol car out there would be enough to stop him from killing her."

Before he went home, Jack helped me rouse a very woozy Travis, and together we settled him into the guest room.

"Frank called," Rachel said as soon as Jack was gone. "He'll call back later. He's not too happy about what's going on."

"You told him?" I asked.

"You'd rather he just didn't find you at home at two in the morning?"

I shrugged. "I guess not. Listen, if he calls again, tell him I'll be back in about an hour."

"Back? It's almost three in the morning. Where are you going?"

"Since I don't think I'll be able to sleep, I'm going to interrupt the beauty rest of the one person who might have led the bomber to my home."

"Oh?"

"A society columnist for the *Express.*"

"I thought you said she didn't know your address."

"She doesn't, but to keep a man happy, she might have made the effort to find out."

Rachel laughed. "Be careful, she may be more dangerous than you think. You know where she lives?"

I nodded. "She throws an annual Christmas party at her place. I haven't been to one in a couple years, but I went to enough of them in my single days to remember how to find her house."

"*Bene,*" she said. "And don't worry, I'll keep an eye on your cousin."

16

Margot Martin didn't live far from me, at least not in miles. But then again, back when people lived in castles, the average scullery maid never lived far from the queen. Rivo Alto Island is a world away from my neighborhood.

The streets of Rivo Alto crisscross over the curving canal for which the island was named. Both the man-made island and its canal were the brainchild of a turn-of-the-century developer who looked at a mudflat and saw money. He wasn't wrong.

Margot's manse was one of the island's more modern ones; someone undoubtedly tore down an older house to build it—not an uncommon practice there. As a result, you'd be hard-pressed to find another area as small as Rivo Alto crowded with so many varieties of architectural style.

The houses are closer together than those in my neighborhood, but larger, and those situated along the canal, as Margot's is, each have private docks. The boats have plenty of space, but it's tougher to get around on Rivo Alto in a car—I ended up double-parking in the narrow lane in back of Margot's place. At three in the morning, I figured I'd be fine until the paperboy tried to squeeze by.

On the way over, I'd thought about everything I knew about Margot Martin. It wasn't all that much, even though we had worked on the same paper for a number of years.

I knew that Margot had become a widow about ten years ago, and that the late Mr. Martin left her a bundle. She was his second wife; he was a widower when they met. She spent her thirties as a corporate wife, serving as Martin's hostess at numerous business gatherings, keeping the peace among the other wives at company golf tournaments.

After several decades of jet lag, intense pressure, rich food and three-martini lunches began to take a toll on Martin, Margot tried to help her husband cope with an attempt at a healthy lifestyle—but all the granola and bran muffins in the world couldn't undo the damage. One evening Martin—having slipped out of the house while Margot was at a Junior League meeting—keeled over in the yacht club bar, breaking, as he fell, a bottle of single-malt Scotch that was nearly as old as he was, ensuring that his passing was accompanied by genuine grief.

Before she became a corporate wife, Margot had briefly held a part-time job on a small regional magazine. When our previous society editor retired, she told our editor that Margot was "an experienced journalist" and asked that Margot take her place. I'm sure one look around the newsroom convinced him that no one else had the wardrobe to do the job.

Being a society writer is not an easy job; Margot often attends five events a week, sometimes two a night, usually dressed to the nines. The circles she moves in are relatively small and all are closely interrelated; no little amount of diplomacy is required when dealing—week after week— with Mrs. X who is bitter about not having that photograph of her in her newest gown in the paper, or Mr. Y who is angry that his daughter wasn't in the debutante ball photo, or Mr. & Mrs. Z who weren't mentioned in the article on the Assistance League fund-raiser. One of the curses of newspaper work is that everyone's an editor—or thinks he should be. In her case, it's compounded by constantly dealing with people who are sure of nothing so much as their own importance.

But whatever sympathy or understanding I might usually be able to muster for Margot was gone that night. It had been a hellish day, and I was fairly sure she must have led the bomber to my home.

Her house was dark. As I came up the walk to the front door, Margot's little Yorkies started yapping.

I smiled to myself. Things were looking up.

I knocked on the door. No answer, but I could hear the snickety-snick of Yorkie toenails scrambling across the marble entryway. The barking got louder, and then there was the telltale thump of a full eight pounds of ferocious protection launching itself against the door. Judging by the sounds, one of them was trying to shoulder it open, making a miniature leaping canine battering ram of himself, while the other was trying to scratch his way through the wood with forelegs that were only slightly slower than a circular saw.

"Nice doggies!" I said.

The barking became frenzied.

A light came on at the house next door. Still nothing at Margot's place. I rang the bell. The dogs went ape wire.

Above the doggie din, I heard Margot's phone ring. Apparently she heard it, too. Soon lights came on at her house, then went off at the neighbor's. "Hush," I heard her call, to absolutely no purpose.

The porch light came on. I already knew she had a video camera set up at the front door, so I looked toward the camera and said, "Open up, Margot, we need to talk. Now."

"Irene?" Barking in the background.

"Yep."

"Quiet!" I heard her snap at the dogs. They lowered their protests to growling. "Just a moment."

I heard her lead them away, probably shutting them up in the downstairs bedroom. She came back, apparently a little more awake and ready to do battle. Her voice was less sleepy now.

"Irene, what's gotten into you?" she said reprovingly. "This is no hour to be calling on anyone."

"Open up, Margot."

"Leave me alone. Go on, don't make me call the police on you."

"Please do call them, Margot. I'd like for them to know how the person who planted a bomb in front of my house learned where I live."

The front door flew open. "A bomb!"

But I was speechless. The thin woman standing bare-footed in front of me was clutching the folds of a blue cotton robe; peeking out beneath it was a worn red flannel nightgown with little lambs on it. She had not brushed her short, not-from-nature-blond hair and—most startling—had some kind of white cream all over her face, everywhere but around her eyes. She looked like a poorly designed Day of the Dead figurine. This couldn't be Margot, could it?

"Well," I said, when I came out of my daze, "at least I know he's not spending the night."

Her hand flew to her head and she said, "Come inside." As she shut the door, she motioned toward a leopard-skin fainting couch in the front room. "Have a seat. I'll be right back down." She paused halfway up the staircase and said, "Make yourself a drink if you like."

"Mind if I turn on some lights?"

"Not at all. I'll only be a minute."

The dogs had switched to an alternative schedule of barking—sporadic outbursts of barking between lengthening interludes of mere growling.

Although she had said she'd only be a minute, I knew Margot wouldn't come back down until she had put herself together, a project that might take some time. I felt a moment's hesitation over what I was contemplating, then thought about Travis and found my resolve. I strolled across her white carpet and out of the front room, trying to remember where I had once seen an office on the first floor.

Trying not to be distracted by the view of moonlight on the canal, or the design of her big open kitchen, I turned to the right, walked down a hallway and opened a door next to a laundry room. A bathroom. I started to close the door, had an inspiration and went to the medicine cabinet first. I found a small box of bandages there and dropped it into my purse.

The dogs started barking again; I began to appreciate the cover their noise provided.

I closed the door, retraced my steps down the hall, turned left this time, and found the office. It was clean and orderly, and during the day it probably had a beautiful view of the canal. The view at night would have been better with a brighter moon; there was just enough light to see Margot's sailboat tied up at the dock. I made myself concentrate on the task at hand. I searched the drawers of the small desk. I looked through a stack of loose papers and invitations, but found nothing of interest.

I had been in this office once before, at one of the Christmas parties, when Margot was giving the grand tour of the house. But this time, all the equipment was new; as I looked around the office, I saw that Margot went in for the latest available models. For the first time, I envied her wealth. The room wasn't outfitted on a part-time reporter's salary—this equipment was better than what we worked with in the newsroom. There was a three-line speaker-phone on the desk. Next to the desk, on a carved mahogany cart, was a plain-paper fax machine; a matching cart held a copying machine. There was a beautiful computer work station with a fancy printer on it. I checked the phone lines running between the phone, computer and fax. The second and third lines were hooked up to the fax and computer.

I looked for an answering machine but didn't see one;

maybe it was in another room. I thought of turning the computer on, but decided that even with this high-tech office, Margot wasn't the type to make computer notes about her boyfriends. I was about to leave when I noticed that one of the line-in-use lights on the phone was lit. Line one. I hurried over to the phone, pressed the mute button so that nothing would be heard from my extension, and picked up the receiver. Whatever number she had called at three in the morning had already answered, and I was only in time to hear a male voice saying, ". . . or enter your phone number and then press the pound key, and we'll get back to you as soon as possible." As I listened, I fumbled in my purse, trying to find a little tape recorder I sometimes use for notes and interviews. There was a long tone, a set of quick beeps, and then the sound of Margot dialing again. I tried to memorize the tune the tones played as she dialed. It was eight tones long. A mechanical voice said, "Thank you," and disconnected. Margot hung up. I quickly followed suit.

It was only then that I found the recorder. I softly repeated the little dialing song into the microphone, hoping I had it right. I was pretty sure it was Margot's number, followed by the pound sign.

I was going to try it out, but since the upstairs phone might also be equipped with line-in-use lights, I hesitated using the office phone while she might be standing near an upstairs phone. I would have to wait to verify that the tones matched her number.

I moved back out into the kitchen. There was a set of hanging baskets near the sink, and one of them held three lemons and a couple of limes. I took one of the lemons, and then, turning to the island in the center of the kitchen, pulled a small paring knife from a wooden block.

I heard water running upstairs just as I passed the kitchen phone. Seizing the opportunity, I set my little treasures down, pulled the recorder back out of my purse, then lifted the handset and replayed the tape. I pressed the numbers that matched the tones.

There were two rings, ones I hoped were not awakening some perfectly nice stranger, then Margot's voice on a recording. Her voice mail. I hung up. The number I had dialed was her own. She had called someone's pager number, entered her own number, and was now waiting for a call back. Because she had a voice mail service, when I called her number from her own phone I got the service instead of a busy signal. It also explained the lack of an answering machine.

Whom did she page? Someone who would respond at three in the morning. A lawyer? Perhaps. Or maybe it was the new boyfriend. And if the man who had been looking for me in the lobby of the *Express* was the bomber, I didn't want to be around if he showed up. I began to wish I had brought Rachel along. I would have done it, but I knew Travis was safe at my home not because there was a patrol car outside, but because Rachel was inside—she would watch over him.

Here at Margot's, my plans had to remain flexible. A lot depended on what Margot did once she came back downstairs.

I quickly searched the rest of the first floor and found one other bathroom. I checked the medicine cabinet—no bandages. I heard a door close upstairs and hurried over to the bar in the front room.

By the time Margot came back downstairs in a blue Chinese silk jacket and loose-fitting slacks, feathery slippers and full makeup, I was mixing an Absolut and tonic. I offered her one, and she accepted.

"I hope you don't mind that I stole one of the lemons from the kitchen," I said, holding it up.

"No, of course not," she said.

I made her drink twice as strong as mine, sliced a couple of pieces of lemon and added them as twists. She sat on the leopard skin. I went for the white leather sofa.

"Now, what's all this about a bomb?" she said.

I told her about the explosion, leaving out lots of details about Travis, merely saying that he was a visiting cousin who was severely burned while trying to rescue my cat. She looked genuinely horrified, which gave me hope for her.

"That's terrible," she said. "But I don't know why you think I had anything to do with it."

"Someone was asking for me in the lobby of the *Express* a few days ago—but you intercepted him."

She blushed, but didn't say anything.

"A man with a similar description—probably the same guy—tried to follow me when I was on my way to see Travis today. He was unsuccessful then, but it seems he finally managed to reach us at the one place where I'd hoped we would be safe—my home. My own home, Margot."

"But you're assuming it's the same person!"

"Margot, did you look up my address for someone recently?"

She set down her drink, placed her hands in her lap. Her nails were perfect.

The dogs took up barking again.

"Yes," she said, wringing the perfect hands, "but he wasn't the one who—he wouldn't have done something like that."

"If you didn't have some doubts about that, you wouldn't have let me in here tonight."

"Of course I would have let you in. We work together."

"Right, we're such close pals. So for the sake of your old pal's health—who is he?"

She looked away from me.

"Who is he?" I asked again.

The phone rang.

She shot up from the leopard skin as if it still had its claws. "Excuse me," she said, hurrying over to the nearest phone—the one in the kitchen. "Probably my neighbor."

Right.

"Oh, hello!" she said in a voice obviously meant to carry to my ears. "I'm so sorry if my dogs awakened you! I know it's very late, but a dear friend from the paper needed to see me. Yes, of course everything is just fine. Sorry to disturb you. I'll try to keep them quiet."

I glanced out the window. The neighbor's lights were still out.

I figured she was talking to her new boyfriend, and decided to resort to Plan B. I walked over to the bar, as if to make another drink. Margot was speaking more softly now, a quick murmur or two before hanging up.

She came back into the room just as I took hold of the lemon, told myself it wouldn't hurt as much as Travis's burn, and nicked my finger with the knife.

"Ow!" I shouted—beyond what the little sting called for. I immediately grabbed my hand and squeezed my finger so that the bleeding looked worse.

"Oh, dear!" she said, quickly looking away.

"Oh! What a klutz! Oh no, I'm going to bleed all over your white carpet . . ."

That snapped her into action. "Come this way, there's a bathroom right down this hallway."

I followed her, and managed to get to the bathroom sink without leaving any DNA on her floor. She was frantically searching for a bandage; of course I didn't tell her there was a whole box of the things in my purse. I was also pleased to note that she scrupulously avoided looking at my hand.

"My God, it's deeper than I thought!" I said. Utter nonsense, but it worked on her.

"Upstairs," she said weakly.

I followed her again.

The master bedroom was huge and featured a king-sized round bed. I didn't get to see much of it before she hustled me into the bathroom, where there were lots of jars and an array of cosmetics out on the counter.

I held my hand over this sink, but still she avoided looking at my savage wound. I was kind of pissed about that, because I figured that if I had known what a daisy she was ahead of time, I wouldn't have cut myself. I could have faked it.

This time, while I surveyed the contents of this larger medicine chest over her shoulder, she found an adhesive bandage. She handed it to me at arm's length, clearly squeamish about the entire business.

"I—I don't think that will do," I said weakly. "Do you have any gauze?"

"Yes, yes." She reached for it, and some tape.

"God, I think I see bone!" I screeched.

She turned white, but shoved the first-aid items at me before stepping just outside the bathroom.

I wrapped the finger rather artistically, then, in the shakiest voice I could manage, said, "I think I'm going to faint."

It was truer of her than of me. "Oh!" Her eyes widened. "Come and lie down for a moment!"

I let her lead me over to the big dot of a bed and did my best to plop my rear down on that part of the circumference next to the fancy telephone on a nearby nightstand. I sat, then put my head between my knees.

"I'll be okay," I said in a muffled voice. I lifted my head a little. "This is so embarrassing. I'll go home in just a minute."

Now she really panicked. "Oh, no, no! Stay here a little longer. I insist."

I groaned. "Oh, maybe you're right. Listen, would you mind getting my drink for me? I left it downstairs."

"Certainly, certainly," she said, happy to get away from the wounded.

The moment she was out the door, I checked out the phone. I didn't bother with the last-number-dialed button—that would just be Margot's own number, entered for the pager. But to my delight, it had one of those "caller ID" features on it, the ones that record and store the numbers of incoming calls. The display showed the last call received as number seventy-five, with date and time stamped but indicating it was a "private call"—meaning her boyfriend had called from a phone that blocked caller ID. I hurriedly scrolled with the "review" button, going back to calls that started on Tuesday, the day she met Mr. Wonderful in the lobby. In the mix of calls, two showed up fairly often, and at hours when her society pals were probably getting their beauty sleep.

Margot had a little notepad next to the phone; I took the top sheet off and slipped it in my pocket, just in case I might need to use old-fashioned methods—raising a number by rubbing a pencil over the indentations. No use outsmarting yourself with technology, I thought. I used the next sheet to write down the two numbers from the caller-ID display.

By the time she had come upstairs, I had made a remarkable recovery.

"Gotta go," I said. "Sitting here reminded me that I'm up way past my bedtime."

She protested all the way down the stairs. At the front door, a little of my smug satisfaction at tricking her left me, and a sense of what I might have set in motion took its place.

"Margot, listen to me. And I mean listen. Your life may depend upon it. If you've called the man who waited for me in the lobby—"

"Called him? At this hour? Of course not!"

"Listen! If you've called him, get out of here. Now. Don't wait for him to come over. He's dangerous. You can see that, can't you?"

"I don't think he's—"

"Fine!" I said. "If you want to wait around here and have Mr. Goodbar make a house call, fine. Invite him in. When they drag the canal and haul up whatever bits and pieces are left of you, I'll tell each and every salt-soaked one of them, 'I told you so!' "

"That's a horrible thing to say!"

"Yeah? Whatever it takes. In fact, if you insist on staying here tonight, at least let me take your Yorkies with me. I'm not as crazy about them as you are, but I hate to see animals suffer."

"Get out!"

"That's what I'm trying to tell you, Margot. Get out."

She opened the door.

"Please, Margot."

"Get out," she said, but it was softer.

I tried to find some measure of hope in that as I drove off in search of a pay phone.

17

Since the nearest pay phones on Rivo Alto were on the single nonresidential street on the small island, I decided to drive a couple of miles farther, to an all-night supermarket on Pacific Coast Highway. The supermarket would be well-lighted and I could phone from indoors; better, for my purposes, than standing out in the open on a street Margot's new boyfriend would be taking to get to her house. I was fairly certain she had invited him to come over.

The phone was near the front entrance of the market. I took a quick look around; at the checkout stand, there was an old man buying a bag of potato chips and a can of dog food, and one young couple with an infant buying baby formula. Otherwise, everyone I saw was an employee. The aisles of the store were crowded with pallets of shrink-wrapped cardboard boxes. Stocking hours.

I went back to the phone and, playing a hunch, rubbed a pencil over the paper I had taken off the notepad. The results were good enough to reveal a third and different number. I dropped a couple of coins in the phone and tried this number first. After two rings, a recorded voice said, "The subscriber on the LA Cellular System that you have called is unavailable, or has left the coverage area. Please try your call again later."

So much for hunches. I tried one of the numbers from the caller-ID display.

It rang for a long time, no answer.

I got lucky with the third number.

"You've reached the voice mail of Richmond and Associates. We're not in the office right now, but you can leave a message of any length, or enter your phone number and then press the pound key, and we'll get back to you as soon as possible."

I hung up. The name Richmond seemed familiar, but then again, it wasn't a rare name.

I had decided to use a pay phone instead of my home phone because my initial plan was to page Margot's friend from a number he wouldn't recognize, and which couldn't be traced back to me. But telling him off over the phone wouldn't get me anywhere, and now a better plan occurred to me. I dropped another round of change into the phone and called the computer room at the *News-Express*.

Jerry Chase answered on the sixteenth ring. The newsroom of the *Express* is usually empty between one and six-thirty in the morning, but those are the hours the computer staff works on repair, maintenance and on freeing up computer memory. Usually there are two computer staffers working those hours, Jerry Chase, who does most of his work in the computer room, and Olivia Sledzik, his recently hired assistant, who is often working in other parts of the building. I had helped Livy get the job, so I had been hoping she'd be the one to answer. Those are the breaks.

Given the time it took Jerry to pick up the phone, I figured I had caught him at one of his three favorite pastimes: going up on the roof for a smoke, talking to his girlfriend on the phone or playing around on the Internet.

"Computer room," he said, a little breathlessly. Rooftop.

"Jerry? It's Irene."

"Oh . . ." It was a sound of relief. I was sorry not to hear the excuse he would have given one of the bosses about the time it took to answer the phone.

"Nice night out. How was the view?"

He laughed. "Terrific. It's their own damned fault for making it a smoke-free building. What can I do for you?"

"I need to find out who owns a phone number. Can you look it up for me?"

"Sure. What are you doing up at this time of day?"

"Long story."

He sighed. "Aren't they all?"

"Yes. Listen, I just need to have you find out who owns a number for me. Actually, I know who owns it, but I need the address and type of business."

"Sure. Local?" I could hear him typing on his keyboard, accessing the database program he'd need to use.

"Yes, within our area code."

"Okay, let me have it."

I read it off to him.

"I love it," he said, almost immediately. "An easy one. It's a business—Richmond and Associates. Licensed private investigators."

"Investigators?" I repeated blankly.

"Yes. By the way—Olivia is great. Thanks for letting us know about her."

Of course she's great, I thought. Livy probably knew more about programming when she was in ninth grade than you did when you got out of college. And she does ten times as much work as you do and . . . and I reminded myself that he was doing me a favor.

"Glad it worked out, Jer."

"Yeah, me, too. I'm learning from her. She's bringing me up to date."

That made me feel a little better about him. "Livy's sharp," I agreed. "You have the address for Richmond and Associates?"

"Yes, in Los Alamitos. Owner is one Harold Richmond."

Suddenly I remembered where I had heard the name "Richmond"—it was in the articles about Gwendolyn

DeMont's murder. Harold Richmond had worked for the police then; he had been the detective assigned to the case.

"Still there?" Jerry asked.

"Yes—sorry."

He read the address to me. I wrote it down, then said, "As long as you're in that program, Jer, could you look up one more number for me? Probably a residence."

"Sure."

I read off the second number, and again he got a quick hit. "Not a residence, though," he said. "The Wharf."

"Someplace down in the harbor?"

"No, it's in Los Alamitos, too. The Wharf is just its name. It's a bar."

"A bar? You're sure?"

"Well, I'm not sitting in it, having a drink and a much-needed smoke, but unless the database is wrong, the place is a bar."

"Sorry, Jerry, I didn't mean to doubt you—just not what I expected. Thanks again for the help."

I stood in the store for a moment after I hung up, thinking about the implications of Richmond and Associates being private investigators, and Margot getting late-night calls from a bar in their town.

I hauled the phone book up from beneath the metal shelf at the booth and flipped back to the Yellow Pages. I looked up investigators, and sure enough, there at the bottom-right-hand corner of the page was an ad for Richmond and Associates:

HAROLD RICHMOND AND ASSOCIATES

CONFIDENTIAL PRIVATE INVESTIGATIONS—24-HOUR SERVICE

SURVEILLANCE   BACKGROUND INVESTIGATIONS

ELECTRONIC DE-BUGGING   MISSING PERSONS

ASSET SEARCHES

FREE CONSULTATION   FULLY BONDED AND INSURED

OWNED AND OPERATED BY FORMER LAW

ENFORCEMENT OFFICERS

A state private investigator's license number was listed at the bottom of the ad.

If he had been the bomber, what did he have against Travis? I could think of only one reason for Harold Richmond to personally dislike my cousin—if he thought Travis had lied to provide an alibi for Arthur Spanning.

But that was years ago. Why this fresh pursuit? And even if he still harbored animosity toward Travis over the alibi, it didn't seem to be something that would drive a former cop to try to kill someone else. If Travis had lied, he wasn't the first person to do so to protect a member of his family. And he had only been a child. Who would have held such a grudge against an eleven-year-old boy?

The more I thought about it, the less likely it seemed that Richmond had placed the bomb in Travis's truck. But I did want to talk to him. I wanted to know why a private investigator—especially one with a connection to the old murder case—had been asking for me at the newspaper.

I drove back to Rivo Alto. Just before I turned onto Margot's street, I noticed that a car was blocking it—a green Olds.

If he had taken a job to investigate me or Travis, it was perfectly understandable that he would try to follow me—understandable, if unnerving. But somehow the sight of that Olds made me hesitate to confront Richmond.

I decided I didn't need that conversation with him after all. At least not now, not alone and at four in the morning.

I'd have it when Rachel was with me. But I was also concerned about Margot—maybe I should stick around, just in case she needed help.

Instead of turning down Margot's street, I crossed the short bridge over the canal. I parked in an alley that ran parallel to the canal, behind the houses across the canal from her own. I got out of the car and stretched.

The air was cool, and the sky was just beginning to lighten. I walked back to the bridge. Near the foot of the bridge, staying on the side of the canal opposite Margot's home, I peered down the waterway toward her house, which was about three houses down from where I crouched.

Water lapped at pilings, ropes creaked and there was the ping-ping sound of sail lines tapping against masts as all along the canal boats bobbed at their moorings. Otherwise all was quiet. No sound of Margot's dogs barking.

I didn't have to watch Margot's place for very long to realize there was something odd going on.

Lights. Lights turning on and off in different rooms, as if someone were searching through the house. I kept watching.

A man. Now I could see his tall, athletic figure every now and then as he moved from room to room. He came back to the first floor, opened the sliding-glass door that led to a small patio between the house and the dock. He turned on the patio light and stepped outside.

He was too far away for me to make out most of his features, but he definitely resembled the man on the tape. And his height, his close-cropped black-and-silver hair, his clean-shaven face—all made me decide that this was very likely the man Briana's neighbors had seen at the apartment building in San Pedro. The man who had been using lock picks, trying to enter her home.

He was looking up and down the canal, and I stayed very

still, hoping it was too dark for him to see me, certain that any movement on my part would give me away. He rubbed a hand over his hair, then turned and walked inside. I stayed still.

He closed the glass door, turned out the light. He also turned out the few lights that were still on inside the house. But I saw him standing at the glass door again, staring out. The sky continued to lighten.

I had already seen what he had just figured out— Margot's boat was no longer at the dock. I prayed that she had taken the Yorkies aboard and gone for an early-morning sail, just in case all my bad feelings about this guy proved to be right.

He moved away from the window. I heard a car start, heard it drive down the street. I waited. It was cool and damp out, and my legs were starting to cramp. I waited a little longer, then walked back to my car, now covered with a layer of dew. The Karmann Ghia made its usual noisy start; I got the windshield wipers and the heater going and put it in gear.

I didn't get far. As I drove around the curve of the narrow alley, I slammed on my brakes. The other end was blocked— by a green Olds. There was no one in the car. I didn't wait to see where the driver was—I threw the Karmann Ghia in reverse. The plastic back window of the ragtop was still covered with dew, so I couldn't back up with any great speed, especially not around the curve. That was just as well—in the side mirror I saw Richmond step out from between two houses behind me, and into the path of the car.

For about half a second I considered running him over, but I stopped. He stood with arms held out to his sides, palms open. I didn't see a weapon, but that didn't mean there wasn't one.

"What have you done with her?" he called out, moving toward my door.

I have to admit the question surprised me. I rolled my window down about half an inch. "Warned her about you," I said, just loud enough to be heard over the motor. "Thanks for shouting. The neighbors will be wide awake when I start screaming for them to call the police."

"Where have you been lately?" he asked sarcastically. "Nobody gets involved any more." He glanced at the houses along the alley. "They'd probably never make the call."

I could smell booze on his breath, but his speech wasn't slurred and his eyes seemed to be focusing just fine. Just now they were boring into mine.

"Wrong neighborhood for that assumption, Mr. Richmond."

He curled his fingers over the top of the window. That bullying gesture annoyed me, and my annoyance began to take the place of my fear.

"So Margot told you my name," he said.

"No, she didn't. Not even when I told her about the bomb."

"Bomb? What bomb?"

It was convincing, I'll admit. Not convincing enough to make me lower the window. "Let go of my car," I said.

"Did someone try to hurt her?" he asked angrily.

Maybe the events of that day had taken the last of my patience, maybe I was just finally feeling exhausted. For whatever reason, that remark sent me over the edge. "No," I said, "no one tried to hurt her—no one except you, you shameless user."

"Now just a minute—"

"Not just any lowlife would pimp himself just to get my address. You're a piece of work, Richmond."

His fingers tightened on the window. "You have no right to—"

"I thought all that business about private eyes sleeping

with somebody for information only happened in pulp fiction and second-rate movies."

He turned red, made a visible attempt to control his temper. "It wasn't—"

"It wasn't like that? Spare me." I leaned closer to the window. "I saw the videotape from the security camera at the *Express,* Harold. If the cops saw that and talked to Margot and a couple of other people, I wonder if they would connect you up to some of the bad luck we've been having in the Maguire family."

All that color drained right back out of his face.

I almost asked him if he'd had a good time at the Wharf, but no use playing all my cards at once. Instead, I simply repeated, "Let go of my car."

His fingers eased open.

"I'll be at your office at two o'clock tomorrow afternoon," I said, putting the Karmann Ghia in reverse again. "If you don't want to lose your license, you'll be there."

"Wait—"

"For what? Don't say another word. This way you have another eight or nine hours to perfect the bullshit excuse you were about to give me." I eased the clutch out.

Just before I headed back over the bridge, I glanced back down the alley. He was standing in the middle of it, watching me, looking lost.

Too damn bad.

I drove home.

18

"Frank has called about half a dozen times," Rachel whispered, handing me a slip of paper with a phone number on it. "He said to tell you to call him no matter what time you got in." We were keeping our voices low; the door to the guest room, where Travis slept, was partially open.

"Is he angry?"

She shrugged.

"How's Travis?"

"He woke up once, took another pill and went back to sleep. He didn't look too great while he was awake, but the pills really knock him out. Probably for the best."

"The patrol car's gone," I said. "I guess I'm not surprised."

"The shift's almost over, and they can't keep a unit here permanently. They'll probably increase the patrols past the house, though."

We moved to the living room. "I tracked down Richmond," I said. "I'll tell you the whole story in the morning. We're going to pay him a visit."

She smiled.

I looked back toward Travis. "I was afraid the dogs would wake him when I came in."

"Naw, that's why he left the door to his room open. He knew they'd come out to greet you. They come out here to check on me every once in a while, but most of the time, they've been with him. Even Cody's in there with him."

"I hope they aren't bothering him."

"Like I said, he isn't aware of too much after he takes one of those pain pills."

"You okay here on the couch? You could have the bed—I'll sleep out here."

"I'm all settled in—you go ahead and take the bed, catch what sleep you can."

"Thanks." I looked at my watch. It was just past four-thirty. "I hate to call Frank at this hour."

"Irene . . . ," she chided.

"Okay, okay."

"See you in a few hours, then. Once you're up, I'll run home and shower and change. Then we can talk."

For all my trepidation before making it, the phone call to Frank was a good one. He had been worried, but apparently Rachel had calmed him down during one of his previous calls.

"Do me a favor," he said. "Think about staying somewhere else. The house in the mountains, or Pete and Rachel's place. Or a hotel."

"Okay," I said, "I'll think about it."

There was a brief silence, probably while he regained his temper. But after that, all the talk was devoted to catching up on his news, and a little of that brand of conversation lovers cherish but others find disgusting, boring or just plain silly.

Because of it, I slept well.

I couldn't sleep much past nine, but discovered that Travis had already awakened.

"He hasn't eaten anything yet," Rachel said drowsily, sitting up on the couch. "He was in a hurry to see Jack."

"Why?"

"Didn't really say. He's been there quite awhile." She yawned. "He's over there with the dogs."

I have this worry that one day Jack will sell his house and I'll be left trying to explain to the new proprietors that regular visits from my dogs are part of the joy of home ownership.

"He also mentioned something about going shopping," Rachel added.

"I can understand that. If he hadn't brought the 'Cosmo' trunk inside the house, nothing from that camper would have been spared."

"Oh, yeah," she said, waking up a little more. "He took that over to Jack's place, too."

"The trunk?"

"Yeah. That upsets you?"

I shrugged. "Maybe he's decided he wants to stay at Jack's place instead."

I called Mary to let her know we had found Travis. She told me to try to take better care of him over the next few hours I spent with him than I had during the first twenty-four, but on the whole she was pleased. She wanted to see him, and I told her I'd call her again later to set up a visit.

I walked next door in time to see Jack leaning over an official-looking document, writing on it as Travis stood by. I saw them exchange a look as I came nearer.

"What are you two up to?" I asked.

"Nothing much," Jack answered. "Your cousin just bought my van."

"Just bought—"

"Yes, and we've agreed that the particulars are entirely between the two of us, Your Royal Nosiness."

"Jack—"

"Everything's fine, Irene. I'll get around on my bike until I decide to buy something less fitting for my image."

I'm now so used to Jack, I don't really notice the black leather outfits, or the scars, tattoos and earrings that frighten most of our other neighbors away from him. Jack, I thought, fit into McCain's scenario of a person of wealth living a simple life—Jack owned a fortune in local real estate, but was happiest riding around on his Harley, or sailing. He's the most generous of friends, but I couldn't allow him to give my cousin his almost-new van, which was completely outfitted for camping.

As if reading my mind though, Travis said, "It's not a gift."

"Strictly business," Jack agreed.

It didn't make me happy, but they were both adults, and I really didn't have any say in the matter. And if I was honest with myself, I had to admit that money wasn't the only reason I was unhappy about the van. "You're going home?" I asked Travis.

He frowned, then shook his head. "Not right away."

"Where is home?" Jack asked.

"Right now, its probably sitting in the police impound yard. What's left of it, anyway."

"You lived in that camper full-time?" I asked.

He nodded, then turned to Jack. "You're sure you don't mind taking care of that other matter for me?"

"Not at all," Jack said.

"He's taking care of your trunk?" I said, mostly to let him know I was on to him.

"Yes, but that's not what I meant."

Perhaps because he knew the limits of my patience better than Travis, Jack said, "I'm picking up a cellular phone for him."

"I could have taken you to do that," I told Travis.

"It will be better this way, I think. But thanks."

Back at my house, I changed the bandage on his wounded hand and watched him as he struggled to eat breakfast left-handed.

"Bring back memories?" Rachel asked.

It did, but I said, "Let's not talk about that."

"About what?" Travis asked.

"Last November I had my right hand in a cast," I said quickly. "Rachel helped me out a lot then."

She folded her arms and raised a brow, but didn't say anything. He looked between us, but apparently decided not to pursue it.

"I'll be back in a little while," Rachel said.

After she had left, he asked, "Where did you go last night?"

I told him.

"I know Richmond," he said.

"You do?"

"Sure. He's hounded us for years. Part of the reason he got demoted from detective was because he harassed us, but he still didn't let up. Mr. Brennan—my dad's lawyer—eventually got a temporary restraining order placed on Richmond. He couldn't come near me or my dad. My mom wouldn't let my dad put her name on the order. But because I was on it, that pretty much kept Richmond away from both me and my mom."

"Was he threatening you?"

He shook his head. "No, just harassing us. He'd follow us around. He was sure my folks were going to get back together." He paused. "But let's not start that death-certificate argument again."

"I don't know much about what your life has been like since . . ."

"Since Gwendolyn was murdered? Actually, you don't

know much about what my life has been like since I was about a month old, right?"

"Right."

He was silent.

"You can punish me like this for another twenty-some-odd years, if that will make you happy," I said. I stood up, started to clear dishes.

He reached over with his bandaged hand, lightly touched my wrist. "No. It won't make me happy. I'm sorry." When he spoke again, there were sharp breaths between the words. "I'm not usually—I guess—everything—that happened yesterday—it's just been a lot to take in, all at once."

I sat down again. "I know."

He wiped at his face, embarrassed, not looking at me. We sat in silence for a few minutes, listening to the kitchen clock tick. He grew calmer.

"I want to go with you and Rachel when you talk to Richmond," he said.

"Okay."

He seemed surprised.

"You were expecting an argument?" I asked.

"I guess so." He was silent again.

"I'll take you shopping if you like, but before we go I need to take the dogs for a walk," I said. "Want to go down to the beach with me?"

"Sure."

The air was cool and misty, the sky was low and gray. A typical June morning; by noon the clouds would burn off, the day would be warm. The crowds would show up then. At this hour, the lack of morning sunshine cut down on the number of beachgoers; other than a surfer here and there, we didn't pass many people as we walked along.

Maybe being out in the salt air made a difference, or maybe the Pacific stretching gray and endless soothed him as it did me.

"I was just thinking that you were only about ten or eleven when you stopped having contact with my father," he said.

"Yes, I guess I didn't know him very well at all. After what you told me last night—I realize I've had these childhood impressions that were wrong."

"You couldn't have known that he couldn't read," he said. "Last night, I told you I'd tell you more about that."

We walked a little farther, then he said, "My father didn't begin to learn to read until he was over forty. He never learned to read very well; his type of dyslexia made it very difficult. When he was in grade school, in the late 1940s and early '50s, no one correctly identified the cause of his problems with reading. He was very bright, but he was always put in the 'slow' groups. Success in school was almost entirely dependent on being able to read and write. He couldn't do either. It was analogous to trying to force deaf students to learn from tape recordings. He had to learn in other ways—you couldn't get through to him with the written word."

"You taught him to read, didn't you?"

"To the extent I could," he said. "It took me a long time to convince him that it was worth trying. He never would have gone back to school. He was too ashamed to let other people know he couldn't read."

"He had dropped out of school?" I asked, remembering the questions I had when I saw Arthur's death certificate.

"Yes," he said. "He wouldn't go to adult school, no matter how hard I tried to convince him it would be different now."

I noticed that he seemed embarrassed about this.

"Who could blame him?" I asked. "I admire him for even trying to learn privately, from you. From what you've told me, school must have been a miserable place for him, a frustrating place, a place where he was made to feel ashamed of something he couldn't help. Becoming an adult wouldn't allow him to suddenly forget that misery, or decide that school might be a wonderful place after all. You shouldn't blame him, either. You know that, don't you?"

He hesitated, then said, "Yes. And the truth is, I do admire him. He had to do so much to compensate for his illiteracy; he came up with all of these tricks and ways to keep other people from guessing the truth. Most people never knew he couldn't read."

"Tell me about him," I said.

After a long silence, he said, "It isn't easy to describe him. When I think of his good qualities, well, he was smart and funny and very generous. He was hardworking. He was good with numbers—they didn't seem to cause him problems in the way letters did. He couldn't write checks or read ledger entries, or he might have been a bookkeeper. My mom paid the family bills, but if I said a group of numbers aloud, he could add them in his head as fast as she could with a calculator.

"If he had been able to go to school to study it, I suppose he might have been an artist—he was very creative. I have some of his drawings and paintings.

"But he liked being outdoors, and loved making things grow. So that was the business he went into. As you know, he was very good at it. He also had—I guess you'd call them 'people skills'—he made other people feel at ease. He was a great storyteller. One reason I never questioned his ability to read was that he could tell these wonderful stories. Who needed something out of a book when Dad could make up a better story?

"Sometimes the stories were on a grand scale—made-up fairy tales of knights and dragons, but mostly they were family stories, or just little tales about someone he had met that day, or something he had seen or done. I loved listening to him."

I remembered that about Arthur, thought that perhaps I

had liked that in him before I took up my father's self-righteous anger against him. I said nothing, though, and after a moment, Travis went on.

"On the other hand, there was always a false front. Even simple things involved deception. When I was very young, if my mother wasn't with us, we ate at places like Denny's and Howard Johnson's—because they had photographs of the food on the menu, and he could get something besides a burger, which is what he usually ordered if there was no HoJo's nearby. That was a safe order.

"I started reading at an early age, so by the time I was seven, I helped him without realizing it. He used to make me feel very important when we ate out together, because he'd say to the waitress, 'This young man is going to pick out something for me. What do you think I'd like best, Travis?' I felt flattered—my father was trusting my judgment.

"There were other tricks he'd use. For example, if a note came home from the teacher, he'd watch me, assess my attitude. He could tell if it was good news or bad news based on my nonverbal cues. He had incredible abilities as far as that went—he might not have learned to read books, but he could read people."

"I can't believe you got in trouble at school very often," I said.

"I did. Ironically, for the same reason he did. I was bored, but for the opposite cause. I was reading ahead of my grade level. I used my spare time to be a class clown."

"And when he got these notes?" I asked.

"If I was giving him reason—nonverbally—to believe it was bad news, he'd smile conspiratorially and say, 'Has your mother seen this yet?' If the answer was no, he'd sigh and say, 'Well, she'll understand. And you better let her be the one to talk to the teacher. As for you and me, we both already know that you're smart enough to figure out how

to do better.' And he'd hug me and tell me not to let it get
me down."

"But he pretended he could read?"

"For many years. He wasn't home every day, of course,
but there was a routine when he was there. Every morning,
he would open the newspaper and browse through it at a
steady pace. He would come across an ad which featured a
woman in a dress and he'd recognize the logo of the store.
He'd say, 'Bree'—that was his nickname for her—'here's
something you might want to take a look at. There's a sale
at Buffum's.'

"Anything like that was her cue. She'd take the paper
from him. 'Oh, maybe I'll go by there,' she'd say, but then
she'd go back to the front page and say, 'I see they're going
to build a marina near downtown,' or comment on whatever
local news was there. Sometimes she'd mention national
news, but usually he'd pick that up from the car radio or
from television.

"While he had been 'browsing,' she had been looking at
other sections for any small items of unusual interest, so
that he could, throughout the day, regale customers or ven-
dors with these. 'Did you see that story about the bank rob-
ber who wrote his hold-up note on the back of an envelope
with his name and address on it?' Stories like that."

"Did your mother always know he was illiterate?"

"Yes—I mean, she knew not long after they met. She was
working for a commercial nursery. He was a friendly person, and she was shy, and he was someone who always
wanted shy people to feel more comfortable. At parties, he
would find the person who was excluded or hanging back,
and bring them into the conversation. He had a way of
doing this so that the other person didn't feel put on the
spot."

"Those people skills you spoke of," I said.

"Yes. I don't mean to say he was universally popular.

There were people like your father, who never liked him from the moment they met him."

I started to say, "That's not true," but it was. Instead I said, "I don't know why my father reacted the way he did."

Travis shrugged. "I think some people could sense he was hiding something from them. Some men didn't like him because women liked him so much. Most women, I should say."

"The vast majority, as I recall," I said, thinking back. "And somehow he did it without really flirting. I don't just think it was his smile or his good looks. If there were two handsome men in a room, your father was still the one with all the women around him."

Again he shrugged. "He always told me that most men would do better with women if they just listened to them. For him it was natural; without being able to read, he had to listen to people to learn what was going on.

"In any case, my mother took a liking to him. One day, her boss came in while my dad was talking to her. He greeted my dad, who was one of his best customers, and slapped a trade magazine down on the counter. It was opened to an article. 'Take a look at that!' he said to my dad. My dad did everything in his power not to panic. There were no photographs with the article.

"He did what he usually did in that kind of situation. He tried to base his response on the other man's attitude. He wanted to say something noncommittal, but still have an appropriate reaction. But I guess my mother's presence made him feel flustered. 'Wow!' was all he managed to say.

" 'What do you think that's going to mean to you and me?' the man persisted. My mother must have seen that something was wrong. She said, 'Let me see that,' and she took the magazine from my dad and read the first paragraph aloud. It was something about the sale of one pesticide company to another.

"From there, my father could manage to participate in the conversation. He was grateful to her. He took her out to lunch. He admitted to her that he couldn't read."

"Who else knew that?" I asked.

"Unless someone guessed and didn't let him know they'd guessed, not many people. W, Gerald, Gwendolyn and Mr. Brennan. I think he said his housekeeper at the other house knew. I didn't realize that he couldn't read until I was about ten."

"Were you disappointed?"

He shook his head. "No. I'm not sure why not, really. It wasn't a revelation, all at once. I gradually began to realize it, and knew it was a secret. At first, I didn't want him to know I knew that secret; maybe I sensed it would hurt him, I don't know. And even then, I thought he just couldn't read very well.

"But one day, the two of us had been out somewhere together and the road he would usually take to go home was closed. There was a sign saying 'Detour, use such-and-so street,' but of course, he couldn't read the sign. When he was working, one of his workers would do all the driving. But with us, he found his way around by memorizing land-marks. Only this time, there were no landmarks. He tried making turns, tried to get back to something familiar. He got lost. I could see he was terrified. Finally, I told him not to worry and pulled out a map and figured out how to get us home. I read the street signs and told him where to turn.

"We managed to get home before my mother came back from wherever she was. He was still shaken by the whole ordeal. So I gathered my courage and told him I already knew he couldn't read, and I'd teach him if he wanted me to. He started crying. I had never seen him shed a tear before then. It scared the hell out of me."

I called to the dogs, and we turned, heading back toward the house.

"He told me about a nightmare he used to have all the time," Travis said. "In the dream he would be driving alone in the car to a place he had been to many times, but then the car breaks down along the way, before he gets to his next landmark. Tough-looking men are watching him—he's in a rough neighborhood. Suddenly he's near a phone—it appears out of nowhere, as things do in dreams—and so he calls the operator and asks for help. She puts him through to the police. The police say, 'We'll send help right way. Where are you?' He has to say, 'I don't know.' They say, 'Read the address on the phone,' and he panics. He lies and says it isn't on the phone, that it must have been torn off. The police say, 'Read the street sign,' and he can't. 'Read the signs on the stores,' and he can't. He finally has to tell everyone, 'I can't read,' and the police start laughing at him and hang up. The tough men are laughing at him, too. Everyone is pointing at him, jeering, and then walking away from him, leaving him, as if he isn't worth bothering with."

"Jesus," I said.

Again we walked in silence.

"This morning, you asked about the time just after the murder," he said. "It was this strange time when we—my father and my mother and I—were actually closer than we had been just before Gwendolyn died. We pulled together to protect my dad. Richmond was the enemy, this monster outside our gates."

"Your mom already knew about the marriage between Gwendolyn and your dad?"

He nodded. "She found out—I never knew how, but she did. She was devastated. I can remember her staying in her room for days on end, not eating, not sleeping, just staring at the ceiling, crying. Wouldn't answer the door or the phone. I took care of things the best I could, did the shopping, things like that. I got her to call my school and tell them I had the flu. Maybe it was just a kid's way of looking at it, but I was afraid to go to school, afraid she'd kill herself if I was away from her too long."

"But you were only—"

"Eleven. I finally told her I was going to get the priest— she begged me not to. She was so ashamed, thought of herself as everything from the world's most gullible fool to a home-wrecker. I guess the threat of my telling anyone about it snapped her out of the worst of the depression. I started going back to school, life settled into a routine. But I don't think she was ever the same after that."

"Your dad—"

"I was angry at him, of course. She wasn't the only one who felt betrayed. When she made him move out, I was glad. At the time, I didn't want him to come anywhere near us. That's what I told myself, anyway.

"They had hoped to settle everything quietly—for my sake, they said. Mom was going to sell the house, move to where no one knew us, tell everyone she was a widow."

"Did Gwendolyn know?"

He shrugged. "I'm not sure, but I don't think she knew. Mom made him swear he would never tell Gwendolyn. She believed they had both wronged Gwendolyn, but that no good would come of revealing the truth to her. It could only hurt her."

"Did your father ever try to explain why he didn't just divorce Gwendolyn? Why he tried to lead a double life?"

He was quiet for so long, I began to regret the question. He looked out over the water.

"He gave different explanations for it over the years. I suppose there is no one answer to that question. He was very young when he married Gwendolyn, and I think his brother pressured him into it—or pressured her into marrying my father, by threatening to expose her as a seducer."

"What?"

"Gerald Spanning. My uncle. When I was becoming—oh,

let's call it *reacquainted*—with my dad, he talked a lot about his younger days, the days before he was married. I've never met Gerald, though."

"Not even when you were little?"

"No. Gerald was part of my father's other life. Introducing us would have meant revealing his secret family."

"But after the secret was out in the open—"

"I don't think Gerald had much to do with my father after the murder. The Kellys weren't the only ones who disowned us."

I let that go by. "Gerald was his older brother?"

"Yes. Gerald is a lot older than my dad—about ten years older. There had been at least a couple of other children born in the years between, but those children had died. They were poor. My grandparents were migratory farm workers."

He smiled at my look of surprise.

"Yes," he said. "A hard life. My dad said that when Gerald was barely out of short pants, my grandfather taught him how to ride the rails. They'd go all over the country, looking for farms that needed workers."

"Are your grandparents still alive?"

He shook his head. "They were killed in an accident on the sugar beet farm. Papa DeMont—that's what my dad called Gwendolyn's grandfather—felt sorry for Gerald and my dad, and let them stay in the house they had been living in on the farm. He also gave Gerald a permanent job. I think Gerald was still a teenager."

"How old was your dad?"

"My dad was very young. Still in elementary school. Gerald wanted him to stay in school, but he dropped out when he was twelve—he was already hopelessly frustrated with it because he couldn't read. He wasn't stupid—in fact, when I think of all he had to do to cope with his illiteracy, his strategies for hiding it . . . well, that's another story."

"So he went to work on the sugar beet farm."

"Yes. I guess Papa DeMont saw that my dad could learn in other ways and took him on as sort of a challenge. My dad used to swear that was how he got his real education—following Papa DeMont around, listening to him talk, watching him work. My father had a natural ability with plants, so I don't think Mr. DeMont regretted hiring him as a gardener."

He cast a quick glance at me, trying to gauge my reaction.

"I don't remember much about your parents' home," I said, "but I do remember the beautiful plants and flowers. I think my mother was jealous of her sister's gardens—Arthur's gardens."

His brows drew together, and he looked away again. After a moment, he said, "Your husband—Frank?"

"Yes."

"You said he planted the garden in your backyard?"

"Yes. Unlike me, he has a green thumb."

He smiled. "My father didn't pass his abilities on to me. I like Frank's garden. When will he be back?"

I shrugged. "Soon, I hope."

I called to the dogs, who were getting a little too far ahead of us. "I've forgotten now—how old was Gwendolyn when they married?" I asked.

"Forty-five. My dad was sixteen."

"She was almost thirty years older than Arthur."

"Yes. They were already friends. I never learned a lot about their marriage, but he did tell me that he was her only real friend. When Papa DeMont—her grandfather—died, she was grief-stricken. I guess she did seduce my father, but he said he thought she turned to him because she was so lonely, so sad. He never seemed to feel angry at her about it."

"But he came to regret marrying her?"

"I don't know if that's the right way to put it. By the time he married my mother, Gwendolyn was about fifty. He was twenty-two. He said he fell in love with my mother when he was old enough to know what it meant. He said he loved her then, and he would love her all of his life. I believe that—I think that was the truth."

He stopped walking and turned to me. "I don't really know the truth about why he stayed married to Gwendolyn. Sometimes he said it was because she was so lonely, and he couldn't bring himself to hurt her. Sometimes he said he loved her in a different way. Once he told me he owed her a kind of debt—one that money couldn't repay. He told me that he was still paying on that debt, but wouldn't explain what that meant. Another time, he just said it was too complex to explain, and we should just get on with our lives."

I didn't say anything, but with his next sentence, he spoke the accusation I had held back.

"It could have been that he wanted the money," he said, "and that divorcing her would have meant giving up a fortune."

"Do you think that's it?"

"I don't know. I don't want to believe that's why, but I don't know. He didn't like talking to me about her, or his life with her, or her money. But I never got the sense that his reluctance to talk about her was because he hated her; it was the habit of keeping those worlds separate, I suppose. His marriage to her was always divided from his life with my mother and me."

I whistled for the dogs, who were wrestling with one another a short distance behind us. Deke and Dunk broke apart, then went barreling past us.

"Your parents were separated," I said, "but he was with you on the night of the murder?"

He hesitated only slightly before saying, "You've seen the scars—the old ones—on my hand. My father was at our home when I cut myself. He carried me into the emergency room. If you don't believe me, there are all kinds of people who witnessed that."

"I'm not accusing you of having lied about that night," I said.

He smiled a little.

"I'm not," I insisted. "I just wondered what he was doing over there if Aunt Briana was so hurt and angry."

"He missed us. He needed us."

"He was trying to patch things up?"

"No," he said slowly, considering the question. "I think he was trying to accept the fact that his whole world was falling apart, but he wanted it to fall apart a little more slowly."

"But the investigation brought you back together?"

"Briefly. Technically, the investigation is still open, of course. But even when the case was actively being investigated, Harold Richmond always refused to believe there was any possibility of another suspect. That was another reason he got demoted—he just didn't do enough to investigate other suspects."

"So he kept pursuing your dad."

"Right. He added to my mother's misery. He would corner her when she was, say, out shopping. During hours I was in school. He'd start out cajoling, then he'd get frustrated and angry with her—sometimes he was drunk. He'd tell her that he knew she had been paid off to lie for my dad, or tell her that he knew my folks had plotted to kill Gwendolyn, and that my mom had better not try to get back together with my dad."

"Why didn't she want her name on that restraining order?"

He shook his head. "She said Richmond was part of her penance. No priest ever assigned it, of course. It was her own idea. She spent a lot of years punishing herself."

"For what?"

He looked down at his hand and shrugged.

I waited.

"For sleeping with a married man."

"She didn't know he was married!" I protested.

"Then for still wanting him, I suppose. For having brought shame to her family. For having a bastard child."

"I don't believe that she was ever ashamed of you."

"How would you know?" he asked.

"Are we back to that again? All right, because I saw how much she wanted you before you were born. Because—"

He held up a hand. "Okay, you're right. Maybe she wasn't ashamed of me. Not of me, personally, but she was ashamed that I wasn't legitimate. She blamed herself for my being a bastard. Every time I got in trouble at school for fighting someone over it, it was her fault—all her fault, she would say."

"But Richmond wasn't really a part of that. Why did she decide he was her punishment?"

He stared at his bandaged hand again. When he looked over at me again, he seemed to be studying my face.

"What?"

"Are you sure you want to know?"

"What are you talking about?"

"The night of Gwendolyn's murder. Do you really want to know the answers to all your questions? What if it means your aunt Briana helped Gwendolyn's murderer to escape? Or that your newly rediscovered cousin is also an accessory after the fact?"

I didn't answer right away. "Maybe you did something wrong when you were very young. Maybe you didn't. I don't know. I do know someone tried to kill you last night, and I'm also certain that the hit-and-run accident that killed your mother was no accident at all. That's what concerns me now. And yes, it all seems to have something to do with Gwendolyn DeMont's murder."

I took a deep breath, let it out slowly and went on. "I don't have much family left, Travis. You're my cousin. That's true whether or not you've done something wrong. But I can't help you if you don't tell me everything you can about anything that has a bearing on the DeMont case."

He stopped walking, studied me again, and said, "All right, Irene Kelly. I'll tell you the truth." He held up his bandaged right hand, and at first I thought he was going to mimic a courtroom oath. But he said, "I saved my father with this hand. That wasn't my idea at the time. In fact, I was enraged with him."

"I don't understand—"

"On the night of Gwendolyn's murder, when he came to our house, my father touched the pane of glass, the one I broke with my fist. He touched it before I broke it. He left a bloody handprint on it."

"A bloody . . . was he hurt?"

He smiled and dropped his hand to his side. "Kind of you to ask that first. No. He wasn't hurt."

"Gwendolyn's blood."

"Yes. For years, I thought perhaps he had murdered her, despite his denials. But one day, he got me to listen to him long enough to ask me a question. And that question made me change my mind."

I waited.

"Let me back up a little—that night, I was watching my father through a window before he tried to come in the house. I watched him for some time. I saw him close up, and after I was hurt—when he came into the house—he held me in his arms." Again he looked out over the water. "My father's question was, 'Before I touched you, did you see blood on me anywhere other than the palm of that one hand?'"

Travis looked back at me. "The answer was no."

19

Before I could respond, he said, "Just think about it for a while. I'm not saying it proves anything, and it may raise as many questions as it answers. When I started thinking about it, I realized I had to set aside a lot of assumptions I had been holding on to for a long time."

We had reached the foot of the stairway leading up to the street. I turned to him and said, "Everything I've learned about Harold Richmond makes me believe he has a copy of the DeMont murder file. I'm going to try to get a look at it this afternoon. With what you've had to deal with lately, are you sure you want to come along?"

"Yes, I'm sure," he said.

"There are some other people we need to talk to as soon as we can. This 'W' guy and your lawyer, for starters."

"Mr. Ulkins and Mr. Brennan," he said.

"Yes. Can you get in touch with them?"

"Sure. Mr. Brennan often spends time away from the city on weekends, but I can leave a message on his service. W— Ulkins—should be in the office today."

"But with your father's death—"

"He works for me as well. If he's gone for the day, I'd still like to stop by the office and check for messages. The office is downtown."

"You have a key?"

"Yes, so that's no problem."

The dogs were getting impatient, starting to stray back down the beach, so I called to them and we began climbing the stairs.

"Who else will we be trying to see?" Travis asked.

We. That was what I wanted, right? "I want to talk to Dr. Curtis and a priest at St. Anthony's."

"Which priest?"

"The one who said your father's funeral Mass."

He stopped climbing. "How could you possibly be sure his funeral Mass was at St. Anthony's?"

"Your mother went to it."

"And how could you possibly know that?" a voice called from above us.

We looked up to see Jim McCain leaning over the railing near the top of the stairs.

"Shit," I said. How long had he been listening?

Travis looked between us.

"Travis Maguire," I said, "meet Detective Jim McCain, LAPD Homicide. He's investigating your mother's death."

McCain smiled and said, "Glad to see you're all right, Mr. Maguire." He looked at the bandaged hand and added, "Or are you?"

"Have you found the driver of the car?" Travis asked.

"No, I'm sorry, not yet. We're working on it, though," he said. "Even on the weekend."

"At the beach?" Travis replied.

McCain stopped smiling. "Wherever it takes me. Perhaps Ms. Kelly would be so kind as to let us continue this discussion in a more private place?"

"Sure," I said. "You never know who might be eavesdropping around here."

"People with nothing to hide—" McCain began.

"—still enjoy their constitutional rights," I finished.

We walked in silence most of the way to the house, but just before we got to the front door, Jack came roaring down the street on his Harley, back from whatever errand he had taken care of for Travis. He stopped in front of the house and called, "Everything okay?"

I nodded, and he watched as we went inside.

The first few minutes were spent with McCain telling Travis almost as little about the accident as he had told me; when Travis complained, McCain looked over at me and said, "Perhaps some other time."

"You suspect Irene?" Travis asked in disbelief.

"This investigation is still in its early stages," he said, and before Travis could say more, asked him if he was aware that his mother had willed her entire estate to me.

Travis stared at him, then laughed. "Of course I know!"

"What?" McCain said.

"My mother made sure I knew all about it." He glanced over at me. "You know the Maguire temper, Irene."

"But . . ." McCain began.

"The date on that will, Detective McCain, will be just before my mother moved to her last apartment." He paused, all the amusement of a moment before gone. "I'm ashamed to say that we parted in anger."

"And why would that be?" McCain said.

"Travis," I said, "maybe you should call your attorney."

He ignored me, and answered, "You know about my parents' bigamous marriage?"

"Yes," McCain said.

"Because my mother never forgave my father for that, she forbade me to have contact with him. When I grew past the age when she could forbid it, she simply resented it. She tolerated it, though, until I told her I was accepting money from my father. At that point she said she would no longer live with me, and told me, quite dramatically, that if I was taking anything from him, I'd get nothing from her. That was when she produced a handwritten will leaving everything she owned to Irene, and waved it under my nose."

"So the last time you saw your mother alive was when?" Detective McCain asked.

Eyes downcast, he said softly, "I helped her to move into her apartment. She didn't speak to me."

Whatever else he might have told McCain was interrupted by my barking dogs, up on their feet and scrambling before I heard an imperious knock at the door.

Rachel came striding in before I could warn her—but apparently she already knew McCain was here. "What the hell is going on here, Mac?"

"Hello, Rachel. I was wondering if I'd get to see you today."

"What's going on?" she repeated.

"A murder investigation. You have a problem with that?"

She made a show of looking around. "I don't see a lawyer."

"Don't need to read the card to anybody at this point—or have you forgotten all about how law enforcement works?"

"I remember exactly how it works. Which is why I'm asking you to get out. Now."

"I was invited in," he said.

Her hands were on her hips. "I don't care who invited you in, I'm inviting you to get out."

"You don't live here."

"Okay," I said, "then I'm the one who's asking you to go."

He started to say something, looked back at Rachel, then shook his head. He stood up, which didn't give him too much height on her, and said softly, "You turning your back on your old friends, Rach?"

"I could ask you the same question."

He turned to Travis. "Mr. Maguire, did Ms. Kelly ever tell you how it was possible for her to know that your mother was at your father's funeral?"

"Out," Rachel said.

"A holy card," I answered, causing McCain to laugh out loud.

"Forgive me, Ms. Kelly," he said, "but that's a new one on me."

Rachel started to speak but Travis held a hand up and asked, "You think a holy card from my father's funeral Mass is something funny, Detective McCain?"

McCain gave Rachel a look of utter frustration, but there was nothing disrespectful in his tone when he said, "No, Mr. Maguire. No, I don't. You happen to have this holy card, Ms. Kelly?"

"It's in your room," I said to Travis. "Mind if I get it from there?"

"Of course not."

McCain started to follow me, but Rachel blocked his way. "Oh, no, Mac. You stay here and keep me company."

Travis went with me. I found the holy card and let him take a look at it. He ran his fingers over it, but didn't speak.

"It was in her coat pocket," I said.

"She always got cold easily," he said, and swallowed hard. "Do we have to give this to him?"

"Yes," I said.

When Travis handed it to him, McCain asked, "Anybody see you find this, Ms. Kelly?"

"Rachel. And my aunt Mary."

He scowled. I felt a little bit of sympathy for him. Sometimes my leads don't go anywhere, either. But Rachel was the one who hit him where it hurt.

"Face it, Mac," she said. "Two things are sticking in your craw right now. One, you did a lousy search of the apartment and missed some important items. Two, Irene found her cousin before you could. You keep wanting to believe she had something to do with her aunt's death, but you don't have shit to prove it. Not even a motive. Well, better luck next time."

He tucked the holy card away, smiled and walked to the front door. He stopped, turned back and said, "Don't be too sure about what I do and don't have, Rach."

He closed the door softly behind him.

"Jimmy, Jimmy, Jimmy," Rachel said quietly.

"Jack call you?" I asked.

"Yes."

"That reminds me—" Travis said. "I'll be at Jack's place for a few minutes."

"We need to get going soon," I said.

"This won't take long," he said.

When he came back, he was carrying a small cellular phone. "It's supposed to be activated," he said. "What's the phone number here?"

I told him and he dialed it. The phone rang.

"Great!"

"You had Jack buy a cell phone for you?" Rachel asked.

"I bought it, but Jack agreed to put it in his name for a while."

"How did you talk him into that?" I asked.

"I gave him the money for it. And I think he knows you won't let me rip him off."

"You've hardly known him for a day. How do you know he won't take your money and run?"

"Same reason—I know you won't let him rip me off. Besides, I could see you trust him. Jack's great."

"Yeah," Rachel said, "Jack's great, but don't do too much more business this way, kid. My heart can't take it."

I laughed. "Better not tell her about the van."

After quickly explaining that purchase to her, he turned to me and asked, "Do you think you could drive it?"

"Sure, but don't you want to?"

He held up his injured hand. "Maybe in a day or two. By the way, Rachel, your friend is still sitting out there, watching the house."

"Oh, he is, is he?" She stood up.

"Wait a minute," I said. "I think I've got a better idea. Travis, give Rachel your cellular phone number, okay?"

He smiled. "I was planning to. I think we're on the same wavelength."

While she wrote the number down, I called Jack.

"One more favor, Jack." I explained what I needed—and got his usual willingness to help out.

A minute or two after I hung up the phone, we saw Jack drive off in his van. We waited another minute or two, then the three of us walked out the front door. McCain watched us, but didn't say anything. When we started going down the steps, Rachel said, "He'll watch for us, don't worry."

There were more people on the beach now, though not as many as there'd be in another hour or so. We walked all the way to the pier, and crossed under it. We took the stairs on the far side, passed the landing leading to a parking lot and continued up to the pier itself. We walked out to the end of the pier, where Rachel said, "He's out of the car, but he stayed at the end of the street. Watching us with field glasses. He's bound to know something's up, especially since you two were just out on the beach, so no need to make too big a show out of being out here."

After a minute or two we walked back down the pier. But when we reached the stairs, we stopped at the landing. Travis and I moved toward the parking lot, Rachel waited.

Jack had already pulled around to the end of the landing. He quickly got out of the van, wished us luck, and hurried over to Rachel.

We drove out of the lot and headed toward downtown along a route of surface streets I doubted McCain—not being a local—would think to try.

"I wish I could have seen his face when he realized who was walking next to Rachel," Travis said.

But I wasn't in such a triumphant mood about McCain. I kept wondering what it was he thought he had on me, and if it would amount to enough for an arrest. I was innocent, but I'm not so naïve as to believe that only the guilty get brought to trial—let alone convicted. And defending one's innocence can be expensive.

Charges alone would make my job as a political reporter extremely difficult—even if the charges were dropped, I could see my sources drying up, people hesitating to open up to someone accused of murdering her aunt. For a reporter—perhaps especially on that beat—if you aren't trusted, you aren't talked to, and you soon have nothing to write.

I didn't want to think about how it might affect Frank's work if his wife faced that sort of accusation.

I tried to look at things as McCain might. My alibi was a solid one, but maybe he thought I had hired someone to kill Briana. He often mentioned the will, but why would I pay someone to kill a woman who had nothing? Nothing other than that will tied me to her though, so . . . so she had to have some money somewhere, or something so valuable, McCain thought I'd kill her to gain possession of it.

I could think of only one way that Briana could suddenly have come into a lot of money. It meant that Dr. Curtis hadn't made a mistake on the death certificate; that Arthur hadn't lied to him. Maybe Briana had married—or remarried—into money.

"Travis, you said a priest helped you move furniture into your mom's apartment?"

"Yes. Father Chris, at St. Anthony's."

"St. Anthony's, here in Las Piernas?"

"Yes. My mom liked him, even though she didn't follow much of his advice."

"What do you mean?"

"He kept telling her to forgive me and my father."

"He knew your father?"

"Yes, they both kept going to St. Anthony's, although never to the same Mass. She always went to the ten o'clock Mass on Sunday. My dad said he never wanted her to feel uneasy about going to church there, so he'd always go to an earlier or later Mass—never the ten o'clock."

"I think she finally listened to her priest."

He just shook his head. "You're still on that kick about the death certificate?"

"Yes. Mind if we try to see the priest before we visit Mr. Ulkins?"

He shrugged, took out the cell phone and called information. He asked for the number for St. Anthony's rectory and pressed a couple of buttons to put the call through from information. He spoke to the housekeeper, who was apparently someone he had met before.

"Thank you, Mrs. Havens," I heard him say. "Yes, I'm glad I had some time with him, too. . . . No, I didn't know you had known him that long. Listen, Mrs. Havens, I need to speak with Father Chris. Is he in?"

There was a wait, then Travis said, "Hi, Chris? Can my cousin and I come by to talk with you for a few minutes? Thanks—you're sure this is an okay time?"

An elderly woman greeted us at the rectory door. She exclaimed and fussed over Travis, asking several times if she could bring him anything, until a handsome, dark-haired man of about thirty came into the room. He was wearing jeans, work boots and a flannel shirt, and said, "Thank you, Annie." She left with some reluctance, and only after Travis assured her he would visit again soon. The man in the jeans turned to us as the door closed behind her, and said to Travis, "She used to work for your father, you know."

"So she's been telling me. How are you, Chris?"

This was Father Chris?

"I'm all right, Travis," he was answering. "Doing better now that I know you're back." He turned to me. "You must be the cousin?"

Travis apologized and introduced me to Father Christopher Karis, who, we learned, had climbed down off a roof to talk to us.

"Happy to be called away from roof repairs," he said, extending a hand. "Which side of the family are Kellys?"

"His mother's," I said.

He smiled. "So she did contact her nieces. At a time like this, it must be such a comfort to Briana to have Travis back, and to be seeing her sister's children again. Travis, what happened to your hand?"

Travis looked as if he had been punched. "Chris . . ." He couldn't manage more.

"I'm sorry," I said to the priest. "Briana was killed three weeks ago, in a hit-and-run accident."

We didn't rush things after that. We gave Father Chris what few details we had regarding Briana's death. His shock and grief kept either of us from asking him any questions for a time, but he quickly became more concerned with Travis.

"But—then you don't know! Travis, they married!"

Travis looked at me, then back at Father Chris. "Why?"

"Why? The best reason in the world. They loved each other."

"But she was so bitter—"

"She let go of that, Travis."

"She forgave him?"

"Yes. Yes, and asked his forgiveness. And I know she sought yours, too. She saw that all of this had been hardest on you, who hadn't done a thing to deserve it. She came to regret those years—"

"I understood!" Travis said. "Didn't she know that?"

"I think she did. She told me that after you started traveling, she started thinking. You brought them back together, you know."

"No, you know she just finally listened to you. But there was so much wasted time!" Travis said.

"Yes, I suppose there was. But does that matter now? Both of your parents found some happiness together. Both were good and generous people—human and imperfect, yes, but good at heart. I sincerely believe they're together now, in a life without pain or suffering, without separation or loneliness."

"Yes," Travis said after a while, "I guess I believe that, too. I just wish—I wish we could have all been together, a family again, even for a little while."

"I know, Travis. And I'm sorry that you weren't able to have that. But you aren't without family—" He glanced toward me. "You have your cousins; perhaps other members of your family will be reconciled. And you have a family here—this parish will always welcome you."

They agreed to meet again soon, and Father Chris told Travis to call him anytime—day or night—if Travis needed to talk or if he could be of help to him in any way.

Travis didn't talk much as we left, other than to give directions to his father's office—his office, too, I reminded myself. The office was in a beautiful old brick building, one that had once belonged to an insurance company. It stood with dignity between two taller, newer and less lovely structures, separated from them by more than the narrow alleys on each side. Travis told me that his father had bought it for a song, made a few repairs and brought it up to earthquake code. The offices took up the entire top story—the ninth floor, he said. Most of the rest of the building was rented out to other businesses.

There were a few people walking around on the downtown street that Saturday morning, but far less than the usual crowd. It wasn't hard to find a van-sized parking space.

"I know what's bothering me," Travis said as I turned off the engine. "But what's bothering you?"

"Beyond seeing how hard all of this is on you?"

He nodded.

"McCain. If your mother received anything—community property, anything—after your dad died, and that holographic will was the last one she made, I'm going to be suspect number one."

"Ulkins will probably know what the situation is," he said. "Mr. Brennan can help us with any legal hassles."

I was out of the van when I realized that although he had opened his door, he was having trouble unfastening the seat belt using one hand. I had just stepped around to his side of the van when we heard glass shatter.

Pebbles of it pelted hard down on us, blue-green gravel from the sky. We hardly noticed the glass, though, for as we turned toward the building an object hurtled onto the sidewalk next to us, spraying us with blood and God knows what else, making a horrible sound, a sort of crackling thunk, as if someone had smashed a carton of eggs by hurling a watermelon at it.

This helpless missile had been a man, a frail old man.

I looked away, looked up to see where he had fallen from, and saw a sight so incongruous, I wondered if my mind had finally snapped. Above us, leaning out through a broken ninth-story window, was a man in a black wetsuit, wearing a ski mask and gloves.

Someone a few feet away started screaming, and soon several people were screaming, shouting, running toward us. I looked to see Travis, bending over the awful mess on the sidewalk, shouting, "No!" He took a breath, filled his lungs, and let it out in a long, loud "No!" again and again and again.

I shoved through the flow of people who came toward us, moved away from my cousin and the remains of a man I already knew must have been Ulkins, ran out of the crowd and into the building, hell-bent to catch the son of a bitch who was seriously screwing up the Maguire family reunion.

20

I got lucky—the lobby was empty, an elevator car was open and waiting. I was in it and on my way up to the ninth floor before my temper cooled off enough to allow me to ask myself what the hell I thought I was going to do when I caught up with Mr. Death in a Wetsuit. I quickly pressed eight, got out on that floor, pulled the STOP button, then the DOWN call button to bring the other car. When it arrived, I did the same thing—pulled the STOP button. If he hadn't escaped already, he wasn't going to take an elevator. That left the stairwell. He might have plans for using the roof, but he'd be obvious—people on the street would be looking up at the ninth floor, the top of the building.

A man running around downtown in a wetsuit would be equally obvious. Anyone who was wearing a wetsuit inside an office building didn't just happen to walk in off the street that way; he planned to wear it, and must have plans for getting out of it and into less attention-grabbing attire. I was counting on that to give me some time to limit his escape options.

I hurried toward the stairwell, to my right. I would just keep an eye on him, I told myself. From a safe distance. I'd stay low until I heard him pass by, then step into the stairwell and get a look at him. Tell the police where he had gone, give as good a description of his street clothes as I could manage. Nothing more. No revenge—yet.

This darkened floor of the building seemed deserted; all the office doors along the long, L-shaped hallway were closed. All was quiet. At the top of the L, far behind me, a tall window at the other end of the hall provided soft low light. The end I was approaching, near the stairwell door, was brighter. As I reached that part of the hall, I saw that the light came from a larger, second window—an old fire escape. I wondered briefly if he would make use of it, but decided he would not—too much exposure, and unlike the stairwell, it made access to other floors more difficult.

As I neared the stairwell door, I heard a soft clicking sound behind me and whirled, but saw nothing. I felt myself break out in a cold sweat. Suddenly, the hallway was filled with a loud ringing, a giant's brass alarm clock, echoing off the walls—the elevators. The stop buttons must have had a timer on them—and now the alarm bells were heralding my presence to anyone one floor above. I ran back down the hallway, got into one of the cars and slammed my palm against the STOP button, then hit the CLOSE DOORS button. Nothing happened. The ringing was so loud in this enclosed space, it made me clench my teeth. I wasn't going to stay in that elevator car.

I considered going into the stairwell, or a nearby janitor's closet, but opted instead for the fire escape. What would have been his disadvantage would be my advantage—and outside the back of the building, I might see any exit the killer made from this side.

The bells kept ringing; the hall seemed to be made of the sound. I stepped closer to the window, took hold of the latch on the sash, and vaguely recognized the reflection of something dark before he grabbed me from behind and yanked me backwards, off balance. A large, black rubber hand, coated in something wet and warm and sticky, covered my face. The smell of it mixed with rubber made me want to pull away, but he held me tight, his much larger arm pinning both of my arms; I felt the weird smoothness of the neoprene suit against my skin, on my neck and arms, as he lifted me off my feet, and even as I kicked at him, turned and slammed my head into the wall.

Dazed, I saw nothing but black wetsuit and the wall as he maneuvered me against it; I made some useless efforts to push away, then felt searing pain on my already aching scalp as he took hold of a handful of my hair and yanked it hard. His other hand took me by the belt; he lifted me from my feet by these two handles and swung me toward the wall again. At the last instant, I realized his intention and tried to shield my face with my arms, twisted my head just enough to prevent myself from hitting completely face-first. It hurt like hell anyway, the impact strong enough to give me a bloody nose. He slightly changed his grip, picked me up, and twisting at the last minute, managed to land another blow to my head. I didn't feel anything after the moment of impact.

I awakened, if you can call it that, to heat, and the smell of something burning. Neoprene. And rubber gloves. And other things. I had no idea how long I had been out, but I could still hear the goddamn elevator bells ringing and took that to be a good sign. People would be coming into the building, they would hear the bells. No, I thought— slowly, it seemed—people don't run into burning build- ings.

I was dizzy, and facedown on the linoleum, which—a few feet away from me—was also on fire. I couldn't see very far. The hallway was filling with smoke. I looked for an exit, but the stairwell and the hallway to the elevators were blocked by a bonfire of sorts. An evidence fire, with what looked like a few items from the janitor's closet thrown in for good measure.

I tried to move, found my hands tied behind my back, but my feet free. Telling myself that being burned alive would hurt worse, I tried to ignore the aching in my head and face and the strain on everything else as I pulled my knees up to my chest, worked my hands down over my rear and feet, then rolled to my back, bringing my hands in front of me. They were bound by an electrical cord, and I decided not to waste time trying to untie them—I needed to get the hell out of the building.

I moved awkwardly toward the fire escape again, staying low, trying to breathe the cooler air near the floor. By the time I had reached the window, the heat was intense, the smoke thickening. As I stood and reached for the window latch, I prayed to God that Arthur Spanning had maintained his building well.

The window opened easily, and set off another loud alarm, but my head was already ringing. I half-crawled, half-fell out onto the fire escape, and only then heard sirens and shouting. I was on my back, looking at the sky, which also had smoke in it, and a helicopter. But although smoke was billowing out after me, compared to the hallway the air here was cool and good, and for the next few moments, all I could do was close my eyes and take big gulps of it into my lungs. Someone in the helicopter said something over a loudspeaker and I'm fairly sure it had to do with me, because soon a fireman was on the fire escape, talking to me, freeing my hands.

"Travis!" I said, sitting up too quickly.

"Someone else in the building?" he asked, apparently pleased I was responding to him.

"No—at least I don't think so. Outside—a young man, with a bandaged hand—"

"Oh, the owner of the building. He's okay. He'll be happy to know that we've found you. Come on, let's get you out of here."

Travis was waiting for me in the alley, and I made no complaint when the embrace he gave me sent a memo from everything that had hit the wall. It was good to know he was safe, still here, that the killer hadn't somehow taken him away, too. When he stepped back, paramedics came toward me—but a familiar voice said, "Irene? Can I talk to you first?"

I turned to see Reed Collins, a Las Piernas homicide detective. I was relieved that Ulkins's death was going to be Reed's case; relieved, not just because I have faith in his abilities but because Reed works with Frank, and maybe as a way of doing penance for his actions when Frank was taken hostage, he has treated me with kid gloves ever since. I needed a break from bullies.

"Sure, Reed," I said, "but I didn't get a good look at him. He came at me from behind, never said a word. He was wearing a wetsuit, but it's one of the things he set on fire up there." Remembering how he had grabbed me, I said, "I think he's right-handed."

I still wasn't too steady on my feet. At the paramedics' suggestion, Reed took me to their big, boxy ambulance so that I could sit down while I talked to him. With Travis hovering nearby, I told Reed what I could.

"A wetsuit?" he asked.

"Yes. It confused me at first, but I think the guy must have heard about hair and fiber evidence or DNA, and was trying not to leave anything behind."

"But he must have been here before, to know that Ulkins worked here on the weekends. He couldn't have visited in a wetsuit every time."

"No, but he could have learned Ulkins's routine without going into the office itself. And today, I think he was already down on the eighth floor when I got there. You might want to check out the tenants on that floor."

When I told Reed that the glove held over my face had

been sticky, he gently took hold of my chin and looked closely at my left cheek, then said, "I need a favor from you." I saw him glance toward a crime scene photographer.

"Oh." The thought of having my photo taken in this state was humiliating, but I knew a photo might help a D.A. get a conviction—for assault if nothing else—provided this guy was ever caught. "Sure, go ahead—but Reed, I need a favor in return."

"Anything I can do—you know that."

"Don't tell Frank—not yet, not while he's away. I'll tell him soon, but right now he can't do anything about it, and it will just torture him. You know how he is."

Reed smiled. "Sure. He has this crazy idea that if he's not around, you'll get into trouble. Dumbass hasn't figured out that you'll get into trouble anyway."

"Thanks, Reed."

They took the photos, and Reed even had one of the lab guys scrape dried blood from different parts of my face. "You think he left some of his blood on my face?"

Reed shook his head, glanced at Travis and said, "Maybe, but most likely it's Ulkins's."

"He tortured him," Travis said angrily. "Tortured that old man!"

I looked to Reed, who nodded. "We need to wait for the autopsy, but he appears to have some electrical burns on him. A few cuts as well."

All of a sudden, I didn't feel so hot.

"Let me get those paramedics back over here," Reed said, watching me.

"Wait—up on that fire escape—once the fire is out—"

"It's already out," he said. "Soon as the fire department gives us the okay, we're going inside to have a look at Ulkins's office."

"Then have someone look for a piece of electrical cord on the fire escape of the eighth floor—the ends are cut. He tied my hands with it. I know it's a long shot, but maybe he handled it before he had the gloves on."

He spoke into a handheld radio, asking someone to look for the cord. "Oh, one other thing," Reed said to me. "There was an LAPD homicide detective here, name of McCain." He smiled. "I thought Pete Baird's wife was going to deck him."

"Rachel's here?"

"Yeah, I get the feeling she's no stranger to this McCain." He watched me for a reaction, but it was a wasted effort. "Anyway," he went on, "I've had words with the guy, a very serious discussion, on the subject of his pulling his head out of his ass, and I do believe he made daylight by the time he left. But he still claims he wants to talk to you and your cousin here. Thinks this has a bearing on a case he's working on. I told him I'd ask you to call him later—if you felt up to it—but for now he needed to go on home like a good boy. He said you had the number."

"I owe you for that, Reed. Thanks—and don't worry, I'll call him."

"He's not the one I'm worried about at the moment. Let me call the paramedics back over, have them take a look at you, get you cleaned up a little, okay?"

"Thanks—and Rachel—"

"No problem. I'll get her now. And if I need to talk to you and your cousin again—?"

"I'll be at home or—Travis, mind if I give Detective Collins your cell phone number?"

Travis read it off to him.

"I called Rachel," Travis told me as Reed left. "I—I didn't know what had happened to you, and I panicked and—"

"It's okay," I soothed, "it's okay." I put an arm around his shoulders.

"I'm sorry," he said. "God, I'm sorry."

"For what? You didn't tell me to run inside. I'm sorry I left you out there alone. I was so relieved to see you were okay."

"Same here, seeing you." His voice came out just above a whisper. He looked down at his hand, rubbed his wrist beneath the bandage.

"The burn bothering you?"

"A little. I'm all right."

After a moment, I asked, "Were you and Mr. Ulkins close?"

"No, but W—Mr. Ulkins—was very close to my dad. He was his interpreter, you might say." He paused, then said, "Imagine doing business in Japan—living there without speaking the language. It's a little like that. For my dad, anything written was a foreign language. Mr. Ulkins translated that language for him—turned written words into spoken ones—and wrote what my father dictated into a recorder. He was sort of a combination secretary, bookkeeper and reader."

"Your father must have had a great deal of trust in him."

"He did. My father didn't want others to know he couldn't read, but he couldn't hide it from Mr. Brennan. Mr. Brennan had the brilliant idea of hiring someone discreet and trustworthy to read correspondence, documents and financial news to my father. W also wrote letters, filled in forms, wrote checks and took care of anything that required reading or writing. Dad said that without W, he never could have run the business."

The paramedics came back then, so we held off talking more about Ulkins. They helped me clean the rest of the blood off my face, and while I held a cold compress to my cheek, told me nothing seemed to be broken, just bruised—that I should probably go to the hospital because of the head injury. But I wasn't seeing double or feeling nauseated, and although my head and one side of my face hurt like hell, the initial feelings of dizziness hadn't returned, so I thanked them for their help and told them I'd take a rain check on the ambulance ride.

By then, Rachel had joined us. "Richmond," I said, once she had been reassured that I'd probably be all right. "It's almost one o'clock. We have to get over there by two, and I don't want McCain coming along for the ride."

"I don't think Mac's going to be a problem," she said. "He's pissed off that we ditched him on the beach, but he knows he brought some of that on himself. And I don't know what Reed said to him, but he's backed way off."

"So let's get going. I need to go home, change clothes."

"You sure you're up to this?"

"He's not going to talk to the two of you—he's probably only talking to me because he's worried I'll cause problems for him with Margot."

"That didn't exactly answer my question."

I didn't say anything.

"I'll call him and tell him we'll see him at two-thirty, how's that?"

She talked me into it.

Harold Richmond's office was on the second story of a strip mall not far from the Los Alamitos Race Course. There was a convenience market and a doughnut shop on the first floor of the small shopping center, so the basic qualifications for a strip mall were met. We had decided to take two cars; Rachel had reasoned that Richmond might need time to copy or retrieve the file we were after if he agreed to supply it. "And one look at you," she said, "tells me you should be back home as soon as possible."

I didn't like to admit it, but she was right. The hot shower had helped, but as I climbed the stairs to Richmond's office, I realized that my bruises were starting to make me feel a little stiff. We walked down the single, exterior hallway, passed a tax accountant's office and a nail parlor before we reached Richmond & Associates. The words were lettered in black on a glass door; the door had a silver glaze on it that reflected an image of our weary faces back at us, but didn't allow us to see in. I had already had a rather disheartening look at my face during my brief visit to my house. I avoided looking at Richmond's door.

"All set?" I asked the others. They nodded. "Remember, Travis—"

"Let you handle it," he said.

"Right."

I pulled at the door; it rattled but didn't open.

"I called him and he said he'd be here at two-thirty," Rachel said. She took out her keys and used one to rap on the glass. A muffled voiced answered something none of us could make out, but after a couple of minutes a rumpled version of Harold Richmond opened the door. He looked hung over. It didn't look as if that was a new experience for him.

"Sorry, I fell asleep," he said.

In the next moment, his eyes widened in surprise as he saw Travis.

"Thought you had killed me?" Travis said, breaking his promise right off the bat.

Richmond scowled and said, "No. I had nothing to do with that." He tapped his chest with his thumb and added, "If I had been trying, I would have succeeded."

Rachel made a show of looking him up and down and said, "We should believe that because you've made such a success out of the rest of your life?"

"Hold on, hold on," I said. "Let's call a truce for now, all right?"

Richmond didn't lose the scowl, but he didn't try for a snappy comeback. I had the feeling I had saved him the trouble of thinking one up. Rachel shrugged and we followed him inside. I was moving a little slower than usual, and let the other two go in first.

"What happened to you?" Richmond asked me, as he got a closer look at my face.

"Diving accident," I said.

He led the way through a small waiting room. Its walls were covered with dark wood paneling of the type popular in the late 1960s. Thumb-tacked to one wall was a yellowing bullfight poster. The rest of the decor consisted of worn gold shag carpeting, a couple of sagging chairs and a dusty end table—which held a single torn copy of *Sports Illustrated*. Rachel picked up the magazine as she passed the table and said, "Holy shit, the Dodgers are leaving Brooklyn!"

Travis grinned, Richmond ignored her, and at my pleading look she said only, "Lighten up."

Richmond led us through a second door and into his office. The room was plain; a metal desk with a computer on it, a bank of old filing cabinets, a safe and a bookshelf. A small metal table held a copier and a fax machine.

There was one chair that looked as if it didn't bring business to orthopedic surgeons, and Richmond plopped down in it as he sat behind his desk. The other three must have been made by the same people who make desks for parochial school students. Travis and I each took one of these, while Rachel stayed on her feet. She's tall, so this made her tower above us. Richmond didn't look too happy as he watched her stalk around his office, but he said nothing.

Travis was also being quiet, giving me hope that he was remembering his end of the bargain.

"Who hired you?" I asked Richmond.

"You know I can't answer that," he said.

"Professional ethics? If you're helping someone who's trying to kill my cousin, you know you'll lose more than your license over it."

He rubbed his hand over his face. "I know my client isn't involved in anything like that."

"You don't sound too sure," Rachel said.

"I'm sure," he said, a little more forcefully. "If they wanted that type of work, they wouldn't have come to me. They know I wouldn't go for it."

"But maybe they handled the rough end of things themselves," she said, "once you located Travis."

"Or hired someone who wasn't so upstanding to complete their plans," I said.

"I don't believe—" he began.

"Before you tell us what you do and don't believe about your clients," I said, "think about Briana Maguire. You put her apartment under surveillance, even tried a little breaking and entering—"

"I didn't—"

"We talked to the neighbors," Rachel said. "Those old women have excellent memories. You made quite an impression on them. We wouldn't need more than that little bit of B-and-E to get your license yanked."

He picked up a pencil and started stabbing it into his desk blotter. He didn't look up at us, just frowned at the little indentations he was making.

"I know a detective in the Los Angeles Police Department who would be interested in hearing what we have to say about your surveillance of her," I said, "especially when we tell him what happened after you started keeping an eye on her son. He might not believe that the Maguires could get so unlucky all of a sudden, or that someone who was watching them so closely had no idea who tried to harm them."

"When I went over to her place, I didn't know she was dead," he said, still not looking up at us. "I just figured she had gone off to try to wheedle a few bucks off Spanning before he kicked."

Out of the corner of my eye, I saw Travis start to get up out of his chair. I was going to reach over, but Rachel had moved behind him, and gently but firmly put her hands on his shoulders. He sat back down, but Rachel kept her hands on him. *"Calma,"* she said softly.

"You're not in any position to be antagonizing us," I said.

It wasn't as easy as it usually is, but I stood up. "Sorry, Travis, I guess our next call is to—"

"Hold on!" Richmond said, then, more quietly, added, "Sit down, sit down."

I stayed on my feet.

"Please sit down." It was killing him.

"He owes Travis an apology," Rachel said.

His mouth became a tight line, but he finally said, "Sorry."

Rachel turned to me. "You hear anything?"

"Nope."

"I'm sorry, kid," he said to Travis.

"Let's get on with this," Travis said to me.

"I'll stay to listen to you," I said, "but don't make me sit back down in that chair."

Richmond didn't say anything. I decided to let the silence stretch a little, but Travis broke it first.

"For the record," he said tightly, "throughout the time they were separated, my mother never took a dime from my father."

"He already knows that," Rachel said quietly.

Richmond went back to jabbing his blotter.

"I can't give you my client's name," he said again. "Report me if you want to."

"There's something else you *can* give us," Rachel said, moving from behind Travis, strolling a little closer to the desk.

He looked up at her. "What?"

"Your files on the murder of Gwendolyn DeMont."

He shook his head, went back to his attack on the blotter. "Open case. You'll have to contact the Los Alamitos Police Department for that information."

She moved so fast, I didn't see exactly how it happened, but within the next few seconds she managed to reach across the desk, snatch the pencil from Richmond's hand and snap it in two.

Richmond looked up at her, slack-jawed.

"Don't push your lousy luck," she said. "Get the files!"

"I'm not turning them over to somebody who stands to gain from that woman's murder!" he shouted.

"You've had over a decade to prove your point," she shot back, "and you haven't come up with jack shit."

"That's not my fault!"

"Oh, really?"

"It's his fault," he said, pointing at Travis. "His and his mother's."

"And all the people in the emergency room that night," I said quietly.

He sat back in his chair.

"You're not going to let go of it," I said. "No one expects you to. But we want to find out who killed her—even if it turns out to be Arthur."

He gave a snort of disbelief.

"If you won't give us the files," Rachel said, "make copies."

"That would take all day!"

"You and I will work on it together," she said. "Irene and Travis have other things to do."

"So do I."

"No, you don't," she said flatly.

He looked among the three of us. He didn't find anyone in sympathy with him.

"Go on, Irene," she said. "I'll drop them off at your house later."

Travis stood up. Richmond looked at his bandaged hand and said, "I didn't plant that bomb. I'd never do something like that, especially not right outside a cop's house."

"So you've checked out our backgrounds," I said.

"Yours," he acknowledged.

"Then I should tell you that not only is Rachel a licensed PI, she's—"

"An ex-cop," he finished. "I could guess that much."

"A former homicide detective," I said.

He looked surprised.

"Phoenix," she said. "Retired."

"You're too young!"

She smiled. "Save your flattery for your society columnist."

He looked at me and said, "You'll tell her, won't you? Margot, I mean?"

"Tell her what?"

"That she doesn't have any reason to be afraid of me."

"I don't know that for a fact, do I?" I said, and left with Travis.

21

"You need to take a pain pill?" I asked Travis, who was look-ing down at his hand as it rested in his lap.

"No. Maybe later." He glanced over his shoulder as we pulled out of the parking lot. "Maybe we shouldn't leave Rachel alone with that guy."

"She can take care of herself. Or are you worried about his safety?"

He smiled a little, then lapsed back into silence.

"What's on your mind, Travis?"

"My uncle lives here in Los Alamitos. He raised my dad, but I've never met him. I guess I was just thinking about what Father Chris said."

"You've never met Gerald?"

"No. I'm not even sure where he lives. I just know it's somewhere in Los Alamitos."

Knowing I was going to hate myself for not going straight home and crawling into bed, I said, "Reach into my purse, and hand me the little notebook you find in there."

He did as I asked, and at the next stoplight, I flipped to the page where I had written the addresses Rachel gave me for the DeMonts and Gerald Spanning. We hadn't reached Spanning's street yet.

"I can take you there right now if you want to go," I said.

"But—you need to rest—"

"A short visit to your uncle won't do me in. Just call

Rachel at Richmond's office and let her know what's up."

He hesitated, then made the call.

When he finished, he said, "Maybe this isn't a good idea."

"Nervous?"

"Yes," he admitted, then added, "I'll be all right."

But a few minutes later he said, "Maybe we should call first."

"The only time I called him, I got the number off the computer, so I don't have it with me."

"You've talked to him?"

"Only very briefly, when I was looking for you."

"Oh."

"He said to ask you to give him a call someday."

"He did?"

There was so much hope in those two words, I wondered if I had set him up for disappointment.

He saw my hesitation and said, "Maybe he was just being polite."

"I don't know," I said, trying for a little more honesty, although polite was hardly the word I would use for my brief conversation with Gerald Spanning. "I hope he's home. I want to talk to him before I talk to the DeMonts."

"Why?"

"Several reasons. Your uncle was around the DeMont family for many years. He must know something about what your father's life with Gwendolyn was like, and that may be of help to us."

He seemed lost in his own thoughts.

As I slowed to search for Spanning's street, Travis said, "You haven't asked me many questions about the money."

"What money?"

"My father's money."

I made a right onto a street lined with a mixture of small wood-frame homes and two-story apartment buildings. "What about it?"

"Aren't you curious about what's going to become of his millions?"

"Millions?" I pulled over to the curb. We were nowhere near the address I was looking for, but this called for some discussion. I turned off the engine and said, "I guess that shouldn't surprise me, but it does."

"Of course, millionaires are fairly common these days—"

"Oh, sure. Thick on the ground."

"You're sitting next to one," he said.

We eyed one another for a moment. I blinked first. "Don't you need to talk to your father's lawyer before you start calling yourself a millionaire? See a will or something?"

"No. Like I said, he gave most of it to me before he died, through trusts. That was one reason my mother and I had a falling out. She told me it was blood money."

He fell silent, brooding for a moment.

"She must have changed her mind about that," I said. "I can't believe she married him if she thought he was a killer."

"Maybe. It wasn't for his money. Mr. Brennan said I had almost everything. When my father became . . ." He faltered, then said, "unable to care for himself because of the illness, he sold his properties, even his home. He kept enough to pay off his obligations. He—he died sooner than expected, so perhaps there was some small amount of money left in his estate."

"So you're this millionaire, riding around in a pickup truck, sleeping in the camper?"

He stared straight ahead, not answering.

"Jesus." I leaned my head back against the headrest. "And here I thought you were smart."

He looked back at me. "What I choose to do—"

"Travis," I interrupted, "why are you wasting your time with Rachel and me?"

"What?"

"You could hire dozens of people to help you out. And a couple dozen bodyguards while you're at it."

For some odd reason, this seemed to amuse him. "If I did," he asked, "would you stop looking for the person who killed my mother?"

"No, but that has nothing to do—"

"Why not?"

"Why not?" I repeated blankly.

He nodded.

I opened my mouth, shut it again.

"Tell me what you were going to say," he insisted.

"You wouldn't like it," I said, then muttered, "Probably wouldn't believe it."

He waited.

In the silence that followed, I suddenly found myself thinking of my mother—not one of the carefully sorted out memories I had of her, but an unbidden, sharp and perfect memory from an imperfect time: My mother is thin and fragile; her skin the color of ashes; her beautiful auburn hair thinned and dulled by chemotherapy; there are dark circles beneath her green eyes. As she lies propped up against the pillows in my parents' bed, she reminds me of a young bird fallen from its nest. Briana is with her, sitting next to her, on the edge of the bed.

Hoping to redeem myself with the angry God who has made her so ill, during these days I'm trying to be helpful, to not argue with Barbara, to be the good and quiet daughter I have never been. I've made tea, brought it in to them. I'm watching my mother. I've felt frightened for her for weeks, but for the last few days especially. She seems so tired, and at eleven, almost twelve, I'm old enough to see that she has considered a previously unthinkable notion— she has thought of giving up, of letting go. And now, entering the room with a small tray, I see that Briana has told her something that has made her cry. I'm upset until I realize they are happy tears.

"You must help us think of a name for your new cousin,"

Briana says, and seeing my confusion, my mother tells me my aunt is expecting a child.

I'm amazed at this news, and look at Briana's stomach, which doesn't look pregnant; I begin to refocus my attention on the adults' conversation only when I hear my mother say, "Yes, of course, I would be proud to be the baby's godmother." And the two of them are looking at one another, my mother's hand clasped in Briana's, as if they have pledged something to one another.

— ⌐

Travis said my name, bringing me back to the present, and I quickly wiped the back of my hand across my eyes.

"Are you okay?" he asked.

"Yes." I started the van again.

"Wait a minute," he said. "What wouldn't I believe?"

I had no idea what he was talking about.

"You said you'd keep looking for my mother's killer," he said patiently, "and that I wouldn't believe your reason for doing so."

"Let's just say it has something to do with who was able to attend my twelfth birthday party," I said. "Or that I owe something to your mother because the two of you once helped me through a rough patch."

He was quiet, then surprised me by saying, "You mean, when your mother was in the hospital?"

"I had forgotten that your mother told you about that."

"Yes," he said. "But she seemed to think she was in your debt for that."

I couldn't talk. I shook my head.

"There are undoubtedly lots of investigators who'd be happy to take my money," he said. "But I'd rather work with you and Rachel than with people who will never really give a damn about my mother."

"Thanks," I managed to say.

I pulled away from the curb again. As we reached the end of the block, I tried to find 12457 Acorn Street, the address Rachel had given me. At first I thought the number didn't exist, since there was nothing across the street from 12456, 12458 and 12460 except a long brick wall. But as we doubled back, I realized why I had missed it—12457 was a mobile-home park.

"There must be over a hundred trailers in there," Travis said. "Do you have a lot number?"

"No, but don't despair."

There were two security gates at the front entrance of the park, one for key card entry, one with a telephone for guests to use. There was a directory of residents last names and first initials. I saw one for "Spanning, G." Code number thirty-six. I picked up the receiver. No dial tone.

I tried entering thirty-six anyway. Nothing.

I sighed, put the receiver back in place.

"Don't give up yet," I said, and pulled the van around to the residents' gate. Travis grinned and we waited in a companionable silence. Within moments, a car pulled up behind me. A man, whose patience quickly wore thin. He honked at us.

"Allow me," Travis said, getting out of the van. He cradled his hand and walked up to the other driver. I kept my window down and watched him.

With a rueful look he approached the other driver and said, "I'm so sorry, sir. I cut my hand, and on our way out to the hospital, I guess we rushed off without our key card. If you'll just back up a bit, we'll move out of your way. My sister is due home from work any time now, and we'll just wait over there—" He began to point vaguely with his bandaged hand, winced, then appeared embarrassed. "Ah, we'll just get out of the way and wait for her to show up and let us in."

The other man was out of the car and inserting his key

card to let us in almost before Travis could get back to the van.

"You take care of that hand now," he said, waving off our profuse thanks.

"You little conniver," I said admiringly, as the gate closed behind us.

He smiled, but said, "Be sure to act like you know where you're going."

"I do."

"What?"

"We're looking for the neatly kept space, with a few flower pots, perhaps a whirligig, but most definitely a little American flag."

"A whirligig?"

"You know, those little lawn decorations that whirl with the wind—from ducks with wind-milling wings to dairy-maids that milk cows whenever a little breeze blows."

"God help us. Whose trailer will that be?"

"Our informant's."

"I thought you'd never been here before?"

"I haven't. But I've had to interview plenty of people who live in trailer parks. You learn."

Most of the homes in the park were double-wides and fairly neatly kept, but we didn't have to go far before we found a trailer that fit the bill; immaculate, appropriately decorated and—best of all—an aged but recently washed Ford Escort was parked in the carport. The owner was prob-ably home. I did a little more cruising around to make sure it was the leading candidate. There were some contenders, but I decided the first one was our best choice.

"She'll have a hat on," I predicted. "And she's already seen us." Travis shook his head, still not convinced that I knew what I was doing. But as I pulled up at the curb, an old woman came warily out of her mobile home. She was frowning.

"Note the straw bonnet," I said to Travis, and heard him choke back a laugh.

He suddenly seemed to enter into the spirit of the enterprise though, saying, "Stay here. My bandaged hand makes me less dangerous, your swollen face makes you scarier."

"Thanks a bunch," I said, but let him have his way. I rolled the passenger window down so that I could hear their conversation.

Travis got out of the van and gave her his most charming smile. She was obviously still suspicious, but that smile seemed to have the effect on her that it did on everyone else—she smiled back.

Travis—suddenly possessed of an accent any matinee buckaroo would take pride in—turned back toward the van and said, "Oh! Look here, Irene. Isn't this the most clever whirligig you ever did see?"

I waved from the van.

He crouched down beside one of them, staring at it as if it were the Shroud of Turin. "Why, it's even better than any of the ones we saw at the fair! Excuse me, ma'am, but where on earth did you find it?"

The object of this acclaim was a harness racer; the horse trotted in the wind, and the wheels of the rig moved. That Travis's admiration marked him as a rank amateur in whirligig appreciation mattered not one whit to the owner of this specimen.

"Oh, honey," she said, shaking her head sadly, "the fellow that made that passed on a couple of years ago. I've never seen another like it myself. He made it for me because I live out here near the track."

"I'm sorry for your loss," he said, without the least bit of insincerity. "But you have something very unique to remember him by, don't you?"

"Yes, yes, I do," she said wistfully.

"I'm Travis Maguire," he said, then gestured toward me. "And that's my cousin, Irene."

"Trudy Flauson," she said.

He cocked his head to one side and said, "I'll bet some school kids used to call you Mrs. Flauson."

She laughed. "Yes—only it's Miss Flauson. But I am a retired schoolteacher. How you guessed, I'll never know."

"Oh, I don't know," he said, apparently becoming bashful, "maybe you just reminded me of one of my favorite teachers. Well, I'm sorry if we disturbed you, ma'am, but I made Irene stop the car when I saw this yard. I just love whirligigs, and here you have half a dozen of them. We were all turned around anyway, so I said, 'Look at that pretty little yard, Irene. I want a closer look at that trotter.' And she said people in California might not like folks snooping around their yards, and were as like to shoot you as look at you, but I'm not from around here, so I said, 'This house is flying an American flag, and the yard so pretty, I'll take my chances that the owner knows varmints from honest folks. What's it going to hurt to stop for a minute?' "

In a lower voice, he said, "Can't blame her for being distrustful. Husband beats her."

She gave me a pitying look. I was going to strangle him.

"My mama asked me to come out here to try to get her to leave him. I'm also supposed to look up a third cousin of ours living here in Los Alamitos." He slaughtered the Spanish, making it sound closer to "Last Tomatoes."

"*Los Alamitos,*" she corrected. "It means 'little cottonwood trees.' "

He looked all around. "Cottonwoods? Where?"

"There used to be lots of them," Miss Flauson said, laughing.

He laughed, too, then suddenly stopped, wincing and holding his hand. He looked up, smiling bravely. "I guess we should get back to business. Thanks for letting me see your whirligigs."

"Honey, is that hand bothering you?"

"Oh, it's nothing."

"Don't let him tell you that!" I called. "Wilbur was going to hit me with a hot iron and Travis stopped him by grabbing it bare-handed."

Her eyes widened, and Travis turned bright red.

"Now, Irene, hush!" he said. "Ma'am, you don't need to hear all our troubles. And I didn't do anything anybody else wouldn't have done."

She winked at me, as if to say she knew a humble hero when she saw one.

"Well," he said, "we'd better try to find our way over to Cousin Gerald's place. He'll wonder why we never showed up."

"Gerald!" she said, scowling. "Gerald whom?"

"Spanning?" he said meekly.

"You mean to say you're looking for Gerald Spanning?"

"Yes, ma'am," Travis said.

"Which one?"

We looked blankly at one another.

"Junior or Senior?" she asked.

"Junior?" Travis said, looking at me with unfeigned surprise.

I stepped into the batter's box and called out, "I told you, Travis, that ever since Cousin Dolores passed on, nobody has been able to keep track of all the births in the family. Sorry, Miss Flauson, we didn't know we had a fourth cousin."

"Well, you may wish you never did learn about it. This one is no blood relations of yours, she's his wife. That's just what we call her around here. Her real name is Geraldine, and she's old Gerald's wife. So we call them Gerald Junior and Gerald Senior. Just nicknames."

"Oh" was all either one of us could manage.

"I have nothing to say against Gerald Senior," she went on. "He is one of the hardest-working men I ever hope to meet on this side of heaven. Drinks a little, but not more than most fellows around here. That's how he met her— she's a cocktail waitress. Mostly they keep to themselves, but Gerald Senior's always willing to lend a hand to a neighbor if need be. But that wife of his is another story." She paused, then said, "Well, I won't carry tales about your family. You'll see for yourself, I'm sure."

"They been married long?" Travis asked.

"No, not so long. Four or five years, perhaps."

"Thank you, ma'am," Travis said. "It would have been awful if we'd acted too surprised when we met her. Uh—I don't suppose I could ask you to point us in the right direction to my cousin's place?"

She was happy to oblige, describing not only the route, but the trailer itself. "I think I may have seen Gerald going to work this morning, but maybe he's back by now."

We thanked her profusely, and she waved to us as we drove off down the lane.

Once we were out of sight, Travis started laughing. "God, you are a sorry liar!"

"Me?"

"Wilbur? Caught a hot iron bare-handed? *Puh-leese*. And we already told her neighbor that I cut my hand. They might talk to one another."

"Oh, yeah? What about the fact that the guy with the cut hand has a sister that lives here? And doesn't have a rodeo accent?"

He grinned and shrugged. "We'll have to be more careful."

"No kidding. By the way—how did you know she was a teacher?"

"She had a small teacher's union sticker on the rear bumper of her car."

I congratulated him, then said, "Going back to the subject of being more careful—how many people know you're already in possession of your father's money?"

"Very few. My parents knew, of course. My father's lawyer, and Ulkins. And now you. That's it."

"You're sure?"

He nodded. "My father didn't trust many people."

We spotted the mobile home Miss Flauson had described to us: a large white double-wide with flower boxes full of red geraniums bordering the carport, which was empty.

"Doesn't look like they're home," Travis said.

"We've come this far; let's at least knock on the door."

There was a small, shady patio on the opposite side of the structure, under which sat two lawn chairs and a small, low table. There were no whirligigs on the Spanning lot, but there were wind chimes hanging from the carport awning.

The area around the trailer was neat and clean, uncluttered. We climbed the steps on the carport side and rang the bell.

The door opened, and as I first looked in through the screen, I thought we were being greeted by a young man. The reddish-blond hair of the person standing before us was shaved in a '50s-style flattop; a half-smoked Lucky Strike dangled from one corner of her hard mouth. She was either part armadillo or had spent too much time in the sun—I figured it to be a fifty-fifty bet either way. She wore absolutely no makeup; her eyes, squinting from the smoke, were small and dark beneath black brows that nearly met over her sharp nose. She was thin, wearing a man's sleeveless undershirt, a wide leather belt, blue jeans and leather work boots. There was a tattoo of a scowling pirate waving a sword near her collarbone on her right shoulder, the words "Pirate's Dream" scrolled above it. If the tattoo was a self-mocking joke, it referred to the old schoolboy's taunt to flat-chested girls: a pirate's dream was a girl with a "sunken chest." The appellation fit. Even with her arms crossed as they were now, she had the door, but absolutely no knockers.

"What the fuck do you want?" she said by way of greeting.

22

Travis gave me the briefest of glances, but enough to make me understand that he wanted to handle this. That rankled a little, but when I thought of how much he had seemed to enjoy playing out his little drama with Miss Flauson, I relented.

He regarded the woman before us now with open disapproval, but without speaking, staring long enough to make her nervously remove the cigarette from her mouth. But before she could speak again, he held up his left hand with an unmistakable air of authority and said, "Oh, no, please don't." The refined diction would have shocked Miss Flauson. He turned to me, slightly inclined his head in a thoughtful manner and said, "Apparently you were given the wrong address. I'm sorry. This is not Gerald's home."

It was all I could do not to bow and say, "Begging your grace's pardon."

He started back down the stairs. I followed.

"Hey," she called, opening the screen, but we kept walking.

"Hey, you!"

We had almost reached the van.

"You looking for Gerald Spanning?" she called.

He stopped and turned. "Do you know where he lives?"

"Right here."

"Impossible," he said.

"What?"

"Gerald Spanning would never greet a visitor to his home in the manner in which you just greeted us."

She scowled, then said, "Don't get your nose out of joint. What's your business with him, anyhow?"

He moved a little closer to her, and said in a low voice, "No one says something so vile as they open the door to complete strangers unless they are—one, intending to put someone's nose out of joint—or two, suffering from Tourette's syndrome. Are you suffering from Tourette's syndrome?"

"What the fuck is that?"

"Hmm. Difficult to say which the case may be—but I don't think I'll leave a message for Gerald with you. I hate to think how it would be translated."

"You look familiar," she said. "Do I know you?"

"As I said, we are complete strangers. Good-bye."

"Hold it, hold it!"

He waited.

"What do you want with Gerald?"

He sighed. "We aren't making progress here, are we?"

"What do you want, an apology? Okay, I'm sorry. There. You've got your damned apology."

"A very heartfelt and handsome one," he said. "Thank you. Now, where might we find Mr. Spanning?"

"He's not home. He's over at the house."

He arched a brow. "I beg your pardon?"

"We bought a house. Over on Reagan Street."

"Here in Los Alamitos?" I asked.

"Yeah, that's right," she said, apparently much happier to talk to me. "We can't live there yet, 'cause he's fixing the place up. Hang on."

She hurried inside. After a few minutes, she came back out with a slip of paper. She handed it to me. It had the number "10682" written on it. "That's the address. When you see him, tell him his wife said to get his—to come home," she amended, after glancing back at Travis.

She looked back at me and seemed suddenly unsure of us, eyeing the scrap of paper as if she wanted to take it back. I quickly put it in my pocket.

"He hit you?" she asked, indicating Travis.

"Do you find that likely?" he asked.

"Who are you guys?"

"Long-lost relatives, looking through the family tree," I said.

"No fooling," she said suspiciously, but then studied Travis. "He does look a little familiar . . ."

Travis thanked her and we were about to leave, when she suddenly shouted, "Wait! Here he comes!"

A big pickup truck with a construction toolbox on it pulled under the carport. A large, gruff-looking man wearing a T-shirt and shorts got out. She ran to him. He was tanned and muscular, his face weathered and his dark hair turning silver on the sides. He picked her up off her feet in a big bear hug, saying, "Hey there, sugar." He looked over her shoulder at us, puzzled for a moment, until he saw Travis.

His eyes widened, and he gently set his wife back down. She was starting to babble out an explanation to him, but Gerald seemed not to be listening. Looking straight at Travis, moving slowly forward, he said, "Good God in heaven . . . you're . . . you're Arthur's boy, aren't you?"

"Yes, sir," Travis said quietly—so quietly, I wondered if Gerald heard him. It seemed to me that all the mischief of a moment ago had been replaced by an anxiousness that he didn't quite manage to hide.

"Travis?" Gerald asked.

Travis nodded.

"Well, Travis," Gerald said, his voice breaking, "you're the spitting image of your dad." By the time he reached us there were tears running down his cheeks. Travis stepped forward, and Gerald extended a hand, but then, seeing the bandages, moved to one side and hugged Travis around the shoulders. "Lord 'a mercy," he said, looking down at his nephew. "Lord 'a mercy."

I watched Travis carefully; he returned the embrace, if a little awkwardly.

"Whew!" Gerald said, dashing away his tears. "Come on in, boy, come on in." Then, seeing me, he said, "Forgive me, I've lost all my manners." Without letting go of Travis, he said, "I'm Gerald Spanning, Travis's uncle Gerald."

"I'm Irene Kelly. Travis's cousin on his mother's side."

After the slightest flicker of hesitation, he smiled. "Yes, we spoke on the phone, didn't we? Well, bless your heart for bringing this boy to see me. Come in, come in. You've met Deeny, right? Her name is Geraldine, but that just confuses the hell out of everybody, so I call her Deeny."

"Better than what some of the old farts around here call me," she said, turning on her heel. She wasn't hiding her unhappiness—she seemed jealous of the attention Travis was getting from her husband—but she led the way into the trailer without protest.

"She's not much older than you are," Gerald confided to Travis, "so it's best you not call her *Aunt* Deeny."

The interior was roomier than might have been expected for a mobile home. It reeked of cigarette smoke, but was clean and neat. The furnishings looked as if they had been purchased in the '70s, although the mobile home itself didn't appear to be that old. Deeny gave a wave of her hand to indicate that we should have a seat. I sat on one of two avocado-green recliners; Travis, having smoothly extricated himself from Gerald's grasp, took the other one. Gerald didn't seem to mind taking a seat on the gold-and-brown couch, separated from us by a heavy, imitation walnut coffee table. There was a paperback on one corner, an action adventure story, with a bookmark near the last pages.

Deeny came back from the kitchen with four cans of

Coors still in their six-pack plastic collar. She sat down close to Gerald and pulled them free, popping tops and shoving a can at each of us without asking if we wanted one.

Gerald lifted his beer can as if for a toast, and Deeny stopped in the act of taking her first swig to hold hers up as well—so Travis and I followed suit.

"Mi casa es su casa," Gerald said, smiling at Travis.

"Speak American!" Deeny complained.

"English," Gerald corrected.

"Whatever," she said sullenly, earning a reproving look from Gerald. Her shoulders drooped a little and she asked, "Well, what did you say in Mexican?"

Gerald smiled at Travis and me, rolling his eyes. Her shoulders fell a little farther and he gave her a quick squeeze. "Oh, now," he said easily, "don't fret. It's just an old way of welcoming someone in Spanish. Kind of like saying 'Make yourself at home.' And that's what I want my nephew here to do—make himself at home."

"Thanks," Travis said.

"I take it Arthur doesn't know you're here?" Gerald asked.

I nearly missed seeing the sharp look Deeny gave him; I didn't know what to make of it, though. Travis, for his part, was remarkably self-possessed.

"I'm sorry to be the one to tell you that my father has passed away," he said.

"Arthur?" Gerald said, his eyes wide. "Arthur's dead?"

"Yes, sir," Travis said.

"No—no it can't be. Why, he's not even fifty!"

"No, sir. He was forty-eight. He died of cancer."

"Cancer?"

"Yes, sir. Last month."

"Arthur, dead a month . . . excuse me," he said, rising.

He walked away from us, down a short hallway, where I supposed the bedrooms were. Deeny got up and followed him, not saying a word.

Travis glanced over at me. "I didn't handle that very well, did I?"

"There's no easy way to tell someone something like that," I said.

"I feel terrible. I should have realized that he wouldn't know. I should have thought about it before we came over here."

I didn't say anything. We waited, neither one of us sure exactly how much time had passed since the Spannings went into the other room. We could hear their muffled voices every now and again, not able to make out any words, nor trying to. Travis grew edgier as time passed.

Sitting was only making me stiffer, so I stood and stretched.

"I don't want this beer," I said. "You want yours?"

He shook his head. He held the nearly full can up to me.

I took it from him, and picked up my own. I carried them into the kitchen and poured them down the drain. I rinsed out the cans and looked around for a recycling bin. I found a plastic grocery sack full of empty cans next to the trash can, and bent to put them in it. As I did, something in the trash can caught my eye.

A church bulletin. From St. Anthony's Catholic Church. I reached in and carefully extracted it from beneath a used wet coffee filter. I heard voices coming into the living room and quickly folded the paper. I had just stashed it in my back jeans pocket when I heard Deeny say, "What are you doing?"

"Just putting our beer cans in the recycling," I said.

I stood up and washed my hands, while she leaned against the counter, scowling at me. I could hear Gerald talking to Travis in the other room, but I couldn't make out what they were saying. When I reached for a hand towel, she said, "Make yourself at home, why don't you?"

"Mi casa es su casa," I said with a smile, taking perverse pleasure in watching her eyes narrow.

In the living room, Travis was sitting close to Gerald on the sofa, their heads bent over something. Gerald had a pair of reading glasses on. As I drew closer, I realized they were looking through a photo album. Travis looked up at me and patted the empty space next to him. "Sit next to me, you'll enjoy this."

I did, then we all scooted over again to allow Deeny to sit on the other side of Gerald. She ended up draping herself over his shoulders, sitting more behind him than next to him, but he didn't seem to mind. He reached up and took her arms in his hands, stroking his fingers along her forearms. He let Travis hold the album.

Travis turned back a few pages. "Look! Here's a photo of my great-grandparents. The Spannings. And that was their farm."

He pointed to a black-and-white photo of an elderly couple standing in front of a Model A. There was a narrow two-story house in the background, and open fields beyond. The photo wasn't well-focused and you couldn't make out much of their features. The man was wearing a hat, the woman a plain and modest dress.

He turned the page forward, pointed out other views of the farm, photos of great-aunts and -uncles. With these, he had help from Gerald, who seemed moved by Travis's enthusiasm. He smiled whenever Travis correctly named the people in the photo, studied Travis with apparent fondness as Travis studied the album.

"That's my grandfather," Travis said of a grimy, barefooted boy in overalls. The boy, about twelve years old, wore a cap at a rakish angle; his charming smile had been passed down to the next two generations of Spannings.

Travis stared at the photo for a long time before turning to another section. There were photos of the maternal sides of the family, and a few of the town in Missouri that was closest to the family farm.

Eventually Travis came to photos of Gerald as a young

boy. There were not many photos of Gerald and Arthur's immediate family. One showed Gerald at about the age of five standing next to a chair shared by two smiling toddlers.

"Those were your aunts," he said softly. "Lizzy and Mary Lee. They never got to be much older than you see them there. Those were the hardest years. Farm was lost and we would just stay wherever we could. I think we were with one of my aunts then. There were two other little babies didn't even live long enough to take a picture of them. A little boy, Charlie, and another girl, Bonita. That about broke your grandmother's heart. I didn't get to know the babies, of course, but I sure missed Lizzy and Mary Lee."

"What happened to them?" Travis asked.

"Oh, the babies just never were likely to live; they were both born in the winter, and one came early. They each only lived a few days. And the girls, they caught a fever and I guess they just weren't strong enough to fight it." He ruffled Travis's hair. "So I was pretty excited when your daddy came along. I'd started to think I wasn't ever going to have anybody else to play with."

Travis smiled and turned to another page. There was a grainy photo of Gerald, about nine, standing with his father and several other men in the doorway of a boxcar.

"Look at that sorry bunch of stiffs," Gerald said, laughing.

"Who took the photo?" I asked.

"Oh, I think it was one of the wives of the other fellows. She stayed with my mother when my mother was pregnant with Arthur. Mama didn't want to leave the sugar beet farm. She said she wasn't going to have any more babies after this one, and she wasn't going to lie down in some hobo jungle to give birth to her last child."

There was a photo of a well-dressed older man standing in what might have been a very dignified pose, had he not had his hand on the shoulder of a grinning young rascal of about twelve.

"That's me and Papa DeMont," Gerald said.

"I've heard a lot about him," Travis said, and studied this photo closely.

Gerald glanced quickly at me, then said to Travis, "Then you know he owned the sugar beet farm. Miss Gwen's daddy. He was good to the children. His permanent workers—like me and your grandparents—lived in little old houses, but compared to what we were used to, they were palaces. Old Papa DeMont always made sure no one went hungry. And he'd bring treats for the children. He was just plain good."

On the next page was a wedding photo. Travis stared at it for a long time. Gwendolyn stood between Gerald and Arthur, her smile faint but serene. She was wearing a simple dress and pillbox hat, not a bridal gown and veil, and she held a small bouquet. She was not an unattractive woman; she had dark hair and big brown eyes. Arthur, tall but clearly hardly more than a boy, stood smiling tensely at her side. There was something different about him in this photo, something that went beyond that tension.

Gerald, who at the time would have been about twenty-six, looked much older than my cousin did now, at nearly the same age. In the photo, Gerald's smile was one of satisfaction. If I hadn't known the history behind the marriage, I would have pointed him out as the groom, though both Spanning brothers were young enough to have been her sons.

"Was Arthur generous with you once he had married Gwendolyn?" I asked.

His eyes narrowed. "Did I get a payoff when they were married, you mean? Hell, no, and I didn't want any, even though I was the one that always took care of Arthur, gave up everything for him. DeMonts wouldn't believe it, so I got together with Gwenie's lawyer and signed an agreement saying I'd never get a penny of Papa DeMont's money."

"So Arthur never loaned you money?"

"His own," he admitted grudgingly, then added, "by that I mean he loaned me money from his own business. That gardening business. DeMonts never could believe that Arthur made a little bit of his own money."

"How well do you know Horace DeMont, Gwendolyn's uncle?" I asked.

"That old good-for-nothing?" Gerald scoffed. "I know all I need to know. He thinks he's better than anyone on God's green earth, but the truth is, he lost every nickel he owned speculating on the stock market, and for a time he was as much a vagabond as any Spanning ever was. In fact, Travis, your grandfather met him on the road, and that's how we came to the sugar beet farm, because even though old Horace was complaining, my daddy could tell there was plenty of work to be had."

"Horace DeMont was a vagabond?" I said in disbelief.

Gerald laughed. "Oh, yes. Him and that brat of his, Robert. In fact, one day when he was looking down his big nose at us, I told Bobby that my daddy had once seen him giving testimony at the Sally Ann in Chicago. He denied that he was ever any mission stiff. But later, when people started romanticizing about what it was like to ride on Old Dirty Face he bragged he had done it, like he was Jack Kerouac himself, to which I said, 'Yeah, except Bobby wasn't a hobo, just an old moll buzzer.' That made him mad as fire."

"Speak English!" Deeny interrupted.

"Oh, sorry honey, I just fall into that way of talking whenever I think about those years on the road. Well, here's how it is: There are hoboes, and there are tramps and there are bums. A hobo is a working stiff—he's a migrant worker, that's all. His labor built this country much as anybody else's. You don't believe it, go pick fruit for a summer, or herd cattle or dig ditches or lay rails. Hoboes did all that. That's what we Spannings did when we were riding rails—

we looked for work, went wherever we could find it.

"Now, a tramp is just a fellow who doesn't believe in working if he can avoid it, but he keeps moving. It's a kind of philosophical thing with some of them, I supposed you'd say. Sometimes they call them scenery bums. That's not the same thing I mean when I call a man a bum, though.

"A bum is a man who stays in the city, usually down on skid row. He's not working, he's not moving, he's on the bum.

"Now, the categories aren't so neat, and any man may take a turn at being one or another of those fellows, mostly depending on how fond he is of old redeye."

"Redeye?" Travis asked.

"Whiskey."

"And Sally Ann?"

"Salvation Army. A mission stiff is a man who spends a lot of time getting saved so that he can get free flops and food."

"Old Dirty Face?" I asked.

He smiled. "A freight train."

"And what's a moll buzzer?" Deeny asked.

"Guy that mooches off women. That's what old Bobby did, and his old man, Horace—why, he probably taught him all he knew. Then they got in some kind of trouble over it out in Boise back in the summer of '40 and the town clowns threw Bobby in the jail. Now, most fellows would see that as part of the deal and not fuss over it. But I think the charges must have been something out of the ordinary vag charges, because old Horace cried to his daddy about it."

"What are town clowns and vag charges?" Deeny asked.

"Oh, sorry, honey. Town clowns are police. And vag charges are vagrancy charges. But they treated old Bobby like he was some kind of yegg, and as much as I don't like him, I don't think he was ever a yegg."

"Which is?" she asked, not hiding her irritation.

"Well, I mentioned hoboes and tramps and bums, but there was another class of people out there, and they spelled trouble for everybody else—the yeggs. Those were the real hardened criminals—safecrackers and gangs of thieves and killers and people who did things I'd just as soon not mention. Horrible things. They were out there riding the rails, running from the law, raising the devil. They were really more dangerous to the hobo than just about anybody, but a lot of the local cops didn't see any difference between a yegg and a hobo, so they treated us all the same.

"Anyway, Horace cried to his daddy and Papa DeMont bailed Bobby out. He brought them home and read Bobby up one side and down the other. Told him to haul himself up by the ass pockets and act like a man.

"I guess somewhere in all that Bobby heard what he needed to hear—but more likely he just had the jam scared out of him when he got arrested. But for whatever reason, Bobby got all respectable after that. Even fought in the war. And I hear tell that old Horace is still alive, but he must just be living on his meanness. Doug, his oldest boy, he died awhile back. I don't know if Bobby's still around or not."

"You must have been fairly young when Bobby was arrested," I said. "How do you remember that?"

"Oh, well, first off, because Papa DeMont liked my dad—Travis's grandfather. And because my daddy knew his way around that part of the country, Papa DeMont sent him up there, along with Zeke Brennan—"

"Zeke Brennan?" Travis said. "He must have been young, too."

Gerald laughed. "I'm talking about Ezekiel Brennan, Senior. He was the father of your daddy's lawyer. Old Zeke didn't drive, but your grandfather did. So they were going up there with the bail money and bring the two of them back. School just got out for the summer, and my dad took me with him. Papa DeMont let my dad take one of his cars, and that was my first ride in an automobile over any great distance. A big old Bentley. That was some car. I suppose that's mainly why the trip stayed in my mind. And Papa DeMont didn't usually lose his temper with people, so it was something to see him so mad at the two of them."

There were a few other photos in the album, but not many. Most were of Arthur and Gerald together. A few were pictures of the sugar beet factory, apparently taken not long before it closed down.

"How long did you work there?" I asked.

"Oh, let's see. We first came out here in 1938, when I was just about to start school. It was after the girls died; your grandmother decided she never wanted to live where it was cold again, and she found work in a café in the off-season, so she stayed here. Your granddad wanted me to get an education."

"Were you able to go to school?" Travis asked.

"Oh, yes, for a time. And some of my schooling was on the road. Whenever work at the factory got a little slow, my father would take me with him and we'd go rambling, hire out wherever we could. I met some amazing fellows in those days. At the time, during the Depression, there were some highly educated men riding the rails. And the road itself will teach all kinds of lessons you won't get in a classroom—some good, some bad. Anyway, we never left for very long at a stretch, because he didn't like being away from your grandmother. I did go to school here pretty regular up until your grandparents died. Then it was up to me to take care of your daddy, and Papa DeMont always made sure I had work on his place after that."

"What do you do for a living now, Uncle Gerald?"

"Oh, a long time ago, your father loaned me some money to start my own business," he said. "I buy old houses, fix 'em up and sell them. I've done well for myself, and I paid your daddy back. He wasn't going to let me, but I did. I think he felt like I took good care of him, so . . ." His eyes clouded up, and he left the sentence unfinished.

He seemed to struggle with himself, then said, "I never did like the way he carried on with your mother. There, I've said it. I thought he was throwing his whole life away, and after Papa DeMont had been so good to us, I just figured your father had shamed our family. It was dishonest, really, and hurtful to someone who had never hurt him. Then he was mad at me, because I guess he did love you and your mother so much, and there were hard, hard words between us after Gwen was killed. We never spoke again."

Travis slowly turned the pages of the photo album back, until the front cover was closed. "Do you think he killed her?" he asked.

"No," Gerald answered without hesitation. "That wasn't your daddy's way. Never think that, not for one second."

I looked at my watch. "We have to be going," I said, to Gerald's dismay and Deeny's too-obvious relief.

"Can't you stay a little longer?" Gerald asked.

Travis's cellular phone rang, and he answered it, then said, "Yes, just a moment." He handed it to me. "It's for you, it's Detective Collins."

I took the phone, and said, "Hi, can I call you back in a few minutes?"

"Sure," he said. "No privacy?"

"No."

We hung up.

"A friend of my husband's," I explained to the Spannings, giving the phone back to Travis.

"We'd better go," Travis said.

When we reached the van, Gerald gave Travis another hug, and this time, Travis returned it easily.

"Come over again," Gerald said. "We have a lot of catching up to do."

"I will," Travis said. "Thanks for showing me the photos."

"I'll have some copies made for you," he said.

"Thank you," Travis said.

"How can I get ahold of you?" he asked.

Travis glanced over at me. "I'm staying with Irene."

"You could stay here if you like," Gerald said. "We've got plenty of room."

Even without looking over at Deeny, who was pouting so openly she was shading her chin with her lower lip, Travis shook his head. "That's kind of you, but I've got some other people to see in Las Piernas, so I might as well stay there. Maybe I'll visit you after things settle down a little."

"Sure," Gerald said. "That's fine."

Travis gave Gerald his cell phone number. Gerald thanked him. "I've worked on a lot of places in Las Piernas," he said to me. "What part of town do you live in?"

"We're near the beach," I said.

"You should see their garden," Travis said.

Gerald smiled. "I'd like that. But mostly I'd like to see you again."

Reed's call was just a warning that Frank had already heard about today's trouble. "But not from me," he swore to me. "You know how it is around here; something this dramatic, the whole office is talking about it. He called in today before I could warn everybody to keep it quiet."

I thanked him for the call and hung up.

The rest of the ride home was in silence.

"Why don't you like him?" Travis asked, as we pulled up at my house.

"Who are you talking about?"

"My uncle."

"Your uncle appears to be a charming man. I have no reason to dislike him."

There was a stubborn set to his jaw, but he didn't argue.

Rachel pulled up as we were getting out of the van. She carried two big envelopes.

"Ah, just one big happy family," she said as she reached us. I've never doubted her powers of observation.

"Anything interesting in the files?" I asked.

"Oh, yes," she said. "I've read through them once, but they deserve some real study."

She quickly coaxed Travis into telling her about our adventures in the trailer park, and his mood lightened. He was a storyteller, and he told this one well.

As he went on and on about his uncle, I realized that for him, this was a vital connection—that Gerald Spanning was someone who could tell him about a group of people his father had been too young to know—grandparents and other relations. He now had a family to identify himself with, a family denied to a bastard child.

I felt the paper folded in my back pocket and found myself wishing I hadn't seen it, wanting to be rid of it, hoping it wasn't important.

In the end, literally, the dogs betrayed me.

23

I walked into the house first, listening to Travis say to Rachel—for perhaps the third time—"You'd really like him." Deke and Dunk came forward to greet us but never moved on to Travis and Rachel, becoming quite fascinated with my rear pocket.

Their intense sniffing of one of my ass cheeks, even as I turned from them and tried to shoo them off, did not go unnoticed by my companions.

"They want whatever that is in your back pocket," Travis said, laughing. "What is it?"

Since Deke showed every sign of being willing to pull the bulletin out of my pocket if I didn't, I reached back and removed it, holding it high and snapping an irritable command at them to get down as I kept moving toward the kitchen.

They obeyed, skulking off with tails down, but casting reproachful looks back at me—making me believe the guilt trip was not, after all, a human invention.

There was a noticeable silence in their wake. Both Travis and Rachel were staring at me. I made myself unfold the coffee-stained paper enough to see that the date on it was the same as the one on the bulletin I had found among Briana's possessions. I suddenly felt tired.

Rachel said, *"Che cosa è?,"* but Travis was closer and he took it from my hand.

"A church bulletin from St. Anthony's?" he said, and I heard Rachel's quick intake of breath.

"Where did you find it?" she asked.

"In the trash can under the Spannings' sink."

"What were you doing looking through their trash?" he asked sharply.

I didn't answer. I went into the living room and tried to make peace with the dogs.

"Travis," Rachel said, "open it up. Read through the announcements."

He stared at her for a moment, then slowly obeyed. All the color left his face. She put an arm around his shoulders, took the bulletin from him, and led him to where I was sitting, putting him between us on the couch. He was looking at me in confusion.

"It announced my father's funeral Mass," he said.

"Yes. Your uncle already knew your father was dead."

"But that means—oh, God!" he said miserably. "It means he was just putting on an act! That goddamned—" But as he said it he looked at me, and I was much handier than Gerald. *"You knew!"* he said angrily. *"You knew* that he was faking grief for my father, and you didn't say anything to me! I asked why you didn't like him and you said, 'Your uncle appears to be a charming man. I have no reason to dislike him!'"

This last was repeated in a mincing la-de-da tone that I have never used in my life. I ignored that, and the anger. "I saw the bulletin in their trash when I was getting rid of the beer cans. It looked like the one I found when I was going through your mom's papers, but Gerald and Deeny came back out into the living room before I could do more than stuff it in my back pocket. I didn't have time to check the date on it. Until just now, for all I knew, that bulletin could have been from a year ago."

"But in the car . . ." He looked away from me. "Never mind, I understand."

"I'm sorry, Travis," I said.

"For what? Sorry that the Spannings are a pack of liars? Christ, there must be something in the DNA. A beguiler's gene."

Rachel laughed, surprising him into smiling back at her. "I do a good job of feeling sorry for myself, don't I?" he said.

"Not especially," she replied easily. "Most people I know, if they had the kind of weekend you're having, they'd be throwing tantrums or getting drunk or locking themselves up in dark rooms for a good long cry."

"All of those ideas sound great to me right now."

"Nobody would blame you. How's the hand?" she asked.

He shrugged. "If I'm distracted, it doesn't bother me. When I was pretending I was someone else at the mobile home park, or looking at the photos . . ."

"You want a pain pill?"

"No," he said. "A distraction."

"Well, I've got the murder files, but are you really up to that?"

He hesitated, then said, "Sure."

She looked over at me and said, "What about you? You're looking a little worn down."

"I'll get a couple of aspirins. I'll be all right."

"I'll get them for you," she said, standing.

Travis turned to me and said, "I'm sorry I snapped at you."

"It's okay. And by the way, I think there are plenty of people to be proud of on the Spanning side of your family."

For a moment I thought that little bit of understanding was going to be his undoing. I saw his eyes tear up, but he struggled to pull himself back under control. I got up to check my answering machine, just to give him a minute to himself. There was a message from Margot, saying she was back home and asking me to stop picking on Harold Richmond. Rachel, overhearing it, rolled her eyes.

"I guess I hadn't really expected her to stay away from him," I said.

There were two messages from McCain, requests to give him a call—polite as usual. Rachel just shook her head at those. I took the aspirin.

Travis was still thinking about Gerald. When we sat back down on the couch, he said, "Why? Why would he lie about something like knowing my father was dead?"

"I'm not sure. Maybe he just wanted a chance to leave the room with Deeny, to talk to her out of earshot. When we first came in, I caught her giving him surprised looks a couple of times. Something was going on there, I'm just not sure what."

"Or he wanted me to believe he really missed my dad, wanted the two of us to share sympathy—have something that would bring us together."

"I don't know. He could have done that without the lie." I thought for a moment while Rachel, who had ignored two empty chairs to sit down on the floor in front of us, began pulling copies out of envelopes. The envelopes made me think of the DeMont inheritance. "I hate to ask this, Travis, but have *you* made a will?"

"Yes. I provided for my mother," he said, and again I saw him struggle for self-control. After a minute he said, "I guess I'll have to make a new one. I'll talk to Mr. Brennan. I—I wanted to talk to him anyway, about setting up an endowment in my father's memory, something for local adult literacy programs."

"That's a good cause," Rachel said absently. "I had an aunt—came here from the old country. She learned to read from one of those programs—adult school, at night."

"Irene didn't tell you?" Travis asked.

"I wanted to respect your confidences—" I began.

"Yes," he interrupted, "and I appreciate it."

"Tell me what?"

"My father was illiterate."

"Really?" She took a moment to absorb this information, then said, "He did so well for himself—your father must have been quite a man."

"Yes, he was. Charming, resourceful and bright. A bigamist, a liar and—well, let's look at the file. You worked in homicide, Rachel. Maybe you can tell me if my father was also a murderer."

24

"I'm not sure," she said. "But I can definitely tell you that you shouldn't hire Mr. Richmond to do any detective work for you."

"Why not?" I asked.

"Oh, he may not be bad at tracking people down, but he should have handed this homicide investigation over to people who knew what they were doing. He sure as hell didn't."

"What did he do wrong?"

"Well, the scene was obviously unnecessarily disturbed before the coroner got there—lots of people moving in and out of the room, touching things they shouldn't have been handling—Richmond, too. Looks like some of that started before he got there, though, so he can't take all the blame.

"The worst thing he did was to break rule one—he had an easy suspect and he worked backwards from there, instead of keeping an open mind while he looked at the evidence. Once he had your dad figured for this, Travis, he wasn't going to budge from that position. He's still defensive about it."

"Why am I not surprised?" Travis said, sighing.

"So tell us what you think," I said.

"Well, let's start with the basics. She was stabbed to death. Someone placed a pillow over her head—apparently not pressing down hard enough to suffocate her, but enough to keep her quiet—and went at her with a knife. No weapon left at the scene, but they could tell it was a knife both from the wounds and because a small piece of the tip of the knife broke off when it struck a bone.

"There were no prints. Arthur's prints were in the house, all right, but not anywhere unexpected. Killer was wearing gloves."

"Wait!" I said, as she was about to go on. "Are you sure?"

"What do you mean?"

"I mean, are you certain the killer wore gloves?"

She picked up one of the stacks of paper and flipped through it. She read one page for a moment, then said, "Yes. There was a lot of blood, and they found bloodstained prints of gloved hands on some of the surfaces in the bedroom.

"Then his hand . . . ," Travis said.

Rachel looked sharply at him. "What are you talking about?"

Travis told her what he had told me on the beach—but in slightly more detail, telling of seeing his father approach the house, and touch the glass—that Arthur's hand was bloody, but not his clothing.

"Why didn't you say something about this before?" she asked angrily.

"Can't you guess why he didn't?" I said.

She calmed down a little. "Which hand? Which hand had the blood on it?"

He closed his eyes. "His left hand."

"You're sure?"

He nodded.

"A few drops of blood, lots of blood, what?"

"It—it coated his palm. When he put it on the glass, it made a hand print. A red hand print. That's what I drove my own fist through."

"How far did you live from the DeMont farm?"

He shrugged. "About fifteen minutes away."

"Less if someone were in a hurry," I said. "And at that time of night, there wouldn't be much traffic."

"Did your dad ever tell you how his hand ended up coated in blood?" she asked.

"He said he had gone into her room. The lights were out, but the room wasn't completely dark. He could make out her shape on the bed. But she wouldn't answer when he called to her, and there was a smell—he said it was an awful smell. He said he leaned his left hand on the mattress as he reached with his right to turn on the lamp near her bed." He stood and demonstrated, using the couch as a stand-in for the mattress, placing his weight on his left hand as he reached out with his right. "It felt damp. When the light was on, he saw that his hand was in a pool of blood, Gwendolyn's blood. He could tell that she was dead. He became frightened and turned out the light, then left. He panicked, he said, and the first person he thought of turning to was my mother, so he drove to our house, but then he realized that it wasn't really his home anymore, and that he had no right to be there. He also felt sure that his own life was in danger, that he would be accused of murder."

"He talked about it that night?"

"What I've just told you I learned later, when I talked to him about the handprint on the window. I know he talked about it with my mother that night—she came downstairs and asked what had happened, and I told her I had cut my hand. He was only worried about me then, but she asked him what he was doing there—it wasn't asked in an angry way. And he said, 'We have to get him to a hospital.' She asked again why he was there, and he said, 'Because I need my family.'

"I have to admit that I wasn't really paying much attention after that, because my hand was bleeding and I was focused on that. I just remember that we got into his car, and my mother drove, and he held on to me in the backseat, as if I were a much younger child, but I remember liking it, feeling safe and—" He paused, then said, "I had a towel wrapped around my hand, but I still bled all over him. I remember watching the stain soak from the towel onto his shirt and telling him I was ruining it. He said not to worry about it, the shirt wasn't important, I was the one who mattered most to him. I remember him trying to soothe me, to keep my mind off my hand. I think he must have told my mother something about Gwendolyn's murder while they first took a look at my hand in the emergency room, because Mom was the one who got rid of the car."

"She what?" I asked, shocked.

He turned red. "Whatever my father is guilty of, my mother engaged in a criminal act that night. When we first got to the emergency room, it was really busy, so they just cleaned my cuts and then put some kind of a temporary bandage on my hand, just to stop the bleeding until the hand surgeon could come in. My dad stayed with me while they were doing that, and Mom went out to the car. She wiped off the steering wheel and the door handle, then took the car to a bar not far from the hospital and left it parked in the parking lot. She said she thought of setting it on fire, but decided that would attract too much attention, and might result in damaging someone else's property. So she just left it there and walked back and waited for us in the waiting room."

Apparently Rachel was just as stunned as I was, because she just sat there staring at him.

"She was really very cool-headed about it. I had seen that side of her before—the protectiveness, I mean. Mom was shy and timid, except in one circumstance: when anything threatened someone she loved. Then she turned into this fierce Irish warrior woman."

I smiled. "My mother wasn't as shy as Briana, but she was just as protective of her family. God help anyone who so much as said a word against any of us."

"So the car wasn't really stolen?" Rachel said.

"Well, yes, it was, but from that lot—not the hospital, I mean. She said she thought it might get stolen, because it was a tough neighborhood. The car was a new T-Bird, and she left the windows down and the doors unlocked. The more my father and I thought about it, the more we realized how dangerous it had been for her to be walking around in that area by herself at two-thirty in the morning. God knows who might have come out of that bar. My mother always said a lot of prayers for that car thief—that he'd keep the car and never steal another. She was grateful to him for putting a little truth in her lies to the police."

"Your dad didn't know what she planned?" I asked.

"No. Neither of us did. We were both amazed when she told us."

"But what if the police had found the car?"

"Well, I suppose she thought that it might help my father's lawyer raise some questions about where the blood came from—if the police had found any traces of blood on it. But mainly she wanted the police in Las Piernas to be able to attest to the fact that my dad was there that night."

"How long were you at the hospital?" I asked.

"Oh, a long time. I had to have surgery, because I had severed a bunch of tendons. I wasn't ready to go home until about ten or eleven o'clock the next morning; then we couldn't find the car. So by the time we talked to the hospital security people and did the police report—they just took the report by phone—and hired a taxi to come home, it was early afternoon on Saturday. We were all exhausted.

"My parents put me to bed, then they stayed up talking for a while. I was really excited, because I thought they were getting back together. Then when I woke up, late on Saturday, my mother told me that Gwendolyn had been murdered, and that my father didn't kill her, but he would be blamed. She said that if anyone ever asked me, my father had been home with us all evening. I guess I knew right at that moment that we would only have a little time together. There wasn't any way that things were ever going to be okay again. Maybe I should have told the truth to the police, but I loved my father—I had figured that out that night, when I got hurt, that even if I was angry with him about some things, I loved him. If he were alive right now," he said, his voice breaking, "I would lie for him again."

Neither one of us said anything. I could tell that his story didn't sit well with Rachel, but she didn't criticize him. I sat trying to imagine what it would have been like to be an eleven-year-old boy in that situation.

"Rachel," I asked, "wouldn't his hand print have remained in the blood on the sheet?"

"It probably was there," she said, "and might still be on the sheet if they've kept it. But as I said, the scene was disturbed. The housekeeper and several other people—including Richmond—were leaning on or kneeling on the bed to look at the victim. It may have gone unrecognized after that."

Travis drew a deep breath and said, "So, back to distraction. What have you got to show us, Rachel?"

Rachel pulled out one of the copies of the crime scene photos. It was a sharp image in black and white—too sharp.

"That's an actual print, not a photocopy," I said.

She smiled. "Switched them on old Richmond. I'll give these back to him when we're done with them."

"Rachel—"

"Hell, he's had over a dozen years to look at these things. If he hasn't memorized them by now, he's a bigger jerk than I think he is."

Travis was half looking at it, half looking away.

As crime scene photos go, it wasn't one of the more gory ones I've seen. It was a shot taken inside Gwendolyn DeMont's bedroom, from across the room, looking toward the bed. The body was not uncovered; there was form under a single, bloodstained sheet. A pillow lay across the face.

Rachel looked at it dispassionately. "There's a lamp here where your dad said he reached for one."

She handed the photo toward him, and when he shrank back from it, she gave it to me. She moved on to the next photo, which was taken directly over the bed. It was easy to see why Arthur knew his wife was dead. The one part of her that could be seen between pillow and sheet was her throat, which lay slashed open like a strange dark mouth.

"That was probably one of the last blows," Rachel said. "Not much bleeding for that type of cut, no arterial spray. I think she was already dead when the killer got around to this slice. The ones over her chest and stomach bled more."

I made myself ask, "What about spatter patterns?"

"That's some of the best evidence—Richmond and the housekeeper didn't touch the walls and ceiling." She thumbed through the photos and handed me several.

"Even though there isn't blood all over the place, you can tell that her killer really went at it," she said. "There's a pattern to the spray—it's called cast-off blood, because it was projected or cast from an object, not the site of the wound; it came from the weapon, not directly from the victim, like this arterial spurting, here and here." She pointed to large spots with long drips running down from them.

"Look at this, then," she said, showing me other, finer drops. "A bloodstain specialist could give you a good estimate of how far, how fast, and at what angle this blood traveled from the knife, and would have been able to count the blows delivered.

"See the way the spray arcs up the walls, even to the ceiling? Look at the close-ups of the spatter—at the shape of the blood drops. See the tails on these drops? They're more elongated as they're more distant from the source. And they indicate two directions—up and back down. He was really putting some swing into it." She demonstrated with a closed fist, making a motion that would bring a knife up high above the killer and back down in a powerful sweeping curve. "I'd say this killer was pissed."

She handed me other photos, not as close up as the previous ones. "Some of the spray is blocked," she said, pointing to places on the photos—on the ceiling and the wall nearest the foot of the bed—where there seemed to be "shadows," or areas where something blocked the spray of blood. "See here?" she said, "and here?"

I nodded, and tried not to think about throwing up.

"There was some spatter on the floor, but according to the reports, this housekeeper had started cleaning up before the scene was secured. Mopped the floor and opened the windows to let some air in. Neither action helped out as far as preserving evidence goes, but the blood traces were found with chemicals used by the lab guys. There was a single bloody footprint impression found on the farther side of the sheets, probably made when he got up off the bed. And in the hallway going to the front door, they did find a series of very faint bloody footprints. So there were probably footprints in the room before she started mopping."

"From a bare foot?" Travis asked.

"No, the sole of a man's shoe."

"So the killer was male?" I asked.

"Yes, probably," she said.

"What size shoe?"

She looked through the file, then said, "Eleven."

"A big man, then."

"Possibly. Most men wear between an eight and a ten-and-a-half."

"Do you know your father's shoe size, Travis?"

He shook his head. "I could probably find out."

I was trying to picture the killer's actions from what she had told us. "He stood on the bed?"

"No. I think the killer straddled her, pinned her arms down with his knees—there was some bruising there—muffled her screams with the pillow—used his left hand to hold the pillow on her face. Her hands were beneath the covers, no chance to scrape or claw him—nothing found under her nails.

"Killer is probably right-handed—see how the left arm blocked some spray? So did his body, as he bent over her. Wounds are all in the victim's upper body. The autopsy studies of the wounds also indicate a righty doing the work."

"Attacker was above the bedding the whole time?" I asked. "No sign of rape or molestation by her attacker?"

"They did all the usual tests during the autopsy—no recent sexual activity." She handed over the next one, which showed the body without the pillow or sheet.

"Excuse me," I heard Travis say weakly, and he hurried out of the room. I was regretting the fact that the house had only one bathroom. I winced and pushed the photos back at her.

"Sorry," she said, but there was an unrepentant gleam in her eye.

"So do you think Arthur told him the truth?"

She lifted one shoulder. "I don't know. It's certainly possible. I guess the old cop in me ain't dead yet, because it pisses me off that these people never spoke up. I guess it never occurred to any of them that someone got away with murdering this woman."

"I think you're wrong about that, Rachel. It probably occurred to them every day, and they felt guilty. I think that's what kept Briana and Arthur apart all those years: Gwendolyn's ghost."

"Maybe, but I still don't like it. They gave false information to people who were only trying to find the murderer."

"You've met Richmond. Do you really believe that? Can you blame them? Arthur would look perfect to any prosecutor. A fortune at stake; an older, reclusive wife; a secret family in another town—"

She sighed. "It's one thing when an adult makes up his or her mind to impede an investigation. Another to force a kid to go along with the program. Who carried the biggest burden in all of this? Your cousin. You think it was right for them to involve him in this?"

"No, but I don't doubt they loved him, and I think they would have avoided involving him if they had thought they could."

"Hmph. Look what's become of him! He's a good-looking young man who hides out from the world by living in a purple camper. Spends his time dressing up and telling fairy tales to kiddies. That's not right."

"I'm not saying he wasn't damaged by all of this—he was. But you shouldn't assume that he's unhappy doing what he does for a living or that there's anything wrong with it. It's important, and he knows that even if you don't." At her frown, I added, "You should have seen him today, whenever he had to take on a role or make up some story—he loved it, Rachel. Besides, if this isn't what he's supposed to do with the rest of his life, so what? He's still young. Give him some time to find his way."

"Find his way? He's wandering all over the map. You gotta give him something to hold on to, Irene. Some roots. Some roots that won't let loose of the earth the first time a little ill wind blows his way."

"Why, Rachel Giocopazzi! You've got a soft spot for him."

"Damned right I do. He's a good kid."

We heard the bathroom door open, and the good kid came back out.

"Whew," he said. "Rachel? Maybe not *that* much of a distraction."

"Sorry, Travis. You want to do something else for a while?"

He shook his head. "I'll be all right—I didn't get sick, I just felt like I might."

She laughed. "Oh, is that all?"

He blushed.

"So, back to work," I said. "Any way to estimate time of death? I think the newspaper said late Friday or early Saturday."

"Right. Body was found on Monday at six in the morning by the housekeeper, Mrs. Coughlin. Rigor mortis had passed off, and there were other indicators that she'd probably died late Friday. More importantly—and here's one of the instances in which Richmond really failed to pursue leads—she talked on the phone twice on Friday night. She was called by her cousin Robert, and she called her brother-in-law."

"When?" I asked.

"Robert called at a little after eight; she called Gerald Spanning at nine-thirty."

"Any idea what the calls were about?"

"According to Robert, he called to ask for a loan. He said she agreed to give him one, and he was going to come by on Monday morning to get a check from her."

"Is that very likely?" I asked.

"Robert said she loaned him money all the time. Richmond didn't check it out. Travis, I'd like to ask your dad's attorney if we can get a look at his old accounts—he had a joint checking account with Gwendolyn, and I'd like to see if she really did write checks to Robert."

"I'll ask Mr. Brennan if he can help us out," he said. "How soon do you need the information?"

"The sooner the better."

He hesitated, then said, "I guess I should let him know what's going on. May I use your phone?"

"Go ahead—use it any time you like while you're here," I said.

He came back in a few minutes and said, "I left a message with his service. They're going to try to reach him and have him call me back here or on my cell phone."

"You said Gwendolyn DeMont also called Gerald Spanning on the night she died?" I asked Rachel.

"He said she called to ask if he knew how to get in touch with Arthur. Gerald said he told her that he didn't, but if Arthur called him, he would tell him to give her a call. She said not to bother, she was going to be turning in for the night. He asked her if she needed anything, or if he could help her, but she said no, she was fine, there was nothing urgent."

"Any signs of forcible entry?" I asked.

"None."

"Who else had keys to the house?"

"Good question. Arthur and the housekeeper, definitely. The housekeeper said the locks hadn't been changed on the house in years. Who knows how many people had access. Richmond didn't check that out, either."

I was puzzled. "But I thought there were walls and security gates?"

Rachel nodded. "There were. But nothing a novice couldn't get past. Fence wasn't electrified or anything like that. It was just a big brick wall."

"How high?"

She shuffled through the photos. "Maybe seven or eight feet." She handed a photo to me. "You can see it here in this shot of the front drive. I'm not exactly sure why they took this photo. Richmond didn't make any notes about it. Maybe just showing the security arrangements."

I looked at it for a moment, then pointed at a marking on the gatepost and said, "What's this, the symbol for the farm? A brand or something?"

She looked at it and shook her head. "I don't know."

Travis took the photo from her, studied it and said, "Do you have a magnifying glass?"

"Yes, in the desk in your room."

"My room?" he laughed.

I went into the guest room, which doubles as a study, and got the magnifying glass out of the desk. I brought it to him. After a brief look at the photograph, he said, "It's a hobo sign."

"Hobo sign?" I asked.

"You know, one of the signs hoboes leave for one another. Some people call them Gypsy signs, some people say they go back to old medieval ritual signs. Wherever they came from, drifters depended on them. They could tell a man where to catch a train or find a camp or a handout. If he knew where to look for them, the signs could tell him a lot about a house—to beware of a vicious dog, or that the owners will care for a man who's sick, or that a man with a gun lives there. A drawing of a cat, for example, means 'A kind woman lives here.' If there are three triangles by the cat, it means 'Tell her a sob story.'"

"What does this one mean?"

He looked up at me. "It means 'Run like hell.'"

25

He handed the photo and the magnifier back to me. I could now see that the mark was drawn in pencil, and looked like an "h" that slanted to the right; it wasn't hard to imagine a stylized runner.

"There's another way to draw that one," he said, as I handed the photo and glass to Rachel.

He borrowed Rachel's pencil and awkwardly used his bandaged hand to draw a circle on one of the manila envelopes. Then, across the circle, he drew two parallel arrows. The arrows pointed right.

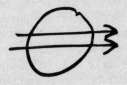

"If you saw that, you knew you should hit the road, and quick!" he said.

"How do you know about these signs?" Rachel asked.

"My dad could understand symbols and pictures, even numbers—he just had trouble with letters and words. His family taught him hobo signs from when he was very young; he taught them to me. If you weren't on the road, of course, they were only good for so many situations. My dad and his brother had other little signs they used if they had to leave notes for one another. My mother and I used them with him, too. That was a big thrill, of course, when I was younger. We pretended to be spies, or to have our own secret language. Took me awhile to realize it wasn't a game."

"Wait!" Rachel said suddenly, and searched through her papers. She handed a photo over to Travis. "I took that at the back of your mother's apartment. Someone tried to break into a window. This was drawn on the window frame, between the bars."

His expression was grim as he said, "It means, 'This is the place.'"

Rachel went back to the murder file photos, looking through other shots, sorting out photos of the exterior of the house. "There aren't any others," she said.

"There probably are others," Travis said, "but you have to know where to look for them. Maybe I should say, there probably *were* others—the whole area where the farm was is now an industrial park. My father had the place torn down years ago."

"Getting rid of memories?" I asked.

"I guess," he said, but I'm not sure he really heard the question. He had taken the stack of glossies from Rachel and was studying them intently, through the glass. He held one out to her, a photo of the front door. "There's another hobo sign in this shot," he said. "Look here—at the little pencil marks on the facing of the front door."

"I still don't see it. What are you looking at?" she said.

"Here," he said, moving to look over her shoulder. "These three slanting lines. They mean, 'This is not a safe place.'"

Rachel handed it over to me, and Travis had to point out the lines to me as well. "What do you make of it?" Rachel asked.

"Assuming they were left on the night of the murder, and left by the murderer, then the killer was warning someone else," I said. "Those two assumptions are big assumptions.

But if the killer left them, then the question is, who was he warning?"

"The DeMonts may have known these symbols?" she asked.

"Yes," Travis said. "If my uncle didn't lie about Horace living on the road, then Horace would have certainly known them. And Robert. I don't know if he taught them to his other kids or not. I don't know if the others traveled with him."

Rachel had another set of pictures. "These were taken of your dad's apartment," she said. "Do you know about these?"

He nodded, looking through the pictures. "My dad rented this apartment when he separated from my mom. He was going to buy another house, but he said he wanted a place where I could visit him in the meantime. At first, I had thought he would just go back to Gwendolyn, but he didn't. I think he also wanted a place that was just his, a place to sort things out.

"When Richmond found out about the apartment, he got a search warrant. One for our house, too. He never found anything."

I was looking over his shoulder at a shot of Arthur's bedroom. Everything was neat and tidy—the bed made, the closet orderly. "Look," I said. "Your mom had a night-light just like that one."

"The Virgin Mary night-light?" he smiled. "No, it's the same one. He gave her that one. She said he told her it might make her feel protected. My mother used to laugh and say she thought it was his way of saying he wanted her to be as pure as the Virgin Mary—that he didn't want her to have any other men in her life."

"Was she afraid of him?"

"No," he said. "Not at all."

"But she didn't let him back into her life—I mean, not until recently."

"No, like I said, she felt tremendous guilt over everything that had happened before the murder. She didn't want to profit from Gwendolyn's death. Once the crisis was over and she felt sure my father wouldn't be charged with Gwendolyn's murder, she felt guilty about lying on his behalf. She decided that no matter how much she loved him, he wasn't good for her or for me. She couldn't trust him again."

"And he went along with this?"

"Think of the threat she could hold over him," he said. "I'm not saying she ever did threaten him, but we both knew that my dad was dependent upon our silence."

So my aunt had exercised her own form of blackmail over those years. Stay away from me and your son, or I'll blow your alibi.

"Once she got an idea in her head," Travis was saying, "it was harder than hell to get her to let go of it. A couple of years ago, she read a passage in one of her Georgette Heyer novels to me, about a shy woman. Heyer had made the observation that shy women often have strong prejudices. She asked me if I thought that was true."

"What did you say?"

"I said the fact that she hadn't spoken to my father in a decade ought to prove that Ms. Heyer severely understated the case."

"This was near the time you had the fight with her over your dad?"

"Yes. I had reached a point in my life when I needed to get to know him. If he was a liar, a cheat, a killer—whatever—I needed to get to know him. The pity was, I had lost ten years during which he was perfectly healthy."

The phone rang.

"Reed tells me I'm not supposed to yell at you," the voice said. "Can I just say I'm worried?"

"Frank! Please don't worry. I'm home, I'm safe, just a little bruised."

"We're leaving Boise tomorrow morning—"

"You're coming home!"

"No," he laughed, "but I'm glad you sound so excited about the idea. We think our guy is in Montana now. We have some pretty solid leads."

"Oh."

"Sorry. I'm anxious to get back, too. Twice as anxious now."

"So where will you be?" I asked.

"I'll call you when I know for sure. We're still working on finding a place to stay."

"Frank, you know how you've been telling me about the people you've met there, with the Boise PD?"

"Yes," he said warily.

"Is there anyone there who might be willing to look something up for you?"

He groaned. "For me, huh?"

"Okay, for me. It's important."

"What is it?"

"I need to know if there's an arrest record for a Robert or Bobby DeMont in the summer of 1940."

"Did you just say '1940'?"

"Yes."

"Irene—"

"Come to think of it," I said, remembering that Gerald mentioned that school had just let out for the summer, "it was probably June of 1940."

There was a pause. "Want to tell me why I should put any new acquaintance of mine to that kind of trouble?"

I told him about the conversation with Gerald Spanning.

"Hmm. Any idea at all what the charges might have been?"

"No, but to send a lawyer all the way to Boise—"

"A lawyer and a bunch of money," he said.

"If it was a violent crime against a woman, it would be

worth it to DeMont to have it hushed up, don't you think?"

"I'll see if I can get anyone interested in it. Spell the name for me again."

I did. "Thanks, Frank."

"Irene?"

"Yes?"

"Be careful, okay?"

"You, too."

"Think about staying somewhere else, okay?"

"I have been, much more seriously," I said. "I'll give you Travis's cell phone number in case you can't reach me here."

He told me that Pete wanted to talk to Rachel, and I put her on.

"Travis," I said, "Frank doesn't think it's a good idea for us to stay here, at least for a while. Do you mind if we stay somewhere else tonight?"

He looked relieved. "I didn't want you to feel insulted. Let me pay for a couple of hotel rooms somewhere, or we could stay in the van. Either way, I'd feel safer."

"I think I know someone who'd probably love to have us stay over at her place. The rooms are small, but the food is great. And wait until you see the gardens."

26

Jack was willing to take care of the pets, so Travis and I arrived on Mary's doorstep about an hour later. Rachel had been invited to join us for dinner but wasn't going to stay overnight.

"Travis!" Mary cried, as he entered the house. Within moments she had instructed him to call her Aunt Mary if he wanted to, because even Frank and Rachel called her that. "So there's no need to stand on genealogical ceremony," she said. "Irene, he must be half-starved, waiting so late for his dinner. Travis, I hope you like beef stew, because I've got a big pot of it simmering on the stove."

I never really think of her as motherly, or even grandmotherly, but as I watched her fuss over him in an agreeable way, I began to realize there were sides of Mary Kelly I didn't always get to see. She might spoil Frank or goad me, but her treatment of Travis was more tender, and solicitous without being oppressively so.

"What happened to your hand?" she asked. His answer earned me a look of reproof from her. "Sweet heavens, Irene! I expected you to take better care of him!"

"Yes, I managed to injure him within twenty-four hours of meeting him," I said.

"That's not true!" he protested. "Irene has been nothing but good to me. And I think she was hurt worse today. I told you what happened, Aunt Mary—my injury was my own fault, not Irene's."

"Well, I'm just thankful you weren't hurt any more seriously than that," she said, turning back to the stove. Travis couldn't see her face from where he sat, so he didn't see her smile. I decided she must have been pleased that he had started calling her Aunt Mary. Maybe that was it.

She then began regaling him (and Rachel) with stories of some of the more ridiculous moments of my childhood. The story of Barbara locking me in my grandmother's outhouse had already been met with hilarity.

It was with some relief, then, that I heard Rachel's cell phone ring in the middle of the story about the time my father took off work to come to my school for a conference with one of the nuns, only to discover that the good sister had been barricaded in the library. Aunt Mary hadn't reached the part about the fire when the phone rang.

It was McCain, trying to reach me through her. I told her I'd talk to him and she handed the phone to me. I glanced over at Travis, who was listening to Mary tell another story. I walked out of the kitchen. Rachel watched me, but didn't say anything.

"I understand you've had a rotten day," McCain said.

"I understand you have, too."

He laughed. "Well, nobody's giving me half a million to cheer me up."

"What are you talking about?"

"Your inheritance, Ms. Kelly. Arthur Spanning remarried your aunt."

"I know," I said. "I just talked to their priest today. He can tell you that neither Travis nor I knew that, by the way."

"He can tell me that you acted like you didn't know."

"Ask Rachel to give you Harold Richmond's number—he can tell you what happens to people who don't let go of one idea. Maybe you've only ever had one in your lifetime, and this is it. But trust me, it's a bad one."

"Why should I doubt that the sole beneficiary of Briana

Maguire's estate should be interested in five hundred thousand dollars?"

"She didn't have five hundred thousand. I doubt she had five hundred."

"You should talk to your buddy Reed Collins about the papers that were found in Mr. Ulkins's office."

I sighed. "That can only mean something came to her through Arthur. Travis should have it. Travis already has most of Arthur's money, and Arthur wouldn't have wanted me to take anything from his estate. I'll talk to his lawyer, if it will make you lay off."

"Where is that lawyer, by the way? No one seems to be able to locate him. And you're keeping your cousin damned close to you, aren't you?"

"Look," I said, "I was going to offer to help you out here, but maybe I'll just have you talk to my own lawyer."

"We'll talk again, Ms. Kelly. By then, you'll need that lawyer."

I walked back toward the kitchen just in time to hear Travis say, "These stories are funny, but they must be embarrassing to Irene. Don't you have any positive stories to tell about her?"

As I stepped into the room, I said, "She's too old to change her habits, Travis."

"I've got all kinds of stories about her," Mary said. "But I don't want her head to swell. She knows I'm proud of her."

"Do you?" Travis asked me.

It was the look of worried uncertainty on Mary's face that made me say, "Of course I do. And the reverse is true as well. She knows I'm proud of her."

"This stew is about to burn," Mary said, suddenly turning away to stir the pot.

I was assigned to the smaller of the two small guest rooms, to sleep on a bed that I had slept in before, and had always found to be comfortable. But on those previous occasions, I hadn't been thrown against a wall a few hours before bedtime.

At about three in the morning, I decided to break down and take half of one of the pain pills I had brought with me, prescribed for an older injury. I rarely took them, but I needed sleep. I got back into bed and was trying to find a tolerable position, trying not to think of Ulkins, when there was a slight tapping at the door.

"Come in," I called.

It was Mary, and by the hall light I could see she had a rather festively colored, comfy-looking robe on. She sat next to the bed, and took my hand. "You poor thing," she said. "Anything I can get you?"

"I'll be all right," I said.

She sat next me, reminiscing for a little while about the numerous childhood injuries I had sustained, recalling some scrapes and bumps and a rather spectacular fall from a tree. All the while she softly stroked my hair the way my father used to do when I was little, whenever I had had a particularly bad day, and I wondered drowsily if she had comforted him in this same way when he was a boy. I don't remember falling asleep or hearing her leave the room.

She didn't wake me the next morning to go to Mass, but she took Travis to St. Matthew's with her while I slept in. Later they dropped me off at my house, where I got into the Karmann Ghia, put the top down and headed for Huntington Beach. They were going shopping—in the Mustang—while I went to talk to the DeMonts.

I took the coast route, even though Pacific Coast Highway was bound to have heavy summer traffic. As it turned out, I didn't have to pay too high a price for choosing it over the inland route; PCH was crowded, but the traffic moved. No local would think of expecting more.

I crossed the bridge over Anaheim Bay, passed the wildlife refuge and took my last good look at nature until I

reached Warner Avenue. For the next few miles, the highway is dominated by a motley assortment of buildings:
houses, bars, surf shops and restaurants.

Technically, Huntington Beach begins on the left side of
the highway just over the bridge, the right side belonging to
Surfside and Sunset Beach. But growing up in an area where
there are now high school classes that will teach you how to
hang ten, I had long ago developed other ideas about true
local geography. For me, the real Huntington Beach begins
when you get within sight of the pier. The two beaches on
either side of that pier boast some of the most well-known
surfing territory on the coast. *That's* Huntington Beach.

Before long, I was at the edge of the oil fields that
brought on the first boom years in Huntington Beach, back
in the 1920s. There were still big platforms just off the
coast, but fewer and fewer signs of drilling on shore. Most
of the oil fields had given way to developments packed
with large, imitation villas in pastel stucco on streets with
names like "Seapoint" and "Princeville" and "Castlewood."

I took a last look at the water before turning left on
Golden West, still thinking about my surfing days, wondering if I'd ever work up the nerve to paddle out again.

The DeMonts lived in a section of the city that was older
that the ones I had just passed; their homes were on one of
the numbered streets between Main and Golden West.
Although the neighborhood was older, that didn't mean the
homes were—it soon became apparent that most of the
original structures on these streets had given way to new
buildings. The result was a mixture of housing: many of the
lots had condos and apartment buildings on them; others,
large single-family dwellings; a few were smaller, older
homes. There was even a strip of colorful faux Victorians.

I turned right on Acacia, found the street I was looking
for and slowed when I came to the address for Leda
DeMont Rose and her father, Horace—a corner lot. I got

lucky with parking and found a space not far away, then walked back to the corner.

It was a large house, though not among the very newest on the street. Judging by its design, I thought it probably had been built in the 1970s. I studied the addresses and realized that Robert's home was on the same side of the street, at the beginning of the next block, on the opposite corner of the intersection. His was a single-story cracker-box that was probably built in the 1940s. My guess was that a similar house had originally occupied Leda's lot.

While Leda's property was neatly kept, her brother's was a little less so. Robert's place could have used a coat of paint, and looking at the brown, patchy grass in his yard, I saw that no one could accuse him of wasting water on a lawn. The place wasn't so far gone that you'd call it an eyesore, but it didn't look like the owner had a lot of domestic enthusiasm.

I stood debating which household I should upset first, and decided that even in my current condition, I could take on a guy who was almost a hundred and live to fight another day. I wasn't sure how old Robert was, but Gerald's story about Robert's arrest was enough to make me decide to save Robert for round two.

There was a low wooden fence around the front yard of Leda DeMont's home; I lifted the latch on the gate and made my way along a set of long, flat platforms set at right angles to one another. The platforms served as steps. On either side of each platform were carefully pruned bushes and shrubs that added privacy as well as greenery. The platforms ended at a deck that was concealed from the street by more plant life. At one end of the deck was a small rock grotto with a stream of water flowing through it. The water pooled at its base; the flow produced a soft gurgling, a not-quite-babbling brook effect.

Tall, ornate double doors stood across from the grotto. Looking at those doors, I made a set of predictions: cathedral ceilings, Italian marble entry, a huge stone fireplace, a loft, white walls and white carpet, and—not really going out on a limb here—lots of tinted windows on the ocean side, which was also the side that faced Robert's place. I rang Leda's doorbell.

I was so surprised when a young woman answered the door, I nearly forgot to congratulate myself on knowing what to expect inside. She looked to be about sixteen or seventeen. She was a pretty girl, with big brown eyes and light-brown hair, which she wore in a long braid. She had on jeans and a red tank top. She was about five-six or so, and slender.

"Hello," I said. "Is Leda DeMont in? No, I'm sorry—is Leda Rose in?"

She pulled her gaze away from my bruised cheek and forehead, smiled and said, "Sure, just a minute." She turned toward a hallway and shouted, "Grandma! It's for you!"

"Who is it?" a voice called back.

"Irene Kelly," I said, knowing the name probably wouldn't mean anything to her.

I heard my name shouted back and forth a couple of times, then the voice in the background said, "I'll be right there."

Taking this for permission to let me enter, the young woman guided me to a seat on a white leather sofa.

"Would you like something to drink?" she asked.

"No, thanks. Do you live here with your grandmother?"

"No, I just come by on the weekends. I help her take care of my great-grandfather."

At this moment, Leda came out of the hallway. "Laurie?" she called.

"Over here, Grandma," she answered.

Leda DeMont Rose was an older and slightly heavier version of her granddaughter. Her hair was cut short and the brown was a little less natural in shade, but their features were very similar.

She smiled at me and said, "I'm sorry, I don't seem to remember where we've met."

"We haven't met," I said, standing and extending a hand. "I'm Irene Kelly." I took a breath and then launched into the story I had decided to use. "I was hoping to speak to you privately about a rather personal family matter."

She raised a brow, then turned to her granddaughter and said, "Laurie, why don't you keep an eye on old Grumpypuss?"

Reluctantly, and as slowly as possible, Laurie left us.

"Now," Leda said. "What can I do for you?"

"Well, this is rather embarrassing, and I hope it won't be too upsetting to you, but I need to talk to someone who might be able to give me some advice. I've been approached by a private investigator, a Mr. Richmond?"

She sat up a little straighter, but said nothing.

"Mr. Richmond claims to have some information of interest to a cousin of mine, Travis Maguire. You may think of him as Travis Spanning."

Her lips flattened, but she didn't say anything.

"The problem is that my own family has had very little to do with Travis. Even though his mother is my mother's sister, we haven't had much to do with her since the death of your own cousin, Gwendolyn."

"The *murder* of my cousin," she corrected.

"Yes. I'm sorry. But you see, my mother died not long after Travis was born, and my father didn't like Arthur Spanning, so we never had much to do with him. My parents are no longer living, and I never heard the full story, so this isn't a personal grudge of my own. My problem is, I suppose I could locate Travis, but before I do, I'd like to be a little more sure of Mr. Richmond. He said he worked for you."

At that her mouth fell open in what was clearly unfeigned amazement. "He did? Why that lying scoundrel! I—I can't believe it! Of all the unmitigated gall!"

"Excuse me?"

"That man—that man is the last person I would *ever* hire to do any detective work for me, I can assure you! Don't do a thing to help him! Oh! I blame him for—oh, for so much!" she finished bitterly.

I waited.

"Mr. Richmond's incompetence has been the cause of a great many ills, not the least of which is that my aunt's murderer remains at large."

"You're speaking of Arthur Spanning?"

"No, of course not!" she said.

I was stunned. This was the last response I had expected.

"I don't know what problem your father had with Arthur, but I can tell you that he never would have harmed Gwen."

"Never harmed her? But he was a bigamist—"

"Yes. Yes, he was. And that was very wrong. Not that I don't understand what led to that, but it was wrong. And that poor little boy—"

She stood up and paced, wringing her hands. "Do you think there is any chance you will find your cousin?"

"A very good chance," I said.

She began pacing again. I decided to stay silent; she was apparently debating something with herself and I was too unsure of the territory to push her into answering questions.

"You've misjudged him, you know," she said at last.

"My cousin?"

"No, Arthur. You've believed Richmond's story, haven't you?"

"Well, until I got here, I suppose I did," I lied. "But I did think there was something about Mr. Richmond that seemed a little strange."

"Forget Mr. Richmond. Perhaps," she said, sitting down again, "I can do a little something to right an old wrong. Are you willing to keep an open mind, Ms. Kelly?"

"Yes, of course. And call me Irene, please."

"All right, Irene." Several moments passed before she spoke again. "First of all, let me tell you that your uncle Arthur never killed Gwen. If Arthur had wanted to end his marriage to Gwen, he would have divorced her. I haven't seen him in years, but I knew Arthur then, my dear, and believe me, he would have never chosen murder over divorce. There was no reason for him to do so."

"Her fortune—"

"Hah!"

"Pardon?"

"I said, 'Hah!' Tell me, Irene, did you see the house across the street on your way in?"

"Yes."

"That's my brother's place. Robert DeMont. Do you know why this house looks better than that one?"

I shook my head.

"Because I married a wonderful man named Elwood Rose, and he wouldn't let my father or brother involve him in any of their harebrained investment schemes. For a number of years, Gwen did not have such a protector, and my father and brother did a great deal of damage to that fortune."

"I don't understand."

She sighed. "You've heard of my grandfather, Quentin DeMont—the man everyone called Papa DeMont?"

I nodded.

"He ruled that farm and everyone on it as if he were a king anointed by God. I loved him, and so did Gwen, but because my father argued with him so often, I wasn't in Papa DeMont's shadow the way Gwen was. You know that my grandfather raised her?"

"Yes," I said.

"Well, my father was on the outs with Papa DeMont. Some of it was my dad's own fault, but a lot of it was just that he wasn't willing to be under Papa DeMont's thumb. I later came to think that was a lucky thing for me."

"How so?"

"Gwen never learned how to stand up to him, or anyone else, for that matter. And I think Papa thought he'd be able to take care of her forever, so he didn't teach her the things she needed to know about life. She was this hothouse flower, you might say."

"So when he died—"

"When he died, she was just about as lost as any one soul could be. Suddenly she was being asked to cope with a set of responsibilities she was totally unprepared for—a business she had never participated in.

"I was younger than Gwen, about fourteen years younger, but I swear to you, I often felt as if our age differences were reversed. I was almost thirty when Papa DeMont died, and Gwen was in her mid-forties. But I was married and raising kids, and you would have thought she was still in high school, for all she knew about getting along in the world." She glanced toward the hallway and said, "I love my father, but I haven't always been proud of him, and I am truly *ashamed* of how he took advantage of her after Papa DeMont died."

"In what way?"

After a long silence she said, "He told her his favorite sad story, the one about how Papa DeMont didn't love him—which was untrue—and what a rough life he had had, and on and on, giving her a spiel just as if he were panhandling back in his tramp days. Pretty soon she felt so guilty, she started opening her checkbook to him."

"Did Arthur know?"

"They weren't married yet. Gerald—Arthur's brother? He used to try to warn Gwen, to tell her that there was a reason Papa DeMont never let my father have money—namely, it was spent before Daddy could fold it up and put it in his wallet. Bobby—my brother—was the same way. Both of them hated Gerald for that."

"So if the handouts stopped when Arthur married her—"

"They didn't. Arthur didn't try to stop them until later. I'm not sure he realized what was going on at first—you know he was only sixteen?"

"Yes. I guess I've often wondered—"

"Why a sixteen-year-old boy would marry a woman that old?"

"Yes."

She thought for a moment before answering. "I guess you would have to have known the two of them, and the situation there on the farm. It was a little world of its own, in many ways. In each of their cases, after their parents died, Gwen and Arthur had no other world, really. Gwen was afraid of most men—most people, really. She was so lonely.

"And Arthur—even as a boy, Arthur was the kind of person who wanted to be helpful. I guess he wasn't any good in school—which I could never figure out, because he was smart, and don't let anybody ever tell you otherwise. So when Papa DeMont let him help out in the gardens, he just—I don't know, I'd say he changed. You could see how much happier he was to be there than at school. I think the schoolkids might have been mean to him, I don't know. He never did like kids his age. He'd rather be around adults."

"Were there any other children on the farm?"

She shook her head. "No. None that Gerald would let him spend any time with. So in his own way, I think he was lonely, too. He tried to make up for it by being helpful, I think, to get the adults to like him. If anyone else needed a hand, even when he was little, Arthur rushed to help them out."

"And so he helped Gwendolyn?"

She nodded. "It was as if he was determined to do whatever he could to make her smile or laugh. To be honest, I don't know anyone who made her smile more often. And when he got to an age where—well, boys get to be men, physically if in no other way, and if he hadn't started thinking about the one thing that seems to take up most of the male brain, he wouldn't have been normal, would he?"

"There weren't any other women around?"

"You have to remember that Gerald kept as tight a rein on that kid as Papa DeMont kept on Gwen. Only I don't think Gerald was above smacking Arthur around. He was a kid raising a kid."

I thought of the photo of the wedding day, and wondered if that was why Arthur looked different—was his face a little swollen?

"Gerald made sure Arthur learned gardening and landscaping—and not the type of farmwork that would put him out in the fields or in the factory," Leda was saying. "Gerald was proud if nothing else."

"Forgive me, but Gwendolyn's—" I hesitated, sought a word. "Gwendolyn's availability might explain why she was his first sexual partner, but it wouldn't explain why he married her."

"Gerald. Gerald pushed that. It surprised me at first. At the time, I thought maybe Gerald figured he could control Arthur and Gwen's money both—prenuptial agreement or no. I don't mean to say that his intentions were bad. He was very fond of Gwen, and since he was one of Papa DeMont's favorites, he was close to her, too. He was protective of her, and he resented what my father and brother were doing."

"You had more than one brother, didn't you?" I asked.

"I had two, but Douglas died in 1980," she said.

"I'm sorry," I said.

"Doug left home early on, and never had much to do with any of us. That may make him the smartest of the bunch. When he heard what had happened to Gwen, he was angry, and he fell for Richmond's theory. But I think anyone who didn't know the whole story would have believed what Harold Richmond was telling them. And of course, my father and Robert backed Richmond all the way."

"Because they wanted the money?"

"Yes. If Arthur had been proven to be the killer, they were the next in line for money—and not just Gwen's inheritance. They could have brought a civil suit against Arthur, and taken his money, too."

"But you seem sure he wasn't the killer. Why?"

"He loved Gwen. Maybe not in the way a husband should love a wife, but they were friends. He had his business. He could have left her a long time before she died and he would have been fine. But I think he was grateful to Gwen. She gave him a way to get out from under Gerald's thumb— that was Gerald's big surprise."

"What do you mean?"

"Well, Gerald sort of bullied Arthur. Ordered him around. Of course, Gerald was the head of the household after his folks died, and he took on a big responsibility at a young age. But he just couldn't seem to understand that Arthur was growing up. Gwen saw it. And after the wedding, she stood up for Arthur in a way that just shocked Gerald— shocked us all, really. She encouraged Arthur to get a driver's license and a car and to travel off the farm."

"All the things she had never done?"

She nodded. "Exactly. And one day—I think this might have even been the day of the wedding—she told Gerald off in a way that maybe she had always wanted to tell Papa DeMont off. I had never imagined she had that much spine."

"So Arthur felt indebted to her."

"Oh, yes. And as he got older, I think he also saw how very much she depended on him. Maybe—"

But before she could finish her sentence, she was interrupted by a loud male voice roaring a random litany of oaths and obscenities that turned the white room blue and Leda Rose's face red. It wasn't just one cannonball of cussing that hit in a single shot; it was a rapid, rat-a-tat-tat, machine-gun-fire swear-o-rama. It was hard not to be impressed.

"Excuse me," Leda said, but she was no sooner off the couch than a leathery wisp of a man wheeled himself into the room. This had to be Horace DeMont. He was closely followed by his great-granddaughter, who had her arms folded and a mulish look on her face.

You could have put three of him into that chair, and still had elbow room. He was wearing a bathrobe and pajamas, his head looked too big for his neck, and most of his hair had abandoned his mottled pate. You might not have thought he had any fire left in him until you looked at his face. There was so much anger burning there, it would probably keep Horace DeMont around long enough to get another look at Halley's Comet.

"My father," Leda said, having recovered her poise. She moved toward the back of the wheelchair.

"Who's this?" he barked. There was nothing wrong with his ability to speak, but a minute earlier I had already heard more than enough to know that.

"None of your business," she said, giving me a warning glance as she grabbed the handles of the wheelchair. "Why are you out here, Daddy?"

"I want apple juice, and that damned girl won't get me any," he said, taking his hands off the wheels, content to be pushed now that he had the attention of his daughter.

"We're out of apple juice," she said, guiding the chair back to the hallway.

Another string of expletives preceded them as they went down the hall, but they lacked the passion of the earlier performance.

"Poor Grandmother," Laurie said, pushing a stray hair out of her eyes. "She has to put up with that all the time."

"She must be very grateful for your help."

She shrugged. "Somebody has to help her. Uncle Bobby's too spaced out, fooling around with his inventions."

"He's an inventor?"

"Not really. To be an inventor, you have to make things that *work,* don't you?"

I laughed. "I don't know. I guess lots of inventors fail more often than they succeed while they're working on their ideas."

"Yes," she said, "but they usually learn something from their mistakes, right?"

I left that one alone. "Do you visit him while you're here?"

"Well, since his car problems, Grandmother has been making things for him to eat, and I bring them over to him. I hate it. He always wants to show me some new thingama-jig that doesn't work, or to be like his guinea pig or some-thing. Nothing that would hurt me or anything, but it's so weird. And then he says, 'No, wait! Wait! Just let me adjust this . . .' and that never works, either, so finally I just have to say, 'Bye, Uncle Bobby, have a nice time!' "

"It sounds like your Grandmother has her hands full. Like I said, she must appreciate your help."

She lifted a shoulder. "I don't know. I've been thinking about maybe becoming one of those people who take care of old people, you know, maybe have a business doing that. It's going to be a big business, you know. Because of all the people who are, you know, your age. The Baby Boomers. You're all getting older."

I laughed. "Not all of us, but for now, at least, I'd rather be in the group that is."

She smiled. "Yeah."

Within a few minutes, Leda came back out, looking weary. "Your great-grandfather is a mean old son of a bitch, Laurie."

"No kidding," Laurie said, apparently used to such proclamations.

"I'm sorry, Ms. Kelly, but I have a brother to feed and a nasty old man to calm down. I would talk to you more, but Laurie and I will be busy for a while now."

"Please don't apologize," I said. "You've been very helpful. And I'll tell my cousin what you said."

"And avoid Mr. Richmond," she added.

"Yes, I will. I wondered—since I'm on my way out anyway, would you like me to take your brother's meal to him?"

Laurie and Leda exchanged a look that clearly said they had found a pigeon ripe for the plucking, and just weren't sure if they had the heart to grab my feathers. "Oh, I couldn't—" Leda began.

"Nonsense. Believe me, this is the least I can do for you after taking up your time today."

"I'll get it ready for you," Laurie said, hurrying off to the kitchen before her grandmother could refuse a second time.

Leda smiled after her.

"You must be very proud of her," I said.

"I am. She's a good-hearted girl." She looked up at me. "And your uncle is a good-hearted man. He deserves your forgiveness."

"Yes," I said, "I'm beginning to see that perhaps he does."

"You know," she said, "I didn't get a chance to finish what I was saying before my father interrupted us. My dad provided a perfect example of what I was going to tell you, though."

"I hope you weren't about to tell me *that*," I said, and she laughed.

"No, no. I meant, his situation is a good example. Until a few years ago, my father was strong and active. People always guessed him to be twenty years younger than he was. Then about five years ago, his health began to fail—and to fail quickly. It was as if those years caught up to him all at once. He hates being sick. He hates being dependent on me. He thinks of me as his jailer, not his helper. But I hate it, too. And I'm as much his prisoner as he is mine."

Her face was set in angry lines as she said this. She looked away from me, and stared out the windows, toward her brother's house. Gradually, her face softened, and her voice was quiet when she spoke again. "You might say, 'Just put him in a home, then.' Maybe someday it will come to that. But right now, while I can still care for him, I can't think of setting him aside, or leaving him to strangers—well," she added with a smile, "not on most days."

"No one could blame you."

"And I can't blame Arthur. Until you've been there—it's hard to understand. But I think Gwen's dependence on Arthur became like that. I think it made him feel confined. His business gave him his first taste of freedom. And Gwen learned to be a little more self-reliant, although if he left her alone too long, Bobby or Daddy came by looking for a handout." She shook her head. "His so-called secret family—your aunt and your cousin—they gave him his real life, a more balanced life. I was so sorry that they didn't stay together after Gwen was killed, although I can see why it would have been almost impossible. I'm sure your aunt felt very hurt and betrayed."

"She did, but—things change," I said faltering for a way to say more without admitting how many lies of one kind or another I had racked up in the last hour. "Leda, there's so much I'd like to tell you, but I think I'll wait until I can bring my cousin with me—if that would be all right with you? Perhaps we can come at a time when your father is sleeping or won't be disturbed by us?"

She smiled. "That would be wonderful. I've never had a chance to meet Arthur's son."

Laurie arrived with a grocery sack but hesitated before handing it to me. "Are you sure?"

"I'm sure." I took it from her, said good-bye, and made my way across the street. About halfway across I had a sensation of being watched, and looked over my shoulder. I couldn't see anyone looking out the tinted-glass windows, but I could have sworn that somewhere on the other side of that glass, Horace DeMont was boring holes in my back with his angry stare.

27

"Come in!" a voice called from a speaker near the front door of Robert DeMont's home. I hesitated only for a moment before trying the door; it was unlocked. But as I opened it, I couldn't see anyone waiting for me in the room beyond. That didn't mean he wasn't there—the room was not one that could be taken in at a glance. I had been able to guess the decor of Leda's home, but even looking at the interior of Robert's place, I wasn't sure what I was seeing. Except for the spaces taken up by windows, the walls were lined with bookcases. Not all of these bookcases held books; many of the shelves were crowded with gadgets and tools. Apparently the books that had once occupied the shelves were stacked on the floor—not much of the floor was visible. A maze of worktables was covered with drawings, metal parts, gears, bottles of adhesives, soldering irons, magnifiers, cardboard boxes, clamps, more tools and a host of unidentifiable objects. The tables each had their own chairs; most were metal folding chairs, a few looked like used office chairs.

To my right was a door that seemed to open onto a hallway, and at the other end of the front room, another doorway, probably leading to a kitchen. No sign of DeMont.

I was about to call his name when I heard a toilet flush. I stepped inside and waited for a respectable amount of time. Just as I was about to call out, "Are you feeling okay?" I heard another flush. And another. About six in succession before he yelled, "Bring my dinner back here!"

Not especially anxious to obey, and wondering why anyone in such apparent gastric distress would want to eat— let alone eat in that particular room—I said, "I'll just leave it on the kitchen table."

"No you won't!" he called, and I could hear him moving down the hallway. He stopped in the doorway and looked at me. "A woman!" he grinned, "That's great! Just what I need! What happened to your face? Oh, never mind, that's a rude thing to ask."

He was a big man, tall and broad-shouldered, probably in his late sixties or early seventies, but in good shape. Having heard that he was an inventor who needed to have his meals delivered, I suppose I had expected someone who would be frail and pale. He was tanned and fit and seemed perfectly capable of taking care of himself. Or anyone else, for that matter.

His hair was white, his eyes blue under snowy brows. He waved his hand to me in a "hurry up" motion and took off back down the hallway. "Come on," he called over his shoulder, "I want to show you an invention that is going to save marriages all across America."

What the hell, I thought, and cautiously followed, keeping my distance.

He walked into the bathroom and moved to the toilet. I was just about to turn right back around when he said, "Watch the toilet seat."

As he stood there, facing the toilet in the classic standing male position, the seat slowly but steadily lifted. He turned to me, beaming. "Now watch!"

He moved away from it with a jaunty step and it flushed.

"Now you try it," he said.

"Uh, no thanks," I said.

He gave me a sly smile and said, "Okay, you big chicken. Watch this!"

He approached the toilet, turned his back on it—as if he were about to take a seat—and slowly but surely, the seat came back down. He lowered himself onto it, grinned at me, and got off. Again the jaunty step, and the toilet flushed.

"You see?" he said excitedly.

"Yes. Amazing."

His grin faded. "What's the problem?"

"What's what problem?"

"What's the problem that is preventing you from being enthusiastic about a product that could revolutionize the sleeping habits of millions?"

"Sleeping habits?"

"Of course!" he exclaimed, as if I were the biggest dunderhead he had ever laid eyes on. "Every night, all across America, millions of women fall onto wet, cold porcelain surfaces. And why? Because some man has forgotten to put the seat back down! Now how is any poor gal going to get back to sleep after something like that happens to her?"

"It's very thoughtful of you to try to be of help—"

"I hear a but coming!" he said.

"I beg your pardon?"

"A b-u-t. You like it, but—" He stretched the last word out.

"But it needs to rise and lower faster. By the time that seat was starting on its way down, most women would have already hit the porcelain. And I don't even want to think about what will happen while a half-asleep man waits for that seat to rise all the way up."

"Well, he better not rush it," DeMont said, " 'cause this thing is operated on an electrical pressure-sensitive mat and if he hits the mat instead of the toilet, he just might get electrocuted."

"Some women might consider that a fitting punishment," I said, "but I don't think Consumer Product Safety is going to give it the old green light. Maybe you need to work a few of those little bugs out."

He seemed so dejected at this, I added, "But I like your front-door setup. How did you know I was there?"

"I didn't know it was you, exactly," he said, reanimated. "But that's a pressure-sensitive mat, too."

"How does it work?"

"Anybody steps on it, it sends a signal to my recorder, which plays a little tape and that's what you hear over the speaker."

" 'Come in'?"

"Yes."

"It greets *everyone* by saying, 'Come in'?" I asked.

"Sure."

"But what if you don't want someone to come in?"

"Why, you just lock the door," he said. "That's all."

Unwilling to argue the possible shortcomings of that system, I said, "Maybe you should eat dinner in another room."

"Okay," he said cheerfully, and led the way to the kitchen.

The kitchen was far less cluttered than the rest of the house, but I had a feeling his sister and Laurie were responsible for its relative state of cleanliness. I set the bag down on the table as he went to a cupboard. I was wondering what story I should tell him to get him talking to me on subjects other than toilet seats and doormats when he said, "Sit down, Irene, I'll get you a glass of my special power drink."

But I stayed standing, and didn't loosen my grip on the bag. "How do you know my name?"

He laughed, but didn't answer right away. I watched him warily as he set two tumblers on the table and moved to the refrigerator. "Let's see," he said, pulling out a pitcher of something that had settled into several layers that were various shades of red. He walked over to a blender, poured the contents of the pitcher into it, put the lid on the blender, then stood back and clapped his hands. The blender began whirring.

"I put one of those doodads on its power supply," he said, speaking up over the whine of the blender, "so you could start and stop it from anywhere in the room."

I didn't bother to point out that remote control of a blender was not worth much if you were already forced to stand next to it to fill it and empty it. I just nodded, watching the liquid in the blender turn a single shade of bright red.

But when he clapped a second time, the blender kept going. "Dag nab it!" he said. Given his father's virtuoso swearing, it surprised me. He tried clapping again, and still it whined on. Finally he went over and pushed a button on the machine. That stopped it. He clapped again, and nothing happened. He pushed a button, and nothing happened. He took the lid off and peered down into it. "Wonder if the dang thing's jammed?" he said, reaching for a knife.

"Uh, shouldn't you unplug it first?" I said.

He turned and smiled at me—a big, immensely pleased smile. "That's it!" he said, banging his hand on the counter.

The blender started up again. I quickly ducked beneath the table, while Mr. DeMont received an object lesson in the power of centrifugal force as the blender sprayed red juice everywhere. He fumbled blindly with the machine, finally turning it off. There was an eerie silence.

I crept up from my sheltered position. Other than a few spots here and there on my clothing I was, for the most part, unscathed. But Robert DeMont looked like he had been doing surgery in a MASH unit.

He reached for a dish towel and wiped the red liquid from his face. He looked over at me, grinned, and then began laughing. It was contagious. When we had brought ourselves back under control, he quickly made me lose it again by asking, quite innocently, "What happened?"

Once I had calmed myself, I said, "I don't think the device could pick up the sound of your clapping while the blender was on. So you turned the blender off at the machine itself. The power to the blender was still on, the machine was off. You clapped again, and this time, without the noise of the machine to interfere, the power was turned off, too. You pushed a button, then, but without power, the blender wouldn't start. That's when you took the lid off. The button was still depressed. You smacked the counter—"

"And turned the power back on! Yes, yes! Now I remember! I smacked the counter because when you said, 'Unplug it,' I realized what the problem was. I just chose an unfortunate way to express my excitement."

He gathered a handful of paper towels and wet them down, I grabbed a sponge and together we managed to wipe up the worst of it. I looked up at the ceiling and winced.

"Don't bother," he said, following my gaze. "I'll bring the ladder in and work on it later. Or maybe I'll leave it as it is. It's more interesting this way." He looked down at himself and laughed again. "I'd better clean myself up a little, though. This stuff is a little sticky. I'll be right back, Irene."

"Not so fast! How do you know my name?"

The sly smile was back. "Over there, by the phone," he said, pointing. Then he hurried out of the room.

I looked through the papers near the phone, and was nearly certain that he was simply stalling again, when I saw an envelope that made me feel a sharp sense of disappointment in a man who only moments ago seemed to be nothing more than a hapless gadgeteer.

It was a stiff nine-by-twelve manila envelope, the name "Robert DeMont" handwritten across its face in large block letters. But it was the return address that caught my eye: Richmond and Associates. There were no stamps.

Walking slowly back to the table, I opened the already unsealed envelope and pulled out a good-sized stack of eight-by-ten color photos. There was a page of text, but for the moment, I ignored it. My attention was fully concentrated on the first photo: Briana, leaving her apartment in San Pedro.

Disappointment gave way to anger. There was no longer any doubt in my mind as to who had hired Harold Richmond. Robert DeMont had a lot to answer for.

I stared at the image of my aunt. I saw her as I had not seen her in life. In photo after photo, here was Briana: Briana walking down the street, cane in hand; Briana coming out of the Reyeses' small grocery store; Briana going into St. Anthony's Church; Briana getting out of a cab in front of St. Mary's Hospital in Las Piernas. My fury rose with each piece of evidence that my aunt had been followed, spied upon. A lonely, shy old woman, vulnerable to the likes of Harold Richmond. Then came the worst of them all, the most intrusive—a photo of her weeping, leaning on Father Chris's arm at a graveside. I heard myself make a strange little choking sound; my eyes blurred. I moved the heel of my hand across them and went on.

The next group were all taken outside my home. Rachel, Travis and me, getting out of Travis's truck. There were photos of the camper, the house and the street, taken from different angles.

The camper—which was only in front of my house for a few hours before it was destroyed.

An odd set of noises I couldn't quite make out seemed to come from several parts of the house all at once. I waited, but heard nothing more. I suddenly realized that I didn't want to sit around chatting with Robert DeMont. I could look at the other photos later. For my own safety, I needed to get the hell away from him—and as fast as I could. What insane notion had led him to reveal the existence of the photos, I'd never guess, but I gathered them together now, stuffed them into the envelope and, taking it with me, hurried to the front door.

No sign of DeMont. I counted my blessings. I reached for the doorknob, turned and pulled. Nothing. Repeated the action, twice again, in the way of a person whose world isn't working the way it should. I looked for some sort of deadbolt. Nothing.

Having once spent a few days having the tar beat out of me while being held captive in a small room, I don't do well with locked doors. Claustrophobia and I have since had an ongoing unpleasant relationship, and DeMont's locked door brought it on in a hurry.

I felt a kind of hysteria rising within me, and fought hard to keep it in check. I turned, telling myself to calm down, to try to find a back door, even as I heard my breath coming in short, quick gasps, as if I been running a race.

Blocking the hallway door was Robert DeMont. He was smiling.

I had an urge to tackle him, but instead I ran through the maze of tables to the kitchen door, hearing him shout, "Stop!"

I found the back door, yanked at it. It wouldn't budge.

"They're all locked," I heard him say from behind me, "but there's nothing to be upset about. I just want to talk to you, find out what you know."

My heart was pounding in my chest.

"Let me out of here," I said, hating how my voice shook. "Let me out!"

"It's one of my inventions," he said. "One button locks all the doors and windows of the house. Once it's activated, I have to enter the secret code to turn it off."

Christ. Trust this to be his one invention that worked. I was sweating. "I have a problem with enclosed spaces," I tried, moving slowly back toward the kitchen.

He frowned, not making any attempt to block my way, but following me. "Are you sure? Richmond didn't mention it in his report."

I didn't answer. I was trembling. My throat was closing up. I began moving toward the front of the house again, my steps shaky, but picking up speed.

"Where are you going?" he said, still following. "Let's talk."

"Open the goddamned doors!" I shouted. I stumbled past worktables, knocking two of them to the floor behind me. I heard DeMont shout something about his work, but paid no attention. My goal, straight ahead, was a set of closed, cream-colored drapes. There was light coming from behind those drapes. A large picture window. I set the envelope down, picked up a metal folding chair.

"Stop!" he shouted. "I'll unlock the door!"

Too late. I had a good grip on the chair and was swinging that son of a bitch at that window as if I wouldn't settle for anything short of a home run. There was a satisfying crash of glass—better yet, a rush of fresh air. Almost immediately I felt myself grow calmer. I yanked the drapes back and, turning my face away, took another couple of whacks at the glass. Now the opening was wide enough for me—I could get through without cutting myself.

I turned to pick up the envelope and saw Robert DeMont looking at me with the same sort of uncomprehending look he had on his face when the blender went wild. "Why did you do that?" he said. "I told you I would open the door."

"First," I said, stepping through the window, hearing the crackle of glass breaking beneath my shoes, "I don't trust you." Once outside the house, I took a deep breath. "Second, you paid someone to spy on my family. That would have been bad enough, but you probably paid for far more than that."

"But I won't harm you!" he said angrily. "Why break my window?"

I looked across the street. Laurie was coming out of Leda's house. She stopped on the sidewalk, looking wide-eyed at the damage.

I looked back at him. "You destroyed our privacy, and now I've done a little damage to yours."

I walked away, not waiting to hear his reply. I wish it would have been in purposeful strides, but it wasn't. I felt sick to my stomach, and my knees were suddenly going rubbery on me. I managed to get to my car, yank the door open and plop myself into the driver's seat. I wanted to start the car and drive off, but I was shaking. Thanking God that I hadn't put the top back up, I just sat there, taking deep breaths, trying to slow down.

I glanced up to see Laurie crossing the street to his house. I folded my arms across the steering wheel and rested my head against them. Now that the adrenaline rush was over, every part of my body that had hit that wall the day before was complaining—but that wasn't what kept me sitting at the curb.

Better not to drive, I knew, when I was feeling like this. When I was feeling like this, my ghosts would rise—the memories would come to me, and I would lose my way in them. I waited.

But while one or two images of my days in captivity quickly crossed my mind, I did not fall prey to them. I wanted to hope that this was some sign that I was making progress, but settled for being grateful that I got off easy this time. I straightened up, felt the warm ocean breeze on my face and was just about to start the car when I heard a voice say, "Are you okay?"

I turned to see Laurie standing next to the car.

"Yes," I said. "Thanks."

"I hope he didn't scare you too bad. You don't look so great."

"I'll be all right in a minute."

"He told me that he had used his locking invention. What a jerk! I'm so glad you broke his window."

"You are?"

"Yeah. He needs to learn that he can't have things his way all the time. He's just an overgrown spoiled brat! He can't go around locking strangers inside his house for no good reason. No wonder it scared you." She suddenly blushed and said, "It's my fault. I should have warned you about the locks. He told me about that invention, but I have to admit . . ."

"You didn't think it would work?"

"No," she said. "It's a first, I think."

I laughed. "I can't blame you. Did he show you the ceiling of his kitchen?"

She shook her head. I told her the story of the blender.

She laughed and said, "Oh, God, that's so like him. He doesn't think about the consequences of his actions. It's all 'I want this,' and 'I want that.' Sometimes he's just a younger version of great-grandfather, only Uncle Bobby doesn't swear. Grandma is stuck taking care of two very selfish old men."

"I hope she won't be upset about the window."

"No, I'll tell her what happened. She'll understand."

I wondered if it were true. She seemed to look out for her older brother. "Does she make meals for him every day?"

She shook her head. "No, she's only doing this until his car is fixed. Before he wrecked his car, he would take care of his own grocery shopping, or, you know, he'd go out to eat. I'm hoping she doesn't spoil him too much."

"What happened to his car?"

She shrugged. "I don't know. He got into some kind of accident a few weeks ago. I guess it, like, kind of embarrasses him. He won't talk about it. He was going to try to fix it himself. God! Can you imagine? Probably have to drive it in reverse all the time!"

A few weeks ago. I tried to respond lightly, to keep the conversation going, but it was difficult to keep smiling. "I take it you talked him out of that idea?"

"No, Grandma had the car towed down to Sun Coast—this body shop on Beach Boulevard. Uncle Bobby was mad, but there wasn't anything he could do about it."

"Maybe he thought it needed to go to a specialist."

"A Camry? I don't think so—hey, are you sure you're okay? You look a little pale again."

A little truth wouldn't hurt. "I'm just not very good about being locked in places."

"No one could blame you for being freaked out. I mean, you go into this dude's house, just bringing him something to eat, and he acts like something out of *Frankenstein*!"

I laughed. "It's the inventor in him."

"Oh, wow, you've seen that movie?"

"I read the book." I steered the conversation back to Robert DeMont. "So your uncle was surprised to find the car gone from his garage?"

"Oh, man, it was so funny when he found out that it wasn't there! He just about died! But if we had waited for him to do anything about it, Grandma'd be fixing him free meals forever!"

"Do you think Sun Coast does good work? I'm thinking of having this car painted."

"Yeah, they're good. But this car is so rad just the way it is—you aren't going to paint it pink or anything like that are you?"

I grimaced. "Not pink."

She laughed and gave me directions to Sun Coast. We talked for a little while longer, then she said she'd better go back to help her grandmother. She stepped away and said, "Hope you'll come back. I could tell that Grandma liked visiting with you."

"I promise I will. Tell her I'll bring Travis."

"Who's he?"

"My good-looking cousin," I said. "Much younger cousin." She smiled. "Cool!"

I didn't think a body shop would be open on a Sunday, but I couldn't keep myself from driving past it. I made my way over to Highway 39, Beach Boulevard. I didn't have far to go before I came to Sun Coast. As expected, it was closed. I pulled up in front and saw several cars locked up behind its wrought-iron fence. None of them were Camrys. I'd have to come back on Monday.

I headed back to PCH. At a traffic light, I moved the envelope on the seat next to me so that it was tucked in more securely. I thought of Travis. With some distance between me and Robert DeMont's house, I began to doubt myself. Maybe I should have stayed and talked to DeMont, should have at least tried to figure out what he was planning next. I could have learned more. What assignment was Richmond working on now, I wondered?

With a little lane changing, I got past some slowpokes on Highway 1. In the clear, I asked for a little more from my old ragtop, and it delivered. I was anxious to get back to my family.

28

"Frank called," Mary said when I returned. "He left this number. Room two fifty-four."

"Where's Travis?"

"Sleeping. His hand was bothering him and—of course, much more than that. Took one of those pills. Sleep will do him good. You look like you could use a little nap yourself."

I did feel weary, but I knew it wasn't caused by a lack of sleep. Remembered precariousness, vulnerability—that was what weighed on me. It was as if I had blindly stepped out over a cliff with one foot, drew back in time to keep from falling, but now, with solid ground beneath me, could only think of that near miss. *Watch where you're going. Watch where you're going.*

"Maybe I'll try to catch some sleep a little later," I told her. "Mind if I use your phone?"

I billed the call to my home number.

"Are you in Montana?" I asked Frank, once I was connected to his room.

"Yes, in Helena." He gave me the hotel name, which I hadn't been able to decipher from the switchboard's mumbled answer. "Thought I'd give you that information on DeMont," he said.

"That was fast—this friend of yours must be pretty efficient."

"I didn't ask for anybody's help." I could hear the satisfaction in his voice. "I looked it up myself—well, Pete and I worked on it together, and I found it first."

"How?"

He laughed. "Same way you would have. I went to the library."

"And to think some women have to worry about how their husbands will spend a Saturday night on the road."

"Be sure you tell Rachel that Pete came with me. The library was open last night and we had some time, so we looked at microfilm—old local newspaper files, just to see if we could find anything. Pete took the first half of June, I took the second half. And I found it."

"Great! Tell me what you learned."

"Okay. June 19, 1940. Robert DeMont and his father were named in the article, and the paper referred to them as 'two drifters from California.' They did some work on a farm owned by a widow, on the understanding that she'd pay them. She wasn't satisfied with the work and was going to give them less than the agreed-upon amount. Robert lost his temper, picked up a kitchen knife and took a couple of swipes at her."

"A knife?"

"Yeah." He paused. "Maybe it's his weapon of choice."

I began to feel a little better about breaking DeMont's window—and a little shaky again.

"Are you there?" he asked.

"Yes—sorry. So what happened then?"

"According to the paper, Horace and the widow struggled with Robert, both trying to get control of him, but he still managed to cut her once. Horace wrested the knife away from him, and then helped the widow bind up her wound."

I had been in Robert DeMont's kitchen. What if he had been in the mood to stab somebody then?

"Apparently it wasn't very deep," Frank was saying, "but naturally, she was upset. A neighbor happened by and the DeMonts got scared and ran off. The neighbor called the police, who managed to catch the DeMonts before they got very far."

"They were both arrested?"

"No, just Robert. But Horace wouldn't leave town without him. There was a second article, a little later on, saying that the charges were dropped, and there's a quote from the widow that made it sound as if the whole thing was a misunderstanding."

"Right," I said. "A misunderstanding that got straightened out once Papa DeMont's checks cleared the bank."

"Probably."

"I wonder how often his money covered some situation like this?"

"I don't know," he said, "but steer clear of these people, all right?"

"I can promise you, I won't go near Horace or Robert DeMont." I didn't tell him I had already learned that lesson the hard way.

"What happened?" he said sharply.

Oh, damn. "Who said anything happened?" I tried, but even to me it sounded feeble.

" 'I can promise you'? You think I just met you yesterday?"

So I ended up explaining.

After a long silence, I heard him let out a deep sigh. "You're sure you're okay? I mean, I know you weren't hurt, but—"

"Yes," I said. "Thanks for asking."

"You're still willing to make that promise? I don't have to have Reed show you a pile of photos of stabbing-wound victims?"

"Not necessary—I promise. I believe absolutely that Robert DeMont is capable of stabbing someone in a fit of rage. I don't want to be next."

"You might also think about the fact that one of the easiest places in the world to buy a wetsuit is Huntington Beach."

I didn't say anything. I was picturing self-involved Robert DeMont—walking past a surf shop, looking in the windows, suddenly inspired; later, pleased with his plan to use the wetsuit, reveling in his invention of a special torture device, eager to try it out.

Frank's voice brought me back from horrific visions. He had changed the subject—apparently he didn't want to end on that note of fear and argument. I didn't either. We talked for a while longer. I thanked him again for the research help, and we agreed to talk again later that night. In the end, I was glad not to be hiding anything from him, and knew that talking about it with him had helped me shake off the worst of my gloominess.

— —

Mary, seeing I wasn't going to take a nap, made a strong cup of coffee for me. I asked to borrow a magnifying glass, and after locating one for me, she went out to work in her garden. One of the things I like about Mary is that she puts a limit on her hovering.

I sat at the kitchen table and took another look through the envelope I had taken from Robert DeMont. This time, I pulled out the note. It read:

Robert—
Rushed these per your request, no time to sort them. I have my own copies, these are yours to keep.

Have already spoken to you re: photos I
took of subject's mother prior to locating him.
Of interest is Irene Kelly, subject's cousin,
who appears with subject and unknown
woman in some shots. Believe Kelly may
have possession of item we seek.

It was signed by Harold Richmond.

The anger kicked in again. I was feeling better and better
about breaking that window. If I hadn't made that promise
to Frank, I would have considered going back and breaking
a few more. But what, I wondered, was this "item" they were
looking for? The murder weapon? But why would they look
for that if Robert DeMont had killed her?

I thought about this. If Robert DeMont had killed
Gwendolyn in a fit of anger, then left the knife at the scene,
who found it? Arthur or the housekeeper, Mrs. Coughlin. If
Richmond believed I had it, he must also believe that Arthur
took it from the scene.

But Richmond thought Arthur, not Robert DeMont, was
guilty. He'd never work for DeMont if he thought Robert
had killed Gwendolyn. Maybe that suited DeMont just fine;
let Richmond pursue it for his own reasons and—and
what? It made no sense. DeMont would not want Richmond
to find the knife—not if the knife could somehow link him
to the crime.

Perhaps the "item" had nothing to do with the crime
scene. I quickly dropped that idea—Richmond's obsession,
his connection to the DeMonts and Arthur and my cousin,
was one event: Gwendolyn's murder.

I set that problem aside and went back to the photos,
started looking through them more slowly.

At the top of the pile were the ones of Briana in San
Pedro. I pulled out my notebook, flipped to my conversa-

tion with Mr. Reyes. According to the store owner, Briana had been wearing a blue sweater on the day she was killed. I sorted through the photos, found the ones taken of Briana when she was walking near the market. A red sweater. Little chance of mistaking one for the other. The photo had not been taken on the day she was killed.

Still, she had been stalked.

I went on to the ones taken at my house—of Rachel, Travis and me getting out of the camper; of the house, street and camper from other angles. The photos were taken during the day; the only daylight hours during which the camper had been at the curb in front of my house were that same afternoon. By later that evening, it had been destroyed.

If Richmond had been taking photographs before he—or Robert DeMont—had rigged a bomb, perhaps one of the people on the street had seen him near the camper, witnessed him fooling around with it.

It was while I was looking at a group of people walking on the sidewalk, slightly down the street from the camper, that I inadvertently made a discovery. The group included a young woman with two small boys. I didn't recognize them, and although they appeared to be giving their mother a hard time, I doubted the kids were young urban terrorists, out to rig bombs in campers. As I idly moved the glass to focus on one boy's impish expression, I saw something odd in the car nearest the group—gradually, I realized that it was a shoulder.

The car was a gray El Camino with dark upholstery. The shoulder, in a white T-shirt, stood out against the dark seat. It belonged to someone who was sitting in the car, ducking out of view from the camera.

In three or four other shots, varying portions of the car and the shoulder appeared, but there was no closer shot of it. It became apparent that Harold Richmond, master detective, had no idea that someone was trying to hide in a car not half a block away from where he was spying on us. A large man with muscular shoulders.

One shot accidentally caught a portion of the man's head, taken as he was either starting to peek up or duck down again. Dark hair, silver on the sides.

Robert DeMont's hair was white. Harold Richmond's hair color was very similar to that of the man in the photo, but Richmond was the camera man. Gerald Spanning's was also dark, going to silver on the sides.

I told myself that from the little that was visible of the man in these photos, there was no way to tell if it was Gerald Spanning in the El Camino. I couldn't convince myself that it wasn't.

That raised other questions. If it was Gerald, how did he learn where I lived? How did he manage to be there on the same day I found Travis, at the same time as Richmond? Had he followed Richmond? How would he even know what Richmond was up to, who he was watching?

There was also the problem of the car. At Gerald's mobile home, he had pulled up in a pickup truck. Parking was limited near his trailer; I hadn't seen an El Camino.

I kept looking at photos. At the end of the stack, I came to one that made my blood run cold.

Mary Kelly's house.

Richmond—and Robert DeMont—knew where to find us.

29

"Mary!" I called, running into the backyard.

"For heaven's sake—"

"Do you have friends you could stay with, someone else you could spend a few nights with?"

She looked puzzled, but said, "Yes, why?"

"It isn't safe here for you, or for us." I found myself looking toward Travis's room, worrying that I would be too late to take him out of harm's way. Hastily, I tried to explain, all the while distracted by my fears, wondering if even now the killer was watching this house, setting new plans in motion.

"What can I do to help?" she asked calmly, after I had told my disjointed tale.

She wasn't going to challenge me, question me at length. Some of the panic lifted. "Help me wake Travis. Pack whatever you'll need. Most of my own things are ready. You have Travis's cell phone number?"

"Yes."

"Take it with you. If you need to reach us, use that number."

"Where will you be?"

"In the van. I'll stay on the move. Safer for us, safer for our friends."

I knocked on Travis's door; he didn't answer. I knocked louder, still no answer. "The pain pills," Mary said, and opened the door.

He slept peacefully on his back, on top of the covers; except for stockinged feet, he was fully clothed. His hands lay palm up at his sides, his mouth slightly open, his face relaxed—but it was not the face of the puckish storyteller in the park. The young man before me had been marked by too much sudden grief, its signs apparent even as he slept.

Reluctantly, I tried to wake him; he opened his eyes, murmured something, fell asleep.

"Let him sleep until we're ready to leave, then," I whispered to Mary. I put his few items of new clothing in his trunk, packed up my own belongings and the cell phone, then took all of it out to the van. I made up the bed in the back.

When I came back in, Mary was ready to go. She gave me a slip of paper on which she had written information about where she would be staying. "Met her in my t'ai chi ch'uan class," she said.

We managed to rouse Travis enough to get him into the van; he promptly fell asleep on the bed.

I hugged Mary, and she pulled me back into a second embrace, giving me a kiss on the cheek and telling me, "Be careful. I will never forgive you if you don't outlive me."

"I feel exactly the same way about you," I said, making her laugh. I watched her walk over to the Mustang and called out, "Will you be able to park that thing in your friend's garage?"

"That," she called back, "was the first consideration in deciding where to stay!"

I watched to make sure no one followed her, then drove off, sparing one last, worried look at my Karmann Ghia. I supposed if Mary could leave her home behind, I could leave my car.

‒ ‒

For a while I drove aimlessly, checking the rearview mirror often. I stopped at a gas station, filled up the tank. Travis slept through it all.

I picked up the cell phone and called Rachel. I asked her to meet me in the parking lot of a grocery store on the east side of town.

I got there first. I opened some windows and the roof vent, so that Travis wouldn't suffocate in the afternoon heat, and stepped outside. I stayed next to the van, even after Rachel parked several spaces away.

She walked over and I explained what was happening. I told her she could look through the photos while I picked up a few things in the store.

I wasn't gone long; I had no idea how many days we'd spend on the road, but being an optimist, I guessed on the low side. Besides, there wasn't much room in the van's little refrigerator.

We stepped outside to talk.

"What are your plans for these photos?" she asked in a low voice.

"I'm going to have a talk with your friend McCain."

She didn't comment on that, or shrug or gesture. That made me uneasy. "You've seen him lately?" I asked.

"Had lunch with him today." After a moment she added, "Talked over old times."

"No kidding."

"Listen, you have something on your mind, say it."

"And get my ass kicked? No thank you."

"I won't touch you, and you know it. So speak up."

I didn't say anything.

"All right, then," she said.

After a long silence, during which neither one of us would look at the other, she said, "You need anything?"

"Just check on Mary once in a while." I gave her the address and phone number. "And one other thing—a big

favor." I handed her my car keys. "Move the Karmann Ghia?
Maybe Jack would help you out."

"I'd rather stay with you, protect the two of you."

I shook my head. "If anything happens to us, I'm depending on you and Mary to make sure Frank starts dating
again."

"Don't talk like that."

"Oh, I'm supposed to tell you that our boys spent
Saturday night at a public library in Boise, Idaho, looking up
that story on DeMont."

She smiled. "The sad thing is, I believe it."

She walked back to her car, then drove it over to where
I still stood outside the van. She rolled down her window,
said, "I shouldn't have to tell you this, but I would never do
anything to hurt him."

She drove off, while I stood there, alone with my shame.

I called McCain.

———

I drove the van to a large park near the eastern side of
town. Part of the park can be accessed for free; I went to
the larger section, the side that charges a low admission
fee. It was that time of day when picnickers were starting
to leave, so when I paid the two bucks to go in, most of the
other cars were going out.

I drove to the far end of the road, to a relatively treeless
section that is mostly a large stretch of uneven ground. Not
enough shade or tables for a picnic, nor level enough for
games. We had it to ourselves. I would easily be able to see
anyone approaching by car or on foot.

Travis still slept, but his sleep was more restless now.
Once, I thought he had awakened, but he was only talking
in his sleep, murmuring half-words that I couldn't understand.

I opened up the side of the van, and set up its attached

awning. This kept the van cool and made a shady spot to sit while waiting for McCain. I set up two chairs under the nearest tree, so that we could talk without waking Travis.

I heard the car even before I saw it, and noticed that McCain was approaching cautiously, as if driving into a possible trap. Suspicious son of a bitch. Not that I blamed him.

He parked some distance away, but that might have been because I had told him Travis was sleeping. I motioned him over to the chairs. He was in a suit, and he hung the jacket on the back of his chair. I offered him a can of iced tea, and he accepted. He seemed to be studying my every move. As I handed him the iced tea, it dawned on me that he hadn't seen me at all the day before, so the bruises and swelling were new to him. He saw that I had caught him staring at me and said, "I didn't realize that guy had roughed you up so much."

I shrugged, and said, "There are worse things that can happen to a person."

"Reed Collins tells me you know about some of those, too."

I took a deep breath. "Not why I asked you over here."

"Well, yes, but this is my awkward attempt at working up to an apology. Sorry I got so hot under the collar yesterday."

"I was a little testy myself."

"Nobody had slammed me against a wall."

"Okay, you win, you were the bigger asshole."

He laughed. "Much better. What can I do for you?"

"I visited Robert DeMont today. You know who he is?"

"Cousin of Arthur Spanning's first wife. We talked to him. Says what everybody says in this case—he hasn't seen Briana Maguire in years."

"Did you visit him at his house?"

"No, just talked to him on the phone."

I held up the envelope. "If I tell you who has the negatives, will you leave these here with me?"

"If they have to do with an ongoing—"

"Oh, take the starch out of your drawers!" I snapped, holding the envelope out of reach.

He seemed taken aback, but then smiled and said, "A compromise. If I can't find the negatives by Monday morning, you hand these over."

"You search diligently before then?"

"Absolutely—if they're worth the search."

I handed him the envelope. "No worries on that score."

He opened it, pulled out the photos, and after a surprised look crossed his face, took out his notebook and said, "Who took them?"

"Harold Richmond."

"The guy with one idea?"

I felt the parts of my face that weren't purple turn red. I explained who Richmond was, told him who had hired him. "I think you'll find that he matches the description of the man who was trying to break into Briana's apartment. The neighbors would probably be thrilled to pick him out of a lineup."

While McCain continued to study the photos, I wrote down Richmond's address and phone number, and told him how to get to Margot's place on Rivo Alto. "You're more likely to find him there," I said, "or at a bar called the Wharf."

As I said this last to him, an idea struck me. Fortunately, he was absorbed in studying the photos, so he didn't see the little lightbulb go on over my head.

"Because there's a connection between your case and the bombing of the camper," I said, "I think the Las Piernas Police are also going to want these negatives. So promise me you'll share them with your good friend Reed Collins."

He looked up then, and said, "You think this man killed your aunt?"

"I'm not saying he did or he didn't. But he was taking her photo in the very place where she was killed."

"And other places as well."

I didn't trust myself to speak.

"You're angry."

"If someone you loved had been photographed at her husband's funeral, all for the entertainment of her spouse's enemies, wouldn't you be a little pissed off?"

"Yeah," he admitted softly. "Yeah, I would."

"One other thing. DeMont owns a Camry that was in a wreck a few weeks ago."

His brows went up.

"I can give you the address of the body shop it's in, if you don't think it's too late to find evidence on it."

"We'll probably find what we're looking for. They may not have started working on it—a reputable shop will report anything that has signs of being in a pedestrian versus vehicle accident."

"But it wasn't in the shop until this week." I explained the situation. "He might have cleaned it up before his sister hauled it off to the shop."

"Don't worry, if you've got the right car, we'll know it." He paused, then said, "You're a reporter—got a strong enough stomach for some details?"

I nodded, not sure that was true.

"Blood, hair and other matter will still show up on a car that's been washed—on the undercarriage, behind the grill and in other places most people wouldn't think of cleaning. As for the time that's passed, sure, we'd like to find any evidence as soon as possible, but even if the blood, fiber and other evidence have been destroyed, the LAPD collected parts of that car from the scene. We've got pieces to match up to the damage, and autopsy observations that will help do the same. And of course, there are the tires."

"The tires?"

"There were tire-tread marks visible on the body."

"Oh."

"I don't tell you this to distress you," he said. "Just to let you know that I think we'll have plenty of ways to link the car to the crime if it's the one that was used to kill your aunt. He could have taken it through a car wash, and we'd still be able to show a jury that it's the one."

He reluctantly handed the photos back, then said, "You know these weren't taken on the day she was killed?"

"Wrong sweater."

He smiled. "You talked to Mr. Reyes." He put on his jacket and tucked his notebook away. He studied me for a moment, then said, "You must get along well with Rachel."

"If I could have chosen my own sister, I would have picked Rachel. You should see who I got instead."

He laughed and said, "Thanks for the help. I need to get going on all of this." He looked around, then said, "You think you and your cousin will be safe out here?"

"Does this mean I'm no longer a suspect?"

"Whoever said you were one?"

I groaned. "Maybe a long talk with Richmond will make you a little less suspicious of me."

"One can always hope," he said, smiling to himself as he walked toward his car.

I put the envelope on the small table in the van, then went back out to get the chairs. When I returned, Travis was standing next to the table, his hair sleep-tousled, a look of bewilderment on his face.

"Where are we?"

"A park on the east side of Las Piernas." I picked up the envelope and explained why we had left Mary's. "We tried to wake you, but the pain pill made that impossible."

"I vaguely remember walking out to the van," he said, rubbing his face, seeming still half-asleep. "How can you be so sure they knew where we were?"

That led to an explanation about my afternoon, and the photos.

"The photos are in that envelope?"

"Yes."

"You said he took photos of my mother?"

"Yes."

"May I seem them?" He said it with a touch of impatience.

Reluctantly, I handed them to him. I stepped outside to take the awning down.

He was silent as he looked through them, but despite visible efforts to control himself, he couldn't hide his grief when he came to one of them. He hadn't looked through all of them, but he set them down, then covered his eyes with his left hand. I stepped inside, finished with the awning, but leaving the door open. On the table, at the top of the stack, was one of the photos of his mother at Arthur's funeral.

He broke down, but this storm was over almost as quickly as it started, as if he only needed its release for it to pass.

I found a box of tissues, and he took it, saying, "I'm sorry, I'm sorry. It's just—God! I should have been there! I should have taken care of her, protected her!"

"Do you think you could have prevented Richmond from spying on her?"

After a moment he shook his head. "I couldn't even prevent him from spying on you and me."

He stepped outside, looked around. "Can we stay here overnight?"

"No. But we should keep moving, anyway."

He glanced back at the envelope.

"Do you think Robert DeMont killed my mother?"

"If he did, McCain will find out from the car."

He was quiet for a moment, then said, "But you don't think he did it."

"I'm not sure."

"Why not?"

"These photos were most likely taken because someone believes your father murdered his first wife."

"Harold Richmond and Robert DeMont both believe that," he said.

"Well, Richmond does anyway." I told him about DeMont's history with knives. "But the more I think about it, the more I wonder why Robert would have killed Gwen. He might have tried to get her to divorce your dad, so that he could go back to raiding her money. But if she was dead and he couldn't pin the murder on your dad, he was out of luck."

"Maybe he found out about us—my mom and me," Travis said. "Maybe he *did* hope to frame my dad, thought the bigamy would convince a jury that my dad was a murderer. Then the other DeMonts would get everything—my dad couldn't inherit."

"Hmm. But that was all settled a long time ago, whether they like it or not. Why hire someone to take photos of you and your mother now? Why attack you, your mother, Ulkins? They won't get anything from the estate by killing you."

"Who would?"

"Your uncle Gerald."

"But he said he can't inherit—"

"Gerald only said he couldn't get anything from the DeMont estate. There could be money that didn't come from her inheritance, and which would be fair game for Gerald. We need to talk to your friend Mr. Brennan to find out if there ever was a prenuptial agreement. I was hoping I could get you to call him again, ask his answering service to tell him that we want to drive out to—where does he stay?"

"Lake Arrowhead."

"So tell him we'll come up to Lake Arrowhead to talk to him."

He made the call. When he hung up, he said, "I know that Gerald lied to me, but think about the things that have happened! This Richmond guy takes photos of my mom in an intersection, and she's killed there! He takes these photos of my camper, and it blows up! What more do you need? I'm not saying I know *why* Richmond and Robert DeMont are trying to destroy us—hell, maybe they think of this as revenge. But Gerald couldn't know you were going to find me that day, or even know where you live."

"You're right about Richmond and his photos, but I'm not so sure what you just said about Gerald is true."

"What do you mean?"

"Something occurred to me while I was talking to McCain, telling him where he could count on finding Richmond. Earlier today, I had been asking myself some of those same questions—how could Gerald know where Richmond was going, and when he'd be there? Richmond might not have noticed that he had a tail on him, but Gerald wouldn't be able to follow him around night and day. He works. And Deeny works, too. But I had forgotten a couple of pieces of information—failed to put them together until I was talking to McCain."

I flipped to the page of my notebook that had the numbers from Margot's caller-ID display written on it, and, next to them, the information Jerry Chase had looked up for me on the *News-Express* computers.

"I want to test a theory," I said. I dialed the phone number. The number hadn't answered the last time I called it—from the pay phone near Rivo Alto. I had called after closing time that night.

Travis looked on, puzzled.

"I'm calling a bar in Los Alamitos," I said. "One that Harold Richmond frequents on a regular basis."

After three rings, a gruff voice answered, "Wharf."

"Hi," I said. "Is Deeny there?"

Travis's eyes widened.

"Naw, she won't be in until five," the voice answered, "but she'll be working—no personal calls. Call her at home, all right?" He promptly hung up on me.

I repeated the conversation to Travis.

"So Richmond gets drunk at this bar and brags about his progress in the case," Travis said. "And she goes home and tells Gerald."

"Right."

"Wouldn't Richmond make the connection?"

"Not unless he sees her with Gerald; if she drives herself to and from work, probably not. And how many men in a bar ever learn a cocktail waitress's last name?"

"I see your point. How did you know she worked there?"

"Our informant in the trailer park told us she was a cocktail waitress."

"Trudy Flauson! Yes, now I remember."

"Richmond the braggart," I said. "Not hard to imagine him telling her about his obsession, especially when there's some exciting news: Arthur is seeing his son again; Arthur is in the hospital; Arthur has legally married Briana Maguire."

The phone rang. Travis answered it, then looked over at me. "It's Mr. Brennan. He wants to give you directions to his house in Lake Arrowhead."

30

We were on the Riverside Freeway, stuck in traffic, when the fight started. It began with what was supposed to be a compliment.

"I have to admit," Travis said, "I've been surprised by the Kellys."

"Finding out we aren't such a bad bunch after all?" I said, trying to keep my tone light, but in retrospect, I'll admit I failed to do so.

"I'm not ready to forgive Patrick, of course," he said.

"Oh, of course not!"

He didn't miss it that time. "Look, I'm sorry, but you weren't living in Las Piernas when all hell broke loose for us. Your father completely turned his back on us."

"Travis, that back had been turned on your family for years. I don't say it was right—it obviously grew out of a terrible misunderstanding. But have you ever thought that your father could have explained what was going on?"

"Oh, right! He's going to tell Patrick Kelly, who has scowled at him from the moment he met him, that he can't read!"

"I'm not saying that what my father did was wonderful. But how hard did anybody on your side of the family work to patch things up?"

"Because he was known to be so forgiving? Look—forget about how he felt about my father. Do you realize how hard life was for my mother, after she split up with my dad?"

"Did she try to make contact with my father?"

"Did Patrick try to contact her?" he shot back.

I tried to count to ten. I got to three, and said, "A moment ago you said I didn't know what was going on in Las Piernas then. You were only eleven. You didn't know what was going on in my father's life then, did you?"

"How could I? He wasn't speaking to us. Besides, it couldn't have been as bad as what was happening to her."

"Oh, no? Well, listen to this, Your Honor, Judge of the Family. He had cancer. How's that for an excuse?"

"He didn't tell us," he said, but he wasn't shouting now.

"No, he was sort of like your own father. He had his secrets, too. He didn't like to appear to be weak. He was the one who had to be strong for everybody else. He didn't let me know about it until he was too sick to work. So I came down from Bakersfield and took care of him."

"But Barbara—"

"Barbara couldn't take it. She still hasn't forgiven him for knowing that, for calling me to come to him. Then again, she hasn't forgiven herself for running away from his illness."

There was a long silence.

"Go ahead," he said. "Ask."

"Ask what?"

"Ask me why I was out riding around in a purple-and-yellow camper—"

"Oh, Christ—"

"—telling children's stories—"

"That's not what I was trying to say!" I protested.

"Telling fairy tales, while my parents were dying."

"You didn't know that!"

"I didn't know what would happen to my mother." He paused, swallowed hard. "But I knew my dad was dying."

"Travis—no, please. I wasn't trying to say anything like that."

"Let me—let me explain." He couldn't go on for a moment, but gradually he pulled himself together and said, "I think I've told you that I reached a point in my life when I wanted to get to know my father—as an adult. My mother didn't like the idea. I don't think, looking back on it, that it was because she hated him then. Even during the worst of it, I think she still loved him. I guess I've always known that.

"But I don't think she was ever a person who found it easy to trust others. She had trusted him, though, and he destroyed that trust. After that, she wouldn't date other men. The one man she loved had caught her up in a thousand lies, and her son was a bastard whose face was a constant reminder of the man who destroyed her life—"

"Travis—"

"No, she said that to me once. 'Every time I look at you, do you know who I see?'"

"She didn't mean it—"

"Yes, she did. I'll admit she was angry, but she meant it. It wasn't so obvious when I was younger, with a boy's face, but as I became a man, I was a reminder." He paused, and added, "I'm not saying she didn't love me. She did. I never doubted that.

"But you can see why," he went on, "the closer my father and I became, the more upset she became. She started issuing ultimatums to me. You haven't known me very long, but I guess you can imagine how well that worked."

I smiled. "Yes, I think so."

"My father had already been diagnosed with cancer when I started to spend more time with him, but he wasn't—he wasn't an invalid. Most of the time, he did his best to make me forget that he was ill. We had a lot of catching up to do. It was clear to me that he still loved my mother. It was the way he would ask about her, the way he would look whenever he'd talk about the years when we were a family."

He fell silent for a while. By then we had reached San Bernadino. Soon we would be in the mountains themselves.

"Once in a while he would have a bad day," he said, coming out of his reverie, "and on those days, he'd ask me not to come over. I'd protest, and tell him that I wanted to be with him no matter what, but he could be stubborn.

"When there started to be more bad days, he sat me down and told me—well, many things. He said that the two of us had more than enough painful memories between us, that he preferred this reunion of ours not to include my seeing him helpless and sick. He said he would always feel he had taken horrible advantage of me if he had only brought me to his side to watch him die. He wanted life with me, he said, not death, and nothing but good memories of our time together to sustain him through whatever was to come."

He was silent again. He reached for the envelope of photographs, pulled out one of the ones of the purple camper and smiled wistfully.

"During one of my earlier visits," he said, "my father had learned that I had studied to be a reading specialist, and asked me about it. He encouraged me to talk about the things I enjoyed doing—and about the things I dreamed of doing. I told him about storytelling, which I had been involved in locally for a number of years. And another time, I told him that I had this urge to travel. That's when I learned more about the hobo side of the family—he said I couldn't help being a nomad, it was the Spanning vagabond in me.

"This last time I saw him, he called in Mr. Brennan, whom I had met when I was younger, but hadn't seen in many years. My father and Mr. Brennan told me about the provisions my father had made for me. I was astounded, to tell you the truth.

"My father told me he was worried that making me this

wealthy would put me in danger, and not just from the DeMonts, but he figured I would understand that, and take care of myself. He said there were members of the family who would try to convince me that I owed them big portions if not all of his money, and he wished I would tell them to go to hell, but if I wanted to hand it over to them, fine. For now, he said, he was the one who had earned it, and so it was his decision to make himself happy by imagining me doing what I wanted to do, making my own choices.

"He asked if I ever thought of taking my storytelling act on the road for a time—and as he went on to describe some of his ideas about it, it wasn't as if he was pushing me to conform to something he wanted. It was—it was as if I had told my most secret dreams to someone, and he had not only not laughed at them, but he had understood them perfectly."

"And given you the power to make them come true."

"Yes," he said. "Yes."

"But your mother didn't like the idea?"

He shook his head. "Hated it. She would have been angry at me for taking a dime from him. She saw it as a betrayal. She even moved to that one-bedroom apartment—a way of saying I wasn't going to find a room for myself when I came back. I guess—I had lived with her for so long, beyond the time when I wanted to move out, because I knew—I knew!—how lonely she'd be . . ."

"So for once in your life, you did something for yourself."

"Oh, not for once," he said. "She made a lot of sacrifices for me."

"Your wanting to leave the nest—it was the natural course of things, Travis. I remember how my father—well, never mind."

"Your father didn't want you to move out?"

"No. But at that time, I felt as if we'd end up hating each other if I stayed. And I think we would have."

"But you came back."

"That's true. It was what he wanted, what he asked for. For me to be there. I did what he asked. Your father asked for something different. You did what he asked."

He was silent.

Ghosts, I thought, then suddenly remembered Travis's e-mail address. "Was he your George Kerby?"

He smiled. "*Topper.* My dad and I watched a videotape of that film one day. He threatened to start calling me 'Toppie' because he said I was just like Cosmo Topper, confined to routine and taking life far too seriously. He said I needed to get out and do the things I wanted to do. He said he'd come back and haunt me if I didn't start living a little. So Cosmo became my storyteller name."

"I wonder if he was also trying to take you out of harm's way for a while."

"What do you mean?"

"Maybe by sending you on the road, making it difficult for people to find you after his death, your father saved your life."

He was thinking that over when his cell phone rang.

"It's Rachel," he said, "but she said I should ask you to pull over before I give you the phone."

"Oh, brother. Once a cop—" I said lightly.

"She sounds upset," he said.

31

I had just started up Highway 18, so I pulled over and took the phone from Travis.

"Rachel? Is Mary all right?"

"Mary's fine. Her house is fine, too, although there was a fire."

"A fire! Her house caught on fire?"

"No, the Karmann Ghia."

"The . . ." I couldn't say it.

"Jack and I went over there to pick it up, there was already a fire truck on the scene."

"Not my Karmann Ghia . . ."

"I'm so sorry, Irene. I know you loved that little car. I know you've had it for a long time—"

"Since college," I said blankly. "Since college."

"Can you forgive me?"

"Forgive you?"

"If I had gone straight over there, after I talked to you—"

"Oh, Rachel. Don't do that to yourself. I'm the one who left it there. What happened?"

"Molotov cocktail."

"We must be rushing him. The bomb on Travis's camper was much more sophisticated."

"Let Travis drive—you're upset."

"Steer a van up mountain roads with one hand? Not if you aren't used to it. But now he's wondering what has happened. Explain it to him, will you?"

I handed the phone to Travis and started up Waterman Canyon. He spoke briefly with Rachel, hung up, then said, "I'm sorry, Irene."

"Just a car," I said, which was such total bullshit, I'm surprised he didn't call me on it. But he fell silent, which is what I needed.

I was grateful for the mountain roads; they required my absolute concentration. The sun was setting, and by the time we reached Mr. Brennan's large, lake-view mountain home, it was dark. I parked along the road, took out a large flashlight that Jack had apparently included in the price of the van, and Travis and I stepped outside. I felt the chill mountain air, heard the crickets sing, smelled the pine fragrance and saw the stars overhead. I promptly bent over double and started throwing up.

"Irene!" Travis rushed over to me.

"Some water, please," I said between dry heaves. "Bottle in the van fridge."

He brought it to me. I rinsed my mouth out. "Is it because of your car?"

"No."

"The curving road?"

"No."

"The altitude?"

"No. The mountains," I said.

"The mountains?"

"I'm—I'm afraid of the mountains."

He stopped asking questions.

"I was taken to a place not far from here once," I said. "Against my will. Locked me in a little dark room. Spent three days beating the shit out me. Haven't been to the mountains since. And if you ever want to see me go nuts, lock me inside any confined space."

He reached over, took my hand. "Why didn't you tell me?"

"You had enough on your mind. Besides, I have to try to get over this sooner or later." I laughed. "Frank is going to be so pissed."

"At me? I won't blame him."

"No, me. He owns property up here. I always make him go without me."

I stood up, took a little bit of time to get myself back together, or what I hoped would pass for together. It was an act, of course, but sometimes you have to make do with an act.

There was a dignity about Ezekiel Brennan that made one approach him calmly and quietly. He was a tall, broad-shouldered man with a full head of perfectly combed white hair, watchful gray eyes—slightly enlarged by the lenses in his pewter-rimmed glasses—a strong nose and chin, a firm mouth. He wore casual clothes when he greeted us at the front door—a light sweater and jeans—but it wasn't hard to picture him in a finely tailored suit, carrying a leather briefcase.

Brennan was gracious to both of us, a perfect host. Travis obviously meant more to him than the average client. It would be easy to assume it was the millions, but even before he started talking about Arthur Spanning, I knew that he looked upon Travis as he might a grandson.

When he first saw my cousin, his smile became much warmer. "Travis!" he said in his deep voice, embracing him with an arm around the shoulder.

"Thank you for allowing us to come to your home on such short notice, Mr. Brennan," he said, returning the embrace.

"What has happened to your hand?!" he asked.

"Oh—that's a long story," Travis said, then added, "I'm so glad to see you!"

The hand on Travis's shoulder gave it another squeeze. "An extremely difficult time for you, I know. I am so very sorry."

"My dad—your friendship was so important to him. He was grateful for all you did to help him over the years."

"That was my pleasure. And his friendship was equally important to me," Brennan said. "I find myself somewhat at loose ends these days—I do miss him."

He showed us into a spacious living room, where a small fire burned in a brick fireplace. Large windows and sliding-glass doors looked out on the lake below. It was too dark to see much more than the outline of the shore, but in daylight, it would be a beautiful view. Travis was watching me nervously. "I'm okay," I said softly.

We declined the offer of a drink. With nothing more than a raised eyebrow, Mr. Brennan indicated to me that he expected to have a private conversation with Travis.

"I want her here," Travis said, reading the look. "She may hear anything you have to say to me."

"Whatever you wish, of course," Brennan said, "but wouldn't it be better—"

"When my father warned me about being bothered by the family," Travis interrupted, "was he referring to the Kellys?"

"No," Brennan admitted. "Your father was referring to your uncle Gerald and his other in-laws, the DeMonts."

Travis studied the lawyer for a moment, then said, "I am willing to explain why I want Irene to be here, but I don't want to upset you—"

"My boy, I am old, but I am healthy, and working in law has strengthened my nerves remarkably. Say what you have to say."

"Irene is helping me to discover who murdered my mother. She needs to hear everything. And she'll have some questions of her own."

But Brennan was still caught on one word. *"Murdered?"*

"Yes." Travis seemed unable for a moment to go on, and said, "Irene—will you please tell him?"

Brennan listened in silence as I told him what we had learned about the hit-and-run accident. He offered condolences to Travis, and seemed genuinely shaken.

"I was there when she married him again," he said. "I was their witness. They were both very happy, despite the circumstances—Arthur was in the hospital, of course. But I must say, Travis, that your mother's presence gave him strength." He paused, then said, "Once, when she had left the room for a few moments, your father spoke of you and your mother coming back into his life, and of—of forgiveness. He said, 'Zeke, never doubt that I will die a happy man.'"

His voice caught on this last and he stopped speaking for a moment while he pulled out a handkerchief, ostensibly to wipe his glasses. He took a few minutes to do this, then said, "She never wanted his money, of course, but he made sure that she would be provided for. When she learned of it, I think her first thought was of you, because she asked me to make a new will for her."

"Tell me that she signed it," I said.

He looked surprised, then said, "Why, yes, she did."

"Oh, thank God!" I said. They both looked at me as if I had lost my mind. "Please call Detective McCain of the LAPD for me," I said. "Although he'll probably tell you that I couldn't have known about the new will."

Travis understood then, and explained to Mr. Brennan, adding, "Most people wouldn't be so happy over losing half a million dollars."

"Peanuts, if it gets McCain off my back."

"I'll have a talk with him, if you like," Brennan said.

"Thank you. Would you please help Travis make out a new will tonight?"

"A new will."

"Yes—and for godsakes, leave me out of it. Travis's will is made in favor of his mother, and I'm afraid there is at least one person who would like to see him die intestate."

"Good Lord."

"In fact, perhaps you could clear something up for us. Do Robert or Horace DeMont have any claim on any portion of Arthur's estate?"

"Absolutely not. But a mere matter of law won't stop those two. Robert and Horace are imbeciles. Their only genius is in their tenacity."

"Perhaps not their only genius," Travis said, and told him of my experiences at Robert's home.

"I should have liked to see that window go!" he said. "But I still say Robert and his father are fools. And I was wrong— they have an additional ability to make the worst investment choices on earth. They have not, either one of them, realized that if it hadn't been for Arthur, there would have been absolutely nothing left of the DeMont fortune by the time Gwendolyn died. There was damned little as it was."

"Leda said something like that," I said.

"Leda," said Brennan, "is so sensible, I believe she must be a changeling. But Robert and Horace! Gwendolyn's naïve trust of them caused a great deal of harm."

"But she was still wealthy when my father married her, wasn't she?" Travis asked.

"When he married her? Oh, yes. Even the DeMonts could not destroy that much money in so short a time. Her fortune was rapidly being decimated, but there was wealth. It was still some time before he took a hand in matters; after all, he was only sixteen when he married her. And there were extenuating circumstances . . ." He looked over at me, then said, "Travis, your father instructed me to tell you the whole story, should you wish to hear it, but I cannot believe he intended—"

"I think he would have trusted me to make this decision, don't you?"

Brennan smiled. "Yes, of course."

"She knows my father couldn't read or write," Travis said, and seeing Brennan's dismay, quickly added, "and I don't believe she thinks less of him for that. If anything" — he glanced at me — "we've cleared up an old family misunderstanding."

"How old was Arthur when he told you, Mr. Brennan?" I asked.

"Near his eighteenth birthday. I shall never, as long as I live, forget that day. I had already become fond of your father, but when he admitted his problem, I thought he showed remarkable courage."

"He told me about that," Travis said. "That was when you found Ulkins for him—oh, my God! You don't know about him either!"

This news greatly upset him; they spoke for a long time about Ulkins.

"My father said W changed everything for him," Travis said.

"Ulkins was well-paid," Brennan said, "and liked your father immensely. As Ulkins himself often said, he only made information accessible to your father. It remained for your father—without the aid of notes, relying strictly on his memory—to process that information and make decisions. He built a fortune. Never doubt that your father was a very intelligent man."

"Did Gerald do all of your father's reading before that?" I asked.

"Gerald or Gwendolyn. Mostly Gwendolyn, by then."

"Mr. Brennan," I asked, "was there any sort of prenuptial agreement signed when Arthur married Gwendolyn?"

"Only as concerned Gerald. He was not to inherit or receive from Arthur any of the DeMont money. Gerald claimed to be happy about it; he said it would prove that his—insistence, shall we say?—on the marriage was not motivated by greed."

"Did you believe him?"

Brennan considered this for a time, then frowned. "Gerald's insistence didn't matter—Gwendolyn wanted the marriage. As for Gerald, I believe that while he has always wanted money, money itself is not what motivates him. He enjoys controlling others. He enjoyed it on that occasion." The frown deepened. "Gerald is, I'm afraid, someone your father worried over."

"In what way?" Travis asked.

"I don't know, exactly, but I do know your father had given your mother something that was supposed to ensure that Gerald never bothered the two of you. When I asked him why on earth Gerald would bother you, he merely said that Gerald was always very fond of Gwendolyn. I took that to mean that Gerald might resent you and your mother, on Gwendolyn's behalf."

"Do you know what it was Arthur gave Briana?" I asked.

"No, he was very evasive on that subject."

"I'm sorry to say that whatever kept Gerald away must no longer exist," Travis said. "Did Gerald come after Dad for money after Gwendolyn's death?"

"No, your father and his brother were estranged. Gerald was not the only person who could not accept your father's bigamy, and Gerald's own regard for Gwendolyn perhaps made him more prejudiced than most. But Arthur loved Gerald—make no mistake about that. Gerald had raised him and was the last remaining member of his family; he spoke many times of the sacrifices Gerald had made for him. Not that having someone make sacrifices for you is all that it's cracked up to be. Gerald was overbearing in those days."

For a moment he was lost in thought, then said, "By the time I first met Arthur, when he was sixteen, he wanted nothing more than independence. It was clear to me that he was genuinely attached to Gwendolyn. No matter how hard I questioned him, he wouldn't deny to me that he wanted to marry her, but over time I grew certain that the marriage was almost entirely Gerald's idea. I even suspected Arthur had received a beating from Gerald over the matter, but could prove nothing. Arthur would never utter a word against his brother.

"Gwendolyn—well, perhaps Gwendolyn felt she had no other chance. And I think she, in her own way, saw an opportunity to help Arthur."

"How so?" I asked.

"She helped him to free himself from Gerald. She explicitly instructed me to do all I could to enable Arthur to get away from the DeMont farm every now and then. And although she never spoke of it specifically, she certainly turned a blind eye to his absences from home."

"You think she knew about us?" Travis asked.

"I'm not certain, of course, but I think not. Your father wasn't careless of her feelings. But even before she married him, she told me that Arthur was never, under any circumstances, to be spied upon. She said he had spent too many years under Gerald's watchful eye, and now deserved an opportunity to get into any sort of mischief he pleased."

"Leda seemed to think Gwendolyn would stand up for Arthur sooner than she would defend herself."

"Definitely," Brennan said. "But Arthur also protected her. Unlike him, she longed for that sort of protection. She disliked business matters; he thrived on them. She wanted to remain a recluse; he was sociable. She hated to leave that farm; he was glad to travel. She liked his company, but I believe she would have been unhappy with a man who was constantly under what she certainly thought of as her roof. Arthur preserved rather than destroyed that private world of hers. She knew he attended to the matters that her various fears would have caused to have been neglected. And so on the whole, I believe she was perfectly content with the marriage."

"How did he start his own business?" I asked.

"With a loan, which he very quickly repaid."

"A loan from the DeMont fortune?"

"No. There were virtually no liquid assets in the DeMont holdings by the time Arthur turned eighteen."

"Nothing that could have been borrowed against?"

"Oh, certainly. There was the farm itself, a few other properties. But Arthur never would have borrowed against the DeMont farm."

"So who loaned it to him?" Travis asked.

Mr. Brennan colored slightly, then said, "I did."

Travis grinned. "Why, Mr. Brennan, it seems I'm much more indebted to you than I imagined."

"Oh, no, Travis. Not at all. The reverse is true. Given access to information, your father was the shrewdest investor I ever met. He was very generous to me over the years. I have no hesitation in telling you he was my favorite client."

"He made his money in the stock market?" I asked.

"Eventually, yes—that and other investments. At first, though, he concentrated a tremendous amount of effort in his own business. He did very well with it, took the profits in hand and promptly doubled them. I was very impressed, until I saw that he was just getting warmed up."

"Mr. Brennan," I said, "during the time of the initial investigation of Gwendolyn's murder, Robert said he had contacted her to obtain money. He said she had agreed to give him a check. I know she loaned him money on previous occasions, but was that still going on by the time she died?"

"No, I don't think so," he said. "As little as she liked business, Gwendolyn was aware by that time that the DeMont fortune had in truth become the Spanning fortune, with, as I say, only the lands themselves untouched. The fields on the farm were planted because Arthur paid to have them planted. He never refused her anything she wished to purchase for herself, but he was so angry with the DeMonts for taking advantage of her, he did forbid any further expenditure on them."

They talked a little longer, Mr. Brennan apologizing for not having any of the papers he wanted to go over with Travis. "They are in my office. Can you come by there tomorrow?"

We agreed to stop by. I excused myself to go outside while they worked on the will. "It's chilly out there," Brennan said. "Wouldn't you rather wait in my library, or some other room?"

"Irene loves fresh mountain air," Travis said.

"This may take awhile," Brennan said. "Would you like directions to the town?"

"No, Travis is right. The outdoors will be entertaining enough."

"Then let me lend you a sweater," he said.

I was grateful for the sweater, but more grateful for the fresh air, the time to think. I found Mary's temporary address and phone number in my jeans pocket, and thought of calling her. I couldn't get a strong-enough signal, though, and gave up. Tired, I went to lie down in the van, thinking of Brennan's offer of directions before I dozed off.

I awoke to see three strangers entering the house.

I made a mad dash for the front door, coming in on their heels, but not tackling anyone when I saw that I was the most threatening individual present.

"Don't worry," Travis said, knowing exactly what had caused me to rush inside. "These are Mr. Brennan's neighbors. One is a notary. The other two will witness the will."

They stared at my bruised face, then turned to Travis, and asked him how he hurt his hand.

Mr. Brennan had already made photocopies of the unsigned will. He gave one of these to Travis, saying, "Perhaps I should keep the only signed copy in my safe for tonight. I can give it to you in Las Piernas if you want to keep it in your own safe-deposit box."

That was agreeable to Travis.

He offered to have us stay overnight, but Travis declined the offer. "We need to get back to Las Piernas," he said.

I thanked him and returned the sweater. He seemed reluctant to see Travis leave. "I hope you know you should call on me any time—and you need not have the excuse of business. I always enjoy seeing you."

I was searching the pockets of the jeans I had worn the day before when Travis came back to the van. I had just found what I was looking for when he said, "I didn't think you'd want to stay up here tonight."

"You're right. Thanks. I do want to go back downhill, but not because of my phobias."

"You're over your mountain phobia already?"

"Sorry, no—progress made, but no cure." I started the van, and pulled away. "That wasn't what I meant. I had a chance to do some thinking while I was outside, and now I'd like to get back to talk something over with Rachel."

"What?"

"First, take a look at this."

He turned the passenger reading lamp on and said, "This was what you got out of your jeans pocket?"

"Yes," I said. "Thank God I haven't had a chance to wash them."

32

"What is it?"

"The little slip of paper Deeny gave me when we were at the trailer park. An address on Reagan Street in Los Alamitos. A house owned by Gerald. I'll bet he doesn't know Deeny gave this to us."

"And I'll bet he wouldn't be happy to know she did," he said. "I had forgotten all about this. We made her think we needed to see Gerald on some important business matter, and she gave us this address." He stared at it for a moment, frowning.

"What's wrong?" I asked.

"Oh, probably nothing," he said.

"Go ahead," I said, "maybe you're thinking the same thing I did. That it was an odd way to tell us where he was. You're wondering if Deeny can read."

"I couldn't possibly tell that from one scrap of paper," he said.

"No one is asking you to make a professional assessment here," I said, concentrating on the road again. "I just wondered about it. When someone gives you an address, they usually write down both the house number and the name of the street. She did something unusual. Maybe because she didn't know how to write it."

"Or maybe for some other reason," Travis said.

I thought back to our visit to their home. "There was a

book inside the trailer," I said, "but maybe Gerald was reading it."

"Or maybe no one was," he said. "My dad used to do that. Put a bookmark in a book and carry it around with him. Part of the ongoing fakeout." He handed the paper back to me and added, "My dad used to do this, too. Just write the numbers. Pretend he was in a big hurry, couldn't write out the rest."

"Whether she can read or not, I'm betting there's an El Camino stashed there."

"A what?"

I told him what I had seen when I studied the photos.

"And if it's at this address?"

"We'll consult Rachel on that. The police can probably tell if anyone has hauled explosives in that car."

He started looking through the photos again.

"One other thing," I said, "I can understand why your uncle didn't ask about my face being bruised. Unfortunately, not everyone will ask a woman where she got her bruises—they may be thinking, 'Leave that husband before he kills you, honey,' but not many people will comment aloud. Brennan and his neighbors didn't ask, several other people didn't ask. But you—have we met up with anyone who didn't ask or comment about your hand?"

He thought for a moment, then said, "Just Gerald."

"Right. And since the prenuptial agreement only covered a fortune that no longer exists, who stands in line to inherit if you and your mother are out of the way?"

"Before this new will, Gerald."

"If he has worked long enough in construction," I said, "he probably knows where he can get access to explosives."

After taking some time to think about all of this, he asked, "What should we do?"

"First, call Rachel. Talk to her about all of this, and tell her we're on our way to her place."

"I don't think this is such a hot idea," I said.

"Let's just see if we can find that car," Rachel said. "We don't need to touch it—but if it's there, we call the police, tell them to bring dogs trained in locating explosives. You can bet they'll be traces of it in the El Camino."

"I don't know—" I said, feeling more cautious than usual.

"You have some dark clothes in that trunk of yours?" she asked Travis, ignoring me.

"Yes," he answered, excited by the prospect of taking some action. "I might even have a dark T-shirt that will fit Irene."

She told us to change into the darkest clothes we could find; she had already done the same. In fact, she was shamelessly outfitted as though she were a burglar.

"You don't want to come along," she said to me, "fine. Stay here."

I let myself be swept along, even as I heard that inner voice say, *Watch where you're going!*

Rachel tried to make up for snapping at me by giving me a long-handled flashlight. I tried not to think about it being just like one I used to keep in the Karmann Ghia. I was putting D-cell batteries in it when Travis came into Rachel's living room, shirt unbuttoned and frustration written all over his face. One-handed dressing. I'd been there once myself.

"You managed the pants," I said, before he spoke. "Shirts with buttons are a nuisance. Let me help."

"It didn't give me this much trouble in the store," he said.

"That was earlier in the day."

He was quiet as I worked on the buttons. He thanked me, then paced while I finished putting the flashlight together. I supposed he was working himself up over the evening's adventures, but I decided talking about it wouldn't make him any calmer.

——

"Take a left here," I said. Throughout the drive to Los Alamitos, that type of phrase had been the extent of our conversation. Now that we were off the main boulevards, the streets we drove on were deserted. Rachel was driving—Frank's Volvo—and slowed to look at addresses. She pulled over to the curb.

"It's not in this block," I said.

"Before we get there, once again let's go over what we're going to do. Travis, you'll watch from the car. Any sign of trouble—if you see Gerald or Deeny, or even their cars—start the car. We'll be listening for it. Don't unlock the doors until we're close to the car. Use your cell phone in case there's real trouble—you just stay inside the car and call the police."

I thought he might protest that he wanted to take a more active role, but he simply said, "All right."

"The other thing you need to do is to watch for a signal from Irene. If she flashes her flashlight twice, start the car and if she flashes it three times, call nine-one-one."

"Since we're breaking and entering," I asked, "what is he supposed to tell them?"

Travis laughed.

"Actually," Rachel said, "that will do fine. Travis, tell them there's a burglary in progress."

"I hope none of the neighbors make the same call before he does," I said.

"You could have stayed home," she said.

Too late now. "Where do you want me posted?"

"We'll figure that out when we get there. You'll be outside the building, watching for anyone approaching on foot."

"What if they're already at the house?" I asked.

"Not sure. Depends on the setup."

"Do you two have weapons?"Travis asked.

"Yes, we're armed," Rachel said, not betraying herself by giving me any meaningful looks.While I knew she carried a gun, I wondered what besides my Swiss Army knife and a big flashlight counted as my weapons.

She pulled back onto the street again.There was an odd mix of buildings on the street; a church, small houses, a few duplexes, some light-manufacturing companies and other businesses.We crossed over railroad tracks that used to run through Papa DeMont's sugar beet farm, passing a lumber-yard.

The house Gerald Spanning had purchased was the only residence on its block.There was a new post office across the street,an abandoned foundry on one corner. There were several vacant lots between the house and the foundry.

The house was completely dark, its exterior illuminated by a street lamp.There were no cars parked in the narrow, unpaved driveway, which led to a pair of old-fashioned, carriage-style garage doors.The garage was separated from the house by a short, cracked and weed-choked walkway. A low,rusted and bowed chain-link fence gaped open near one corner of the front yard it enclosed. The lawn had been mowed, but the flower beds were dry and empty.The dark paint on the house and garage was peeling. One of the screens on a front window was torn. If he was fixing the place up,Gerald was working on the interior first.

I noticed there were no trees on the lot."Very out in the open, isn't it?" I said.

"Yes," she said. "Not much cover, but no neighbors to speak of—no one with a view of this place. Looks like there's an alley in back. Let's check it out."

She drove around the corner and stopped the car just at the alley's entrance, illuminating it. There were no cars parked in the alley.

We drove slowly down it, past the graffiti-covered, empty

corrugated tin buildings of the foundry, along the backyard of the house. There was less light here, but we could see two more double doors on this side of the garage, and a cluttered yard. An old bathtub, a sagging clothesline, a broken swing set and other objects were surrounded by weeds. The back screen door was off, propped up against one wall of the house. The chain-link fence on this side of the house was slightly taller than the one in front; there was another short drive leading from this end of the garage to the alley, but it didn't look as if it were much used; the weeds were taller, and a large padlock and heavy chain held a double gate shut.

We continued past the house; the opposite side of the alley was a high cinder-block wall, the back of a shopping center. The other end of the alley let out onto a street bordered by warehouses and a truck yard.

Rachel pulled around to the front of the house, parking on the opposite side of the street again. She seemed to be trying to make up her mind about something. She moved the car a few feet, and said, "This will give you a better view of the back gate, I think. If you need to move the car a little, do it when we first get out, okay? Otherwise you'll start it up and we'll be wetting our pants over nothing."

We all got out of the car. I walked around to the driver's side just as Rachel handed him the keys.

I was feeling uneasy, but when I looked at Travis, he seemed more worried than I was. He got into the car and rolled down the window.

"You okay?" I asked.

"Yes. Be careful." He looked over at Rachel. "Both of you."

"We'll be fine," I said.

"Piece of cake," Rachel said. "This shouldn't take long."

She never should have said that. Later I told her I thought she put the jinx on the whole deal right then and there.

33

We crossed the street quietly. Following Rachel, I could see that she was much better prepared for this adventure: she wore gloves, a holstered gun and an equipment belt that wasn't bulky but kept her hands free—it held her flashlight and a few tools. Her dark pants had lots of pockets.

My pants were dark, too, but while my pocketknife was tucked away in one of the four pockets, I had to carry the flashlight. I hadn't thought of the knife as anything more than a last-ditch sort of weapon; I brought it because it might come in handy as a tool. Rachel would have—quite rightly—counted my carrying a gun in the liability rather than the asset column. I hadn't thought of gloves.

I whispered this last concern to Rachel when we reached the foot of the driveway.

"You won't be touching anything—a lookout, remember?" She glanced down at my shoes. "Good—running shoes—that's all you need. You see Gerald, just warn me and then get the hell out of here."

At the corner of the building, she asked me to stay close to her. "Don't get involved in watching what I'm doing, just keep your eyes moving on the local scenery."

She checked each side of the building, then moved to a door on the side facing the house. While the double doors at each end of the garage were locked with heavy padlocks, this door was locked with a much smaller lock.

"Watch the windows of the house, too," she whispered. "Just in case anyone is home."

She had pulled out something that looked like an eyeglasses case. Less than a minute later, I heard a snick, and saw that she had managed to pick the padlock. She pocketed it, tried to open the door, and found the knob locked as well. This took even less time than the padlock.

"Stay out here," she said. "If you hear or see anything, tap lightly on this door, then get yourself back to the car."

She went inside, closing the door behind her. I walked a few feet, looked quickly down the alley, walked back. I kept watching the house. There wasn't a sound to be heard from the garage. I heard the sound of a car, looked, realized it was on another street—the street at the end of the alley. I waited, but the car kept moving, didn't stop near the alley or Reagan Street.

What the hell was taking so long? It should have only taken a few seconds to see if there was an El Camino in the garage, get its plate number and leave. Plates could be taken off or switched, though, so maybe she was getting the vehicle identification number instead. I moved around a little, checked the other side of the building, came back to the door. It shouldn't be taking so long.

It was with more than a little relief that I saw her open the door again and step outside. I was relieved until I saw her face. She looked angry; there was a harsh determination in her eyes and the set of her mouth.

"The car's not there?"

She had bent to open one of the pockets on her trousers, was pulling something from it. "The El Camino? No." She straightened up, held out a pair of latex gloves. "Here, put these on. You think you can go in there without being bothered by—you know, the confined space?"

"I'll be okay." I took the gloves, started putting them on. "What's in there?"

"I'll show you, but we have to hurry. I don't want to keep Travis waiting."

She stepped inside, I followed. She closed the door behind me. She turned on her flashlight. The garage was more orderly than the backyard, but was nevertheless crowded with lawn equipment, tools and lumber. A fixed wooden ladder led to a half loft above us, where more lumber was stored. I couldn't see much of it, and wasn't really interested in the supplies for the renovation. My attention was focused on the dusty, dark-colored Camry sitting in the middle of the garage. The front bumper was off, and on a workbench, but it was clear the car had been in an accident.

"The right headlamp has been replaced," she whispered. "But the old one is in that barrel—he's using it as a trash can." She moved the light toward a large cardboard drum with a metal rim. "I had a look underneath. There's blood, hair and fabric. It should be enough. You want to look?"

"No," I said, feeling sick.

"Okay. We'll lock up and call the local cops. I'll refer them to McCain. He should—" She suddenly stopped talking. We had both heard it. The sound of the Volvo starting up.

And then, almost immediately, the sound of breaking glass.

34

Rachel's eyes widened. She turned and reached the door before me, peeked out, motioned me to stay back. "Listen!" she said. "Hide in here. I'll come back for you. If not, take that crowbar off the wall and pry the hinges off the door from the inside. Or smash your way out with a sledgehammer—whatever it takes."

"Rachel—!"

But she was shoving me back from the door, and to my horror, I heard her locking it.

"No!" I whispered, but I could hear her moving away from the door.

Do what she asked you to do, I told myself. Concentrate on that. I narrowed the beam of the flashlight, tried to work my way back from the door to find a hiding place. I heard a car door slam. I managed to get to the double doors facing the street; I turned the flashlight off and looked through the crack between the doors.

It didn't afford much of a view, but enough to see Travis being held at gunpoint by Gerald Spanning. As I watched, Spanning took hold of Travis's injured hand and jerked it hard behind Travis's back. Travis made a sharp cry of pain, stumbled slightly. The gun was pressed ruthlessly beneath his jaw. It was then I noticed that his face was bleeding.

It was all I could do not to launch myself against the doors in rage.

Spanning forced him across the street, toward me. Behind them I could see the Volvo, the driver's side window smashed out. Spanning stopped at the foot of the drive and said, "Come on out, all of you. I won't hesitate to shoot this bastard."

Rachel didn't answer. I had a frantic impulse to shout back at Spanning, to do something, anything. Given the distance and the darkness and the fact that she had nothing more than a handgun, I knew Rachel was waiting for a better opportunity to act—but would she wait too long?

Spanning jerked at Travis's hand; Travis's face contorted and he made a soft sound, but he did not cry out. Spanning, not satisfied with this, changed his grip slightly and made another motion, and this time Travis gave out a sharp bark of pain.

I couldn't see or hear Rachel.

A second voice called out from the direction of the alley. "Drop it, lady, slow and easy. I'm a good shot."

Deeny.

Spanning laughed. "She's a damned good shot."

"Put your hands on your head and walk away from the building, slowly," Deeny said.

I saw Rachel come into view.

"Careful, Deeny!" Spanning said. "There's another one of 'em around here somewhere."

"Irene?" Rachel said with scorn. "You think she'd come along with us after that whipping you gave her?"

Spanning didn't look convinced.

"Yeah, that's what she told *you*," Travis said bitterly—perfectly. "But she wouldn't have anything to do with a Spanning if she could help it. They've always snubbed us. If she wasn't hoping to get her hands on my money, she wouldn't give me the time of day. My dad told me the Kellys always thought they were better than the Spannings." He smiled a little. "You should have seen her face when I asked her to come with me to a trailer park to help me find my uncle."

"Yeah? I'm sorry, kid," Rachel said, moving a little closer to them. "Some people are just born snobs. You should have heard what she had to say when she got back from that trip. And when I told her she had probably just visited the guy who kicked her ass, she was shitting herself."

"I know," Travis said. "I thought she'd never shut up."

"Yeah?" Gerald said. "Well, I'll tell you whose gonna shut up right now—and that's the two of you. And you," he said to Rachel, "stay back."

He moved Travis a little farther away from her.

"Deeny," he called out, "come on over here."

So, I thought, it worked; they were convinced Rachel and Travis came alone. But unarmed and locked in the garage, I might as well have been at home.

My narrow view did not allow me to see Deeny, but apparently she covered Rachel as Gerald roughly bound Travis's wrists behind his back. Next he gagged his mouth, saying, as he tightened the strip of cloth, "This is just until we get a few things settled, then you and me are going to have us a nice, long talk." He took the injured hand and squeezed it hard, pressing his thumb into Travis's palm; Travis made a horrible sound behind the gag, fell to his knees. Gerald kicked him over, onto his face in the dirt.

I saw Rachel make the slightest shift of position, the only sign she gave of being affected by what was being done to Travis. I don't think either Gerald or Deeny saw it. Gerald was now taking Rachel's gun and tucking it into his belt. He handed a piece of rope and a gag to Deeny and told her to tie Rachel's hands. I began to wonder if she would submit to being tied up. She was perfectly capable, even unarmed, of taking at least one of them out of action, if not both. But could she do it before one of them killed Travis?

Apparently, she decided to wait for a better opportunity,

because when Deeny—having given her shotgun into Gerald's care—began tying Rachel's hands, Rachel stood silently and put up with it.

They were now standing so that I could see only Rachel's back, and Deeny as she worked on removing Rachel's equipment belt and then binding her wrists together. The two women were fairly close to me, only a few feet away. I moved back slightly from the door, and still it seemed that if Deeny turned suddenly, she might catch me staring out. But all of Deeny's concentration was spent on tying a thin rope around Rachel's wrists, a task that seemed somewhat daunting to her.

Rachel was taller than Deeny, and when Deeny tried to reach up to gag her, I heard Spanning say, "No, that will ruin that lovely mouth, and I might have a use for that mouth a little later on."

Deeny dropped her hands and tucked the strip of cloth into one of her back pockets, but I wondered if Spanning would have thought her such a tame conspirator if he had seen her face at that moment.

I heard a scuffling sound, a grunt of pain and then Gerald's laughter. "What do you know? Arthur's pup has some fight in 'im. That your girlfriend there, little bastard? That your girlfriend?" Another grunt of pain. I felt my nails digging into my palms, even through the latex gloves. "Well, being as we're family, you won't mind sharing her with me, will you?"

There was no mistaking the look of anger on Deeny's face as she stood behind Rachel's back. I began to wonder if she was purposely hiding behind the taller woman, not wanting Gerald to see her reactions.

"Shit," Gerald was saying. "Little fucker passed out on me. Goddamn it, I don't want to carry his ass into the house. You people are making more damned work for me. Search those pockets, Deeny. Oh—and by the way—this your cell phone?"

Rachel didn't answer. I heard the sound of something being smashed, probably my hope of sneaking out to the car and phoning for help.

Rachel had still not said a word to him, and she stayed silent as Deeny started emptying the pockets of her trousers.

"Goddamn, woman," Gerald said, "you're a damned pack mule."

"No," said Deeny, opening the case of lock picks. "She's a thief."

35

"A thief?" Rachel laughed. "A thief has to take something. That's not why I'm here."

"Shut up!" Gerald barked. "Deeny, check the locks on the garage."

Deeny dutifully turned and rattled the padlock just in front of me, then moved to the back of the garage and rattled at the lock on the alley side.

I heard Travis groan. Rachel, just in front of me, made a circle of her thumb and forefinger at her back. An "okay" sign.

There was another groan. It didn't sound as if he was okay to me. "Just stay still now, boy," I heard Gerald say.

Deeny had moved to the side door, the one we had entered by, and pulled at that lock. "It's still locked up," Deeny said. "It hasn't been opened."

"Maybe, maybe not," Gerald said. "Could have already been in and out again. Of course, that depends on how long they been here, right?"

"Oh, not long," Rachel answered easily. "I'm kind of curious about how you managed to know we were here at all." Deeny had come back now, and moved toward Gerald. Rachel moved slightly, and now I could see both Deeny and Gerald, too. Travis was still out of my line of vision. There was a mess of broken plastic near Gerald's feet—the cell phone.

Deeny took her shotgun back from Gerald, who still didn't move any closer to Rachel.

"Well, when Deeny here got off work tonight, she happened to remember that she made the mistake of telling somebody about this place. You do see that was a mistake now, don't you, Deeny?"

She didn't answer.

"I'm a fellow that just can't rest when something like that stirs me up. I decided we might need to come by and take a look," he said. "Just check on things. We drove past the street and saw a familiar car sittin' over there. Just what made you decide to pay a call, darling?" he asked.

"Looking for a car," she said, and I was gratified to see both of them widen their eyes. After a slight pause, Rachel added, "But I don't see the El Camino here. Where is it?"

Their relief was visible. She sent them straight back into hell.

"We have some excellent photos of it, of course. Taken on the day Travis's camper had a little problem with its remote key. Plate numbers, everything. And I suspect that a good police lab could do wonders with the image of the driver. Lord knows how many people have copies of Mr. Richmond's photos."

"Richmond!" Deeny said scornfully. "As if we need to worry about that has-been. I'll buy him a couple of drinks at the Wharf and he'll hand the negatives over to me."

"That's enough, Deeny!" Gerald said sharply. "Damn it, I'm going to put a gag in *your* mouth in another minute."

Deeny gave him a mulish look, then went back to emptying Rachel's pockets. "Here's her ID," she said. I was afraid it would be Rachel's investigator's license, but as Deeny held it up, I could see it was only her driver's license.

"What's her name?" Gerald asked, then laughed at the look of fury Deeny gave him. "All right, all right. Bring it to me."

He glanced at it and said, "Rachel—holy shit, some kind

of a dago name even *I* can't read." A sound in the distance made him suddenly look around. "No use standing out here where God and everybody might come by—you cover her while I get the boy inside."

I tried not to think about the sounds I was hearing as Spanning took Travis inside the house. Despite little gestures from Rachel, meant to calm me, my nerves were rubbed raw by the time I heard Gerald speak again.

"Okay, give me the shotgun," he said to Deeny. "I'll take her in. You gather up all this shit you took out of her pockets and lock it up in the garage, and while you're there, make sure she hasn't already been in there."

She began to argue with him, apparently unwilling to let him be alone with Rachel.

"What, after you've been boning Richmond?" he said.

"I have not!" she screeched.

He slapped her. "Keep your voice down."

She held a hand up to her face where he had hit her, and gave him a sullen look, but said nothing more to him. I wanted to hide, knowing she was about to come into the garage. At the same time, I didn't dare move yet; if I bumped into something in the dark, I'd be shouting out my presence.

Gerald and Rachel went in the house. Deeny stood with arms crossed, watching them. She added to her rebellion by taking out a pack of cigarettes, lighting one up.

I risked the narrow beam of the flashlight, holding it low and taking a path back toward the door. I moved to the workbench, avoided touching the bent and bloodied bumper, searched quickly and found something that would help me create a distraction—a red china marker. I said a little prayer of thanks and made my way to the passenger side of the Camry. I marked the window with three red, slanting slash marks, then stood near the door.

It seemed to me as if I waited a long time, but I know it

could not have been more than a few minutes before I heard Deeny cussing at the lock as she tried to open it. It took her longer with a key than it had taken Rachel to pick the lock. I finally heard it give, and quickly moved farther back behind the door. She seemed to take a long time with the knob lock as well, but finally, the door opened slightly.

She fumbled for the light switch and snapped it on; after the darkness, the single overhead bulb seemed to make the room very bright. I had a sudden sensation of being visible to her, even though the door was between us. But as she stepped farther into the garage, her arms full of Rachel's tools and other paraphernalia, I saw that her attention had been caught by exactly what I had hoped would catch it: the hobo sign on the Camry window. She moved closer to it.

Carefully closing the door enough to block the view from the house, I stepped forward with one lunging step, like a batter meeting a ball and—trying not to shut my eyes as I did it—swung the back end of my flashlight and the weight of all those D cells down on the back of her head. My D cells won out over her brain cells, and I caught at her as she pitched forward, not able to keep her from falling, but slowing it, and guiding her away from the most dangerous objects she might have struck on her way down. I quickly turned and shut the door all the way, hoping Gerald had been too busy to notice the noise made when her armload of Rachel's tools went clattering to the floor with her.

I locked the knob, and after assuring myself that I hadn't killed her outright, went back to the workbench. I found a roll of duct tape, pulled out my Swiss Army knife and went to work. Within a few minutes, I had tied the gag in her back pocket over her mouth, then bound her wrists and ankles with the duct tape.

It would have been nice to feel a sense of triumph at that point, but I didn't. Her face already swelling from the place where Gerald struck her, pale from the blow I had given her, she seemed more a pathetic foolish girl than a vanquished worthy adversary.

Then I thought of the sounds I had heard Travis making, remembered that Ulkins had been tortured, and decided I would have to indulge in sympathy for Deeny some other time.

I wondered where I could leave her that would not be too close to sharp objects; ones she might use to free herself. I searched her pockets, found her pack of cigarettes and a book of matches from the Wharf on one side, a pair of shotgun shells in the other. I took both of these objects. I searched the items on the floor and found her keys. I found the Camry key, unlocked the car and opened the passenger door. I lowered the seat back and—with some effort—dragged her into the car. I rolled the windows down a little, locked the doors and took the keys with me.

I quickly studied Rachel's tools, didn't see anything of much interest to anyone who wasn't breaking into a building. I didn't know how to use them, so I left them there.

Time was running out, I knew. Sooner or later, Gerald would notice that Deeny had been absent too long. She had made things worse by stalling. I looked around the garage, gathered together a few pieces of wood, a canister of oily rags, five cans of spray paint and a can of charcoal lighter fluid. Nothing like your average garage when you're on the hunt for a good set of fire hazards.

I turned out the light, waited for my eyes to adjust to the darkness, then crept outside with my hands as full as Deeny's had been coming into the garage. I forced myself to overcome a paralyzing certainty that Gerald was watching my every move, shotgun in hand. Crouching low, I made my way toward the old bathtub on the back lawn. I set all the combustible materials—save the matches and the cartridges—into the tub, trying to stack the wood up so that it would burn well. I opened the can of lighter fluid, sprinkled a goodly amount of it over the wood, tossed my now flammable latex gloves on top it of all, then moved as quietly as possible toward the house.

Gerald had turned a light on in what I soon realized was the living room. I moved from window to window until I found one with a blind that didn't reach the bottom of the sill. Once again I found myself looking through a narrow, slotted view, this one horizontal. What I saw made me wish I had waited a little longer to take a look.

Gerald was in the process of smacking Travis hard across the mouth. Travis's gag was no longer in place, and Travis and Rachel were each tied to wooden ladder-back chairs. The blood from the wound on Travis's forehead had dried, but now fresh blood came from a split lip. I took some solace in the fact that Gerald had not thought either of them dangerous enough to tie their feet or legs, and had not set up any electrical torture devices.

Gerald was talking—loudly, it seemed, but I couldn't make out what he was saying.

I moved to the back of the house, thought of lighting the fire, hesitated. I crept up the back-porch steps, slowly put what I hoped was the right key into the lock and turned it. It opened with a click that sounded like a shot to me, but apparently Gerald didn't hear it over his own voice. Slowly, cautiously, waiting for a creaking noise that would send him gunning for me, I opened the back door. There was no squeak of hinges. I made myself breathe again, and I went inside.

I was in the kitchen. I could now hear Gerald very clearly.

"Don't look at me like that!" he was saying. "Your daddy used to look at me like that. 'Don't hurt me.' Don't hurt *him!* You know what I did for him? You know what I did? Everything. I fed him. I put clothes on his back and a roof over his head. I read for him. I wrote for him. You know that? You know your own father couldn't read or write?"

"Yes," Travis said wearily. "I knew."

"Well, then! Maybe he told you who it was that was always doing everything for him! Always giving up everything for him! I raised him, tried to make sure he stayed out of trouble. And he was always in trouble! I had to go in and spend my time talking to the teachers when he was flunking everything. I was the one who saved him, you see? Whenever he was in trouble, I saved him. Then I had to find something to do with his sorry ass when he dropped out of school—didn't even finish elementary school!

"Old Papa DeMont, he used to try to teach him things just by talking to him. If it weren't for Papa DeMont, he wouldn't have known a thing. That sweet old man used to let him follow him around like a pup. Taught him all kinds of things. I'm not saying Arthur was stupid, he wasn't. He was about as dumb as a fox, and twice as sly. I'm out there working my ass off, and Arthur's running around in Papa DeMont's pocket, soaking up everything that old man will show him or teach him.

"And you know how he repaid that kindness? By fucking the man's daughter! That's how! Now, I'll admit, he was just a kid, and he can't bear the blame entirely, because she was always tempting him. That was her way, to tempt and tease a man."

"Sounds like you wished you'd got there first," I heard Rachel say.

There was an ominous silence, then Travis shouted, "Don't hurt her!"

Gerald laughed. "Listen to him. 'Don't hurt her!' " he mimicked. "I want to, but I got plans for that dirty mouth of yours, you wop slut, so I'll teach you some manners later."

I moved slowly toward the door that led from the kitchen to the living room. It was open, but I flattened myself against the wall. I had my flashlight ready. If I had the chance, I'd give Gerald the same treatment I gave Deeny.

"You once thought of marrying Gwendolyn?" Travis asked, distracting him from Rachel.

"Before I learned what she was really like, yes, I did. I loved her once." He stopped talking, then suddenly said, "You look so much like him. Your daddy. For a bastard, I'm surprised how much you come up looking like him. Nobody on earth I loved as much as him. Not even her, and I proved it. I always looked out after him, protected him. I made sacrifices. I told Arthur, he had to protect her like I protected him, against Horace DeMont and his brats. Course, he wasn't man enough to do it."

"But he made his own fortune," Travis said, "and he provided for her from that."

"For her?" Gerald said. "Or for a whore and the bastard he got off of her?"

"For all of us," Travis said. "Even you."

There was another sound of a blow. I must have moved, because the floor suddenly creaked beneath my feet. I got the flashlight ready.

"Why do you keep beating on him?" Rachel asked. "Just 'cause he reminds you of his dad? I mean, what the hell is the point of all this? Is this all because we were looking for the El Camino?"

"He knows what it's about!" Spanning said.

"I don't—" Travis said, but there was another blow. I wasn't sure I could stand by, just listening, if Spanning kept at it.

"You know, this is getting us nowhere," Rachel said. "If I knew what the hell it was you wanted, maybe I could help you out."

He paced. "Where's Deeny?!" he shouted.

I could hear him moving, heard him open the front door, heard the squeal of the spring on the screen door as he opened it. In a soft voice, he called, "Deeny! Deeny!"

"She's gone off on one of her pouts," he said, coming

back in, the screen slamming shut. There was the sound of the front door being shut. "Shouldna hit her, I guess."

"What is it you're looking for?" Rachel said.

"That whore's the one that had them," Gerald said. "His mother. Arthur gave them to her. He told me so. Arthur told me he gave them to this little asshole's mother! You trust a man, you do everything in the world for him and what does he say? He needs protection from me. From me! When I was the one protecting him! They're proof, you see? I helped Arthur. He was going to divorce her, you know."

"My mother?" Travis asked.

"No! She wasn't even married! Not really! She was just a whore."

"Who then?" Rachel asked.

"Gwenie. He told me he was going to divorce Gwenie, just to marry that whore and give this brat his name. Gwenie would have taken everything and given it all to her uncle Horace." I heard him pace to the front door again.

The door opened, then the screen door. This time, I heard him step outside. I stepped into the doorway of the living room. Travis's eyes widened, but Rachel shook her head and mouthed the word "no." She jerked her head toward another doorway—one closer to her chair.

I moved back into the kitchen just as I heard Spanning open the door again. He was silent. Someone started making stomping noises, and I used that to cover my progress across the kitchen and into the hallway. I was halfway down the hall when I heard Spanning shout, "What the fuck are you doing?"

"My feet fell asleep," Travis said.

"You're going to be asleep *permanently* if you don't cut it out!"

"Did I ever tell you what happened on the night Gwendolyn DeMont died?" Travis said.

Spanning was silent.

"It was a hot June night," Travis said, his voice taking on a slightly different quality. "So hot. Much hotter than tonight. All the windows were open, but there was no breeze. It was very late. Everything was still and quiet. But in the middle of this still and quiet night, I was awakened by a noise. It wasn't a big noise, just a soft little noise, but I heard it. I was just a boy, already in bed, in my pajamas. But the noise woke me.

"I went downstairs, very slowly, and I saw a light on in the study. My father's study. I was scared until I saw him. He was sitting at his desk.

"At first, I was so happy to see him, so pleased to think that he had come home. He hadn't been there in so many days. Every night, I had waited up for him. Every night, I had hoped he would come back. But he didn't, not until that night. I wanted to run to him, to say, 'Daddy! You're back! You're back home again!' But then I saw that he was crying."

"Crying?!" Spanning said.

"Yes, crying. I ran up to him and hugged him, but it was almost as if I wasn't there. I asked him what had happened to make him so sad. He said, 'Do you know who loves me more than anyone else in the world?' "

There was silence, then Spanning scoffed, "You probably said it was your mother, because God knows she had him by the balls."

"Yes, that's exactly what I said, but I was wrong."

"Then it must have been you."

"No—you know that isn't true."

"Well, if he said it was me, he was right, but he sure as hell didn't give a damn about me. He was too busy with you and your mother to bother with me."

"But he didn't see me for a dozen years," Travis said. "If he loved me so much, he would have done for me what you did for him, right?"

Spanning didn't answer.

"If you love someone, you take care of them and protect them, right?"

"Of course you do!"

"You didn't run away from your responsibilities, did you?"

"Goddamned right, I didn't."

"You were more of a father to him than he was to me."

"Some ways."

"He could be selfish, couldn't he?"

"*Could be?* I never met a more selfish man."

"But even so, he loved you. We all knew that. He always talked about how much you had done for him. He knew. In his heart of hearts, he knew. He knew you'd do anything for him. He knew you even gave up the woman you loved for him. She could have had you, and everything would have been fine. But she wouldn't take you, would she?"

There was a long silence. "You see?" Spanning said. "You see? You know, don't you? I thought he might not have shown them to you. You were just a kid. But he came home that night and showed them to you, didn't he? Now, where are they? I just want them back. Your mother wouldn't give them to me, so I was going to get them myself."

"But then those old biddies at the apartment building called the cops on Deeny, right?" Rachel said.

"Yeah. And then this cousin—one of the damned Kellys who turned their noses up at him! The whore's family! A Kelly goes in there and takes everything out of the apartment. But then I see how it works. You planned this, Travis. You're staying with your cousin. I know you know about them. I even tried to get old Ulkins to tell me. You saw what happened to him. Now tell me—where are they?"

"I wonder how pissed ol' Deeny is," Rachel said, apparently knowing what the follow-up would be if she didn't distract him from whatever "they" were. "Maybe she's fetching the cops on you as we speak."

He laughed. "She's in this as deep as I am."

But evidently it made him worry, because once again he went to the door. I opened my pocket knife to the sharpest blade. I heard him go out on the front porch again, and I came around the corner of the doorway. I tried to cut the ropes on Rachel's wrists, but she whispered, "Give it to me and get out of here!" I placed it in her hand, blade side against the ropes. The screen door squeaked open and I pulled back.

"None of this whispering between yourselves!" Spanning shouted.

I heard him cross the floor, then a loud crash, and trying not to think about what was happening, hurried to the back door.

"I didn't touch you! What'd you fall over for?" I heard him saying.

"I thought you were going to hit me." Travis's voice.

"Well, if you think I'm going to let loose of this gun to pull you up, you whispered for nothing, because you can stay down there for all I care!"

After that, I was outside again.

I wouldn't have gone, except that I had decided to light the fire. It was a moment's work. One match and it was blazing. I threw the shotgun cartridges in and ran toward the front of the house. I wasn't sure how long it was going to take the shells to explode, or if they would, or what would happen to them, but if those spray-paint canisters were going to do what I thought they would, I didn't want to be looking into the fire when they blew.

I never found out if it was the stench of the burning latex, the smoke of the other substances, or the rather fantastic banging that the paint cans made in that bathtub, but Gerald Spanning ran out of his house, and I ran in.

Rachel was already up and cutting Travis's bonds.

"That story you told him about the night Gwendolyn died—" she was saying.

"Total bullshit," he said, and she laughed as we helped him to his feet.

Outside I could hear Gerald swearing at Deeny—whom

he blamed for starting the fire—and turning the hose on.

"Get Travis out of here," Rachel said to me. "Spanning will be back in here in no time."

Travis, holding his ribs and leaning very heavily on me, said, "We aren't leaving you."

"Then stay the hell out of my way."

She had no sooner said this than we heard Spanning come charging back in through the kitchen door.

She was ready for him. As he came running into the living room, she hit him with a kick in the face that dropped him in place. I don't think he had a clear idea what had happened to him at that point, but she had disarmed him by the time he was slowly getting back up on his feet.

He shook his head to clear it.

"Nobody," she said, "has called me a wop since third grade."

He charged toward her. A mistake.

She took hold of his arm and with one smooth, beautiful twisting motion, threw him head over heels. He came down so hard and so fast, I'm surprised the floor withstood the blow. One of the chairs didn't.

He stood up again, this time with fists raised, and took a few clumsy steps forward. He didn't stand a chance.

Both of her feet and both of her fists connected with him about four times each—if I counted the sounds of the blows right—before he hit the floor again. This time he stayed down.

She hadn't broken a sweat.

Travis said, "You're a cruel woman, Rachel Giocopazzi."

"Why?" she asked, already tying Spanning up. "Because I knocked this piece of shit on his ass?"

"No," he said. "For trying to get us to leave without seeing you do it."

36

Without Ezekiel Brennan's help, I'm convinced we wouldn't have been able to get home as early as we did, which was noon on Monday.

We didn't call the police until Rachel had retrieved and hidden all of her illegal tools. Travis insisted on going with us to the garage to help, even after we warned him about the Camry. Deeny, it turned out, was awake, and not a little angry. When Travis saw the window, he said, "The hobo sign for 'This is not a safe place.' You gave her fair warning, Irene."

When Rachel opened the car door, Travis said to Deeny, "Your husband controlled my father the same way he controls you. If you want to talk to the lawyer who helped my father, maybe he'll help you." He paused, then added, "You're going to need a good lawyer."

We saw the wisdom of it ourselves, and called Brennan right after we called the police.

We didn't tell the entire truth to the Los Alamitos Police, but we kept our stories straight. We had come to the house to look for the El Camino, a vehicle which might contain traces of the explosives used to destroy Travis's camper. Rachel supplied Richmond's photos of the El Camino taken on the day the bomb was put in place. When she mentioned that Harold Richmond was involved, there was a change of attitude—his infamy lived on in the department.

I told them that they might contact Detective McCain of the LAPD about Mr. Richmond's whereabouts. This was a success, and reached while being interviewed in Detective McCain's office, Richmond confirmed that he sometimes talked about his business to the cocktail waitress at the Wharf. No, he didn't know what her last name was.

McCain was pleased to hear where he could find the Camry. We knew, from what we had shown them when they arrived on the scene, that the Camry would prevent Gerald from walking out of the station.

The police were still curious about our activities, especially given our attire. On that subject we said nothing. Mr. Brennan's arrival resulted in Travis's release; he was not being charged with any crime, and Mr. Brennan insisted that Travis receive immediate medical attention. Deeny, who was being released by the hospital into police custody as Travis walked in the Emergency Department doors, called out, "I want to talk to my lawyer!"

"I'll be right with you," Mr. Brennan replied.

Her cooperation led to first my release and then Rachel's—and oddly, Deeny did not seem to recall much of anything that happened just before she was hit on the head, but specifically denied seeing any special burglary tools on Ms. Giocopazzi's person, no matter what was claimed by Gerald. By then McCain and Detective Reed Collins from Las Piernas had made the trip to Los Alamitos, and Gerald was officially placed under arrest.

I called the paper and phoned in a story that made Morey decide I could be excused for another day or two while I healed a little. The acting news editor told me he was assigning a couple of other people to write follow-up stories from less personal angles. Fine with me.

Mr. Brennan drove Rachel over to the hospital, where she arrived not long before Travis was ready to go home with us.

"I want to grow up to be like my cousin," he said to me, walking stiffly and trying to act as if the broken ribs, black eye, fat lip and lump on his forehead were nothing. He held

up his cleanly swathed right hand. "And look, you don't
have to change the bandage for me today."

"We have a specially air-conditioned Volvo to take you
home in," I said, and after we all thanked Mr. Brennan again,
we were on our way, sans driver's side window, but happy.

— —

We arrived at my house to see two men getting out of a
Yellow Cab. "Oh shit," said Rachel. "Now we've had it."

"Who is it?" Travis asked.

"Our husbands."

But she was wrong if she thought they were angry. After
several hours of trying to reach us at every possible number, they were so glad to see us, they didn't even bitch
about the cab fare from LAX.

— —

I awakened at about seven in the evening, as the last of the
early summer sunlight was fading. After a few moments of
enjoying the sensation of being held possessively by my
sleeping husband, I gently extricated myself from his grip. He
rolled over but didn't awaken, and soon was snoring again. I
stood and listened to it for a while after getting dressed.

I checked on Travis, who was sleeping soundly, despite
being propped up at the angle the broken ribs required.
Uncomfortable, but better than getting pneumonia, the doc-
tors said.

I fed the animals and started making dinner. I put a
chicken in the oven and started straightening the living
room. I came across the Virgin Mary night-light and smiled.
It reminded me of one my mother had once had, too. I tried
plugging it in, but it didn't light up. I unplugged it, and
unscrewed the base—no bulb.

I went into the kitchen, checked on the chicken and,
after a brief search, found a spare night-light bulb. My hus-

band came out of the bedroom, and I became distracted by some nuzzling until he said, "Uh-oh. What papist trappings are you decorating the house with now, Catholic girl?"

I laughed and told him that the night-light was apparently the one gift that had survived the years during which my aunt purged her home of every other reminder of Arthur, save Travis himself. He cocked his head to one side for a moment, but made no wisecracks, so I went back to replacing the bulb.

Travis came slowly down the hall and Frank, who had already taken a liking to him, offered to help him get settled in a chair.

"No thanks," Travis said. "The thought of trying to get up again makes me want to stay on my feet." He saw what I was working on and smiled a misshapen grin. "What are you doing to the Virgin Mary?"

"I was going to surprise you," I said, trying to concentrate on what was becoming a frustrating effort to reattach the base to the statue. "You know—replace the bulb and set this in your room—have you wake up to a glowing religious night-light."

Frank groaned.

"Hey, Mr. Episcopalian," I said, handing the two parts to him. "Instead of making rude sound effects, why not see if you can get this back together?"

Frank took it from me as Travis said, "Well, you do almost have to grow up with it, Irene."

"Tell that to her sister," Frank said, peering up the hollow Virgin Mary's plastic gown. "She keeps trying to talk me into converting."

"Maybe I'll put off meeting Barbara," Travis said, and Frank laughed.

Frank started poking a finger into the statue. "Hold it," I said. "There's a limit—"

He looked back into the bottom of the statue, ignoring me. "Get me a pair of tweezers."

"Tweezers!"

"Please."

Well, it was the magic word, after all.

With tweezers in hand, he began picking at something inside the statue.

"What is it?" Travis asked.

"The reason the bulb won't fit. There's something rolled up inside here."

Travis looked over at me.

"Travis, you said this was the only thing among your mother's possessions that your father had given to her . . ."

"And he gave it to her to protect her," he said softly. "To protect her from Gerald?"

Frank soon began complaining that if we didn't give him some elbow room, he wouldn't be able to get the object—something made of metal wrapped in paper—out without tearing the paper.

But a few minutes later he succeeded, and handed a short flat key and what at first appeared to be a scroll of thick paper to Travis.

"Is that a safe-deposit box key?" I asked.

"Too short," Frank said. "Maybe a cash box, something like that."

Travis, who had taken a seat next to Frank on the couch, handed the scroll back to him. "Could you help me unroll it?"

Frank carefully unrolled the scroll, which turned out to be a small envelope. It was the size of the envelopes invitations and thank-you notes sometimes come in, about four-by-six inches, and it was addressed to Arthur Spanning at an address I didn't recognize at first, but marked "Personal."

The address was written in black ink in a rough hand. There was no return address, no stamps, no postmark, but

at the top of the envelope, a different hand had penciled in
the number twenty-five and circled it.

"The office address?" I asked Travis, finally remembering.

"Yes. He told me that he had most of his mail sent there,
not only because W would read it to him, but because it was
the one place he would be every day—otherwise, he alter-
nated between our house and the farm, and later between
his apartment and the farm. But even if he couldn't get into
the office during the day, most evenings, he stopped by to
check his mail."

"Ulkins was there all the time?"

"No. Ulkins would tape-record the mail, usually just sum-
marizing it. See this number twenty-five? Ulkins wrote that.
He numbered the envelopes, then said on the tape, 'Letter
one is from so-and-so, regarding x and y . . .' and so on. My
father would listen to it as soon as he got a chance, whenever he had a moment. Sometimes that was in the afternoon, but usually it was late in the day."

He explained who W/Ulkins was to Frank as he turned
the envelope over. There were two red ink marks on the
back, from a pair of rubber stamps. One was the figure of a
hand.

"Hand-delivered," Travis said, pointing to it.

The other stamp was a date—all numerical. "Date
received," he said.

"The day Gwendolyn DeMont was murdered," I said.

"Should I—should I be handling this?" Travis asked.

"Probably no prints, but just to make sure, here," Frank
said, and using the tweezers but making the barest contact
otherwise, he removed five index cards and the page of a
calendar from the envelope. All were as curled as the envelope, but using the eraser end of a pencil to hold down one
end and the tweezers to hold the other end, Frank held
them open.

The calendar page was from the same date, the day of

the murder. On it, someone had drawn a crescent moon.

"This doesn't have anything to do with the actual phase of the moon," Travis said. "It means 'This night.'"

On each of the five index cards, symbols had been drawn.

"What do they mean?" I asked Travis.

He pointed to a simple house shape with other symbols within it.

"I'm not sure. The symbols on the inside of the house shape mean, 'Rich people live here.' When we used to leave the notes for one another, our house was drawn like this, but with a heart inside."

"Maybe it was a symbol for the DeMont farmhouse," I said. "Especially if Gerald and your dad devised it before your dad lived in it."

Frank held the next one open. "A zero?" I asked.

"Yes, in a way," Travis said. "It means 'Nothing to be gained here.'"

The next one also seemed familiar. "A diamond?" Frank asked.

"No, see the little protrusion at the bottom?" Travis point-ed to it. "It's a hobo sign for 'Hold your tongue.'"

Neither of us guessed at the next one.

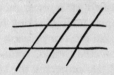

"This means 'A crime has been committed here,'" he said. "And this last one means 'Be ready to defend yourself.'"

"He killed her," Travis said. "Gerald kept hinting about this great favor he had done my father, but he didn't really admit killing her."

"He warned your father with hobo signs. These papers are what he was looking for," I said. "And this key."

We had told Frank about our encounter with Gerald, but only the basics. Now Travis filled him in on the details, then said, "I know he'll be convicted of murdering my mother, and maybe even charged with attempted murder for trying to kill me. Killing Ulkins, the way he hurt Irene, and tried to kill her—there may be convictions for that, too. He should go to jail for a long time, and I should be satisfied.

"But if Gwendolyn's murder is left as an open case, it isn't enough." He paused, then added, "I feel sorry for her, but I'd be kidding myself if I said I wanted justice for her sake. It's more selfish than that.

"I want to clear my father's name. I mean, he was a bigamist, yes—that I admit. But he didn't kill his wife. My family—my father, my mother and I—we paid for that murder. We were punished for it, even though my father was innocent." He stopped himself, shook his head. "No, that's not true. He didn't kill her, but he wasn't innocent."

"Your father protected Gerald," Frank said.

"Yes," Travis said. "He protected the killer."

"His only brother," I said. "A man who had raised him."

"His brother's keeper," Travis said. "And God knows, Gerald was his keeper in every sense of the word." He turned to Frank and said, "Is there any hope of using these to convict him of murdering Gwendolyn?"

Frank looked at the curling papers in silence for a time, then said, "Using them as evidence? There are some problems. Even if you could find prints or DNA on the envelope, there's the problem of where the evidence has been all this time, who's had a chance to tamper with it, and so on—not that I think they've been anywhere but in this night-light, but a defense lawyer would probably have them thrown out in no time."

"Oh."

"But that doesn't mean the police can't make use of them," Frank said. "I know some of the guys over in Los Alamitos. Let me talk to them about it. Gerald was obsessed about getting these from your mother and you. A good interrogator might be able to show this to him without saying a word, and maybe he'll give it up."

Travis didn't say anything.

Frank said, "Used to be, we could use the methods of some of these wild women private eyes out there, and smack the bad guys around until they confessed—but those days are over."

Travis smiled a little.

"Fortunately for us," Frank went on, "Rachel made him polish her shoes with his face, ribs and ass, so I think his spirits will be a little low. Trust me, I have experience dealing with this kind of turkey."

The next day, Travis asked me to go with him to St. Anthony's to see Father Chris, to learn where Arthur had been buried. As we drove to the church, I thought of our last visit there, and of the housekeeper's warm welcome. That in turn reminded me of things she had said then, and suddenly several pieces of information I had heard over the last few days fell into place.

I looked over at my cousin, whose errand had put him in a somber mood. He was sitting stiffly, his injuries undoubtedly making the ride uncomfortable.

"Travis," I asked, bringing him out of his reverie, "do you remember when Mrs. Havens was your family's housekeeper?"

"We never had a housekeeper at our house," he said. "Mrs. Havens kept saying she worked for my father. She must have worked for my dad after my parents separated."

"I think she may have worked for your father and Gwendolyn, before Gwendolyn died."

His eyes widened. "What?"

"Father Chris called her 'Annie.' The housekeeper at the DeMont farm was named Ann Coughlin. Different last name, but maybe she remarried, or changed it. I just think it's unlikely that your father had two different housekeepers named Ann."

"But that would mean she was the one who found Gwendolyn's body . . ."

"More than that. Suppose she hadn't mopped the floor where your father walked, or disturbed the place on the bed where your father put his hand into Gwendolyn's blood?"

"He would have been arrested for murder. Dad's alibi wouldn't have mattered much if Richmond had found that evidence intact."

I shrugged. "Richmond might have blown it in some other way. I'm beginning to doubt that Mrs. Coughlin was just some befuddled old lady who messed up a murder scene, though. I think Richmond assumed that's all she was, and she took advantage of that."

She greeted us at the rectory door, again fussing over Travis. Father Chris had been called out to a sick parishioner's house, she explained to us. Would we please wait? Travis and I exchanged a glance. We were brimming with questions for her; Father Chris's absence would make asking them less awkward.

"I'm so glad you're safe!" she said, seating Travis in the most comfortable chair she could find. "I read the stories in the paper." She gave me a wink. "If I wasn't gray already, that would have done the trick." She propped a pillow behind him, then looked between us.

"She may be your cousin," she said to him, "but I don't see much of your mother's side of the family in her. And I still say you look just like your father. Oh, I don't mean all bruised and so, but I thought so even when I saw you as a baby."

"You saw me as a baby?" he asked warily. "But my father didn't have a housekeeper then."

She hesitated only slightly before saying, "Oh, he did, just not at your mother's place."

"You worked for him at the DeMonts'," I said.

She sighed. "Yes, you've figured that out, haven't you? Well, I don't guess I'm obliged to keep these secrets after all that's happened. Yes, I worked for Mr. Spanning at the DeMont place, and for Papa DeMont and Miss Gwen before him."

"Ann Coughlin?" I asked.

"Yes, that was my first married name. Mr. Coughlin died and I later on married Mr. Havens. Mr. Havens, God rest his soul, died a few years back. Mr. Havens was always good to me.

"But Mr. Coughlin! He used to lose his temper with me every now and again, and he wasn't above using his fists on me. Called it 'teaching me a lesson.' Probably would have killed me one day, except young Arthur—oh, he must have been about eighteen then—he found out about it and put a stop to it. Told Mr. Coughlin there'd be none of that on the DeMont place, or he'd give him a lesson of his own—one that would make him feel like he'd been to college." She laughed. "Mr. Coughlin never laid a hand on me after that. Well, all I'm saying is, I knew who helped me, didn't I? And I never forgot it. And I was proud to be able to help him whenever he needed it."

"When Gwendolyn was murdered—" Travis began.

"Yes, I helped him then, too. I was shocked, of course, but I knew he wasn't the one that had done the killing."

"But you couldn't be certain!"

"Who on earth could be any more certain, I ask you? I spent more hours in that house with the two of them than I did in my own home. Arthur was never anything but kind to Miss Gwen. There wasn't a mean bone in his body. And he never would have done anything to harm her." She paused, then added, "I knew your daddy and I knew his brother, too—from the time your daddy was a little boy."

"If you saw Travis when he was a baby," I said, "you must have known about Arthur's other life."

"Yes. As I say, you can't hide much from the person who cleans your house and washes your clothes. I'm sure there are plenty of people on this earth who will judge him harshly for what he did, but I won't be one of them. That's all I have to say about that. He helped me when everybody else just pretended not to see anything wrong—that man got me out of a living hell. I would have done anything to try to repay him for that."

She turned to Travis. "I was always begging him to work it out so that I could see you, so proud he was of you. So one day, I told Miss Gwen I had some shopping to do, and he told your mother he had some shopping to do, and I got to see you! Oh, I was thrilled. You could just see how much he loved you, how precious you were to him. I told him then and there, he was right, having you was worth the world. The very world."

"Thank you, Mrs. Havens," he said softly. "For telling me that, and for—well, thank you for everything you've done for us."

"Travis," I asked, "do you have the key with you?"

"The key!" she exclaimed. "But surely you can't need it now! I read where they caught him! He's locked up, right?"

Travis pulled the little key from his pocket. "Gerald? Yes, Mrs. Havens, but we want to make sure he stays locked up."

She frowned, then said, "Wait here, I'll be right back."

By the time she came back, her new boss had returned. That's how it worked out that when we opened the small strongbox, a Catholic priest happened to be present. I wasn't surprised to find a knife with a broken tip and dark stains on it. But I was surprised to see it resting on a pair of stiff, blood-stained gloves.

"Don't touch anything in that box," I warned the others.

"How did my father get these?" Travis asked.

"Well, you don't have an older brother, so there's no

way you could know," she said. "But one thing a younger brother always knows about an older one is where he likes to hide things. Arthur found these that Sunday, he told me, and I helped him hide them before the police even knew she was dead. Gerald was fit to be tied, of course, but Arthur told him if he ever brought any harm to you or your mother, someone else would turn that over to the police, along with some notes. I was the someone else!"

"But—but Mrs. Havens!" Father Chris said, looking at his elderly housekeeper in an entirely different way. "This was evidence! The woman lay there murdered for a full day after you knew about it!"

"I loved Gwen, Father, but she was dead. Wasn't going nowhere, right? And what was more important, to protect three innocent people's lives, or let the likes of Harold Richmond use that evidence to hurt them? And before you say another word, Father, ask yourself if Arthur Spanning could have possibly paid a higher price for loving his brother as himself. If anything, that man loved his brother too much!"

And with that, she turned on her heel and walked out. She was back less than a minute later to say, "Two weeks notice, Father. Time I retired. Travis, you call me."

▬ ▬

I'm still not sure if it was the notes, the knife or Reed Collins's bold assertion (made without checking with any lab) that DNA could easily be lifted from the inside of Gerald's gloves that made the difference. Reed liked my theory that Gerald's wetsuit trick indicated a certain fear about leaving DNA around, and put it to the test.

Personally, I think having his ass kicked by a woman so disordered Gerald's way of looking at the world, he took one glance at the notes, knife and gloves and started unburdening his conscience. This, I'm told, took the form of a lot of ranting about bitches who could have been happy with him, traitorous brothers, whores and bastards—but the district attorney, a judge and a jury of his peers were able to sort it all out and find him guilty.

▬▬

I took Travis to meet Leda DeMont Rose and her granddaughter. They quickly set him at ease, and by the end of the visit, they were well on their way to becoming friends, even though Laurie's first glimpse of my badly mauled cousin must have made her believe I had lied about his good looks.

Horace DeMont died the day after Travis visited them, and I have still not convinced him that it was not his fault.

Robert DeMont, though disappointed that he had not found a way to get his hands on the small remaining portion of the DeMont fortune, was able to sell an improved version of the toilet-seat invention to a novelty manufacturer, and realized enough from the sale to work on other innovations, as well as to pay an auto body shop bill.

I envied him, as well as Rachel and Frank, and everyone else whose car came back from the body shop. Like Travis's camper, the Karmann Ghia was gone forever. I still miss it.

▬▬

Long before any of that came to pass, Frank and I made another visit to Holy Family Cemetery. We stood near my parents' graves, but we weren't alone. Great Aunt Mary and her caretaker friend, Sean Grady, were nearby. My sister Barbara, and Rachel and Pete were there. Travis was there, too, as were Zeke Brennan, Father Chris and Ann Havens, the latter two having forgiven one another. Father Chris presided over a reburial of Arthur's remains, next to those of Briana. They had been in the same cemetery, as it turned out—but separated from one another. Now there was a new stone in place, their names together. Though tears were shed, it was, on the whole, a celebration.

I thought I saw McCain's car in the parking lot, but I may have been mistaken.

Travis was staying with us for a while, having realized that we really didn't care that he could afford to stay elsewhere. What you can afford in money, we had learned, you can't always afford in time.

That day, putting fresh flowers on my parents' graves, I felt sorry that they had lost time with Briana and Travis, had not welcomed Arthur. Perhaps if we had offered our family's strengths to him, or a little more forgiveness, we would not have been lost to one another in that tangled, strangling web of pride and shame and deceit.

I looked out across the cemetery and set aside my regrets. No time, no time for regrets. Who teaches that better than the dead? All that lingered was the first real sense of peace I had felt at my parents' graveside. Something has been made right, I thought, some wound healed.

It was at that moment that my sister, Barbara, knelt down next to me.

I looked up at her, saw the expression on her face and said, "Don't say it, Barbara."

"Well, I *did* want that spot. Now where am I going to be buried?"

"Next to me," I said.

"Next to you!" She stood up, clearly appalled. "Then don't bother writing 'Rest in Peace' on my tombstone!"

"As if death could calm her down," Frank said, watching her go.

He took my hand and we walked back to the car, speaking, as lovers will, of the benefits of cremation.

Notes and Acknowledgments

I spent part of my adolescence in Los Alamitos; I am happy to report that the city survived that particular bit of turmoil and recently celebrated its centennial. However, the Los Alamitos in *Liar* is by and large a fictional version of the city. And although a sugar beet factory played a major role in the city's history, the factory and the surrounding sugar beet farms were not owned by a single individual—in *Liar*, the DeMonts, the Spannings and all other characters from Los Alamitos are entirely a product of my imagination.

—~ ~

While I am solely responsible for any errors in *Liar*, I am indebted to a number of individuals who helped with research. Alice Littlejohn of the CSULB University Library helped me to find examples of hobo signs. Sharon Weissman is a sharp observer, and her recounting of an incident she witnessed inspired part of this tale. I also thank her—along with Sandra Cvar and Tonya Pearsley— for reading and rereading the manuscript.

Steve Kingston, aka "the real Rockford," is a private investigator who patiently explained to me several aspects of wills, probate and the task of locating heirs. His help in these and other areas, as well as his lively conversation, are deeply appreciated.

Other help came from the Los Alamitos Museum, Debbie Arrington, Kira Bauman, Bill Valles, Tonya Pearsley, Louise Krause, John Pearsley, Jr., Bill Pearsley, John G. Fischer, Bill Mitts of the California Department of Motor Vehicles, and Sharon Oropeza. Father Angus Beaton provided answers to my questions about past and current Catholicism. Dr. Jim Gruber and Dr. Ed Dohring helped with medical questions.

Several students of the Long Beach School for Adults spent time talking to me about the challenges facing adults who cannot read; these personal experiences were often painful to recall, and I thank them not only for their candor and courage in speaking to me about incidents in the past, but also for inspiring me with their steadfast determination, their hard work and their hope for a better future. I have the highest regard for them, and for their dedicated teachers, most especially Judy McCall and Michelle Davidson.

The children's librarians and acquisitions librarians (including Amy, Judith Rosenberg, Caren Soltysiak, Sarah Flowers, Toni Walder, Paula Belair, Marlyn Roberts, Anne Paradise, Debra Eisert, Ginger Armstrong, Mary Miller, Ann Pentecost and others) on Internet mystery list DorothyL were helpful in advising me on a number of matters concerning Travis's work. They also told me of PUBYAC, started by Shannon VanHemert. Ms. VanHemert, with Dr. Margaret M. Kimmel, graciously allowed me to refer to it within the story. My thanks also to the real Irene Galwan, and the Valley Plaza Branch Library in North Hollywood.

Esthela Alarcón-Teagle helped with the Spanish; Lia Matera with the (clean) Italian phrases; both women gave me friendship and support through some of the more trying moments of writing the manuscript.

Senior Constable Ken Lyons, South Australia Police— Major Crash Investigation Section was a great help with accident investigation information.

My thanks to those who have given me so much support at Simon and Schuster, especially my editor, Laurie

Bernstein, who—this time under amazing circumstances—was once again able to provide invaluable insight and suggestions. (And welcome to the world, Benjamin!) Nancy Yost, in addition to being a hardworking agent, laughs at my jokes—which may be the hardest work of all.

And as for Tim Burke—if I had used up all my luck just meeting you, I'd still be lucky.